g ε γ 73

Georgette Heyer

THE
FOUNDLING

P9-AQI-857

AN ACE BOOK

Ace Publishing Corporation
1120 Avenue of the Americas
New York, N. Y. 10036

The Foundling, Copyright, ©, 1948 by Georgette Heyer.

An ACE STAR Book
by arrangement with G. P. Putnam's Sons.

Printed in the U.S.A.

Into the room stepped a vision of loveliness. The Duke caught his breath, and stood staring. He was not prepared for anything as superb as this creature who was making his senses swim for a dizzy moment.

The Duke swallowed once, and waited. Her melting gaze widened a little as it rested on him, but the lady said nothing.

"Did not Mr. Ware promise you marriage, my love?" prompted Mr. Liversedge.

"Yes," said the vision. "Oh, yes, he said I should have a purple silk dress when we were married." And two large tears welled over, and rolled down her face.

"No, no, don't be unhappy Miss—" said the Duke, terrified lest she dissolve into tears. "What is your name?"

"Belinda," she answered with a look of surprise.

"Your surname?"

"Oh, I haven't any other name! I'm a foundling."

"Have you no relatives to whom you can turn for help?"

"Oh no!" she said, shaking her head so that her golden curls quivered. "Foundlings don't you know."

"What in heaven's name am I to do with you?" said the Duke, looking harassed.

"You might wish to give me a purple silk dress," she suggested.

If the Duke had been dizzy before, his senses now reeled. Some instinct warned him that he beheld Trouble. . . .

Also by Georgette Heyer:*

*Available in ACE STAR Editions.

CHAPTER 1

WHEN the young gentleman strolling through the park with
his gun on his shoulder and an elderly spaniel at his heels
came within sight of the house it occurred to him that the
hour must be farther advanced than he had supposed, for
the sun had sunk below the great stone pile, and an autum-
nal mist was already creeping over the ground. Amongst
the trees the mist had been scarcely perceptible, but when
the gentleman emerged from their shelter on to an avenue
which ran through undulating lawns to the south front of
the mansion, he perceived that the vista was clouded, and
became for the first time aware of a chill striking through
his light nankeen jacket. He quickened his steps a little, but
instead of pursuing his way to the main front, with its handsome colonnade of the Corinthian order, and cupola sur-
mounting the central compartment, he turned off the avenue,
and, traversing an elegant flower-garden, embellished with
various classical statues, approached a side-entrance in the
east wing.

The house, which occupied the site of an earlier building,
destroyed by fire half a century before, was a comparative-
ly modern edifice, designed in the classic style, and executed in stone and stuccoed brick. A four hundred and
fifty foot frontage made it impressive, and its proportions
being extremely nice, and its situation agreeable, it was held

5

by every Travellers' Guide Book to be worth a visit of inspection on such days as its noble owner allowed it to be thrown open to the public. The enquiring traveller was informed that while the park and the pleasure-grounds were sumptuously adorned with works of art, these embellishments were not obtrusive, scarcely any object occurring to violate the principles of modern taste in garden-arrangement. The park, very richly timbered, was also adorned by water; it measured above ten miles in circumference, and was traversed by an avenue three miles in length. The gardens, which were varied and extensive, bespoke the attentions of an extremely skilled gardener, with underlings who permitted no weed to show its head, and no hedge or border to grow ragged. Formal beds were arranged with propriety of taste, and even the wilderness, beyond the Italian Garden and the shrubbery, was kept under decorous restraint.

"Sale Park," read the Guide Book, "the principal seat of his Grace the Duke of Sale, is a spacious and handsome structure, with colonnades connecting the wings with the central elevation, and a grand portico supporting a richly ornamented pediment." The visitor was then adjured to pause awhile to admire the ornamental water, the luxuriant growth of noble trees, and the view to be obtained from the south, or main front, before turning his gaze upon the stately mansion itself and absorbing all the glories of Corinthian columns, pediments, cupolas, which rendered it worthy of study.

The Guide Book bestowed some very warm praise upon the Grecian Temple, erected at enormous expense by the fifth Duke, but the young gentleman in the fustian pantaloons, and nankeen shooting-jacket passed it without a glance. Indeed, he seemed to be quite indifferent to the beauty and the grandeur of his surroundings, treading rather carelessly over neat grass borders, and permitting his spaniel to stray on to the flower-beds at will.

In his person as much as in his dress, which besides being of great simplicity included a shot-belt (an article of attire not at all in favour with gentlemen aspiring to elegance) he scarcely accorded with his stately setting. He was slightly built, and of rather less than medium height. He had light brown hair, which waved naturally above a countenance which was pleasing without being in any way remarkable. The features were delicate, the colouring rather pale, and the eyes, although expressive, and of a fine gray, not sufficiently arresting to catch the attention. He carried himself well, but without any air of consequence, so that in a crowd it would have been easier to have passed him over than to have distinguished him. His address was well-bred, and a certain dignity attached to his bearing, but either from the circumstance of his being only twenty-four years of age, or from a natural diffidence, his manner, without being precisely shy, was quiet to the point of self-effacement. In fact, tourists to whom he had occasionally been pointed out generally found it impossible to believe that such an unassuming figure could really be the owner of so much wealth and magnificence. But he had owned it for twenty-four years, together with Sale House, his town residence in Curzon Street, and eight other country seats, ranging from Somerset to a draughty castle in the Highlands. He was the Most Noble Adolphus Gillespie Vernon Ware, Duke of Sale and Marquis of Ormesby; Earl of Sale; Baron Ware of Thame; Baron Ware of Stoven; and Baron Ware of Rufford, and all these high-sounding titles had been his from the moment of his birth, for he was a posthumous child, the only surviving offspring of the sixth Duke, and of the gentle, unfortunate lady who, after presenting her lord with two stillborn children, and three who did not survive infancy, expired in giving birth to a seven-months male child of such tiny size and sickly appearance that it was freely prophesied of him that he would join his little brothers and sisters in the family vault before the year was out. But the wise choice of a wet-nurse, the devotion of the Chief Nurse, the unremitting attentions of his doctors, the strict rule of his uncle and guardian, Lord Lionel Ware, and the fond solicitude of his aunt, had all combined to drag the seventh Duke through every phase of infantile disorder; and although his boyhood was rendered irksome by a delicacy of constitution that made him liable to take cold easily, and to succumb with alarming readiness to every infectious disease, he had not only survived, but had grown into a perfectly healthy young man, who, if not as stout as could have been wished, or of such fine physique as his uncles and cousins, was yet robust enough to cause his physician very little anxiety. The chief of these had more than once asserted his belief that the little Duke had a stronger constitution than was supposed, since his hold on life had throughout been so tenacious; but this was an opinion not shared by the anxious relatives, tutors, and attendants who had the Duke in their charge. It was some years since he had suffered any but the most trifling ailment, but his entourage still laboured under the conviction that he was a being to be cosseted and protected against every wind that blew.

It was therefore not with surprise that the young Duke, as he reached the east wing of his house, found that his approach had evidently been watched for. The door was flung open before he had set his foot upon the first of the stone steps that led up to it, and various persons were seen to have assembled in the passage to receive him. Foremost amongst these was his butler, an impressive individual whose demeanour gave the initiated to understand that if his Grace chose to demean himself by entering his house by a side door giving on to a narrow passage it was not for him to criticize such eccentric behaviour. He bowed the Duke in, and perceiving that he carried, besides his gun, a heavy game-bag, silently gestured to a footman to relieve his master of these unbecoming burdens. The Duke gave them up with a faint, rueful smile, but murmured that he had the intention of cleaning his barrels in the gun-room.

His head-keeper took the gun, a fine Manton, from the footman, and said reproachfully: "I shall attend to it myself, your Grace. If I had known that your Grace was desirous of shooting to-day I would have sent up a loader, and——"

"But I didn't want a loader," said the Duke.

Mr. Padbury shook his head forbearingly.

"I think," added the Duke, "that I might now and then—just now and then, you know, Padbury!—clean my guns for myself."

Even the footman looked shocked at this, but, being only an underling, could only exchange glances with the fellow footman who had accompanied him to the side entrance. The butler, the steward, and the keeper all directed looks of deep reproach at the Duke, and the middle-aged man in the neat garb that proclaimed the valet exclaimed: "Clean your guns for yourself, your Grace! I should think not indeed! And your Grace wet through, I daresay, with only that thin jacket!"

"Oh, no!" said the Duke. He looked down at the muddied spaniel, and added: "But Nell must be rubbed down well."

He was assured that this should instantly be done; the keeper began to say that he should lose no time in treating the damp gun-stock with a particular preparation of his own; and the steward, prefixing his intervention with a discreet cough, informed his master that my lord had been asking if he was not yet come in.

The Duke had listened rather absently to his valet's and his keeper's remarks, but this had the effect of claiming his attention. He appeared to abandon his intention of going to the gun-room, and asked in a slightly apprehensive tone if he were late for dinner.

The butler, who, although officially the steward's inferior, was a man of far more commanding personality, replied somewhat ambiguously to this question that my lord had gone upstairs to change his dress above half an hour ago.

The Duke looked startled, and said that he must make haste; whereupon the butler, relaxing his severity, assured him benignly that dinner would be held for him, and went in a stately way down the passage to open the door that led into the main hall of the house.

But the Duke again disappointed him, this time by electing to run up the secondary staircase at the end of the passage.

His bedroom was an immense apartment opening out of the upper hall, and as he crossed this to his door he encountered his uncle, a fine-looking gentleman in the early fifties, with an aristocratic cast of countenance, and rather fierce eyes set under strongly marked brows.

Lord Lionel Ware, who prided himself on belonging to the old school, had changed his customary country habit of buckskins and top-boots for the knee-breeches considered *de rigueur* in his younger days, and carried an enamelled snuff-box in one hand, and a lace handkerchief. When he saw his nephew, his brows shot up, and he enunciated, in a sort of bark: "Ha! So you are come in, are you, Gilly?"

The Duke smiled, and nodded. "I beg pardon, sir! Am I late? I shall not keep you waiting above twenty minutes, I promise you."

"No such thing!" said Lord Lionel testily. "Dinner will await your convenience, but you are a great fool to be staying out after dusk at this season. I daresay you will have taken one of your chills!"

"Oh, no!" replied the Duke, in the same sweet, absent tone he had used to his valet.

Lord Lionel ran a hand down the sleeve of that nankeen jacket, and appeared to be not dissatisfied. "Well!" he said. "I don't wish to be for ever coddling you, boy, but I desire you will make haste out of those clothes. You will have got your feet wet in those half-boots. You had better have worn gaiters. Nettlebed! Has his Grace no gaiters to wear out shooting?"

"His Grace will not wear his gaiters, my lord," said the valet, in condemnatory accents. "And his Grace did not send for me to lay out his clothes, nor apprise me of his intention to go shooting," he added, less in self-exculpation than in sorrowful blame of his young master's imprudence.

"I am glad you do not wish to be waited on hand and foot," said Lord Lionel severely, "but this habit you have of slipping off without a word said is nonsensical, Gilly. One would suppose you were afraid someone might prevent you!"

A gleam of humour lit the Duke's eyes; he said meekly: "I think I must have a secretive disposition, sir."

"Nothing of the sort!" said his lordship. "It is high time you realized that you are of age, and may do as you please. Now, be off, and don't neglect to change your stockings! I hope you have been wearing flannel ones, and not——"

"Lamb's-wool," said the Duke, more meekly still.

"Very well, and now make haste, if you please! Unless you wish to keep town-hours at Sale?"

The Duke disclaimed any such desire, and vanished into his bedchamber, where Nettlebed had already laid out his evening dress. The room, although of vast size, was very warm, for a fire had been lit in the grate much earlier in the day, and the windows closed against any treacherous fresh air. Curtains of crimson damask shut out the fading daylight, and the great fourpost-bed was hung with the same stuff. Branches of candles stood on the dressing-table and the mantelpiece; and a silver ewer of hot water had been placed in the wash-basin, and covered with a clean towel. The room was furnished throughout in crimson damask, and mahogany, and hung with a Chinese paper of the style made fashionable some years previously by the Prince Regent, who used it extensively in his summer palace at Brighton. Everything in it semed to be made on rather too large and opulent a scale for its occupant, but it was not an uncomfortable apartment, and, during the day, was generally flooded with sunshine, since it faced south, commanding a view of the avenue, the formal beds and lawns beyond it, the sheet of ornamental water which the Guide Book so highly commended, and, in the distance, the noble trees of the home park. The Duke had slept in it ever since the day when his uncle had decreed that he was too old for petticoat government, and had removed him from his more homely nurseries, and installed him, a small and quaking ten-year-old, in it, telling him that it was his father's room, and his grandfather's before him, and that only the head of the house might inhabit it. As his Grace had been further informed by various members of his household that the fifth Duke had breathed his last in the huge bed, he could only be thankful that his frailty made Lord Lionel deem it advisable to set up a truckle-bed for a reliable attendant in the adjoining dressing-room.

Nettlebed, who might have been considered by some to be rather too elderly a valet for such a young man, began to bustle about, scolding fondly as he divested his master of his coat, and shot-belt, and grey cloth waistcoat. Like

10

nearly everyone else who waited upon the Duke, he had previously been employed by the Duke's father, and considered himself privileged to speak his mind to his master whenever he was out of earshot of other, less important, members of the household, before whom he invariably maintained the Duke's dignity in a manner that daunted the Duke far more than the affectionate bullying he employed in private.

He said now, as he laid aside the shot-belt: "I wonder that my lord should not have said something to your Grace, if he noticed you was wearing this nasty, low belt, more fit for a poacher, one would have thought, than for a Gentleman, let alone one that was born, as the saying is, in the Purple. But, there! tell your Grace till Domesday you'll never mend your ways! And why would you not take a loader, pray, not to mention Padbury? I can tell your Grace he was quite put about to think you should be off without him, and very likely needing a beater as well."

"No, I didn't need a beater," said the Duke, sitting down to allow Nettlebed to pull off his boots. "And as for my shot-belt, I daresay you may consider it a very vulgar appendage, but it spares my pockets, and is, I think, as quick a way of loading as any that I know."

"If you had taken a loader with you, as was befitting, your Grace would not have needed any such," said Nettlebed severely. "I could see his lordship was not best pleased."

"I am sure he was not displeased for any such cause," responded the Duke, walking towards the washstand, and lifting the towel from the ewer. "He is a great advocate for a man's being able to do everything for himself that may come in his way."

"That," said Nettlebed, frustrating the Duke's attempt to pick up the ewer, "is as may be, your Grace." He poured the water into the basin, and removed the towel from the Duke's hand. "But when his lordship takes a gun out, he has always his loader, and very likely a couple of beaters besides, for he is one as knows what is due to his position."

"Well, if I do not know what is due to mine I am sure it is not for want of being told," sighed the Duke. "I think it would have been very pleasant to have been born one of my own tenants, sometimes."

"Born one of your Grace's own tenants!" ejaculated Nettlebed, in an astonished tone.

The Duke took the towel, and began to wipe his wet face with it. "Not one of those who are obliged to live in Thatch End Cottages, of course," he said reflectively.

"Thatch End Cottages!"

"At Rufford."

"I do not know what your Grace can be meaning!"

"They are for ever complaining of them. I daresay they should all be pulled down. In fact, I am sure of it, for I have seen them."

"Seen them, your Grace?" said Nettlebed, quite shocked. "I am sure I do not know when you can have done so!"

"When we were in Yorkshire, I rode over," replied the Duke tranquilly.

"Now that," said Nettlebed, in a displeased way, "is just what your Grace should not be doing! It is Mr. Scriven who should attend to such matters, as I am sure he is willing and able to do, let alone he has his clerks to be running about the country for him!"

"Only he does not attend to it," said the Duke, sitting down before his dressing-table.

Nettlebed handed him his neckcloth. "Then your Grace may depend upon it there is nothing as needs attending to," he said.

"You remind me very much of uncle," remarked the Duke.

Nettlebed shook his head at him, but said: "Well, and I'll be bound his lordship has told your Grace there isn't a better agent than Mr. Scriven in the length and breadth of the land."

"Oh, yes!" said the Duke. "Nothing could exceed his care for my interests."

"Well, and what more could your Grace desire?"

"I think it would be very agreeable if he cared for my wishes."

A slightly weary note in his master's quiet voice made Nettlebed say with a roughness that imperfectly concealed his affection: "Now, your Grace, I see what it is! You have tired yourself out, carrying that heavy game-bag, and your gun, and you're in a fit of the dismals! If Mr. Scriven don't seem always to care for your wishes, it's because your Grace is young yet, and don't know the ways of tenants, nor what's best for the estate."

"Very true," said the Duke, in a colourless voice.

Nettlebed helped him to put on his coat. "Your Grace's honoured father had every confidence in Mr. Scriven, that I do know," he said.

"Oh, yes!" said the Duke.

Feeling that his master was still unconvinced, Nettlebed began to recite the numerous virtues of the agent-in-chief, but after a few moments the Duke interrupted him, saying: "Well, never mind! Have we company to-night?"

"No, your Grace, you will be quite alone."

"It sounds delightful, but I am afraid it is untrue."

"No, no, your Grace, it is just as I tell you! You will find no one below but my lord, and my lady, and Mr. Romsey, and Miss Scamblesby!" Nettlebed assured him.

The Duke smiled, but refrained from making any remark. He submitted to having his coat smoothed across his shoulders, accepted a clean handkerchief, and moved towards the door. Nettlebed opened this for him, and nodded to an individual hovering in the hall outside, who at once withdrew, apparently to spread the news of the Duke's coming. He was the Groom of the Chambers, and although more modern households might have abolished this office, at Sale Park a pomp belonging to the previous century was rigidly adhered to, and the groom continued to hold his post. During the long period of the Duke's minority he had had little scope for his talents, but he was now hopeful of seeing the great house once more full of distinguished guests, all with their exacting personal servants, and their quite incompatible fads and fancies, driving a lesser man to suicide, but affording Mr. Turvey an exquisite enjoyment.

The Duke walked down the stairs, and crossed a vast, marble-paved hall to the double doors that led into the gallery. Here it had been the custom of the Family to assemble before dinner since the Duke's grandfather had rerebuilt the mansion. As the gallery was over a hundred foot long, it had sometimes seemed to the Duke that some smaller apartment might be a preferable assembly room on any but Public Days, but a mild suggestion made to this effect had been greeted by his uncle with such disapproval that with his usual docility he had abandoned any hope of making a change.

Two liveried footmen, who appeared to have been trying to impersonate wax effigies, suddenly sprang to life, and flung open the doors; the Duke dwarfed by their height and magnificence, passed between them into the gallery.

Since September was drawing to an end, and the evenings were already a little chilly, a log-fire had been kindled in the grate at one end of the gallery. Lord Lionel Ware was standing before it, not precisely with his watch in his hand, but presenting the appearance of one who had but that moment restored the timepiece to his pocket. Beside him, and making a praiseworthy if not entirely successful attempt to divert his mind from the lateness of the hour, was the Reverend Oswald Romsey, once tutor to the Duke, now his Chaplain, and engaged in the intervals of his not very arduous duties in writing a learned commentary on the Epistle to the Hebrews. On a straw-coloured brocade sofa, wholly shielded from the fire's warmth by her husband's stalwart form, was disposed the Duke's aunt, a lady fashioned in a generous mould which the current mode of high waists and narrow skirts could not have been said to have flattered; and sitting primly upright in a chair suitably withdrawn from the intimate circle was Miss Scamblesby, a spinster of uncertain age and nebulous relationship, who was always referred to by Lady Lionel as "my cousin," and had been an inmate of Sale Park for as long as the Duke could remember, performing the duties of a lady-in-waiting. As Lady Lionel was extremely kind-hearted, she was not in the least overworked, or browbeaten, the only ills she had to endure being her ladyship's very boring conversation, and his lordship's snubs, which last, however, were dealt out so impartially to every member of the household as to make her feel herself to be quite one of the family.

But the Duke, who had, his uncle frequently told him, too much sensibility, could not rid himself of the notion that Miss Scamblesby's position was an unhappy one, and he never neglected to bestow on her a distinguishing degree of attention, or to acknowledge a relationship which did not, in fact, exist, by addressing her as Cousin Amelia. When his uncle pointed out to him, not in a carping spirit, but as one who liked accuracy, that being only some kind of a third cousin to Lady Lionel her connection with the Ware family was of the most remote order, he merely smiled, and slid out of a possible argument in a manner rendered perfect by years of practice.

As he walked down the gallery, he smiled at her, and enquired after the headache she had complained of earlier in the day. While she blushed, thanked, and disclaimed, Lord Lionel crushingly remarked that he did not know why people should have headaches, since he himself had never suffered such an ill in his life; and Mr. Romsey pleased nobody by saying: "Ah, my lord Duke has a fellow-feeling, I daresay! I am sure no one has suffered more from an affliction we more hardy mortals are exempt from!"

"Stuff and nonsense!" said Lord Lionel, who very much disliked to have his nephew's delicacy of constitution mentioned by anyone other than himself.

Mr. Romsey's well-meaning if unfortunate remark had the effect of arousing Lady Lionel from her customary lethargy, and she began to enumerate, with a surprising degree of animation, all the more shocking headaches her nephew had endured during his sickly boyhood. The Duke bore this patiently, but Lord Lionel pshawed and fidgeted, and final-

14

ly broke in on a discourse that threatened to be never-ending, saying crossly: "Very well, very well, ma'am, but this is all forgotten now, and we do not wish to be reminding Gilly of it! Were you hedgerow-shooting, my boy? Had you any sport?"

"Three brace of partridges only, and some wood-pigeons, sir," responded the Duke.

"Very well indeed," said his uncle approvingly. "I have frequently observed that for all it may not be real game, as we understand it, the wood-pigeon gives some of the hardest shots of all. What shot did you use?"

"Seven," said the Duke.

This made Lord Lionel shake his head a little, and point out the advantages of a four or a five. His nephew, having listened politely, said that he would grant him an accidental shot at long distance with his heavier shot, but that a well-breeched and properly bored gun would shoot Number Seven better than any other. As the Duke was a very pretty shot, Lord Lionel allowed this to pass with no more than a glancing reference to newfangled fads, and asked him if he had taken one of his Purdeys out.

"No, a Manton," said the Duke. "I have been trynig Joseph Manton's New Patent Shot."

"I have bought my shot from Walker and Maltby any time these thirty years," declared his lordship. "But the old ways will never do for you young men! I suppose you will tell me this New Patent has some particular virtue!"

"I think the shot is more compact, and it is certainly cleaner to handle," replied the Duke.

"I hope, Gilly, that you did not get your feet wet?" said Lady Lionel. "You know, if you were to take a chill it will go straight to your throat, and I was thinking only the other day that I cannot recall the name of that very obliging physician who recommended electricity. You were only a child, so I daresay you might not remember, but it was very excellent, though your uncle disliked it very much."

"Does Borrowdale not know that you are ready for dinner?" demanded Lord Lionel loudly. "It will be six o'clock before we sit down to it!"

"There was quite a fashion for electricity at that time," pursued his wife placidly. "I am sure I know of a dozen persons who took the treatment."

"It was what the Captain calls all the crack," said Miss Scamblesby, prefixing her remark with the titter which never failed to irritate his lordship.

Lord Lionel was both fond and proud of his son, but he did not propose to submit to having his words quoted to

15

him, and he immediately said that he had the greatest dislike of cant expressions. Miss Scamblesby's subsequent confusion was only relieved by the entrance of Borrowdale, who came in at that moment to announce that dinner was served. The Duke then assisted his aunt to rise from the sofa, Miss Scamblesby draped a Paisley shawl round her shoulders, Mr. Romsey handed her her fan and her reticule, and the whole party filed out into the hall, and across it to the dining-saloon.

Here the Duke took his place at the head of the table, in an immense carved oak chair, and Lord Lionel installed himself in a similar chair at the foot. Lady Lionel sat at her nephew's right hand, and Miss Scamblesby and Mr. Romsey established themselves opposite to her, with only one footman between the pair of them.

Lord Lionel being an advocate of what he considered a neat, plain dinner, only two courses were served at Sale Park when the family dined alone. The first of these consisted of a tureen of turtle, removed with fish, which was in its turn removed with a haunch of venison. Several sidedishes, such as pork cutlets with Rober sauce, larded fillets of beef, tenderones of veal and truffles, and a braised ham, graced the board, but since his lordship was a moderate trencherman, and the Duke had a notoriously small appetite, the only person who did justice to the spread was Miss Scamblesby, who had (so his lordship had more than once remarked to his nephew) the inordinate appetite of all poor relations.

While the first course dragged on its way, conversation was of a desultory nature. The Duke looked tired; his aunt rarely troubled herself to make conversation; and Lord Lionel seemed preoccupied. When the first course was carried out in procession, however, he roused himself to say: "Well! You are all very dull to-night!" a remark which not unnaturally bereft the assembled company of any conversational ideas they might have had.

"Well, Gilly!" said his lordship, after a pause of which no one showed any sign of wishing to take advantage. "Have you nothing to say for yourself?"

A slightly apprehensive look came into the Duke's eyes. Mr. Romsey said kindly: "I fancy you are tired, my lord."

"No, no!" Gilly disclaimed, almost shrinking from the imputation.

It had the effect of softening Lord Lionel. "Tired? I am sure I do not know why you must all be for ever supposing him knocked up by the least exertion! Let me tell you, it is very irksome to a young man to have such nonsense talked

16

of him! You are bored, Gilly! Yes, yes, you need not trouble to deny it, for I do not wonder at it! You should have invited some few of your Oxford friends to come down and shoot with you. It is dull work for you here alone."

"Thank you, I am very happy, sir!" Gilly stammered. "You —I mean, *we* have invited several parties for the pheasant-shooting, I believe."

"Well, well, that is looking some way ahead!" said his lordship indulgently. "You will scarcely wish for any large shooting parties until November!"

The second course here made its appearance, and a fresh array of silver dishes was set out. Some pigeons and a hare constituted the main features, but there were besides a quantity of vegetables, and several creams, jellies, and cakes, including, as Miss Scamblesby was quick to perceive, a Gâteau Mellifleur, to which she was extremely partial.

Lady Lionel helped herself from a dish of artichoke bottoms in sauce. "I have been thinking," she said. "If you should care for it, Gilly, we could get up a rubber of whist after dinner. I daresay we might prevail upon our good Mr. Romsey to take a hand, and if he does not care to, Amelia does not play so very ill."

Her husband set his wineglass down rather hurriedly, and said with more haste than civility that she must know that Gilly disliked whist. Then, perceiving quadrille in her eye, he added: "Or any other game of cards. Besides, I have just recollected that Chigwell brought up the mails from the receiving-office this afternoon, and there is a letter for you from your Uncle Henry, Gilly. I will give it to you after dinner."

The Duke's entertainment having been thus provided for, Lady Lionel was able to relapse into indolence, merely wondering in an idle fashion what Lord Henry could be writing to Gilly about. Miss Scamblesby said that it seemed a long time since they had had the felicity of seeing dear Lord and Lady Henry Ware at Sale; and Mr. Romsey asked if Mr. Matthew was not now a freshman up at Oxford.

"No, he is entering on his third year," the Duke replied.

"But not, I fancy, at *our* college, my lord?" Mr. Romsey said playfully.

As Mr. Romsey was a Balliol scholar, and the Duke had been at Christ Church, the possessive pronoun could only be taken to refer to the circumstance of his having accompanied his pupil to Oxford to keep a watchful eye on his health and his associates. The Duke, who had suffered as only a sensitive youth could under such an arrangement,

17

found the reminder so irritating that he was obliged to close his lips on an unkind retort.

"My nephew is at Magdalen College," said Lord Lionel shortly. "As for not having seen my brother and his wife here, they spent six weeks with us in the summer, and brought all the children, as I for one am not likely to forget very readily! They cut up the south lawn with their cricket, and if they had been sons of *mine*——"

"But they asked my permission, sir, and I gave it," Gilly said, in a soft voice.

Lord Lionel opened his mouth to utter a blistering reproof, recollected himself, shut it again, and, after a slight pause, said: "Well, it is your lawn, and you may do as you wish with it, but I own I cannot conceive what you were about to give permission!"

A rather mischievous smile lit the Duke's eyes: he looked under his lashes at his uncle, and replied: "I think it was perhaps because I have wanted very often to play cricket there myself."

"Yes! and you would thank me for it to-day, I daresay, had I allowed you and Gideon to ruin one of the finest pieces of turf in the country!" said his lordship.

Miss Scamblesby having by this time disposed of her portion of the Gâteau Mellifleur, Lady Lionel heaved herself up out of her chair. The Duke picked up such small articles as she dropped, the doors were held open, and both ladies withdrew to leave the gentlemen to their wine.

The covers having been removed, the cloth swept away, and decanters set upon the table, the servants left the room, and Lord Lionel settled down to enjoy his port in what he termed comfort, and his nephew thought great discomfort. The fire behind him was beginning to be unpleasantly hot, the ornate carving of his chair made leaning back in it a penance, and he was not fond of port.

Lord Lionel began to talk of some improvements to one of the Duke's estates, which the agent-in-chief thought might be advantageous. "You should see Scriven yourself, Gilly," he said. "You know, you must not forget that in less than a year now you will have the management of everything in your own hands. I am very anxious you should acquaint yourself with all the business of your estates."

"Dear me, yes!" said Mr. Romsey, sipping his wine delicately. "It is very true, though I may scarcely credit it! My dear lord, you will indeed be twenty-five next year! Yet it seems only yesterday that I was so fortunate as to be chosen to be your chief guide and preceptor!"

"I have never had the least doubt that I made a wise

choice," said his lordship graciously, "but what I am saying is that my nephew must not look to be guided for many months more. You have a thousand amiable qualities, Gilly, but you lack decision of character!"

The Duke did not deny the accusation. He felt it to be true, but he could scarcely repress a shudder at the thought of the painful scenes that must have taken place at Sale had he been endowed with the same forceful personality that distinguished his uncle. His cousin Gideon had it in some measure, and had certainly won his father's respect with it; but Gideon had always been a robust and pugnacious boy, and was quite untroubled by sensitive nerves. He had cared for being thrashed as little as for being rated. The Duke had never known which of the two fates he dreaded most. Fortunately for him, Lord Lionel had used him with far more gentleness than he showed his son, so that he was not really at all afraid of him. But a naturally sweet disposition, a dislike of quarrelling, and of loud, angry voices, combined with a rueful appreciation of the very real devotion to his interest and welfare that inspired his uncle's strict rule made him submit docilely where his cousin would have flamed into revolt.

"You are the head of the family, Gilly," Lord Lionel said. "You must learn to assert yourself. I have done all that a man may to train and educate you for the position you must occupy, but you are by far too diffident."

Mr. Romsey shook his head reminiscently. "Indeed, there are few young men to-day who can boast of my lord Duke's advantages," he said. "But I for one feel sure, sir, that he will prove himself worthy of your unremitting solicitude."

The Duke thought of the period of his boyhood, spent largely at his house near Bath, so that he might derive the benefit of the waters there; of three trammelled years at Oxford; of two more trammelled years upon the Continent, with a military gentleman added to his entourage, to teach him horse-manage, and manly sports; and suddenly he made up his mind to assert himself, even if only in a small matter. He pushed back his chair, and said: "Shall we join my aunt now?"

"Really, Gilly, you must see that I have not yet finished my glass!" said Lord Lionel. "Do not, I beg of you, get into a scrambling way of doing things! You should always make sure that the company is ready to rise before you give the signal."

"I beg your pardon, sir," said the Duke, abandoning the attempt to assert himself.

CHAPTER II

WHEN the gentlemen at last joined the ladies, they found them established before the fire in the Crimson Saloon, one of a handsome suite of reception rooms on the first floor. Lady Lionel had sent for some working-candles, and her embroidery-frame, upon which latter Miss Scamblesby was engaged in setting stitches in various coloured silks. Her ladyship rarely occupied herself with anything more fatiguing than the knotting of a fringe, but by constantly desiring to have her embroidery brought to her, choosing the silks, and criticizing the design, she was easily able to persuade herself that she was an indefatigable worker, and would receive compliments upon her skill with perfect complaisance.

Mr. Romsey went over to Miss Scamblesby's side, to observe what progress she had made; and while Lady Lionel informed him for perhaps the tenth time that the work was destined to form an altar-cloth for the Chapel, her husband gave Gilly the letter from his younger uncle, and waited expectantly for it to be handed over to him when Gilly had finished his perusal of it.

Gilly read it in some little surprise. Lord Henry, who was of a saving turn of mind, had managed to avoid the cost of an enclosure by compressing the intelligence he wished to convey on a single, crossed sheet. He wrote to inform his nephew of a very desirable connection he was about to form, through the betrothal of his eldest daughter to a scion of a distinguished family. He contrived to squeeze a number of details into his single sheet, and ended by expressing the hope that the proposed alliance would meet with his nephew's approval.

The Duke gave up this letter to Lord Lionel in a mechanical way, and his lordship, casting his eye over it, said: "Ha! I suspected as much! Yelverton's son, eh? Pretty well for a chit not out of the schoolroom!"

"I cannot conceive why he should write to tell me of it," remarked the Duke.

Lord Lionel looked up from the letter to direct an admonishing frown at him. "Naturally he would do so! It is a very proper letter. You will write your felicitations, of course, and say that you are very well pleased with the connection."

"But he will not care a button whether I am pleased or not," objected the Duke, with a touch of impatience.

"Pray do not let me have these odd humours!" begged

20

his lordship irascibly. "One would suppose you do not attend to anything that is said to you, Sale! I have been telling you for ever that you are the head of the family, and must learn to take your place as such, and now you talk rubbishing stuff to me of your uncle's not caring a button for your approval! If you are so lost to the sense of what is due to your position, you must perceive that he is not! A very pretty letter he has written you: expresses himself just as he ought! I must say, I had not thought he would have contrived such an eligible match for that girl—not but what it is not precisely what I should have cared for myself."

"No," agreed Gilly, taking his letter again. "My cousin is not yet seventeen, and I am sure Alfred Thirsk must be forty if he is a day."

"Well, well, that need not signify!" said Lord Lionel. "The thing is that I have never fancied that brood of Yelverton's. There is a damned vulgar streak in them all; came into the family when the old man—Yelverton's father, I mean: you would not recall—married some rich Cit's heress. However—it is none of my business!"

The Duke said a little impishly: "Very true, sir, but if it is mine I think I should inform my uncle that I do not like the match. Poor Charlotte! I am sure she cannot wish for it!"

Lord Lionel audibly drew a breath. In the voice of one restraining himself with a strong effort, he said: "You will not, I trust, be guilty of such a piece of impertinence, Sale! Pray, what should a young man of your age know about the matter?"

"But you told me, sir, that I must learn to assert myself," said the Duke meekly.

"Let me assure you, Gilly, that that kind of nonsense is beyond the line of being pleasing!" said Lord Lionel sternly. "You must be perfectly well aware that this very proper letter of your uncle's is the merest formality, and not to be taken as an excuse for you to be putting yourself forward in a very unbecoming way! A fine state of affairs it would be if a man of your uncle's age and experience is to be told how he is to manage his household by a young jackanapes of a nephew! You will write to him as I have directed, and mind you write it fair, and not in one of your scrawls! You had better let me see the letter before it is sealed."

"Very well, sir," said the Duke.

Perceiving that he had quite banished the smile from his nephew's eyes, Lord Lionel relented, saying in a kindlier tone: "There is no need to be cast into a fit of dejection because I am obliged to give you a scold, boy. There, we shall say no more about it! Give the letter to your aunt to

21

read, and come into the library with me. I have something I wish to say to you."

The Duke looked extremely apprehensive on hearing these ominous words, but he obediently handed over the letter to Lady Lionel, and followed his uncle downstairs to the library on the entrance floor. Since the candles had already been lit, and the fire made up, it was apparent to him that this interview had been premeditated. Insensibly he braced himself to meet it with becoming fortitude, wishing that he dared light one of the cigarillos which his cousin Gideon had very reprehensively bestowed on him. But as Lord Lionel objected strongly to the vice of smoking, both on the score of its being a vulgar, dirty habit, and of its being excessively injurious to the lungs, he did not dare.

"Sit down, Gilly!" said Lord Lionel, treading over to the fire, and taking up his favourite position before it.

This command was less unnerving than earlier ones (delivered in ferocious accents) to stand up straight and put his hands behind his back, but the prospect of having to sit in a low chair while his uncle loomed over him was almost equally daunting. The Duke's apprehensive look deepened, and although he did sit down, it was with obvious reluctance.

Lord Lionel, who did not include the taking of snuff amongst the vulgar and dirty habits engendered by the use of tobacco, helped himself to a generous pinch, and shut his box with a snap. "You know, Gilly," he said, "that letter of your uncle's comes remarkably pat."

The Duke's eyes lifted quickly to his face. "Yes, sir?"

"Yes, my boy. You will be of full age in less than a year now, and it is high time we were thinking of settling your affairs comfortably."

The Duke was aware of a sinking sensation in the pit of his stomach. He kept his eyes fixed on his uncle's face. "Yes, sir?"

For once in his life, Lord Lionel seemed disinclined to come speedily to the point of his discourse. He opened his snuff-box again, and said: "I have always tried to do my best for you, boy. I daresay you may sometimes have thought me harsh——"

"Oh, no!" said the Duke faintly.

"Well, I am happy to hear you say so, for I am very fond of you, Gilly, and always have been. I have no scruple in telling you that apart from your health, and a want of spirits in you, you have never caused me anxiety."

The Duke, feeling that a response was expected, stammered: "Th-thank you, sir!"

"I don't say that you are as wise as I could wish," said

22

Lord Lionel, tempering his praise, "or that you have not a great many faults, but on the whole I fancy your poor father might have been not dissatisfied with his son, had he lived to see you to-day." Here he took another pinch of snuff. As Gilly was unable to think of anything to say, an uneasy silence prevailed. Lord Lionel broke it. "Your father left you to my guardianship," he said, "and I think I may say that I have in every way open to me followed out what I knew to be his wishes. I even had you christened Adolphus," he added, a slight sense of grievance overcoming him, "although it is one of these new-fangled German names that I very much dislike. However, that was a small thing, and you know I have never called you by it. And I have never permitted your uncle Henry to interfere in your education, for all he has been one of your trustees. I have nothing to say against your uncle, and no doubt his notions do very well for his own sons, but they will not do for me, and they would not have done for your father either, and a thousand pities it was that his name should have been included in the Trust. But there is no sense in repining over that, and I hope I know how to deal with my own brother."

The Duke, drawing upon his recollection, could not feel that this hope was misplaced, but he did not think himself called upon to say so. Instead he uttered an indistinguishable murmur.

"There is no reason why you should be treated like a child, Gilly," said Lord Lionel, in a burst of candour, "so I shall not conceal from you that I have a very poor opinion of your uncle's judgment! He does not want, precisely, for sense, but you must know that he never partook of your father's and my sentiments as one could have wished he might have done, and when he married that foolish woman —but I do not wish to dwell upon that, and if he chose to ally himself with a female out of a canting Methodist family, and to breed a pack of ill-conditioned brats who can think of nothing better to do than to ruin a lawn it has taken fifty years to bring to perfection, I am sure it was not for me to cavil. Although, mind you," he added admonishingly, "I told him how it would be at the outset. But Henry was never one to listen to those who might be supposed to be a little wiser than himself. I trust you will not turn out to be the same, Gilly."

The Duke assured him that he would not.

"No, well, I fancy I have drilled a few proper notions into your head," agreed his uncle. "But all this has nothing to do with what I have to say to you!" He bent his austere gaze upon Gilly's downcast face, and was silent for a moment. "I am speaking of your marriage, Gilly," he said abruptly.

The Duke looked up, startled. "My marriage, sir!"

"There is nothing to be surprised about in that, surely!" said Lord Lionel. "It is not, I fancy, unknown to you that I have already made certain arrangements on your behalf. I do not believe in making a secret of a very ordinary business, and since I am quite as much concerned with the question of your future comfort and happiness as with the very important one of securing the succession, I have been careful to choose for you a bride who will bring you, besides the necessary advantages of birth and fortune, a reasonable chance of harmony in your future life. In this, I hope you will realize, my boy, that I have had all these modern notions with which I make no doubt you are imbued in my head. You are not to suppose that my mind was irrevocably fixed upon the first and most obvious choice. I have had several young females in my eye, but I believe they will not do for you, and it is now some years since I have entertained any other idea than that you should, as soon as you had come of full age, marry Lady Harriet Presteigne."

The Duke got up suddenly, and said in some little agitation: "Yes—no! It had not been unknown to me. But the succession cannot be in danger, sir, while my cousin Gideon and, indeed, my Uncle Henry's five sons——"

"Do not talk to me of your Uncle Henry's sons!" commanded Lord Lionel wrathfully. "If they are all to take after the eldest of them, who, I am hearing, is for ever in some disgraceful scrape, as I have very little doubt they will do, for what can one expect, if a man will marry a Methodist?—I can only say that I am astonished you should entertain the notion of seeing one of them here in your shoes for as much as a moment!"

"But I should not see them in my shoes," pointed out the Duke reasonably. "And really, you know, sir, Matt's scrapes cannot be called disgraceful! And in any event I am sure that Gideon would fill my shoes far better than I could ever do. Surely——"

"You may put that out of your head once and for all!" said Lord Lionel, in his sternest voice. "Understand me, Gilly, I have never thought to see my son in your place, and nothing could more distress me than the knowledge that it must come to that in the end! I venture to say that Gideon shares my sentiments to the full. I do not know what cause he can have given you to suppose——"

"None! Oh, none!" Gilly said hurriedly. "I only meant—

24

I only wished to say—that it cannot be thought *necessary* for me to marry so soon!"

"So soon?" repeated his uncle, raising his brows. "My dear boy, it has been an understood thing between myself and Ampleforth any time these five years! I make no doubt the young lady herself is fully aware of it, for her mother is a woman of great good sense, and will have made it her business to prepare the girl for the position she is destined to occupy."

"You think that Harriet herself knows of it?" the Duke said, in a stunned voice.

"Certainly. Why should she not?" replied his uncle. "If you have some romantic notion in your head, I advise you to rid yourself of it, boy. Romantic notions do very well in a trashy novel, and I daresay they may not come amiss amongst the lesser ranks of society, but they are not for persons of our order, and that you may depend upon. Yes, yes, you think me very unfeeling, I daresay, but you may believe me when I tell you that I have seen more unhappiness arising out of a so-called love-match than from any other cause in this world. I dare swear you, at twenty-four, and with your head full of nonsense, have not half as much idea of what will suit you as I have. But don't imagine, Gilly, that I would tie you up to someone for whom you feel the least degree of dislike! You cannot have failed to notice that your aunt and I have taken every opportunity of inviting the Ampleforths to Sale. I have encouraged you to visit them, and you have not been backward in accepting invitations to Ampleforth. I have made it my business to observe you narrowly, and I own that I shall be surprised to learn that you are wholly indifferent to Lady Harriet."

The Duke grasped the back of a chair. He looked even paler than was natural in him, and acutely unhappy. "No, indeed! I have the greatest regard—She has always been most amiable—But marriage——!"

"Come, Gilly!" said Lord Lionel, a little impatiently, "you do not mean to tell me that you had never considered the question! You knew very well that the matter was arranged!"

"Yes," the Duke said, in a hollow tone. "Yes, I did know. Only I hoped—I thought——"

"Well, and what did you think and hope?"

"I don't know," said the Duke helplessly. "Only that perhaps something would occur—or some other man offer—or—or that it might not be quite yet!"

His uncle looked shrewdly at him. "Have you a *tendre* for some other female, Gilly?" he asked.

The Duke shook his head.

"Well, I thought you had not, for you have never been in the petticoat-line, but you need not scruple to tell me so if I have been mistaken." He waited, but the Duke only shook his head again. "Then what is the matter? Be open with me, I beg of you!"

The Duke took out his handkerchief, and pressed it to his lips. "I hardly know. I do not mean to say anything in Harriet's disparagement! I have always been excessively attached to her, ever since we were children. She is everything that is amiable and obliging. Indeed, she is all compliance and good-nature, and is very pretty besides, but—but I had thought that when I came to marry I should choose a wife for myself, a lady for whom I felt—with whom I might be in love, sir!"

"Oho! Here is a high flight!" said his uncle, rather amused. "And where is this fine lady?"

"I have not met one. I——"

"I am happy to hear it, for if any one thing is more to be depended on than another is that she would be quite ineligible! We have all our youthful fancies, Gilly, but it will not answer to be fashioning our lives on them. Now, you are not a schoolboy. You have been about the world a little: I took care that you should do so. You have been presented at Court, you have taken your seat in the House, you have travelled, you have had a season in London. Had you formed an attachment for some female it would not have surprised me in the least, and had your affections become fixed upon an eligible object you would not have found me unreasonable. But although you have met any number of young females of *ton*, none has succeeded in capturing your fancy. I do not feel that in urging you to come to the point with Ampleforth I am tying you up in matrimony before you have had time to know your own mind."

"Do you mean that I shall never feel—a—a stronger degree of attachment for a female than—than——"

"My dear Gilly, this is being foolish without permission! In plain terms, the sort of passion you have in mind has little to do with marriage. I grant that to be obliged to live with a woman whom you held in aversion would be a sad fate, but we need not consider that. You own that you are not indifferent to Lady Harriet. For a female, I believe her to have a superior understanding. Her disposition is amiable, and if you mean to object that there is a want of spirits in her I would point out to you that you have very odd humours yourself, and would find less rational comfort with a woman of more vivacity than with a quiet girl who would,

26

I am persuaded, partake of many of your sentiments, and study to please you."

"Oh, yes, yes!" interrupted Gilly. "But——"

Lord Lionel held up his hand. "No, listen to what I have to say to you, my boy! You think I do not enter into your feelings upon this occasion, but you are mistaken. I shall be plain with you. In Lady Harriet you will not find yourself saddled with a wife who will expect more from you than you are inclined to give. She is a very well brought-up girl; and while, on the one hand, I am satisfied that she will conduct herself, as Duchess of Sale, with propriety and discretion, she will not expect you to be always at her side. If you choose to mount a mistress, she will know how to look the other way, and you will not be obliged to face the reproaches which might be levelled at you by a woman of lesser breeding. In short, you may be assured of a well-conducted household with an amiable woman at its head, and may indulge what romantic fancies you please out of it."

"Do you suppose, sir," said Gilly, in an extinguished tone, "that it is with such sentiments as these that Harriet thinks of marriage with me—or—or with another?"

"I have been acquainted with Augusta Ampleforth any time these twenty years," responded Lord Lionel readily, "and I entertain no fears that Harriet has been allowed to fill her head with romantical stuff and nonsense. I daresay Lady Ampleforth may have some faults——"

"I have always thought her the most unfeeling woman I have ever met!" the Duke said.

"Well, well, now you are in your high ropes again! She is an ambitious woman, but she has a great deal of common-sense, after all!"

The Duke released the chairback, and took a turn about the room. He was evidently agitated, and his uncle allowed him to walk about for a few minutes before saying: "If you dislike it so very much, Gilly, you should have told me of it earlier. To draw back at this late date will be as bad as to declare off."

The Duke turned a startled face towards him. "Oh, no, surely not!"

"It has been understood between the two families for some years, and from what I hear the announcement of your engagement is pretty widely expected."

The Duke looked quite horrified. "But it cannot be! I have never offered—never said a word to Harriet, or given anyone the least reason to suppose that my affections had become fixed!"

"My dear boy, in our world these affairs are generally

27

known. Ampleforth has refused one offer for Harriet's hand already, and I have little doubt that her ladyship will have dropped a hint or two abroad. It would be a great piece of folly to pretend that you are not a splendid matrimonial prize, Gilly, so we will not indulge ourselves with any humbug about that. In fact, except for Devonshire, who must be nearing thirty by now and seems to be a settled bachelor —besides he is extremely deaf—I do not know of one to equal you. Depend upon it, Augusta Ampleforth will not have been able to resist the temptation of telling her friends —in the strictest confidence, of course!—that she has such large expectations for her daughter. She must be the envy of her acquaintance!"

The Duke passed a hand through his fair locks. "I had no idea of this! Do you tell me that the Ampleforths—Harriet—have been expecting me to declare myself?"

"Oh, well, no, I do not say that," replied Lord Lionel. "In fact, I told Ampleforth I would not have you established too early in life. Your health was too uncertain, and I wished you to have time to look about you before making your choice."

"My choice!" Gilly ejaculated. "It seems I have none at all, sir!"

"You have certainly made none," said his uncle dryly.

There was a defeated silence. After a few moments, Gilly said: "I do not know what to say. I must see Ampleforth, and—and Harriet too. Until I am persuaded that she does indeed expect me to offer—Well, I must see her!"

"Not before you have spoken with her father!" exclaimed Lord Lionel.

"Oh, no!" Gilly said wearily.

"There is no need for you to be in a hurry," said Lord Lionel. "I believe the Ampleforths are in London at present, but they will be removing into the country at any moment now, I should suppose. Ampleforth is bound to invite you to one of his *battues*, and you may then——"

"No, no, I would rather by far visit him in town!" Gilly said. "I had been thinking that I would go up to see my cousin. If you do not object, sir, I will do so."

"Object! Pray, why should you always be supposing that I may object to what you wish to do, Gilly?" demanded Lord Lionel. "But you will find London very thin of company at this season, and I own I do not like the fogs for you, and they will soon be starting, you know. However, if you like to go for a few days it can very well be arranged. I will send an express to Scriven, to warn him to

have Sale House in readiness fo[r]
company you, and——"

"I should like to go alone—and to an[?]
Duke desperately.

"Alone and to an hotel!" repeated his uncle, [?]
struck. "Next I shall be told that you would like to [?]
to town on the stage-coach!"

"No, I don't wish to travel on a stage-coach, but I do not
want Romsey!"

Lord Lionel eyed him speculatively. "Now, what mischief are you up to, Gilly?" he asked, not displeased. "Do
you mean to go raking in town?"

The Duke smiled rather perfunctorily. "No, sir, but I find
Romsey very tedious, and I am very sure he will find me a
dead bore, for I mean to see a good deal of Gideon, and
you know that they could never agree! And I thought I might
shoot at Manton's, and look in at Tatt's besides, and that
sort of thing is not in Romsey's line at all."

"No, very true," agreed Lord Lionel. "So you mean to
buy another horse, do you? What is it you want? Something showy to lionize a bit, eh? You had best find out
Belper, and desire him to go with you. Not that I mean to
say you are not able to judge a horse for yourself, but
Belper can advise you."

The Duke was too thankful to have scaped the company
of his clerical tutor to jeopardize his position by demurring
at having his other bear-leader thrust upon him. Captain
Belper might override him in the matter of choosing a horse,
but he was not likely to moralize, and he would not be
staying under the same roof as his erstwhile pupil, and so
would not be able to keep his movements under strict
surveillance.

"You will tell Scriven to draw on Child's for whatever
money you may require," said Lord Lionel. "No need to
trouble yourself about that. But as for staying in an hotel,
certainly not, Gilly! I would not vouch for the way they air
the sheets even at the Clarendon, and when you have a very
good house of your own it would be the height of absurdity
not to use it. Borrowdale may go to London ahead of
you——"

"I do not mean to entertain largely. Should Borrowdale
not remain with you, sir?" said the Duke.

"We shall do very well with the under-butler. Naturally
Borrowdale and Chigwell go with you. You must not blame
me for keeping only a skeleton-staff at Sale House, Gilly.
While you were under age I should not have considered it
proper to squander your fortune in keeping up several

29

. . . must be kept up when you
. . . ed so little in London that it
. . . —But that must all be looked
. . . s me in mind of something else!
. . . marriage settlements with Ample-
. . . not expect it of you. You are of
. . . y much better to leave all such mat-

. . . ke.

. . . to say against your being with your
. . . hope you will see as much of him as you
may, . . . let yourself be drawn into that military set,
boy! Gi . . . older than you, and can be trusted to keep
the line, but there are some fast fellows amongst them, such
as I would not wish to see you associating with too freely.
And you never know where that kind of society may lead
you! Park-saunterers, and half-pay officers, hanging out for
invitations: toad-eaters of that style! It will not do for you by
any means."

"No," said the Duke.

"And if you take my advice, Gilly, you will be a little on
your guard with Gaywood!" further admonished his lordship. "I hear that he is being very wild, and if once he gets
it into his head that you are to marry his sister I should own
myself very much astonished if he did not try to borrow
money from you, or some such thing. I do not mean to be
dictating to you, mind! But if he tries to introduce you to
one of these pernicious gaming-houses, do not go with him!"

"No," said the Duke.

"Well," said his lordship, glancing at the clock, "I do not
think there is anything more I wish to say to you at present,
and I see that Borrowdale will be bringing in the tea-tray
in a few minutes. We had better go back to join your aunt."
He nodded graciously at his nephew, and added, a little
inaccurately, but in great good-humour: "We have had a
comfortable prose together, have we not?"

CHAPTER III

FOUR days later, the Duke of Sale set out from Sale Park, in
the Midlands, for London, driving in his own chaise, with
liveried postilions, and outriders to protect his person and
his chattels from possible highwaymen. He was followed by
his valet, in a second coach piled high with baggage; and
preceded by his steward, his butler, his head groom, and
several underlings, all of whom were considered by his

uncle and his steward to be absolutely necessary to his comfort. Upon the day following his decision to visit the Metropolis, a servant had been sent post to London, to warn his agent of his approaching arrival. The man had carried with him a letter addressed by Lord Lionel to one Captain Horace Belper, half-pay officer, desiring this gentleman to render his Grace all the advice and assistance of which he might be thought to stand in need, so that whatever plans the Duke might have entertained of escaping a visit from the Captain were foiled at the outset.

He had been seen off by his uncle, his aunt, his Chaplain, and his old nurse. His aunt and his nurse had confined their parting counsel to reminders to him to take James's Powders on the least suspicion of internal disorder; to beware of damp socks, and over-rich foods; and not to hesitate to call in that eminent physician, Dr. Baillie of Grosvenor Street, if he should chance to take a chill. His Chaplain recommended him not to miss the opportunity of attending a forthcoming lecture at the Royal Society on Developments of the Nebular Hypothesis, recently advanced by the Marquis de Laplace. His uncle, having testily informed his other well-wishers that no young man setting forth for London on a visit of pleasure wished to receive a clutter of such foolish advice, said that he was to beware of French hazard, not to play billiards except in select company, or roulette in any company at all, and to make a point of visiting his dentist.

Fortified by this send-off, and aware that he had at least one person in his train who would do what lay in his power to persuade him to follow out all the more disagreeable orders laid upon him, the Duke left Sale Park, a prey to dejection, and a great many rebellious thoughts.

For the first half of the journey, he indulged his fancy by forming several impossible schemes for shocking and confounding his relatives, but as soon as the absurdity of these struck him he began to be amused at himself, and his ill-humour, never very durable, lifted. He might chafe at his uncle's domineering ways, but he could not be angry with him. He thought it must indeed have been a wearing task to have reared such an unpromising specimen as himself, and for perhaps the hundredth time resolved that it should not be a thankless task as well. Lord Lionel might have been, in the past, a severe guardian; he might cling to strict, old-fashioned ideas, and insist on having these conformed to; he might often have been over-anxious, and have irked his ward with restrictions and prohibitions; but the Duke knew well that he had acted throughout on the

31

highest principles, and had for him an affection perhaps as deep as for his own son. He had certainly taken far greater care of him, and shown him more partiality. It was Gideon who had received the blame for any boyish escapade—with a certain amount of justice, reflected the Duke, smiling to himself, as he recalled various instances of his elder and more enterprising cousin's exploits. Gideon was sent to Eton, but Lord Lionel dared not expose his sickly nephew to the rigours of public school life, and engaged for him a resident tutor, and any number of visiting instructors, from a French dancing-master to a Professor in the Art of Self-Defence. It had been solicitude, not mistrust, which had prompted him to send Gilly up to Oxford under the aegis of Mr. Romsey, and Gilly had most unfortunately taken a chill which (owing, his lordship was convinced, to neglect) had developed into an inflammation of the lungs which had nearly carried him off. There could be no question after that of sending him up to Oxford alone.

Only his obstinate conviction that no gentleman who had not spent a few years on the Continent could be considered to be more than half-educated had prevailed upon Lord Lionel to take the hazardous risk of exposing his nephew, upon his coming down from Oxford, to the dangers of travel. But the long war with France having terminated in the glorious battle of Waterloo (in which action Gideon had sustained a wound that caused his father no particular anxiety), the Continent was once more open to English travellers, and Lord Lionel steeled himself to send Gilly on a tour which should conform as nearly as possible to the Grand Tours of his own young days. With this end in view, he engaged Captain Belper to share with Mr. Romsey the duties and responsibilities of bear-leading the Duke through France, Italy, and such parts of Germany as had not been ravaged by war.

The Duke was well aware that in choosing Captain Belper to instruct him in all manly exercises Lord Lionel had meant to place him in the charge of one who, while old enough to hold authority over him, should not be too old or to staid to be a companion to him. Unfortunately, the quiet young nobleman found that he had little in common with the bluff soldier, sometimes came near to disliking him, and never accorded him more than the gentle courtesy he used towards Mr. Romsey.

He had spent two years abroad, and although these had not been altogether enjoyable they had certainly done much to improve the state of his health. He wondered sometimes how any two persons could have been prevailed upon to undertake the task of following out the conflicting orders laid upon Mr. Romsey and Captain Belper by Lord Lionel. He commanded them to indulge any reasonable wish their charge might express; he warned them to teach my lord Duke to study Economy, and on no account to keep him short of money; he forbade them to coddle him, but instructed them to discover the name and direction of the best doctor in any town they might chance to visit, never to allow my lord to play tennis or to ride, after dinner, or to neglect to change his clothes after taking exercise. They were to encourage him to mingle freely in society, but they were to remove instantly from any town in which he seemed to be in danger of forming acquaintances not of the highest *ton*.

He was to be initiated into the mysteries of gambling, but kept away from the Palais Royale. They were to remember that he was not a schoolboy but a young man; and they were to keep his lordship informed of every detail of their tour.

On the whole, reflected the Duke, they had not managed so very ill. Mr. Romsey had been the more zealous to conform to my lord's instructions, but Captain Belper had been the better guide for a young gentleman setting foot on a foreign shore for the first time. And since they were mutallly antagonistic, and very jealous of each other besides, their charge had not experienced much difficulty in winning the support of one of them when he wished to run counter to the other's judgment.

Upon his return from his travels, the Duke had been a good deal taken aback by his uncle's proposal to install Mr. Romsey as Chaplain at Sale. He did not dislike his tutor, but he had certainly hoped to be rid of him at last, and had supposed that one of the many livings in his gift would be bestowed on him. But Lord Lionel said that none of these was vacant, and that when old Mr. Gunnerside, who had been Chaplain for so many years, had died, he had purposely kept the post free, so that Romsey might fill it in reward for the years of his faithful services. "You would not wish to be ungrateful, Gilly," had said his lordship.

No, Gilly had not wished to be ungrateful, and Mr. Romsey had got his Chaplaincy, and perhaps, in the course of a few more years, he might forget that his patron had once been his pupil. "For God's sake, Adolphus, give that prosy old fool a set-down!" had begged his cousin Gideon.

But the Duke did not like giving set-downs to persons who wished him nothing but good, and had too much sensibility to be anything but courteous to those whose situation in life obliged them to accept without retort the snubs of their patrons.

"Adolphus, you cannot continue to employ such an anti-quated valet as Nettlebed!" expostulated Gideon. "Pension him off, child! pension him off!"

"I cannot!" said the Duke despairingly. "It would break his heart!"

"Can you never bring yourself to hurt anyone's feelings, my little one?" asked Gideon, with his crooked smile.

"Not the feelings of people who are attached to me," answered Gilly simply.

"Then there is no hope for you!" said his cousin.

Gilly was unhappily inclined to believe him.

And now it appeared that there was another person to be added to the list of those whose feelings the Duke could not bring himself to wound. He did not know whether his intended bride was fond of him, but she was gentle, and shy, and, if his uncle were to be believed, she was depending upon him to make her a Duchess. The Duke had not been made a member of various clubs, and participated in a London season, without assimilating certain social facts. He had very little doubt that Lady Harriet's chances of securing him for a husband were being freely betted upon at White's, and to blast all her hopes, to set her up to be the butt of every ill-natured wit in town, would, he realized, be conduct wholly unbefitting a gentleman.

His mood of dejection deepened. Lying back in one cor-ner of his chaise, his eyes on the bobbing forms of the postilions, he tried to think about Lady Harriet, and found it difficult. She had been so very correctly brought-up, had been of late years so zealously chaperoned, that he could not feel that he knew very much about her. There had been a great deal of intercourse between his family and hers; she had very often stayed at Sale Park, or at Cheyney, his house near Bath; and when they had been children he had liked her very well—better, in fact, than the more assertive chil-dren of his acquaintance. He still liked her very well, but the easy intercourse they had once enjoyed had latterly dwindled, perhaps from his own consciousness of the future laid down for them both, perhaps from the lady's increasing shyness. He had squired her to the Opera, and danced with her at Almack's; he found it easier to talk to her than to any other lady of his acquaintance; but she was not the bride of his independent choice, and although he had no very clear idea of what this imaginary damsel might be like, he felt sure that she did not resemble poor little Harriet.

But since he knew, naturally, that he must marry a lady

of impeccable lineage, he was forced to own that Harriet would suit him decidedly better than any other marriageable young female of his set. Only it was all very dull; and without having the least ambition to marry to disoblige his family, as the saying was, he did wish that he could have found a wife for himself, and that not a lady whom he had known from his cradle.

He wondered what it would have been like not to have been born in the purple, but to have been some quite unimportant person—not of too lowly a degree, of course, for that would certainly have been uncomfortable. He might have been obliged to live in Thatch End Cottages, for instance, with a leaking roof; or have been snapped up by the press gang; or even, perhaps (since he had always been undersized) have become the slave of a chimney-sweep. It was undoubtedly better to be the seventh Duke of Sale than a sweep's apprentice, but he was much inclined to think that to have been plain Mr. Dash, of Nowhere in Particular, would have been preferable to either of these callings.

He began to picture the life of plain Mr. Dash, and was still lost in a pleasant, if slightly ill-informed, reverie when his chaise swept into the forecourt of his house in Cruzon Street.

He came down to earth with a thud. Mr. Dash inhabited one of those cosy little terrace houses in a quiet corner of the town, and when he returned to his dwelling after a convivial evening spent with his cronies, playing French hazard, and getting his feet wet, he let himself into his house with his own key, and found no one at all who cared a button where he had been, or what he had been doing. None of his servants had ever known his father. In fact, he had very few servants: just a cook, and a housemaid or two, supposed the Duke, and—stretching a point—possibly a groom to look after his horses. Stewards, butlers, footmen, and valets were encumbrances unknown to Mr. Dash. Nor had he any relatives. Or had he one or two cousins? The Duke could not make up his mind on this point, for although the right style of cousin would undoubtedly be a comfort to Mr. Dash, cousins carried uncles in their wake, and Mr. Dash had no uncles—not even an uncle who lived a very long way from London, and never stirred out of his own house. And, thought the Duke, warming to his theme, Mr. Dash had no Chaplain, and no agent; no tradition to uphold; no dignity to maintain.

It was at this moment that the Duke returned to earth. His chaise had drawn up, and he found himself looking, not at a cosy little house in a terrace, but at the imposing

35

portico of Sale House. As he blinked at it, the great doors were opened by unseen hands, his butler's portly form appeared; and two footmen and the porter came down the steps to open the door of the chaise, let down the steps, remove the rug from across his Grace's knees, and assist his Grace to alight. They were followed by Mr. Chigwell, th steward, who kept a sharp eye on their movements, and was the first to offer a respectful welcome to his Grace.

The Duke began to laugh.

The elder of the two footmen, who figured on Mr. Scriven's account-books as "the Duke's footman," continued to stand with his arm crooked for his master to lean upon as he descended from the coach, and his face rigidly impassive; but the younger footman found the Duke's low laughter so infectious that he so far forgot himself as to grin in sympathy. Mr. Chigwell, himself a trifle startled, made a mental note of this, and silently rehearsed the words of stern reproof he would presently utter.

The Duke picked up his ebony cane, ducked his head to avoid knocking his tall, curly-brimmed beaver against the roof of the chaise, and jumped lightly down, ignoring both the steps, and the proffered arm. Mr. Chigwell and the porter both surged forward to prevent a possible fall, uttering in shocked accents: "Your Grace!"

"Oh, don't, pray!" besought the Duke, in a shaking voice. "You will set me off again!"

Mr. Chigwell bowed politely but in a good deal of bewilderment. He said doubtfully: "I am glad to see your Grace in spirits. Will your Grace enter the house? You will be tired after the journey, I make no question. Refreshments have been laid out for your Grace in the Blue Saloon."

"Thank you," said the Duke.

He trod up the steps, smiled mechanically at Borrowdale, who bowed him in, and found that three more persons were waiting to welcome him. These were the groom of the chambers, the agent-in-chief, and a stalwart, smartly attired gentleman, who darted forward with his hands held out, exclaiming joyfully: "My dear, dear lord! You must let me be amongst the first to bid you welcome to London! How do you do? But I can see for myself that you are in good health!"

All desire to laugh abruptly left the Duke. He halted dead on the threshold, staring up in dismay into the florid countenance that loomed before him. Then, as he recollected himself, he blushed faintly, and held out his hand, saying, with a little stammer: "F-forgive me! I did not know you had been informed of my coming to town. It is excessively obliging in you to have come to meet me, Captain Belper."

"Why, I could not keep away, my dear Lord!" the Captain said, warmly shaking his hand. "I had the news from your good uncle, and excellent news I found it. I have not set eyes on you since I know not when! But come in out of the draught, sir! You see, I do not forget your old weakness! We must have no sore throats to spoil your visit to the Metropolis."

"Thank you, I am very well," the Duke said, disengaging his hand, and turning to bestow it upon the agent.

Mr. Scriven, a middle-aged man in a neat black suit, bowed very low over it, and said that it was a happiness to him to see his Grace. He hoped that everything would be found to be in readiness at Sale House, and begged his Grace to pardon any shortcomings. "Your Grace must know that we have not a full staff of servants here at present," he said. "And I own that I am not perfectly happy in the Chief Confectioner." His grave face relaxed into a smile. "But your Grace did not give me very long warning of this visit!"

"I am sure I shall do very well," said the Duke. "I did not mean to put you to a deal of trouble. I daresay I could have been tolerably comfortable without a Chief Confectioner."

Everyone realized that the Duke had uttered a witticism, so those who social status permitted them to laugh, did so, in a discreet way; and Mr. Scriven said that he hoped his Grace would not find his house to be quite so ill-prepared as *that*. He then added that he should hold himself in readiness to attend upon his Grace as soon as he should be needed; and bowed himself away to the set of offices in one wing of the mansion, where he conducted the business of the Duke's many estates and large fortune.

The Duke turned to find Borrowdale waiting to assist him to take off his long, multiple-caped driving-coat. He handed his hat, and his gloves, and his cane to his personal footman, allowed Borrowdale to remove his driving-coat, and stood revealed in fawn pantaloons, well-polished Hessian boots, and a blue cloth coat of Weston's excellent tailoring. As he did not belong to the dandy-set, his shirt-collar points were not excessively high, and his neckcloth, although arranged with propriety, did not aspire to the niceties of the Mail-coach, the Osbaldestone, or the Trône d'Amour. A single fob hung at his waist; he did not carry a quizzing-glass; and except for a plain pearl pin in his tie the only other adornment he wore was the heavy sardonyx signet ring which had belonged to his father. The shank had had to be made smaller to fit his finger, and the ring seemed to be a trifle too large for so delicate a hand, but the Duke was fond of it, and rarely wore any other.

He accompanied Captain Belper into the Blue Saloon, where a fire had been lit, and a table spread with such light refreshments as might be acceptable within a few hours of dinner.

The Captain declined food, but took a glass of Madeira. He said: "Well, and what brings you to town, my lord? Your uncle writes that you mean to buy a horse!"

"Yes, I think I may do that," replied the Duke.

The Captain lifted quizzical brows. "I think I know you a little too well to stand upon ceremony with you!" he said. "Thought I to myself, Aha! that is a tale for Lord Lionel! Is he still as—careful, shall we say?—as ever?"

"Oh, yes! But I need a new hunter," replied the Duke tranquilly.

"You know I shall be happy to give you my advice. It will quite bring back old times. And for the rest you mean to do a little junketing about the town, eh? But the high *ton* parties are at an end, I fancy. Everyone is gone out of town."

"I hope to see something of my cousin."

"Of course! he is stationed here! I think I caught sight of him the other day, devilish smart in his regimentals! These Lifeguardsmen! Hyde Park soldiers, we Peninsular men used to call them!" He laughed heartily as he spoke, but as the Duke had heard this pleasantry a good many times before he did not accord it more than a perfunctory smile. The Captain crossed one leg over the other, with the air of one who had no immediate intention of removing, and said: "Well, my lord, and what is the news with you? I did not see you at Egham races, although they tell me Lord Lionel was there. I was sorry to have missed the chance of paying my compliments to him."

"Yes, my uncle was staying at Oatlands He does so every year."

"But still does not take you along with him!"

"I was in Yorkshire."

"I should have known it indeed! You would not miss the grouse-shooting, I'll wager! I daresay you would not have been amused as well as at Oatlands: nothing but whist, and the company rather elderly nowadays. *Très polissons*, moreover: not at all what his lordship would wish for you!" He drank some of his wine, and set the glass down on the table at his elbow. "Well, you are wanting to hear all the town-gossip, I expect. There is very little to tell you. The old Queen seems to have recovered from the spasm she suffered in the spring. They say it was provoked by hearing that the Duchesses of Cambridge and Cumberland had met and embraced. Her physicians thought her rage would have carried her off! Then we had Clarence's marriage in July: a shabby affair! Lord, what laughing-stocks they do make of themselves, the Royal Dukes! Three of them bolting into matrimony helter-skelter, one after the other. Entering for the Heir-to-the-throne Stakes, I call it! No doubt we shall be celebrating three Interesting Events next year. What else is there to tell you? Upon my word, I know of no particular tit-bit of scandal! The Regent drives his tilbury in the park every day, with his groom sitting up beside him: it doesn't take well: the sobersides think he should have more dignity. You did well to stay out of town for the general election: you know Castlereagh got pelted? A bad business: came near to rioting in some parts. But you will have heard all that!"

In this fashion the Captain rattled on until interrupted by Borrowdale, who came into the room to enquire if it would suit his Grace to dine at eight o'clock, or whether he wished to visit a theatre. The Duke had meant to call at his cousin's chambers that evening, but he knew that the Captain hoped to be asked to dine with him, and he could not bring himself to disappoint him. Upon receiving the invitation, the Captain protested half-heartedly that he was wearing his morning-clothes, but allowed himself to be easily persuaded into remaining. The Duke, feeling that a whole evening of his conversation could not be borne, said that they would dine early, and go to the theatre. This necessitated ordering the town carriage, selecting the play to be seen, and despatching a footman to procure a box—arrangements which the Duke found pompous, and the Captain, who was generally obliged to attend to all such details himself, agreeably luxurious.

They did not part until the Captain had wrung an assignation for the following morning out of the Duke, but a decided hint that they should also spend the afternoon together was countered by the Duke's saying that he had some calls he must make.

At breakfast next day, the Duke bethought him of his agent, and desired one of the footmen to carry a message to him. Mr. Scriven, who had been expecting the summons, speedily presented himself in the library, bringing with him a formidably bulging brief-case; and the next hour was spent by the Duke in glancing perfunctorily over accounts; listening to suggestions for the improvement of several of his estates; and having it respectfully explained to him why his own ideas could not possibly be put into execution. Mr. Scriven was very kind to him—indeed, almost fatherly; and he said that it was a gratification to him to find his young master taking such a proper interest in his affairs; but he contrived to make him feel very ignorant. The interview ended with his saying that in anticipation of the Duke's needs he had drawn a cheque on Child's Bank, and would his Grace care to take all or part of the money into his own charge at once? The Duke thought he would not need more than a hundred pounds for the present, so this was counted out, in bills, and the sovereigns that still seemed so very new and strange; and the Duke went off to Manton's Shooting Gallery, to meet Captain Belper.

Here he did some very pretty shooting at a wafer, and fell in love with a handsome pair of duelling-pistols, which he purchased. The Captain cut several sly jokes about this, affecting to believe that he must have come to London to fight a duel over some unknown Fair One, and offering himself as a second. The Duke received these in good part, and by dint of employing evasive tactics, managed to shake him off without making any definite arrangement for a further meeting. The Captain said he should wait upon him next day; the Duke made plans for leaving his house at an early hour, and not returning to it until late at night.

CHAPTER IV

AN hour later, the Duke had formally offered for Lady Harriet Presteigne's hand in marriage, and had been accepted.

He had been lucky to have found his future father-in-law at home, he was told. The family was on the point of leaving town, the household, in fact, was in a pucker with the business of packing-up already, for while Lord and Lady Ampleforth, with the younger children, were off to Staffordshire, Lady Harriet was going to pay her annual visit to her grandmother in Bath. If the Duke had come but one day later, he would have found the shutters up, and the knocker off the door.

Lord Ampleforth, who was a kindly, harassed man, generally thought to be under the complete dominance of his wife, pushed matters to a crisis not quite bargained for by the Duke by saying almost at once: "I can guess why you are here, Gilly: I have been having some correspondence with your uncle. But I wish you will consider well, my dear boy! I shall not pretend to you that I do not like the

40

alliance. Indeed, there is none I could like half as well, for setting aside the position my girl would occupy, I know of no one who would, I believe, make her happier. Your poor father was one of my closest friends, too! But do you wish it, my boy? Are you quite sure you have not been pushed into this by your uncle? I know Lionel well! an excellent fellow, and means nothing but good, but overbearing—very overbearing!"

Taken aback, and at a loss for anything to say, the Duke flushed hotly, and stammered: "No, no! I mean——"

"You see, Gilly," said Ampleforth, fidgeting about the room, "I am very much attached to you, both for your father's sake, and for your own, and I should not like to think—Well, I was always very much against arranging such a thing before either of you were out of the nursery! And what I wish to say to you is this! If your heart is not in the business, I would not have you go a step farther in it. You need not regard anything but your own inclination, and I beg of you not to allow yourself to be swayed by considerations that do not matter a button! If expectations have been raised, they were not raised by *you*. I have always deprecated Harriet's being encouraged to suppose—But I need not say more upon that head!"

He had certainly said enough. The Duke pulled himself together, and in a composed voice said that he entertained the deepest regard for Lady Harriet, and should think himself fortunate indeed if his suit were accepted.

Doubt and relief struggled for supremacy in Lord Ampleforth's breast; relief won; he said: "Well! If your mind is set on it, what can I say but that my girl must count herself honoured to receive so distinguishing a proposal? I am sure —that is, I fancy there can be no doubt—But you will wish to hear her answer from her own lips! Do but sit down, Sale, while I discover if my lady is able to see you! I know she will wish to do so, but with the house at sixes and sevens—— But I will not keep you waiting above a little while!"

He almost thrust his guest into a chair by the fire, and hurried off in search of his wife. He found her in her dressing-room, in conference with the housekeeper, and surrounded by a litter of bandboxes. She was a handsome woman, dressed in the first style of elegance in a Rutland half-robe, with a striped zephyr shawl, and a somewhat formidable turban. Her nose was high-bridged, and her blue eyes at once penetrating and cold. One glance at her spouse sufficed to make her dismiss the housekeeper; and as soon as this portly dame had curtsied herself out of the room, she said: "Well, Ampleforth? What it it?"

"I have Sale downstairs," he said. "He has been with me this past half-hour."

"Sale!" she exclaimed, her eyes narrowing.

"My love, he has made me an offer for Harriet's hand. He expressed himself with the greatest propriety: I think you would have been pleased to have heard him."

"I was beginning to think he meant to cry off!" she said, in the outspoken way which always made her lord wince. "So he has offered at last! He could not have chosen a more awkward moment! The drawing-room is under holland covers already, and it is quite out of the question for us to be asking him to dine. We have only the under-cook here."

"Upon my word, I had thought you would have been glad of the news!" said his lordship, quite astonished.

"Pray do not talk to me in that foolish manner, Ampleforth! You know very well that I am excessively glad of it, but why he might not have made his offer at a more seasonable time I have not the remotest conjecture. We should have held a dress-party, and the announcement should have been made at it. People will think it a shabbily contrived business!"

"You forget, ma'am," rather feebly suggested his lordship, "that we are still in black gloves. It will not be thought wonderful that we do not——"

"Cousin Albinia, and I know not how many times removed, besides having been as mad as Bedlam for years! I assure you I should not have regarded that! However, it is of no use to repine! The thing is that Sale has been brought up to scratch, and heaven knows I must be thankful for that, for I don't scruple to tell you, my lord, that I have been fearing Harriet was to be obliged to wear the willow. Where have you put him?"

"He is in my book-room. I said I must first speak with you."

"Very well, I will come directly. I daresay Harriet dressed all by guess this morning, for we are in such an uproar, with half the servants already gone to Ampleforth!" said the lady, tugging vigorously at the bell-pull. "Do not be loitering here, my lord, I do beg of you, but go back to Sale, and say Harriet will come down presently. Oh, is it you, Mrs. Royston? No, I did not precisely wish for you, but it doesn't signify! Be good enough to desire Lady Harriet and Miss Abinger to wait on me here directly! Pray, what do you stay for, Ampleforth? Go down to Sale at once, and entertain him until I come!"

The Lady Harriet was discovered to be in the school-room, helping to keep her younger sisters amused while the nurse busied herself with the packing of their many trunks. At a table in the window, the governess, Miss Abinger, was endeavouring to instruct two stout lads in frilled shirts and nankeen pantaloons in the use of the globes. When Lady Ampleforth's message was delivered by the panting housekeeper, Harriet jumped up from the floor, where she had been sitting, and instinctively put her hands to smooth her soft brown curls. "Mama wants me?" she said in a scared voice. "Oh, what is it, Royston dear?"

The housekeeper beamed at her knowingly. "Ah, that is for her ladyship to tell you, my lady! But what would you say to a lovely young gentleman's being closeted with your papa?"

Lady Harriet's large blue eyes dilated; she said faintly: "Oh, no!"

Miss Abinger, a sensible-looking woman in the late thirties, rose from her seat, saying in a commonplace tone: "Lady Harriet will come to her ladyship directly. You will do well to tidy your hair, my dear. Come into your bed-chamber and let me draw a comb through it. You know your mama likes you to be neat in your appearance."

"Harry, don't be gone for ever!" begged Lady Maria, a buxom twelve-year-old. "Ten to one it is only one of Mama's fusses!"

"Oh, hush, love!" Harriet whispered.

"Good gracious, Harry!" exclaimed Lady Caroline, who at sixteen bade fair to resemble her mother very nearly, "you don't suppose it is Sale, do you?"

Harriet, blushing furiously, ran out of the room. Miss Abinger said severely: "You will oblige me, Caroline, by writing out in your fairest hand, and without blots, fifty times, *Whoso keepeth his mouth and his tongue, keepeth his heart from troubles.*" She waited for a moment to be sure that her pupil dared not venture on any retort, and then followed Lady Harriet out of the room, and down one pair of stairs to a bedchamber at the back of the house.

Here, the abigail who was folding her young mistress's dresses in silver paper, betrayed by her air of barely sup-pressed excitement that the rumour that was already run-ning through the house had reached her ears. She greeted the governess with a gasp, and an involuntary question: "Oh, miss, is it true?"

Miss Abinger ignored this impertinence, and trod over to the dressing-table, before which Harriet had seated her-self. "You have crushed your gown a trifle, my dear, but it

43

will not do to keep your mama waiting, and we must hope that she will not notice it. Let me take that comb!"

Harriet permitted her to remove it from her singularly nerveless grasp. "Oh, Abby, you do not think——?"

"I think your mama will not like it if you do not bestir yourself, Lady Harriet," replied the governess calmly.

Harriet said, in a helpless way: "No," and submitted to having her hair combed and tidied. She then rose, and with trembling knees followed her preceptress downstairs to Lady Ampleforth's dressing-room.

Her ladyship cast one comprehensive glance over her daughter, and exclaimed in exasperated accents: "Exactly so! Your old plain muslin, and I daresay everything packed up already! Well, it will not do! Miss Abinger, oblige me by seeing to it that Lady Harriet changes her dress immediately! The cambric muslin with the double scallop work at the bottom is what she should be wearing, or if that is not readily procurable, the new sprig gown, with the sleeves drawn at the top with coloured ribbons! My love, Sale is below, with your papa. You will allow mama to be the first to felicitate you upon the very flattering offer that has been made you!"

"Gilly!" Harriet uttered, in a voice so suspended by surprise as to be barely audible. "Oh, no! surely you must be mistaken, ma'am!"

A look of annoyance seemed to sharpen Lady Ampleforth's features. "There is no occasion that I know of for these die-away airs, Harriet!" she said. "You are very well aware of your papa's and my intentions for you!"

"Oh, yes! But I had not supposed—he has never been particular in his attentions—Mama, I did not think Gilly loved me!"

"I can only conclude, Harriet," said Lady Ampleforth, with a condemnatory glance at Miss Abinger, "that you have been taking novels out of some circulating-library, which is a thing I have never permitted."

"Oh, no, Mama!" Harriet faltered.

"Then I am at a loss to understand where you can have learnt such trumpery notions, and I beg you will not make a figure of yourself by mentioning them again! Sale has expressed himself very properly to your papa, and if he and I are satisfied *you* have surely nothing to cavil at! He is waiting to address you himself. I trust you know your duty well enough to make it unnecessary for me to tell you in what terms you must answer him."

"Oh, Mama, pray——!"

"Harriet, what is this nonsense?" demanded her ladyship

irately. "I will allow it to be a most inconvenient time for Sale to be declaring himself, but so it is always! Men have not the least common-sense! But if you mean to tell me that you hold him in aversion——"

"Oh, no, no!"

"Precisely so! You should be grateful to your papa and to me for having permitted you to become pretty well acquainted with Sale, instead of presenting him to you a complete stranger, as might very often happen in my young days, let me assure you! I did not look for this missishness in you, and I can tell you that it is not at all becoming. You have been a little taken by surprise, and that is forgiveable: I was quite thunderstruck myself. But you will have time to compose your mind while you change your dress, and I am confident you will conduct yourself just as you should. Now, do not be dawdling here any longer, my dear! Bustle about a little, if you please! I shall come up to your bedchamber to fetch you myself in half an hour, and I hope you do not mean to keep me waiting. Miss Abinger, be so good as to accompany my daughter, and to make sure that she is dressed just as she should be! Her maid has no head, not the least in the world!"

"Certainly, Lady Ampleforth," said Miss Abinger, in her colourless way. "Come, Lady Harriet!"

She laid her hand on Harriet's trembling arm, and almost propelled her to the door. When she had firmly closed this behind them, she said in a warmer tone: "My dear, try to compose yourself! What is the matter?"

"Oh, Abby, I don't know!" Harriet replied, in some agitation. "Only I did not look for this, and I do not wish—I do not think——"

"Forgive me, but I had not supposed that you were indifferent to the Duke."

"Not indifferent, no!" Harriet said, averting her face. "But he——!"

They had reached the half-landing before Miss Abinger replied. She said then: "I believe the Duke entertains feelings of the warmest regard for you, my love. He is a very amiable young man, and one who will not fail to treat you with all the courtesy and consideration one could wish for you. Indeed, I think you are to be envied! I know your mind to be of too nice a tone to care for such things, but you will occupy a position of the first consequence, and you will enjoy great wealth. Reflect that in addition to this you will have a husband who partakes of many of your sentiments, and is, I am persuaded, the model of compliance and good-nature."

"He does not love me," Harriet said. "It is his uncle's doing, and Mama's. I know it, Abby!"

"I shall not dispute with you on that head, my dear Lady Harriet, and I believe it will not serve to discuss it. Yet I must venture to tell you that I do not by any means despair of your happiness in this alliance. You know, it is not commonly the thing for persons in your station in life to make what is called a love-match."

"No," Harriet agreed dejectedly.

They had reached the upper floor by this time. As Miss Abinger grasped the door-handle of Harriet's bedroom, she added deliberately: "You are not always quite at your ease in your home, dear Lady Harriet. I fancy you may be happier in an establishment of your own. But I have said too much, and we shall soon have your mama coming up to fetch you!"

Harriet coloured, but was silent. While Miss Abinger directed the maid to unpack her mistress's cambric muslin, she waited, looking out of the window between the lace blinds. Her colour faded gradually, and she was able in a few minutes to reply to a chance question with tolerable composure.

It was by no means Miss Abinger's business to dress the hair of her pupils, but she elected to do so, and with so much taste that when Lady Ampleforth came into the room presently she nodded approvingly, and said: "Very well, indeed! I could wish that you had a trifle more countenance, my love, but you look very becomingly. But hold yourself up, if you please! An air of languor can never be pleasing in a girl, remember! Now, if you are ready, we will go downstairs."

"I am quite ready, Mama."

Lady Ampleforth preceded her out of the room, but paused at the head of the stairs to take her hand. "There is no need for you to feel the slightest embarrassment, Harriet," she said kindly. "Sale is a very pretty-behaved young man, and his manners reflect the greatest credit on his upbringing. I only wish your brother had them! I daresay he will do or say nothing to make you blush. Besides, I should not think of leaving you alone together, so have no fears on that score!"

"No, Mama," said Harriet.

Lord Ampleforth and the Duke were standing in front of the fire in the book-room, conversing in a desultory and uncomfortable fashion. Lord Ampleforth was looking rather more harassed than before; and half an hour of his future mother-in-law's brisk, managing talk had so much oppressed

46

the Duke's spirits that he bore the appearance more of one about to face a severe ordeal than of a hopeful suitor. He directed an anxious, questioning look at Harriet, but she kept her eyes lowered, and did not perceive it.

"Ah, my child!" said Ampleforth, going to meet her. "I think your mama has told you that I have just received a very flattering offer for your hand." He took it as he spoke, and gave it a fond squeeze. "But I have told Gilly that I will not have you constrained, and you shall give him your own answer."

He drew her forward; the Duke, miserably tongue-tied, managed to utter a few formal sentences; and Harriet, ready to sink, curtsied, and whispered a reply of which "very much obliged," and "most truly sensible of the honour," were the only audible words.

Her father, apparently taking these to mean consent, held out her hand to the Duke, who took it in his own ice-cold one, and kissed it. He said: "You have made me very happy. I beg you to believe that I shall do everything in my power to—to make you happy too, Harriet!"

"No one who knows you could doubt that, Gilly, I am sure!" Ampleforth said. "I don't scruple to say that you are two very fortunate young persons. I am sure I do not know which of you has the better disposition! Lady Ampleforth, I have something I wish to say to you! We will beg Gilly to excuse us for a minute."

Her ladyship was so much astonished at having such tactics employed against her that she could think of nothing to say, except what she was too well-bred to say in front of a guest. Her husband was holding open the door, and she saw nothing for it but to leave the room with him. The Duke and his betrothed were left shyly confronting one another.

Neither of them spoke for a moment. Then the Duke saw how pale Harriet was, and how much her hands trembled, and compassion made him forget his own ill-ease, and he said; "I hope you do not dislike it very much! I shall do my utmost not to give you cause for any unhappiness. You won't find me exacting, I promise, or—or——"

"No, I do not dislike it," Harriet answered, in a low voice. "I shall try to be dutiful, and to behave just as you would wish. I—I have always had a—a great regard for you, Gilly."

"And I for you, dear Harriet," he responded at once. "I do think we—we may suit very well. It shall not be my fault if we do not."

She looked up at that. "I hope—oh, I hope it may never

be mine! Forgive me! I find myself a little overcome! I had not the expectation—that is, I did not think you were in London, or that—you entertained for me those feelings which——"

She broke off in confusion. He possessed her himself of her hand again. "Indeed, I am excessively attached to you!" he stammered. "I wish you were not going out of town immediately! It must have been my—my earnest endeavour to show you—— But I may come to Bath, and you will allow me to squire you to all the dress-balls!" he added, with an attempt at lightness.

A smile trembled on her lips. "Oh, yes! You know how well our steps suit!"

"Yes, indeed! I am sure there is no one I am happier to stand up with, for you never make me feel myself to be such a miserable dwarf of a fellow!"

"Oh, Gilly, how can you? You are no such thing!"

He laughed. "Ah, you should hear my cousin Gideon on that head!"

"You should hear Gaywood!" she retorted, gaining confidence. "He calls me a poor little dab of a creature!"

"Brothers! We shall not care a fig for them, or cousins either!" he said. He saw that she was looking less pale, and ventured to kiss her cheek.

Lady Ampleforth came back into the room in time to witness this embrace. Her sharp eyes detected Harriet's blush, and the way her hand went up as though to clasp the Duke's coat collar. She said: "Well, I make no doubt you have settled it all between you! It is an unfortunate circumstance that we should be going out of town at this precise moment, but I shall look to see you at Ampleforth, Duke, next month. Harriet must go to Bath: there is no getting out of that, for old Lady Ampleforth expects her, and we must not cast her into one of her pets, you know."

The young couple fell apart guiltily; constraint descended upon them again; and by the time her ladyship had discussed various convenient dates for the wedding-ceremony, and estimated the length of time it would take her to procure Harriet's bride-clothes, the Duke was thankful to take his leave.

When he had been bowed out, Lord Ampleforth, who had been observing his daughter narrowly, said: "My dear Harriet, are you quite happy in this engagement? You must not hesitate to tell me if your mind has any misgiving!"

"No, Papa, I am quite happy," she said.

"Good God, Ampleforth, what can you be thinking of?" exclaimed his wife. "Pray, what more could any girl desire,

I should like to know? To be Duchess of Sale! That is something indeed! Harriet, I wish you will come up to my dressing-room, for there is a great deal I want to say to you!"

She swept her daughter out of the room, saying as she closed the door: "Your papa has some odd fancies, but I trust I have brought you up to know your duty! It was an awkward business, his calling me out of the room as he did, but I returned to you as soon as I might. Sale looked to be in tolerably good health, I thought."

"Yes, Mama."

"He was the sickliest child! I am sure no one thought to see him survive! He is not as well-grown as one could wish, but he is very well made, and has excellent manners. Perhaps he is not precisely good-looking, but there is nothing in his air or countenance to disgust one."

"I think him very good-looking, Mama," Harriet said, in a subdued voice.

Lady Ampleforth entered the dressing-room, thrust an empty band-box off a chair, and sat down. "Yes, very likely, my love, and that brings me to what I wish to say to you. Shut the door! Now, sit down, and attend to me a little!" She waited until this command had been obeyed, and then said, twitching her shawl round her shoulders: "I have often observed, Harriet, that you have just a little nonsense in you which will not do. I shall speak frankly to you, and I daresay you may thank me for it one day. I did not quite like to see you hanging so upon Sale, as you were when I came into the book-room just now. You know, my dear child, he will not be looking for you to wear your heart upon your sleeve: in fact, I can think of nothing more likely to disgust him. I must surely have told you a dozen times that a lady of quality must not behave as though she were Miss Smith of Heaven knows where! I shall never forget my own dear mama's telling me how the Duchess of Devonshire —the first wife of the late Duke, I mean!—actually sat down upon his Grace's knee once, when she was but a bride! And her mortification when he repulsed her! It quite makes one blush to think of it. But I believe Lady Spencer—she was one of those blue-stocking women, you know!—brought her daughters up in the oddest fashion! I should not like to think that *you*, my dear Harriet, would so far forget yourself. Such manners may do very well for parvenues, but whatever your brother Gaywood may have told you, they will not do for you. Sale has not been reared in this modern style, which permits all kinds of license, and, depend upon it, he will expect his wife to conduct herself with fitting decorum. It has been very justly observed, my love—I forget by whom—that if you meet with tenderness *in private* from your husband, you will have no cause for complaint."

Harriet clasped her hands tightly together in her lap. "Mama," she said, fixing her eyes on Lady Ampleforth's face, "may not a lady of quality—*love?*"

Her ladyship laughed. "As to that, my dear, I daresay she is no harder-hearted than the rest of her sex! But she must always be discreet, and I cannot too strongly impress upon you that nothing of *that* nature must be thought of until you have presented your husband with an heir! You must never give your parents cause to blush for you, Harriet, and I am sure you will not, for you are a good girl, and you know what is due to your position."

"Oh!" said Harriet faintly, lifting a hand to her hot cheek. "I did not mean that! Mama—were you not in love with Papa when you married him?"

"I was a great deal too young to know anything of the matter. He was presented to me by my parents: I doubt if I had clapped eyes on him above half a dozen times in my life. But I became very sincerely attached to him, as I hope you may do to Sale. But be upon your guard, my child! You have a romantical disposition, I am afraid, and you are a great deal too fond of showing when you feel a strong partiality for anyone. And that, you know, may lead you into jealousy, which will never do! A man may have his *chères-amies*: they do not concern his *wife*. She must turn a blind eye towards such little *affaires*."

"Perhaps," said Harriet, turning away her face, "he may welcome caresses from his *chères-amies!*"

"Very likely, my love. It is something I am happy to think neither you nor I can know anything about. A man of Sale's breeding will expect a different style of conduct of his wife, that I can vouch for! Remember it, Harriet!"

"Yes, Mama," said Harriet unhappily.

CHAPTER V

THE Duke, returning to Sale House, spent an unprofitable half-hour, trying to draft an advertisement for the *Gazette*. He gave it up finally, exclaiming aloud: "It seems I need a private secretary besides all the rest!"

The door into the library opened. "Your Grace called?" said his footman.

The Duke stared at him in gathering wrath. "Were you standing outside the door?" he demanded.

The man looked quite scared. "Yes, your Grace!"

50

"Then don't do it!"

"No, your Grace! I beg your Grace's pardon! I thought your Grace had called!"

"I did not!"

"No, your Grace!" said the footman, much discomposed, and preparing to bow himself out again.

"When I need you, I will ring for you," said the Duke. "At this present I want nothing! At least—Yes, I do! If Mr. Scriven should not have left the house, desire him to come to me, if you please!"

"Yes, your Grace!"

It seemed that Mr. Scriven had not left the house, for in a very few minutes he presented himself in the library. He found the Duke sitting at the big carved desk, biting the end of a quill, and regarding with dissatisfaction a scrawled sheet of paper. Several screwed-up balls of paper cast in the direction of the fireplace bore witness to frustrated literary endeavour.

"You wished to see me, my lord?" said Mr. Scriven, advancing into the room.

The Duke looked up, a boyishly rueful smile in his eyes. "I can do not the least thing for myself, Scriven!" he said. "Here have I been wasting I know not how long trying to write the simplest notice, and making the sorriest work of it!"

"You know you may depend upon me, my lord, to do anything for you that you desire," said Mr. Scriven, in a soothing voice. "May I know what it is that is giving you so much trouble?"

"Merely the notice of my engagement for the *Gazette!* You would say a simple matter, but only see what a botch I have made of it!"

Mr. Scriven had been moving towards the desk, but at these words he halted. "Your engagement, my lord!"

"Yes, to the Lady Harriet Presteigne. It must be announced, you know, and I shall be very much obliged to you if you will draft a suitable notice for me."

"May I say, my lord Duke," said Mr. Scriven, deeply moved, "that there is no task you could lay upon me which I could undertake with more gratification? I hope your Grace will permit me to offer my sincerest felicitations upon this most happy event!"

"Thank you: you are very good."

"I shall take advantage, my lord, of my long association with the House of Sale, to say that nothing could afford those who have your interests at heart greater satisfaction than this intelligence. And I venture to say, my lord, that there is no one amongst your dependants who has *not* your interests at heart."

"Thank you!" said the Duke again, startled, but a little touched.

"Your Grace may safely leave this matter in my hands," said Mr. Scriven. "The notice shall be sent immediately to all the society papers: I shall attend to it myself. May I enquire when the Happy Date is to be?"

"I do not precisely know. In the spring, I think: nothing is fixed yet!"

Mr. Scriven bowed. "We shall have to see to the refurnishing of the Duchess's apartments," he said. "In fact, there will be a great many details to be attended to, my lord. You may rely on me!"

The Duke, who felt that he had listened to enough plans for his marriage for one day, said hastily that he was sure of it, but that there was time and to spare. Mr. Scriven thereupon bowed again, and went off to enjoy himself very much in drafting an advertisement in terms grandiloquent enough to satisfy his sense of what was due to his noble employer's dignity.

The Duke, who had previously ascertained that his cousin was on guard-duty that day, thought that he might perhaps be dining at White's, and determined to seek him there. He did not succeed, however, in leaving the house without encountering a good deal of opposition, first from his valet, who took it amiss that he did not mean to change his pantaloons for knee-breeches and silk stockings; then from Borrowdale, who had not supposed that his Grace meant to dine from home, and thought that it looked like rain; and lastly from Chigwell, who, forbidden to send a message to the stables, was horrified, and exclaimed: "But your Grace will have the carriage!"

"I do not need it; I am only going to White's," replied the Duke, taking his cane and gloves from his footman's hands.

"Your Grace will not go on foot, and alone! Only let me call a chair!"

"Chigwell, I am not a child, nor shall I melt for a drop or two of rain!" said the Duke.

"No, indeed, your Grace, but they say the town abounds with pickpockets, and street-robbers! I am sure his lordship would desire you to take a chair, and a linkboy!"

"I shall take neither, however."

Chigwell and Borrowdale both looked very much upset. "But, your Grace, you will be very much more comfortable in your carriage!" protested Chigwell. "It can be brought round in a trice, and——"

"*No!*" said the Duke, with sudden and unaccustomed violence.

They fell back, and the porter, who had been standing all the time by the door thought well of opening it.

"As your Grace wishes!" said Chigwell feebly. "At what hour will your Grace be returning?"

"I have not the smallest notion," said the Duke, drawing on his gloves.

"No, your Grace. Quite so! And your Grace would not wish to have the carriage call for you——?"

"I would not!" said the Duke, and ran down the steps into the forecourt, leaving his faithful henchmen to stare after him in great surprise, and no little perturbation.

He did not find his cousin at White's, but just as he was ascertaining from the porter that Captain Ware had not been seen in the club that day, Viscount Gaywood walked in, and instantly pounced upon him. "Sale! By God, I was in half a mind to call at your place! My dear fellow, how do you do? I have just heard the news! Never more glad of anything in my life! Come and dine with me!"

Lord Gaywood, who was tall, lanky, and a great rattle, bore little resemblance to his sister Harriet, but had a beak-like nose that brought Lady Ampleforth forcibly to mind. He was said to be a severe trial to his parents, and had certainly occupied his adult years in tumbling in and out of a great many scrapes. He swept the Duke upstairs to the coffee-room, saying cheerfully: "Well, this is a capital go, old fellow! But what a complete hand you are! I was ready to swear you were not hanging out for a wife yet awhile! Why, I don't believe you ever so much as gave Harry's hand a squeeze at hands across!"

"Well, do not shout it to the whole world!" said Gilly.

"Oh, no one ever attends to me!" replied his lordship. "You know, it's not for me to puff m'sister off, but she's a devilish good girl, Sale, and deserves her fortune. The shyest thing in nature, mind you, but you're a trifle in that line yourself! I'm glad you didn't declare off: don't mind telling you my mother was thrown into gloom when you left town without coming up to scratch! What a business it is! They will be trying their hands at finding a bride for me next, I daresay. Do you want to buy a horse?"

"Yes, but not one of yours," said the Duke frankly.

"What do you mean, not one of mine?" demanded his lordship, affronted. "I've got a prime bit of blood I wouldn't mind selling you. Show's off, well; complete to a shade!"

"Touched in the wind?" asked the Duke, taking his seat at the table.

"Devil a bit of it! Perfect in all his paces!"

"I may look like a flat, but I'm not such a green one that I'd buy one of your breakdowns, Charlie," said the Duke.

Lord Gaywood grinned. "Well, it ain't a breakdown, but I never crossed a greater slug in my life! fit only to carry a churchwarden!"

"Thank you!" said the Duke.

"Oh, well, there's no saying! he might have taken your fancy! What made you take this bolt to the village, my tulip? You did not come merely to offer for Harriet!"

"That, and to buy a horse—not your horse."

"Gilly, you skirter! Don't try to come Tip-Street over me! If you have run away from that devilish uncle of yours, I don't blame you! The most antiquated old fidget I ever saw! Quite gothic, my dear fellow! I'm frightened to death of him. I don't think he likes me above half."

"Not as much," replied Gilly. "In fact, I think he classes you with park-saunterers, and other such ramshackle persons."

"No, no, Gilly, upon my word! Always in the best of good *ton!*" protested his lordship. "Park-saunterers be damned! I'll tell you what, my boy! I'll take you along to a place I know of in Pickering Place after dinner. All the crack amongst the knowing ones, and the play very fair."

"French hazard? You know I haven't the least taste for gaming! Besides, I'm going to visit my cousin Gideon."

Lord Gaywood exclaimed against such tame behaviour, but the Duke remained steady in refusing to accompany him to his gaming-hell, and they parted after dinner, Gaywood crossing the street to Pickering Place, and the Duke going off to Albany, where Captain Ware rented a set of chambers. These were on the first floor of one of the new buildings, and were reached by a flight of stone stairs. The Duke ran up these, and knocked on his cousin's door. It was opened to him by a stalwart individual with a rugged countenance, and the air and bearing of an old soldier, who stared at him for an instant, and then exclaimed: "It's your Grace!"

"Hallo, Wragby! is my cousin in?" returned the Duke, stepping into a small hall, and laying his hat and cane down upon the table.

"Ay, that he is, your Grace, and Mr. Matthew with him," said Wragby. "I'll warrant he'll be mighty glad to see your Grace. I'll take your coat, sir."

He divested the Duke of it as he spoke, and would have

54

announced him had not Gilly shaken his head, and walked without ceremony into his cousin's sitting-room.

This was a comfortable, square apartment, with windows giving on to a little balcony, and some folding doors that led into Captain Ware's bedchamber. It was lit by candles, a fire burned in the grate, and the atmosphere was rather thick with cigar-smoke. The furniture was none of it very new, or very elegant, and the room was not distinguished by its neatness. To the Duke, who rarely saw as much as a cushion out of place in his own residences, the litter of spurs, riding-whips, racing-calendars, invitation-cards, pipes, tankards, and newspapers gave the room a charm all its own. He felt at his ease in it, and never entered it without experiencing a pang of envy.

There were two persons seated at the mahogany table, at which it was evident they had been dining. One was a fair youth, in a very dandified waistcoat; the other, a big, dark young man, some four years older than the Duke, who lounged at the head of the table, with his long legs stretched out before him, and one hand dug into the pocket of his white buckskins. He had shed his scarlet coat for a dressing-gown, and he wore on his feet a pair of embroidered Turkish slippers. It was easy to trace his relationship to Lord Lionel Ware. He had the same high nose, and stern gray eyes, and something of the same mulish look about his mouth and chin, which made his face, in repose, a little forbidding. But he had also an attractively crooked smile, which only persons for whom he had a fondness were privileged to see. As he looked up, at the opening of the door, his eyes narrowed, and the smile twisted up one side of his mouth. "Adolphus!" he said, in a lazy drawl. "Well, well, well!"

The fair youth, who had been staring a little moodily at the dregs of the port in his glass, started, and looked round, as much as he was able to do for the extremely high and starched points of his shirt-collar. "Gilly!" he exclaimed. "Good God, what are you doing in town?"

"Why shouldn't I be in town?" said the Duke, with a touch of impatience. "If it comes to that, what brings *you* here?"

"I'm on my way up to Oxford, of course," said his cousin. "Lord, what a start you gave me, walking in like that!"

By this time, the Duke had taken in all the glories of his young cousin's attire, which included, besides that amazingly striped waistcoat, an Oriental tie of gigantic height, a starched frill, buckram-wadded shoulders to an extravagantly cut coat, buttons the size of crown pieces, and a pair of

Inexpressibles of a virulent shade of yellow. He closed his eyes, and said faintly: "Gideon, have you any brandy?"

Captain Ware grinned. "Regular little counter-coxcomb, ain't he?" he remarked.

"I thought you had a Bartholomew baby dining with you," said Gilly. "Matt, you don't mean to go up to Oxford in that rig? Oh, my God, Gideon, will you look at his pantaloons? What a set of dashing blades they must be at Magdalen!"

"Gilly!" protested Matthew, flushing hotly. "Because you are never in the least dapper-dog yourself you need not quiz me! It's the pink of the fashion, bang up to the nines! You should have a pair yourself!"

"Above my touch," said the Duke, shaking his head. He looked up at Gideon, who had dragged himself out of his chair, and now stood towering above him, and smiled. "Gideon," he said, with satisfaction. "Oh, I think I was charged with a great many messages for you, but I have forgot them all!"

"Do you mean to tell me, Adolphus, that you have slipped your leash?" demanded Gideon.

"Oh, no!" said Gilly, sighing. "I did think that perhaps I might, but I was reckoning without Belper, and Scriven, and Chigwell and Borrowdale, and Nettlebed, and——"

"Enough!" commanded Gideon. "This air of consequence ill becomes you, my little one! Is my revered father in town?"

"No, I am alone. Except, of course, for Nettlebed, and Turvey, and—— But you don't like me to puff off my state!"

"This," said Gideon, lounging over to the door, and opening it, "calls for a bowl of punch! Wragby! Wragby, you old rascal! Rum! Lemons! Kettle! Bustle about, man!" He came back to the fire. "Tell me that my parents are well, and then do not let us talk about them any more!" he invited.

"They are very well, but I am going to say a great deal to you about your father. I think I came for that very purpose. Yes, I am sure that I did!"

"You have never given Uncle Lionel the bag?" exclaimed Matthew.

"Oh, no! He saw me off with his blessing, and an adjuration to visit the dentist. I have never yet succeeded in giving anyone the bag," said Gilly.

Gideon looked at him under his brows. "Hipped, Adolphus?" he said gently.

"Blue-devilled!" replied the Duke, meeting his look.

"What a complete hand you are, Gilly!" said Matthew

impatiently. "I only wish I stood in your shoes! There you are, your pockets never to let, everything made easy for you, all the toad-eaters in town ready to serve you, and you complain——"

"Peace, halfling!" interrupted Gideon. "Sit down, Gilly! Tell me all that is in your mind!"

"Too much!" said the Duke, sinking into a chair at the table. "Oh, that reminds me! Would you like to offer me your felicitations? You won't be quite the first to do so, but—but you won't care to be backward! I have this day fulfilled the expectations of my family—not to mention those of every busybody in town—and entered upon a very eligible engagement. You will see the notice in the *Gazette,* presently, and *all* the society journals. I do hope Scriven will not forget any of these!"

"Oh!" said Gideon. He pitched the butt of his cigar into the fire, and cast another of those shrewd, appraising looks at the Duke. "Well, that certainly calls for a bowl of punch," he said. "Harriet, eh?"

The Duke nodded.

"I don't wish to enrage you, my little one, but you have my felicitations. She will do very well for you."

The Duke looked up quickly. "Yes, of course! What a fellow I am to be talking in such a fashion! Don't regard it! She is everything that is amiable and obliging."

"Well, I'm sure I wish you very happy," said Matthew. "Of course we all knew that you were going to offer for her."

"Of course you did!" agreed Gilly, with immense cordiality.

"Charlotte has contracted an engagement too," observed Matthew. "Did you know it? It is to Alfred Thirsk."

"Certainly I knew it," replied Gilly. "In fact, I very nearly withheld my consent to the match."

"Very nearly withheld your consent!" repeated Matthew, staring at him in the liveliest astonishment.

"Well, I had the intention, but, like so many of my intentions, it came to nothing. Your father wrote me a very proper letter, expressing the hope that the alliance met with my approval. Only it does not: not at all!"

Matthew burst out laughing. "Much my father would care! Stop bamming, Gilly!"

"Bamming? You forget yourself, Matt!" Gilly retorted. "Let me tell you that I am the head of our family, and it is time that I learned to assert myself!"

Gideon smiled. "Have you been asserting yourself, Adolphus?"

"No, no, I am not yet beyond the stage of learning! I am so bird-witted, you know, that I can never tell what is asserting myself, and what is putting myself forward in a very pert fashion that will not do at all."

Gideon dropped a hand on his shoulder, and gripped it, but as Wragby came in just then, with a laden tray, he said nothing. The Duke lifted his own hand to clasp that larger one. "All gammon!" he said jerkily. "I told you I was blue-devilled!"

Gideon smiled down at him in his lazy way, and shook him gently to and fro. "Wretched little snirp!" he said.

"Mackerel-backed dragoon!" retorted the Duke, with an effort at liveliness. "Brew your punch!"

Matthew seized one of the lemons, and sliced it in half, chanting: *"One sour, Two sweet; Four strong, And eight weak!* Shall you add a dash of pink champagne to it, Gideon?"

"I shall not," replied Gideon, releasing the Duke's shoulder, and beginning to measure out the rum. "Arrack, my child, nothing but arrack!"

"Only rustics use arrack instead of champagne," said Matthew, in a lofty way, which he instantly regretted.

"Listen to our rasher-of-wind!" Gideon recommended, with a nod at Gilly. "Proceed, Matt! Any more airs of the exquisite to play off?"

Young Mr. Ware's ready colour surged up again. "No, but it *is* so! Gilly, you go to all the *ton* parties! It should be pink champagne, shouldn't it?"

"Yes, of course, only Gideon has such nip-cheese ways!" responded the Duke, lifting a spoonful of well-pounded sugar from the bowl, and letting it shower back again. "Does Charlotte really wish to marry Thirsk, Matt?"

"Lord, yes, she's in high gig!" replied Matthew cheerfully.

"Good God!"

"Well, she will have a very creditable establishment, you know! Oh, you are thinking that Thirsk is a bit of a loose-screw! She won't care for that as long as he don't spy too closely after her, and I dare swear he won't, for he's got a mistress in keeping, and has had for years. At least that's one of the *on-dits* of town, and I should think it would be true, would not you?"

"But what a charming match!" said the Duke.

"Oh, well!" said Matthew charitably, "no one could blame my father for nabbling Thirsk, after all! Devilish plump in the pocket, you know, and there's the title besides, and four more of my sisters to be provided for! As for Charlotte, it's all very well for you to cavil, Gilly, but you are your own

58

master, and may do as you please. *You* don't have to live at Croylake, dangling after my mother, and having to pour tea for a parcel of humbugging Methodies five evenings out of the seven! I can tell you, there's no bearing it!"

The kettle had boiled by this time; Gideon lifted it from the hob, and poured the sherbet he had brewed in it on to his spirit. A fragrant aroma rose from the bowl. He stirred the mixture, his attention fixed on it. But the Duke, catching the note of bitterness in Matthew's voice, looked at him rather searchingly. Matthew averted his eyes with a little laugh, and began to boast of Oxford larks.

Gideon, who rarely paid the least heed to him, interrupted his chatter without ceremony. "How long do you mean to stay in town, Adolphus?"

"I don't know. As long as I am permitted, I daresay!"

"No time at all, in fact." He began to ladle the punch into three glasses. "Did you tell me you had Belper toad-eating you? What the devil made you advise him you were in London?"

"Don't be so bacon-brained, Gideon!" Gilly implored. "Of course I never did so! *That* was left for my uncle to do. And he did it. I found Belper awaiting me on my doorstep."

"If you had as much sense as a pullet you would have kicked him off your doorstep!" commented the Captain.

" 'I would I had thy inches!' " retorted the Duke ruefully.

"Resolution is all you stand in need of, my child."

"I know. But I fancy he's none too well-breeched, and when a man is so damned pleased to see one—well, what *can* one do?"

"What, indeed?" said Gideon sardonically. "I suppose if all the scaff and raff of London were to show pleasure at the sight of you you would throw your doors open to them!"

"I daresay I should," said Gilly, with a short sigh. "How like my uncle you will be one day, when those beautiful whiskers of yours are no longer so black or so glossy! How right he was to warn me against seeking your company! And how little he knew how right he was!"

"*What?*" ejaculated Gideon. "He never did so!"

"Well, no!" admitted Gilly. "But he did warn me against letting myself be drawn into the sort of company you *keep*. Very justly, I daresay. You Lifeguards—Hyde Park soldiers, Belper calls you: did you know?—you're such a fast set of fellows, and one never knows where military society may lead one, does one? He warned me against Gaywood, too. He said *he* might lead me into gaming-hells, and this is precisely where he did try to lead me, only I was mindful of my orders, and I didn't go with him."

59

"Humdudgeon, Adolphus! You didn't go with him because gaming don't amuse you. No playing off your tricks to me, little cousin!"

The Duke ladled more punch into his glass. "Don't interrupt the head of the family, Gideon! Remember what is due to my position!"

"A little more, and that will be head downwards in my wine-cooler!" said Gideon.

"I warn you, it will be two to one against you, for Matt—if not too castaway—will stand my friend."

Matthew, who had been sitting in a brown study, started. "I'm not castaway!" he said. "A fellow can't be talking all the time!"

"You cannot know Belper, or you would not say so, Gideon. I shall be of full age next year, and my uncle says I must learn to manage for myself. I have a thousand amiable qualities, but I lack resolution. So I thought I would interest myself a little in my estates, but my notions were so nonsensical they made Scriven smile, and put my uncle out of all patience with me. I wish—oh, how much I wish!—that my guardian had been a villain, and my agent a fool, and that the pair of them had tried to ruin me!"

"I don't see any sense in that!" objected Matthew, blinking.

"And I wish," continued Gilly, disregarding the interruption, "that no one about me wished me well, or cared for my interests, or had a particle of affection for me! But they have! God knows why, but they have! Do you know what Borrowdale, and Chigwell, and Nettlebed, and my footman—no, not my footman! Heaven reward him, for he did not know me in my cradle, and does not care a fig what may become of me! He is a splendid fellow! I wonder what wage I pay him? It must be doubled!—But the rest of them—oh, yes, and Turvey, too! how came I to forget him?—the rest of them are waiting for me to come home, and fretting themselves to flinders because I would not have my carriage ordered, and so may have been set-upon by footpads, or taken a chill! They will all be sitting up for me, you know. Borrowdale will offer me a hot posset, I daresay, and I am quite sure that Nettlebed will give me a scold!" He jumped up, and began to stride restlessly about the room. "Gideon, I have been wondering what it would be like to be plain Mr. Dash, of Nowhere in Particular!"

"Try it!" recommended his cousin.

"How can I? We are not living between the covers of a romance, but in this dead bore of a Polite World! And I am going to be married! Give me some more punch! Or had

60

you better perhaps warn me that my digestion was never of the strongest, and it may very likely set up some disorder, for which it will be necessary to summon Dr. Baillie?"

"Go to the devil!" said Gideon, refilling his glass. "You may be as ill as you please, as long as you are not ill in my chambers. I shall bundle you into a chair, and tell 'em to carry you home."

"I like you so much," sighed the Duke, "and there is no virtue in you! You lie, Gideon, you lie! You would have half the Faculty here within an hour of my collapse!"

"Not I!"

"I wish you will stop twaddling for ever!" suddenly exclaimed Matthew, sitting up with a jerk. "I can tell you this, Gilly! It would do you a deal of good *not* to be a Duke, and *not* to have all the money you need, and scores of servants to wait on you, and *not* to have a stable full of blood-cattle, or a pair of sixty-guinea Mantons, or people to manage your affairs, or—or any of the things you *have* got, and don't so much as think about!"

"Yes, I think it would," agreed Gilly, arrested by this outburst. "Would you like to change places with me?"

"By God I would!"

"Well, you can't," said Gilly, sitting down again. "I've suddenly bethought me that if we changed places I should have Uncle Henry for my father, and although I don't wish to offend you, Matt, I don't want him."

"Adolphus, you are three parts disguised!" said Gideon severely.

The Duke smiled at him, but shook his head. "No, I am quite sober. But Matt is right! I have twaddled enough! Matt escort me home through our perilous streets! Where are you putting up?"

"Reddish's, but I don't mind going along with you," replied Matthew, draining his glass.

The Duke went out into the hall to pick up his coat. Gideon accompanied him, and helped him to put it on. "Come and dine with me to-morrow, Adolphus," he said. "I'll have none of our cousins here to meet you."

"Yes, I wanted to find you alone," said Gilly.

"You shall, my little one. Eight o'clock. Do not cut your throat before then!"

"Gideon, Gideon, you don't suppose that I shave myself, do you?" riposted Gilly, much shocked.

CHAPTER VI

For some few minutes after he and Gilly had left Albany, Matthew kept up a flow of alarmingly light-hearted conversation. It did not deceive his cousin, and at the first opportunity he broke in on the chatter, and said: "Are you troubled about anything, Matt?"

The flow ceased abruptly. After a moment, Matthew said: "Troubled? Why should I be?"

"Well, I don't know, but if you are I think you might tell me."

"Oh! Now you are back at that Head-of-the-House stuff!" replied Matthew, with an unconvincing laugh.

"I hadn't thought of that, but now you put me in mind of it I might as well justify my position. Are you under a cloud, Matt?"

"Oh, lord, yes, but that ain't it! At least, in a way it is, but not as you think. My snyder is one of the faithful, thank God!"

Correctly interpreting this mystic phrase to mean that Mr. Ware's tailor gave him long credit, the Duke said, "What's the figure?"

There was a long silence. Mr. Ware broke it. "If you want to know, I need five thousand pounds!"

"Oh!" said the Duke. "I haven't such a sum on me at the moment, but I daresay I could find it."

Matthew began to laugh. "Gilly, you fool! As though my uncle would let you!"

"He has never kept me short of money. In any event, since I was twenty-one I have been at liberty to draw what I please. It is only my principal I may not tamper with."

"Well, if he would let you I would not! I am not such a sponge! I was only bamming!"

"Matt, what is it?"

Another long silence followed this question, but the sympathy in his cousin's voice won Matthew's confidence. "Gilly, I am run off my legs—all to pieces!" he said, sounding very much more like a scared schoolboy than a young gentleman about to enter on his third year at the University.

The Duke tucked a hand in his arm. "We'll raise the wind, Matt, never fear! But what is it? You are not scorched to that figure!"

"Oh, no, it's not debt! But I don't know what to do! It's breach of promise!"

The Duke was somewhat staggered by this revelation.

"Breach of promise! Matt, I don't know what you have been doing, but who the devil could be suing you for such a sum as that?"

"Not *me!* Suing *you!* Through my father, I daresay. To keep our name out of court! Everyone knows how rich you are!"

"What a fool I am!" said Gilly slowly. "Of course! But did you make an offer of marriage to this female?"

"Well, yes, I suppose I did," said Matthew wretchedly. "You know how it is when one writes a letter!"

"Did you write her letters?"

"Yes, I did, but I never thought—— And she did not answer one of them!" said Matthew, on a note of ill-usage.

"Matt, has she many of your letters?"

"It isn't she: it's a fellow who says he is her guardian. He says he has half a dozen of my letters. I do not know how I came to write so many, for in general, you know, I am not much of a dab in that line! But she was so excessively beautiful——! You can have no notion, Gilly!"

"Where did you meet her? Not in London?"

"Oh, no! In the High! She was looking in at a shop-window, and there was a lady with her—well, I thought she was a lady, but when I came to know her better of course I saw that she was not quite the thing, but that didn't signify, and she said she was her aunt, and her name was Mrs. Dovercourt, but I daresay it was not. Anyway, Belinda dropped her reticule, and of course I picked it up, and—and that is how it all began!"

The Duke, feeling a trifle bewildered by this not very clear account of his cousin's entanglement, suggested that they should thrash the matter out in the privacy of his library at Sale House. Matthew agreed to this, but said with a heavy sigh that he did not see what could be done about it. "I won't let you pay, Gilly, and that's an end to it! It's all very well to say you may draw what money you please, but what a flutter there would be if you drew such a sum as that! It would be bound to come to my uncle's ears, and he would tell my father, and then I should have nothing to do but to jump into the river, and that would not anwser, because I am a pretty strong swimmer, and I daresay I shouldn't drown at all! Of course, if I were like you, and could afford to keep my own phaeton, or curricle, or some such thing, I could drive to the devil, and break my neck, but I should like to see anyone driving a job-horse and gig to the devil! Why, you couldn't do it! Job-horses are all slugs! I suppose I *could* blow my brains out, but it would mean purchasing a good pistol, and I'm not too well-

63

blunted at this present, and to tell you the truth, Gilly, I don't above half fancy the idea."

The Duke, realizing that Captain Ware's punch had something to do with this despairing utterance, replied in soothing terms, agreeing that among his own many advantages must be ranked the means of putting a period to his life in an expensive way, and drew his young relative on towards Curzon Street. The walk did much to clear Mr. Ware's clouded intellect, but nothing to lift his depression. When he entered Sale House in Gilly's wake, he made an effort to appear sprightly and at his ease, but achieved such an alarming result that had the Duke's upper servants had eyes to spare for anyone but their master they must have noticed it, and have wondered what could be in the wind. But in the event Borrowdale, Chigwell, and Nettlebed were far too much taken-up with conveying to his Grace by innuendo a sense of anxiety he had caused them to labour under all the evening to have any attention to spare for Mr. Matthew.

The Duke bore all the solicitude that met him with his usual patience, disclaiming any feeling of chill or of fatigue, and desired Borrowdale to bring wine and biscuits into the library. "And you need none of you wait up for me!" he added. "Leave a candle on the table, and I shall do very well."

The steward bowed, and said that it should be as his Grace wished, but Borrowdale and Nettlebed were instantly drawn into a temporary alliance, and exchanged speaking glances, expressive of their mutual determination to sit up all night, if need be.

The Duke led Matthew into the library, and installed him in a chair by the fire; one of the footmen came in with a taper, with the zealous intention of lighting all the candles in the wall-sconces and chandeliers with which the room was generously provided; and Borrowdale soon followed him with a silver tray of refreshments. Having restrained the footman, and assured Borrowdale that he should want nothing more that night, the Duke got rid of them both, and took a seat opposite his cousin's. "Well, now, Matt, tell me the whole!" he invited.

"You won't blab to my father if I do, will you?" said Matthew suspiciously.

"What a fellow you must think me! Of course I will not!"

His mind relieved on this score, Matthew embarked on a long and somewhat obscure story. It came haltingly at first, and with a good many rambling excuses, but when he found that his cousin had apparently no intention either of exclaiming at his folly, or of blaming him for it, he abandoned his slightly pugnacious and extremely self-exculpatory manner, and became very much more natural, unburdening his troubled soul to the Duke, and feeling considerably the better for it.

The tale was not always easy to follow, and in spite of its length, and wealth of detail, there were several gaps in it, but the salient points were not difficult to grasp. The Duke gathered that his impulsive cousin had fallen in love at sight with a female of surpassing beauty, who was visiting Oxford with a lady who might, or might not, be her aunt. This lady, so far from discouraging the advances of a strange gentleman, had most obligingly given him her direction, and had assured him that she would be happy to see him if he should chance at any time to be passing her lodging. And of course Matthew had passed her lodging, and had received a flattering welcome there; and, finding that the lovely Belinda was even lovelier than his memory had painted her, lost no time in plunging neck and crop into an *affaire* which seemed to have run the gamut of stolen meetings, passionate love-letters, and wild plans of a flight to Gretna Green. Yes, he admitted, he rather thought he had mentioned Gretna Green.

The Duke knit his brows a little at this. "But, Matt, I do not perfectly understand!" he said apologetically. "You say she is threatening to sue you for breach of promise, but if you were willing to marry her I do not see how this comes about! Why would she not go with you?"

"Well, I daresay she would have," said Matthew. "She—she is a very persuadable girl, you know. But the thing is that it costs the devil of a sum to hire a chaise to go all that way, and what with having sustained some losses, and its being pretty near the end of the term, I was not at all beforehand with the world, and I didn't know how to raise the wind. You know what my father is! He would have kicked up the devil of a dust if I had written to ask him for some more blunt, and ten to one would have asked me what I wanted it for, because he always does, just as though I were a child, and not able to take care of my affairs! And I never thought of writing to you, Gilly—not that I would have done so if I had, for it might have come to my uncle's ears then, and that would have been worse than anything! So what with one thing and another, it came to nothing, and, to own the truth, I was afterwards very glad of it, because I don't think Belinda would do for me at all—in fact, I know she would not!"

"Did she seem much distressed at your plan's coming to nothing?" asked the Duke curiously.

"Oh, no, *she* did not care! It is all this Liversedge, who writes that he is her guardian. Stay, I will show you his letters—he has written to me twice, you know. I did not answer the first letter, and now he has written again, threatening to bring an action against me, and—oh, Gilly, what the devil am I to do?"

He ended on a decided note of panic, and, thrusting a hand into his pocket, produced two rather crumped letters, written by someone who signed himself, with a flourish, Swithin Liversedge.

The Duke, perusing these, found Mr. Liversedge's epistolary style slightly turgid, and not always quite grammatical. Some of his periods were much involved, but there could be no mistaking his object: he wanted five thousand pounds for his ward, to compensate her for the slight she had endured, for the loss of an eligible husband, and for a wounded heart. Mr. Liversedge ended his first letter by expressing in high-flown terms his belief that neither Mr. Ware nor his noble relatives would hesitate to recognize, and meet, the claims of one whose blighted hopes seemed likely to drive into a decline.

His second letter was not so polite.

The Duke laid them both down. "Matt, who *is* this Liversedge?" he demanded.

"I don't know. He says he is Belinda's guardian."

"But what sort of a fellow is he?"

"I tell you I don't know! I've never clapped eyes on him. I didn't know Belinda had a guardian until I received that letter."

"Was he not with her at Oxford?"

"No, and neither Belinda nor Mrs. Dovercourt ever mentioned him that I can remember. It came as the greatest surprise to me!"

"Matt, it all sounds to me excessively like a fudge! I don't believe he is her guardian!"

"I daresay he might not be, but what's the odds?"

"Well, I am not very sure, but I think he can't bring an action against you. Unless, of course, it is she who brings it, and he merely writes for her."

Matthew considered this. "I must say I should not have thought it of Belinda," he said. "But there is no knowing, after all! I daresay she was hoaxing me all the time, and was no more innocent than a piece of Haymarket-ware."

The Duke glanced at the letters again, and got up, and walked over to the table, to pour out two glasses of wine.

Matthew watched him, saying after a minute: "And whatever he is, you can see one thing: he means to make himself curst unpleasant, and there's no getting away from it that he has those damned letters of mine!"

"No," agreed Gilly. "It's a devil of a tangle."

"Gilly," said his cousin, in a hollow voice, "even if it did not come to an action, it will reach my father, and my uncle too, and that would be just as bad!"

He did not address himself to deaf ears. The Duke almost shuddered, "Good God, it must not be allowed to reach them!"

Matthew dropped his chin in his hands, his elbows propped on his knees. "If only I could think of what I had best do!" he groaned.

Gilly held out one of the glasses to him. "Here, take some wine! Does Gideon know anything of this?"

Matthew accepted the wine, and drank some. "No. I did mean—that is to say, I half thought that I might, if all else failed—But you know what Gideon is!" He saw a surprised look on the Duke's face, and added: "Oh, well, I daresay you don't, for he likes you! But he has a damned cutting tongue! What's more, he is for ever roasting me about something or other, and I'd as lief—However, if you think I ought to tell him——"

"No, I don't," said Gilly, with sudden decision. "It has nothing whatsoever to do with Gideon!" His eyes began to dance. "I must learn to manage for myself: my uncle said so!"

"Oh, Gilly, don't start funning!" begged Matthew. "It ain't your affair any more than it is Gideon's!"

"But it is my affair! You said as much yourself!" Gilly pointed out. "Liversedge knows well you could not afford to pay him half of such a sum, or my Uncle Henry either! You may depend upon it he has acquainted himself very perfectly with the circumstances. It's my belief the whole thing was a deep-laid plot, down to the girl's dropping her reticule when you were passing! *I* am the pigeon he means to pluck! Very well, then! I'll attend to the matter myself, and I think I must be a great fool if I allow myself to be plucked by a person who cannot write the King's English!"

"But, good God, Gilly, what are you meaning to do?" demanded Matthew.

"I am not very sure yet," confessed the Duke, "but don't worry, Matt! Whatever happens I won't let it come to your father's ears, or my Uncle Lionel's either! Where does this fellow write from?" He picked up one of the letters as he spoke. "The Bird in Hand—yes, but I am *not* a bird in hand, Mr. Liversedge! Address to the receiving-office at Baldock. I suppose he fetches his letters. But why Baldock? I should have thought he would have lurked in London! Perhaps he has his reasons for not coming within reach of Bow Street. Very likely that is so, for if ever I smelled a Greek——!"

"Did you?" asked Matthew sceptically.

"Oh, lord, yes, very adroit ones too! A young man with my fortune draws 'em like a magnet. They clustered round me when I was upon my travels—until they had taken Belper's measure! Poor Belper! he had his uses!"

Matthew sat up. "Gilly, do you think perhaps Belper would——?"

"No, certainly not! We shall keep this strictly within the family. Besides, it is the only time I have ever had the chance of doing anything for myself!"

"I do wish you will tell me what you have in your head!" Matthew said.

"I am going to pay a call on Mr. Swithin Liversedge—if I can find him!"

"Gilly, for God's sake——!" exclaimed Matthew, now seriously disturbed.

"I must know what sort of a fellow it is we have to deal with."

"But you must be mad! If *you* go to see him, he will know you mean to buy him off, and he will very likely double his price!"

"But he won't know I'm Sale!" replied the Duke, his face alive with mischief. "I shall be the Honourable Matthew Ware! You said you had never clapped eyes on him, so he won't know it's a hoax!"

"Gilly, you *are* mad! Even if he don't know what I look like, he must know I don't drive about the country in a chaise with crests on the panels, and half a dozen servants, and—Oh, I wish you will be serious!"

"I am serious. Of course, I don't mean to travel like that! I shall go by the mail, or the stage, or some such thing. It's famous! I have never driven in anything but my own carriage in all my life!"

"Well, you need not think there is anything so vastly agreeable in going by stage-coach!" said Matthew, with some asperity. "If you had done it as many times as I have——"

"But I have not, and I should like to find out for myself what it is like to rub shoulders with the world!"

"Nettlebed would send off an express to my uncle on the instant!"

"I make no doubt he would, and so he may, but he won't know where I have gone to, so much good may it do him!"

"You would not go without your valet!"

"Without anyone! Plain Mr. Dash, of Nowhere in Particular! Gideon told me to try it, and, by God, I will!"

"No, Gilly, you must not! I wish I had not said a word to you about it!"

The Duke laughed at him. "Matt, you fool! I am not going into a lion's den! Besides, it will only be for a day or two. I don't mean to be lost for ever, you know!"

"No, but—What if Liversedge recognizes you? He might well!"

The Duke frowned, over this for a moment or two. "But I don't think he will," he said at last. "If he was prowling round Oxford when I was up, he *may* have seen me, but I have altered considerably since then, you know. And I only came back to England last year, and have been at Sale for the better part of my life since then."

"You were in London in the spring!"

"To be sure I was, but not in any company that Liversedge keeps, I'll swear! If you saw me once in the street, would you know me again, beyond question? Now, if I were a big, handsome fellow like Gideon——! But I am not, Matt! You must own I am not! Has not your father said times out of mind that it is a sad pity I am such an insignificant figure of a man?"

"Yes, but—I mean, no!" Matthew corrected himself hastily. "And in any event——"

"In any event, I mean to go! When do you go up to Oxford?"

"I did mean to go to-morrow, but term hasn't begun, and now that you have taken this crazy notion into your head I think I had best stay in town. Gilly, Uncle Lionel would tear me limb from limb if he knew of this!"

"Well, he shan't know, and you had best go to Oxford, so that nobody may suspect you of having anything to do with my having slipped my leash!" recommended the Duke. "I'll write to you there, to let you know how I've fared. But don't get in a pucker, either on my behalf or your own! If I have to buy Liversedge off, I'll do it, and as for the rest —what in the name of all that is wonderful do you imagine can befall me?"

"I don't know," said Matthew uneasily, "but I have the horridest feeling something *will* befall you!"

69

THE Duke awoke on the following morning with a pleasurable feeling that something agreeable lay before him. When he remembered what it was, he was obliged to own to himself that to negotiate with Mr. Swithin Liversedge might not prove to be an altogether delightful experience; but the prospect of escaping from his household, for as much perhaps as three or four days, was attractive enough to make him feel that any possible unpleasantness with Mr. Liversedge would be more than compensated for. He felt adventurous, and while he waited for Nettlebed to bring the hot chocolate with which inmates of any house under Lord Lionel's direction still regaled themselves before getting out of bed in the morning, he lay revolving in his head various plans for his escape.

It was plainly impossible to divulge to Nettlebed the least particle of his intentions; for Nettlebed would certainly insist on accompanying him on any journey which he might undertake. And if he refused to allow Nettlebed to go with him, Nettlebed would assuredly inform his uncle of his revolutionary behaviour without a moment's loss of time. How Nettlebed was to be prevented from telling Lord Lionel of his nephew's disappearance, he had no very clear idea, but he trusted that one would present itself to his mind during the course of the day. And if none did, and Lord Lionel did discover his truancy—well, he would be back at Sale House again before his lordship could do anything unwelcome, and although he might have to endure one of his tremendous scolds, he would at least have enjoyed a brief spell of freedom.

Money presented no difficulties. He had scarcely broken into the hundred pounds Scriven had drawn for him on his bank, so that he would not be forced to arouse suspicion by demanding more. The hardest problem, he soon realized, would be the packing of a valise to take with him.

He had not the smallest notion where his valises and trunks were stored. This was a severe set-back, and he wasted some minutes in trying to think out a way of discovering this vital information before it occurred to him that he could very well afford to buy a new valise. Probably his own bore his cypher upon them: he could not remember, but it seemed likely, since those who ordered such things for him had what amounted to a mania for embossing them either with his crest, or with a large and flourishing letter S.

He would need shirts, too, and his night-gear, and ties, wrist-bands, brushes, combs, razors, and no doubt a hun-

dred other things which it was his valet's business to as-
emble for him. He had a dressing-case, and a toilet-
battery, but he could not take either of these. Nor could
he take the brushes that lay on his dressing-table, for they
naturally bore his cypher. And if he abstracted a few ties
and shirts from the pile of linen in his wardrobe, would
Nettlebed instantly discover their absence, and run him to
earth before he had had time to board the coach? He decided that he must take that risk, for although he knew he
could purchase soap, and brushes, and valises, he had no
idea that it might be possible to purchase a shirt. One's
shirts were made for one, just as one's coats and breeches
were, and one's boots. But to convey out of Sale House,
unobserved, a bundle of clothing, was a task that presented
insuperable obstacles to the Duke's mind. He was still trying to hit upon a way out of the difficulty when Nettlebed
came in, and softly drew back the bed-curtains.

The Duke sat up, and pulled off his night-cap. He looked
absurdly small and boyish in the huge bed, so that it was
perhaps not so very surprising that Nettlebed should have
greeted him with a few words of reproof for the late hours
he had kept on the previous evening.

"I never thought to see your Grace awake, not for another two hours I did not!" he said, shaking his head. "The
idea of Mr. Matthew's sitting with you for ever, and keeping
you from your bed until past three o'clock!"

The Duke took the cup of chocolate from him, and began
to sip it. "Don't be so foolish, Nettlebed!" he said. "You know
very well that during the season I was seldom in bed before
then, and sometimes much later!"

"But this is not the season, my lord!" said Nettlebed unanswerably. "And what is more you was often very fagged,
which his lordship observed to me when we left town, and
it was his wish you should recruit your strength, and keep
early hours, and well I know that if *he* had been here Mr.
Matthew would have been sent off with a flea in his ear!
For bear with Mr. Matthew's tiresome ways his lordship
never has, and never will! And I think it my duty to tell
you, my lord, that the piece of very gratifying intelligence
your Grace was so obliging as to inform me of last night, in
what one might call a confidential way, is known to the
whole house, including the kitchenmaids, who have not
above six pounds a year, and do not associate with the
upper servants!"

"No, is it indeed?" said the Duke, not much impressed,
but realizing from long experience that Nettlebed's sensitive
feelings had received a severe wound. "I wonder how it

can have got about? I suppose Scriven must have dropped a hint to someone."

"Mr. Scriven," said Nettlebed coldly, "would not so demean himself, your Grace, being as I am myself, in your Grace's confidence. But what, your Grace, can be expected, when——"

"Nettlebed," said the Duke plaintively, "when you call me your Grace with every breath you draw I know I have offended you, but indeed I had no notion of doing so, and I wish you will forgive me, and let me have no more Graces!"

His henchman paid not the least heed to this request, but continued as though there had been no interruption. "But what, your Grace, can be expected, when your Grace scribbles eight advertisements of your Grace's approaching nuptials, and leaves them all on the floor to be gathered up by an under-servant who should know his place better than to be prying into your Grace's business?"

"Well, it doesn't signify," said the Duke. "The news will be in to-morrow's *Gazette*, I daresay, so there is no harm done."

Nettlebed cast him a look of deep reproach, and began to lay out his raiment.

"And I told you of it myself," added the Duke placatingly.

"I should have thought it a very singular circumstance, your Grace, had I learnt it from any other lips than your Grace's," replied Nettlebed crushingly.

The Duke was just about to apply himself to the task of smoothing his ruffled sensibilities when he suddenly perceived how Nettlebed's displeasure might be turned to good account. While Nettlebed continued in a state of umbrage, he would hold himself aloof, and without neglecting any part of his duties would certainly not hover solicitously about him. He would become, in fact, a correct and apparently disinterested servant, answering the summons of a bell with promptitude, but waiting for that summons. In general, the Duke took care not to permit such a state of affairs to endure for long, since Nettlebed could, in a very subtle way, make him most uncomfortable. Besides, he did not like to be upon bad terms with his dependants. Lying back against his pillows, he considered the valet under his lashes, knowing very well that Nettlebed was ready to accept an amende. Nettlebed had just laid his blue town coat tenderly over a chair, and was now giving a final dusting to a pair of refulgent Hessian boots. The Duke let him finish this, and even waited until he had selected a suitable waistcoat to match this attire before—apparently—becoming aware

of his activities. He yawned,
"I shall wear riding-dress to-day.

At any other time, such waywa
he had attended since his twelfth
from Nettlebed a rebuke. He woul
tered into his master's plans for the
down a message to the stables for him. B
ly folded his lips tightly, and without utt
stored the town raiment to the wardrobe.

This awful and unaccustomed silence wa ned throughout the Duke's toilet. It was only broke en the Duke rejected the corbeau-coloured coat being held up for him to put on. "No, not that one," said the Duke indifferently. "The olive coat Scott made for me."

Nettlebed perceived that this was deliberate provacation, and swelled with indignation. Scott, who made Captain Ware's uniforms, and was largely patronized by the military, was an extremely fashionable tailor, but the Duke's father had never had a coat from him, and Nettlebed had disliked the olive coat on sight. But he only permitted himself one glance of censure at his master before bowing stiffly, and turning away.

"I shall be out all day, and don't know when I may return," said the Duke carelessly. "I shan't need you, so you may have the day to yourself."

Nettlebed bowed again, more stiffly than ever, and assisted him to shrug himself into the offending coat. The Duke pulled down his wrist-bands, straightened his cravat, and went down to the breakfast-parlour, feeling very like his own grandfather, who was widely reported to have been a harsh and exacting master, who bullied all his servants, and thought nothing of throwing missiles at any valet who happened to annoy him.

But his cruelty attained its object. When he ventured to go upstairs again to his bedchamber there was no sign of Nettlebed. The Duke trod over to his wardrobe, and opened it.

He seemed to have so many piles of shirts stacked on one of the shelves that he thought it unlikely that Nettlebed would notice any depredations, provided he took a few from each pile. He took six, to be on the safe side, and began to hunt for his nightshirts and caps. By the time he had made a selection amongst these, and had added a number of ties, and other necessaries, to the heap on the bed, this had assumed formidable proportions, and he surveyed it rather doubtfully. By dint of asking an incurious under-footman for it, he had been able to procure some wrapping-

...ne without incurring question, but ...that it was not going to be an easy task ...these articles of apparel into a neat bundle. He ...e right. By the time he had achieved anything ap-...aching a tolerable result he was slightly heated, and a good deal exasperated. And when he looked dispassionately at his bundle he realized that it would be quite impossible for him to walk out of his house carrying such a monstrous package. Then he bethought him that if he did not leave his house quickly he would very likely fall into the clutches of Captain Belper, and fright sharpened his wits. He sent for his personal footman, that splendid fellow who did not care a fig for what might become of him. When the man presented himself, he waved a careless hand towards the bundle, and said: "Francis, you will oblige me, please, by carrying that package round to Captain Ware's chambers, and giving it into his man's charge. Inform Wragby that it contains—that it contains some things I promised to send Captain Ware! Perhaps I had best send the Captain a note with it!"

"Very good, your Grace," said Francis, with a gratifying lack either of surprise or of interest.

The Duke pulled out his tablets from his pocket, found a pencil, and scrawled a brief message. *"Gideon,"* he wrote, *"pray keep this bundle for me till I come to you this evening. Sale."* He tore off the leaf from his tablets, twisted it into a screw, and gave it to Francis. "And, Francis!" he said, rather shyly.

"Your Grace?"

"Do you think," said the Duke, with a faint, rueful smile, "you can contrive to leave the house without Nettlebed's seeing you, or Borrowdale, or—or anyone?"

"Certainly, your Grace," said Francis woodenly.

"Thank you!" said the Duke, with real gratitude.

He would have been surprised had he been privileged to read the thoughts in his footman's head. This impassive individual had not been a year in the employment of the gentlest-mannered master he had ever served without developing a lively sympathy for him. It was his opinion, freely expressed to his intimates over a heavy-wet, that there was never a lad so put-upon as the little Duke, and that it fair made a man's blood boil to hear old Gundiguts and Muffin-face a-worriting him, not to mention my Lord Stiff-Rump, treating the lad to enough cross-and-jostle work to drive him into Bedlam. So far from not caring a fig for what became of the Duke, he was extremely curious to know what mischief he was up to, for mischief he would go bail it was.

It would be a rare treat to slumguzzle Gundiguts and Muffin-face, and he was only sorry that his training forbade him to offer his master any further assistance he might need in hoodwinking them and all the rest of the household, rump and stump.

The Duke drew his watch out, and glanced at it apprehensively. The menace of Captain Belper loomed large. He dived into his hanging-wardrobe, found a long, drab-coloured driving-coat with several shoulder-capes, a high collar, and large mother-of-pearl buttons; and a high-crowned beaver hat. He thought that he might perhaps be glad of a muffler, so he searched for that too. He could not think of anything else that he might need, so having assured himself that the visiting-card he had wrested from his unwilling cousin Matthew was safely tucked into his pocket-book, he left his room, and walked sedately down the great staircase.

The porter, who was sitting in a large leather chair by the front-door, got up as soon as he saw him, and told him that a package had just been delivered at the house from Joseph Manton's. This instantly put the Duke in mind of the absolute necessity of taking a good pair of pistols with him upon his hazardous adventure. In spite of the danger of being caught by Captain Belper, he was quite unable to resist the temptation of carrying Manton's package into the library, and unwrapping his purchase. The pistols, a really beautiful pair, lay snugly in their leather-case, looking very slender and wicked. The Duke lifted one from its velvet bed, and tested its balance lovingly. No one could expect him to leave such peerless acquisitions behind! He slid the case into his capacious pocket, and the ball and powder thoughtfully provided by Mr. Manton, in another pocket, telling himself that Baldock would be the very place for a little practice.

He went out into the hall again to find that Borrowdale had sailed into it from his quarters at the back of the house, attended rather regally by two footmen. Borrowdale wished to know if his Grace would be dining at home, and—with a glance at his Grace's top-boots—whether his Grace desired his horse to be brought round.

"No," said the Duke jauntily. "No, thank you, Borrowdale. I do not desire anything at all. And if Captain Belper should call—you do not know when I shall be returning."

"Very good, your Grace," bowed Borrowdale. "And when *does* your Grace expect to return?"

The Duke smiled at him. "But if you knew that you would not be able to tell Captain Belper that you did not, would you?" he said gently.

Before Borrowdale had recovered from his surprise sufficiently to disabuse his master's mind of its curious misapprehension, the Duke had left the house.

His first objective was the General Post Office in Lombard Street. He drove to the City in a hackney carriage, which was an adventure in itself, since he had never ridden in one before, but a disappointment awaited him at the Post Office, where he discovered that as the mails all left London over-night he must be prepared to leave town at half-past eight that evening if he wished to avail himself of their services. A burly citizen in a low-crowned hat took pity on his inexperience, and directed him to a stage-coach-office, at the Saracen's Head in Aldgate High Street. He seemed amused when the Duke, thanking him, asked the way to Aldgate High Street, said that he was a regular Johnny Raw, and begged him not to let himself be smoked by any fly-coves whom he might meet.

The Saracen's Head was a big, busy hostelry, with two tiers of galleries running round a paved courtyard. Even at eleven o'clock in the morning, with most of the outgoing coaches departed long since, it was the scene of considerable activity, and quite a number of persons were waiting in the coach-office to book places on one or other of the many coaches which had their headquarters at the Saracen's Head. The Duke, when it came to his turn, was successful in obtaining the box-seat on the Highflyer, which was due to leave London at eight in the morning, on its long journey to Edinburgh, and would arrive at Baldock at about noon. He then engaged a room at the inn for one night, and, evading the urgent entreaties of a lady who held a bunch of watercress under his nose, and refusing the offer of a one-legged man to sell him a doormat, he set off to look for a shop where he could buy a valise.

This was soon accomplished, and having arranged for the bag to be delivered at Captain Ware's chambers, the Duke was able to turn his attention to such minor matters as the purchasing of soap, and tooth-powder, and a razor. He was directed to Bedford House, where he was most surprised to find for what a small sum he could buy hair-brushes, and combs, and other such articles. In the end, he made so many small purchases that he was obliged once more to make use of his cousin's chambers.

It was just before eight, having whiled away the afternoon as best he could, that he entered the precincts of Albany. As he strolled up the Rope-Walk, an acquaintance who was sallying forth in evening attire, levelled a quizzing-glass at his top-boots, and said: "Just arrived from the country, I see, Duke! I did not know you were expected in town. Are you on your way to your cousin? You will find him at home: I saw him come in above an hour ago."

"I am dining with him," the Duke replied.

"Well, I shall see you at White's to-morrow, I daresay."

The Duke agreed to this somewhat mendaciously, and passed on.

When he was admitted into Captain Ware's chambers, his cousin met him in the hall with a ribald demand to know whether he took his lodging for a receiving office.

The Duke smiled up at him engagingly. "Oh, I could think of nowhere else to have them sent!" he said. "You can have no notion how busy I have been!"

"But, Adolphus, has it come to this, that you are obliged to fetch your linen home from the washerwoman?" asked Gideon, pointing to the unwieldy bundle on the floor.

"So Francis contrived to smuggle it away! Good!" said the Duke, casting off his greatcoat. "Gideon, I have slipped my leash!"

"Capital!" approved his cousin. "Come and tell me the whole!"

The Duke followed him into his sitting-room, but said: "Well, no! I think I will not, if you do not mind it very much!"

"Then tell me nothing at all," said Gideon, handing him a glass of sherry. "Not, believe me, Adolphus, that I would cast the least rub in your way!"

The Duke, with the nature of his adventure in mind, was not so sure of this. His big cousin could be depended upon to aid and abet him in kicking over his irksome traces, but let him catch but one whiff of Mr. Liversedge and his demands and he would without any doubt at all cast very much more than a rub in the way. So he smiled again, and sipped his sherry.

Gideon, who knew that sweet, abstracted smile, said accusingly: "Adolphus, you are brewing mischief!"

"Oh, no!" said Gilly. "I am just very tired of being myself, and I am going to take your advice, and try how I like being plain Mr. Dash. To be Duke of Sale is a dead bore!"

"I am aware. Did I so advise you? My father will want my head on a charger!"

"Last night. I have made a start already, for I have been doing all manner of things that I never did before. A man I met in the City took me for a Johnny Raw. And I think he was right: I am shockingly green! But I shall soon learn. I am going out of town, you know."

"So I had supposed. Does that infamous bundle contain your raiment?"

"Yes, and such a work as I had to get it away without Nettlebed's seeing it! Gideon, I think perhaps Nettlebed may seek me here. Do, pray, assure him that I am safe, and keep them all from flying into some absurd pucker!"

"You may rely on me, Adolphus,—if not to do quite what you would wish—at least to afford your retinue no clue whatsoéver to your whereabouts. In fact, I shall deny all knowledge of you."

"Poor Nettlebed!" said Gilly. "I fear he will be in despair. I offended him this morning, and left him quite out of charity with me. I suppose it is a great deal too bad of me to put him in a fright, but I can't bear it any longer, Gideon! They treat me as though I were a child, or an imbecile! I cannot move a step without one or other of them running to call my carriage, or hand me my gloves, or ask me when I mean to return! Yes, yes, I know what you will say! But I cannot do it! I *have* made the attempt, but the devil of it is I can't but remember how Borrowdale used to give me sugar-plums when I was in disgrace, and how dear, good Chigwell told my uncle it was he who broke the window in the Red Drawing-room, and how Nettlebed has nursed me whenever I have been ill—oh, and a hundred other things of the kind!"

Gideon's crooked smile flickered. "Very well. So, since you cannot bring yourself to tell them that you are a man, and can fend for yourself, you mean to show them that it is so. Is that it?"

"I suppose it is. That is, I didn't think of it, but perhaps it may answer! I only thought how much I wished to be free! But I own if the chance had not offered I should still be talking fustian about being blue-devilled, and making not the least push to assert myself! I must be the dullest, most spiritless dog alive!"

"Oh, without doubt!" agreed Gideon. "But has this humdrum age suddenly offered you adventure, Adolphus? I had not believed it to be possible!"

"A very small adventure!" the Duke said, laughing. "I have found something to do for myself, and perhaps I can do it, and perhaps I cannot, but at all events I mean to try. And for once in my life I am going to see how it would be not to be a Duke, with servants puffing off my consequence wherever I go, and toad-eaters agreeing with every ill-considered word I utter, and inn-keepers bowing till their noses touch their knees, and the common-world saying nothing but Yes, your Grace! and No, your Grace! and As your Grace pleases! Do you think I shall make a sad botch of it?"

"No, my little one, I think you have a very good understanding, and will manage tolerably well for yourself, but whether you will enjoy the experience of having none to wait on you is another matter," grinned Gideon. "It won't harm you, however: you have been kept well-wrapped in lamb's-wool for too long. I hope you will have very exciting adventures, and slay a great many giants and dragons. I wish I might see you!"

"Oh, no, that would never do!" Gilly said, shaking his head. "You would think me very slow in killing my dragon, and soon fall out of patience with me, and end by pushing me out of the way, and slaying the beast yourself!" He added with a gleam of humour: "And I have a melancholy suspicion that if I had you within call I shouldn't take the trouble to think of anything for myself. Oh, I am sure I should wait for you to tell me what I must do next, for that is always what I used to do, and habits, you know, are damnably hard to break! And you are a very peremptory, autocratic, and overbearing fellow, Gideon!"

"Alas! Shall you give me a sharp set-down when you come back from your adventure?"

"Very likely," said Gilly, putting his empty glass down.

Wragby came into the room to set the dishes on the table. His master told him that he need not wait, and the Duke said, as he took his seat: "How snug this is! Shall I carve this bird? I can, you know! My uncle says a man should know how to carve anything that is set before him. I can shoe a horse, too. Now, why do you suppose he should have thought I must learn such a thing as that? He is the strangest creature! How angry he will be with me when he hears what I have been about! It makes me shake like a blancmanger only to think of it."

"Amongst the many odd fancies that come into my head, Adolphus," said his cousin dryly, "is the fancy—I have often been conscious of it!—that in spite of your meekness you do *not* shake like a blancmanger before my father!"

"No, of course I don't: he is a great deal too kind to me. But I do not like it when he storms at me, and arguing gives me the headache. I always try to slip away, and being so small and unremarkable I can in general manage to do so," said the Duke serenely.

Gideon smiled. "Your elusive ways are well-known to me. And, by God, it is just what you are doing, now I come to think of it! Don't try to gammon me with your hints of adventures to be embarked on! You are merely slipping away

79

to rather more purpose than usual. What lying story have you fobbed your devoted servants off with?"

The Duke looked up with rather a guilty twinkle in his eyes. "Well, to tell you the truth, I haven't," he confessed. "You cannot slip away unobserved if you tell people you mean to go!"

"Gilly, for God's sake——! Have you left them without a word?" exclaimed Gideon.

The Duke nodded. For a moment Gideon sat staring at him with knit brows. Then he burst out laughing. "It's the maddest quirk I ever heard tell of, and who—*who* would have guessed that you had it in you to do it?" he said. "Adolphus, I no longer despair of you! You will undoubtedly set your whole household by the ears, from my father down to your lowliest footman, and it will do them a great deal of good! Don't come back too soon! Let them learn their lesson past fear of forgetting it: you may then enjoy some peace hereafter. Fill up your glass! We'll have a toast to your emancipation. No daylights, no heel-taps!"

Then Duke obeyed, and pushed the bottle across the table. "No, we shall drink to the adventures of Mr. Dash!" he said.

"Anything you please!" grinned his cousin, and tossed off his wine with a flourish.

The Duke followed suit. As he lowered his glass, the ring on his finger caught his eye. He drew it off. "Keep that for me!" he said, handing it to Gideon. "It quite ruins my disguise!"

CHAPTER VIII

The Duke did not enjoy a very restful night's repose in his room at the Saracen's Head. The feather-bed upon which he twisted and turned seemed to be composed largely of lumps; and no one else in the inn appeared to go to bed at all. The noise in the tap-room went on until far into the night; doors banged; footsteps clumped down the passages; and an occasional clatter suggested that kitchenmaids enjoyed no respite from their labours. He was also very much too hot, the bed being piled high with blankets, and having been warmed for him by a chambermaid who was directed to take up a warming-pan for the Quality in No. 27 as soon as he arrived in his hackney from Albany.

He had remained with his cousin until an advanced hour, and was consequently tired when he reached the inn. If he had owned the truth to himself, which he resolutely refused to do, he would not have been ill-pleased to have found Nettlebed awaiting him, ready to have unpacked his valise, pulled off his boots, and poured out hot water for him to wash his face and hands in. His bedchamber, which was small, and rather stuffy, seemed oddly friendless when he entered it, and was lit by only one candle, which was set down on the dressing-table by the boots who escorted him upstairs. Had Nettlebed been with him, he would have found his familiar belongings already laid out for him, his own sheets upon the bed, and—but had Nettlebed been with him he would not, of course, have been staying at an inn of this class, but at some posting-house which despised stage-coach travellers, and catered only for the Nobility and Gentry. The Duke firmly banished Nettlebed from his mind, and put himself to bed.

It naturally did not occur to him that he must ask to be called in the morning, but fortunately the boots took his measure, and suggested to him that he should state the hour at which he would wish to have a jug of shaving-water brought up to him. In the event, he underestimated the time it would take him to shave, dress himself, and pack his valise, and it was consequently in a somewhat flurried and breathless state that he ran down to the coffee-room to partake of a hasty breakfast. As he had forgotten to set his top-boots outside his door, these had not been cleaned, and looked, to his fastidious eye, very dull and dusty. But when he came out of the coffee-room into the yard, he found that amongst the many irrelevant persons assembled there was a shoe-black, of whose services he instantly availed himself.

While this individual laboured upon his boots, he had leisure to observe the activities going on around him, and was so much entertained that any regrets he might have had that he had embarked on such an impulsive adventure left him.

The Highflyer, upon which he was to travel, had been dragged into the yard, and was being loaded with all manner of baggage. All the heavy cases were hoisted on to the roof, and the Duke's eyes widened as corded trunk after corded trunk was piled up, until it seemed as though the coach could scarcely escape an overturn at the first bend in the road, so top-heavy had it become. While this was going forward, several persons were assisting the guard to stow into the boot all manner of smaller packages, including the Duke's valise. When this was full, all the articles which still littered the yard, such as a basket of fish, several bandboxes, and some parcels done up in paper, were lashed to the hind axle-tree, or to the lamp-irons.

Meanwhile, the coachman, a burly gentleman in a multiplicity of coats, and with an enormous nosegay in his buttonhole, stood at one of the doors leading into the inn enjoying a flirtation with a housemaid. He paid no heed to the equipage he was about to drive until the ostlers led out from the stables a team of chestnuts, when he ran his eye critically over them, and delivered himself of various scraps of advice and instruction, which included an alarming command to take care not to let the near-wheeler touch the roller-bolt.

The passengers were most of them engaged in arguments with the guard, and in fretfully waving away half the street-criers of London, who, for reasons which the Duke was unable to fathom, had assembled in the yard for the purpose of offering travellers every imaginable comfort upon their journey, from Holland socks, at only four shillings the pair, to hot spiced gingerbread. He had himself been obliged several times to refuse a rat-trap, a bag of oranges, and a paper of pins. One or two of the travellers, notably a thin man, muffled in a greatcoat, muffler, and a plaid shawl, seemed inclined to be querulous; and two elderly ladies were fast driving the guard to distraction by their repeated and shrill enquiries as to the exact location of a number of bandboxes and string-bags. Two of the gentlemen proposing to travel had not found the time to shave; and another was engaged in an acrimonious altercation with the jarvey who had driven him to the inn in a hackney.

The horses having been poled-up, the coachman took a regretful leave of the housemaid, and rolled into the centre of the yard, casting an indulgent eye over his way-bill. The Duke thrust a silver coin into the shoe-black's hand, and mounted on to his seat on the roof; the thin man besought the coachman to assure him that the near-wheeler was not an arrant kicker; the two elderly ladies were cast into a flutter of agitation; and the guard warned everyone to make haste, as they were about to be off, and the Highflyer didn't wait for no one.

The coachman, having cast an experienced eye over his cattle, and warned an ostler in corduroy breeches and a greasy plush waistcoat not to take off the twitch from the young 'oss's nose until he gave him the word, crammed the way-bill into his pocket, and mounted ponderously on to his very uncomfortable box-seat, and gathered up the reins. He was apparently contemptuous of the passengers, for, having taken his whip in his hand, he commanded the ostlers to let 'em go, without troubling himself to cast more than a casual glance behind. A brief recommendation to the passengers to look out for themselves was all the notice he deigned to bestow upon them; and it was left to the guard to warn them to mind their heads as the coach passed under the archway into the narrow street.

The morning was damp and misty, and the Duke was rather sorry that he had not had the forethought to provide himself with a rug. But the coachman, who, after a side-long scrutiny, had decided that he would be good for half a guinea, assured him genially that the day was going to be a rare fine one by the time they reached Islington Green.

While the coach wended its way through the London streets, the coachman was too much taken up with avoiding collision with market-carts, and occasional droves of cattle that were still coming into town, to have leisure for conversation, but when they began to draw out of the Metropolis, he responded to the incessant fire of nervous questions from the thin man, who was seated just behind the Duke, saying with great good-humour that he had worked a coach for thirty years, and never had an upset. The thin man said severely that if he should attempt to race any other coach encountered upon the road he should report him to his proprietor; and informed the company at large that it was his usual practice to travel upon the Mail, in which excellent service armed guards were provided, and the dragsmen very strictly watched for any infringement of the rules. The coachman favoured the Duke with a wink, and began to tell a number of hair-raising stories about the terrible accidents met with by mail-coachmen, all of whom, he asserted, raced one another with an utter indifference to the safety or comfort of their passengers. And as for the guards provided by the Post Office, why, he could tell the thin man that time was when not a highwayman upon the road as *was* a highwayman would have failed to have had a touch at the mails.

The first advertised stage on the road was Barnet, where those passengers who had not yet breakfasted would be allowed fifteen minutes in which to eat and drink what they could; but when the turnpike at Islington was passed, and the tall elms on the green came into sight, the coachman reined-in. From the number of coaches standing outside the Peacock Inn, or pulling away from it, it seemed that this halt was customary. An ostler shouted out the name of the coach as it drew up; a man came hurrying out of the inn, buttoning up his coat, and clutching a carpet-bag in one hand; and a woman with a shawl drawn over her head entered into negotiations with the guard for the delivery of two ducks at some point further along the road. The thin man said suspiciously that he dared say the man with the carpet-bag was not on the way-bill; but his neighbour, a more tolerant man, retorted that a bit of shouldering hurt nobody. This led the coachman into a bitter dissertation on the ways of informers, who, if he was to be believed, lurked at every point on the road, spying on honest coachmen, and trying to snatch the bread from their mouths. The Duke responded sympathetically, and the business with the beshawled woman being by this time concluded the coach set off again, passing the village pound, where a solitary cow lowed, and a small shop which offered in large lettering to beaver old hats.

The Holloway road was soon reached, and gave the coachman the opportunity of curdling the thin man's blood with a series of reminiscences of all the desperate characters who had ever frequented it.

"Was it not on this stretch that Grimaldi was once robbed?" asked the Duke, who, as a small boy, had been regaled with all these stories.

"Ah, that it was!" nodded the coachman approvingly. "And only ten or so years ago! But ven they took his vatch, d'ye see, it had his phiz drawed on it, a-singing of 'Me and my Neddy', and they gave it to him back again, because he was werry well-liked."

"I saw him once," the Duke said. "At Sadler's Wells, I think it was. I remember he made me laugh very much."

"Vell, and so he would do, sir, seeing as that was his lay, in a manner of speaking. And how far am I to have the pleasure of carrying of you, sir?"

"Only to Baldock," the Duke replied.

The coachman shook his head, and said that it was a pity, as there were few stretches of road this side of Biggleswade where he would care to run the risk of handing over the reins to one, who, he clearly perceived, was fair itching to tool the coach. The thin man, who overheard this, instantly raised such a storm of protest that the Duke felt obliged to set his mind at rest, and assure him that he had no desire to take the reins. The tolerant man, who seemed to have taken a dislike to his neighbour, gave his dispassionate opinion of spoilsports in general, and Friday-faced ones in particular; and a consequential gentleman embarked on a long story about a spirited team of blood-horses which he was in the habit of driving.

When Finchely Common, with all its lurking dangers, had been safely passed, most of the passengers were feeling too sharp-set to think of much beyond the breakfast awaiting them in Barnet; and when the coach drove into the yard of the inn at Barnet, nearly everyone hurried into the coffee-room, where a couple of over-driven waiters were running about with piled trays, and mechanical cries of "Coming directly, sir!"

The Duke had consumed little more than a running banquet at the Saracen's Head, but he did not feel inclined to join in the scramble for coffee and ham, and instead wandered a little way up the street to stretch his legs. On his previous journeys to the north, he had changed horses at the Red Lion, but this noted house did not condescend to stage-coaches, although its landlord resorted to some extremely low stratagems to snatch custom from his hated rival at the Green Man, farther up the street. It was not an unknown thing for his ostlers to rush out into the road to intercept some private carriage whose owner had no notion of changing horses, and to drag it into the yard, and forcibly to provide a fresh pair for it. The Duke had the good fortune to witness a spirited bout of fisticuffs between two of the yellow-jacketed post-boys hired by the Red Lion against three blue-habited ones from the Green Man; and watched with amused appreciation the efforts of an old gentleman in a chaise-and-pair to convince the ostlers of the Red Lion that since he was only travelling as far as to Welwyn, he stood in no need of fresh horses.

When he returned to the coach, and climbed again on to the roof, the Duke found that everyone but the coach-man, who had been regaled in the yard with strong drink and flattery, was in a ruffled frame of mind. Even the tolerant man said that to be asked to pay the full price for breakfast when one had had barely time to swallow two scalding mouthfuls of coffee, and had been unable to eat the ham for want of a knife and fork, was a scandalous state of affairs which ought to be looked to.

The Duke had long since discovered that riding on the roof of the stage-coach did not agree with his constitution. It had held the amusement of novelty for a few miles, but the swaying and lurching, added as they were to a very uncomfortable seat, soon made even the coachman's instructive conversation pall upon him. His head had begun to ache; he had never, he remembered, been a good traveller. Baldock seemed to be a very long way off; and by the time Stevenage was reached, and the coachman attempted to lure him into making a bet as to which of the famous Six Hills were the longest distance apart, he refused to humour him, merely replying wearily: "The first and the last. I learned that when I was still in short-coats."

The coachman was disappointed in him, for this time-honoured catch was generally good for a drink at the next halt. He began to think the box-seat passenger a mean-spirited young man, but revised his opinion when, upon setting him down outside the White Horse at Baldock, he received a guinea from him. He decided then that the Duke was half-flash, and half-foolish, and was sorry to be seeing the last of him.

The guard having unearthed the Duke's valise from the recesses of the boot, his Grace was left standing with it at his feet in the road, waiting for someone to run out and carry it into the inn.

But it appeared that inns patronized by stage-coach travellers were not staffed by servants falling over themselves to wait upon guests, so the Duke was obliged to pick up the valise, and to carry it into the inn himself.

The front door opened into a passage, leading at the back of the premises into a lobby, from which the stairs rose to the upper floor. The coffee-room and the tap-room both gave on to the passage, the former of these being an old-fashioned apartment with only one table, which ran its length.

The Duke set down his valise, and as he did so a door opened at the back of the house, and a stout landlady issued forth. She greeted the Duke civilly, but sharply, saying: "Good-day, sir, and what may I do for you?"

"I should like to hire a room, if you please," said the Duke, with his gentle dignity.

Her eyes ran over him. "Yes, sir. How long would you be staying, if I may ask?"

"I am not perfectly sure. A day or two, perhaps."

Her quick scrutiny having taken in every detail of the quiet elegance which characterized his dress, she directed her gaze to his face. She seemed to like what she saw there, and allowed her features to relax their severity. She said, still briskly, but in a tone that held a hint of motherliness: "I see, sir. A nice front bedchamber you would like, and a private parlour, I daresay. You won't care to be sitting in that noisy coffee-room."

The Duke thanked her, and said that he thought he should be glad of the parlour.

"Come from London on the coach, sir?" said Mrs. Appleby. "Nasty racketing things they be! Shaking all your bones together until you're fair wore-out with holding on to the side to stop yourself falling off. I can see you're tired, sir: you look downright hagged!"

"Oh, no!" Gilly said, blushing faintly. "I have just a touch of the headache, that is all."

"I'll fetch you up a pot of tea directly, sir, for there's nothing like it, and I've a kettle right on the boil at this very moment. Myself, I could never abide the way those coaches sways over the road: it makes a body's stomach rise up against them, and that's the truth. Polly! Ned! Take up the young gentleman's bag to No. 1, Ned; and you, my girl, get some kindling and set a fire going in the Pink Parlour! Bustle about, now! Don't stand there gawping!"

"Thank you, but I shan't need a fire: it is quite warm," said Gilly.

"You'll be more comfortable with a bit of a blaze in the grate, sir," said Mrs. Appleby firmly. "Very treacherous these autumn days are, and you don't look very stout to me, if you will pardon the liberty. But no need to be afraid of damp sheets in *my* house, and if you *should* happen to fancy a hot posset going to bed you have only to pull the bell, and I shall brew it for you, and with pleasure."

The Duke perceived suddenly that he had escaped from Nettlebed only to fall into the clutches of Mrs. Appleby, and gave an involuntary laugh. Mrs. Appleby smiled kindly at him, and said: "Ah, you're feeling better now your stomach's beginning to settle, sir! I'll take you up to your bedchamber. And what name would it be, if you please?"

"Rufford," replied Gilly, choosing one of his titles at random. "Mr. Rufford."

"Very good, sir, and mine is Appleby, if you should want to call me at any time, which I beg you will do if there is anything you would like. This way, if you'll be so good!"

He followed her upstairs to a dimity-hung room overlooking the street. The furniture was all old-fashioned, but everything seemed to be clean, and the bed looked as if it might be comfortable. He laid his hat down, and pressed his hands over his eyes for a moment, before casting off the muffler from round his neck. Mrs. Appleby, observing this unconscious gesture, instantly recommended him to lay himself down upon the bed, and promised to fetch up a hot-brick to put at his feet. The Duke, who knew from bitter experience that the only cure for his shattering headaches was to lie in a darkened room, said that he would go to bed for a little while, but declined the hot-brick. But Mrs. Appleby reminded him so forcibly of his old nurse that he was not really surprised when she re-entered the room shortly afterwards carrying the promised brick wrapped in a piece of flannel. The boots shortly appeared with a tea-tray; and Polly was sent off to fetch up the vinegar, so that the poor young gentleman could bathe his face with it. With three people ministering to him, the Duke could almost have fancied himself back at Sale House, and although a spiked cartwheel seemed to be revolving behind his eyes, he could not help giving another of his soft laughs. Mrs. Appleby stood over him while he drank his tea, telling him that her son, who was in a very good way of business at Luton, had suffered from just such sick headaches when he was a lad, but had grown out of them, as Mr. Rufford would doubtless do also. She then drew the curtains across the window, picked up the tea-tray, and departed, leaving Gilly divided between annoyance at his own weakness and amusement at her evident adoption of him.

CHAPTER IX

ALTHOUGH the Duke's headache had not quite left him by the time a medley of fragrant odours arising from downstairs announced the dinner-hour to be at hand, it was materially better, and he got up from his bed, and unpacked his valise. By the time he had disposed his belongings in the chest of drawers, his attentive hostess was tapping on the door. He assured her that he was much restored, and she escorted him to a small parlour, where a fire burned, and the table was already spread with a cloth, and laid with some bone-handled knives and forks.

The Duke dined off some small collars, a serpent of mutton, and a boiled duck with onion sauce, and afterwards tried the experiment of lighting one of the cigars he had brought with him. The waiter, who had been about to bring him a spill, watched with deep interest the kindling of a match with Promethean fire from the machine which the Duke carried in his pocket, and ventured to say that he had heard tell of those things, but had never before seen one.

The Duke smiled in his absent way, and asked: "Is there an inn in Baldock called the Bird in Hand?"

"It's wunnerful what they think of," said the waiter. "They do tell me they even has gas-lamps in Lunnon nowadays. Bird in Hand, sir? Not in Baldock, there isn't. Leastways, I never heard tell on it, and it stands to reason I would have if there were sich a place."

"Perhaps it may be a little way from the town," suggested Gilly.

"Ah, very likely," the waiter agreed, beginning to pile up

the dishes on a tray. "There's no saying but what it mightn't be so."

"And perhaps," further suggested Gilly patiently, "there may be someone in the tap-room who may know of it—if you were to ask them."

The waiter said that he would do this, and went away with his tray. He was gone for some time, and when he came back, although he had collected a quantity of information about a Bird in the Bush, a Partridge, and a Feathers Inn, he had not discovered anyone who knew the Bird in Hand. Gilly rewarded him suitably for his efforts, and said that it did not signify. He did not feel equal to pursuing his enquiries further that evening, so when the waiter had withdrawn he stretched his legs out before the fire, and opened the book his cousin Gideon had given him to read upon his travels. The preface somewhat quellingly advertised the work to exhibit "the amiableness of domestic affection, and the excellence of universal virtue," but Gideon had warned him not to allow himself to be daunted by this unpromising start. The book was anonymously published, and had, of course, been cut up by the *Quarterly*. It was entitled *Frankenstein, or the Modern Prometheus*. The Duke blew a cloud of smoke, crossed one foot over the other, and began to read.

The candles were guttering in their sockets, and the fire was burning very low when the Duke at last tore himself from the tale, and went to bed.

He saw, on consulting his watch, that it was past midnight, and when he opened the door of the parlour he found the inn in darkness. Guarding the flame of his bedroom candle with one hand, he trod along the passage, not precisely expecting to meet a man-made monster (for he was no longer a child, he told himself) but with a shudder in his flesh. He must find some indescribably horrible tale to bestow on Gideon, in revenge for his having given his poor little cousin a book calculated to keep him awake all night, he decided, smiling to himself.

But with every expectation of having his rest disturbed by nightmares, he slept soundly and dreamlessly all night, awaking in the morning to hear cocks crowing, and to find sunlight stealing between the closed blinds of his room. All trace of his headache had left him; he felt remarkably well, and thought there must be something salubrious about the air of Hertfordshire.

He had told the boots he would have his shaving-water brought to him at eight o'clock, but when this worthy came into his room to waken him, he found him standing by the window in his great coat, interestedly watching a herd of bullocks being driven down the street. It seemed to be market-day, and the Duke had never come into close contact with a market before, and consequently found it most entertaining. He turned his head when the boots entered, saying: "Is it market-day? What quantities of pigs and cows and chickens have come into the town! You must have a very large market here!"

"Oh, no, sir!" said the boots pityingly, setting down the jug of water on the corner-washstand. "*This* ain't nothing! Missus said to ask if there was anything as you would be wanting."

"Thank you—if you would be good enough to have my coat brushed!" the Duke said, picking it up, and handing it to him.

The boots bore it off carefully. It seemed a very grand coat to him, made of superfine cloth, and lined with silk. He told the waiter, whom he happened to meet on his way to the boot-room, that he suspicioned No. 1 was a high-up gentleman, one as had come into the world hosed and shod, for he had thrown his good shirt that hadn't a spot on it on to the floor, and a necktie with it, like as if he meant to put on a fresh one. "Which is a thing, Fred, as none but the nobs does. And what queers me is what brings him to this house!"

"Perhaps the Runners is after him," said the waiter. "He's killed his man in a bloody duel, that's very likely what he's done, and he's a-hiding of hisself."

"Gammon!" said the boots scornfully. "He no more killed no one in no duel than a babe unborn!"

"Maybe there's a fastener going to be served on him," said the waiter doubtfully. "Though he do seem to be a well-breeched cove as isn't likely to have got into debt."

"No, he ain't!" retorted the boots. "He come here on the stage, and he wouldn't have done that if he hadn't run aground. Swallowed a spider, that's what he's done. Missus ought to make him show his blunt, but she's taken one of her fancies to him, and likely he'll chouse her out of his reckoning."

"He don't look like a downy one to me," objected the waiter. "And if he'd swallowed a spider he wouldn't have handed me a fore-coachwheel only for asking of silly questions for him, which he did do."

"What's a half-crown to the likes of him?" said the boots disdainfully, but he was impressed by this proof of open-handedness in the Duke, and made up his mind to give his top-boots an extra polish before carrying them upstairs.

When he had partaken of breakfast, the Duke picked up his hat, and sallied forth to find the post-receiving office, where he enquired the direction of one Mr. Liversedge. The clerk said that he did not seem to know the name, and he rather thought he had handed a letter or two to a gentleman calling himself that, or something like it; but he declined to admit any knowledge of the Bird in Hand. No deliveries were made by the Post Office to any such hostelry, and if it existed at all, which he seemed loftily to doubt, it was possibly a common alehouse outside the town, such as would not be frequented by literate persons.

The Duke then bethought him of the market, and made his way there. It was the scene of considerable bustle and business, and in the excitement of watching a young bull, which seemed to have escaped from its tether, being rounded up; six pigs knocked down to a farmer in a red waistcoat; and a large gander putting to rout two small boys and a mongrel cur, he rather forgot the object in view. But when he had been strolling about the market-place for some time, he remembered it, and he asked a man who was meditating profoundly over some fine cabbages whether he knew where the Bird in Hand was to be found. The man withdrew his mind from the cabbages reluctantly, and after considering the Duke for a time, said simply: "You'll be meaning the Bird and Bush."

The Duke received very much the same answer from the next five people whom he qustioned, but the sixth, a jolly-looking farmer with a striped waistcoat and leggings, said: "Why, sir, whatever would the likes of you be wanting with sich a place as that?"

"Do you know it?" asked the Duke, who had begun to think that Mr. Liversedge had been mistaken in his own direction.

"Not to say *know* it," responded the farmer. "It ain't the sort of place *I'd* go to, and what's more, unless I'm much mistook, it ain't the sort of place *you'd* go to either. For it ain't got a good name, sir, and if you'll take my advice, asking your pardon if not wished for, you won't go next or nigh it."

The Duke looked such an innocent enquiry that the farmer became fatherly in his manner, and recommended him to keep out of bad company. He said that if he were to call the Bird in Hand a regular thieves' ken he wouldn't be telling any lies, and added if it was plucking the Duke was after there were those whom he would very likely meet at the Bird in Hand who would leave him without a feather to fly with. He had to be coaxed to divulge the locality of the inn, and finally did so with a heavy sigh, and a warning that he would not be held responsible for whatever ill might come of it. "It's betwixt and between Norton and Arlesey," he said, "a matter of three or four miles from here, more, if you was to go by the pike road till you come to the road as leads to Shefford, and turn down it. But if you're set on going there's a lane which'll take you right past it, and it goes by way of Norton, off the Hitchin road."

Armed with this information, the Duke returned to the White Horse and sought out Mrs. Appleby, and asked her if she knew where he could hire a gig, or a riding-horse. It then transpired that if only he had told her earlier that he would be wanting a gig he could have had hers, and with pleasure, and old Mrs. Fawley, to whom she had lent it, might have gone to visit her daughter any other day, and not a mite of difference which. However, when she heard that the Duke only wished to drive quite a short distance, her brow cleared, and she said that if it should not be too late for him the gig was bound to be back in the stables by four o'clock, and could very well be taken out again. The Duke thanked her, and accepted this offer. She then firmly sat him down to a luncheon of cold meat, which he did not in the least want, and did her best to persuade him to let the waiter fetch up some porter, a very strengthening drink which would set him up rarely. But the Duke hated porter, and was resolute in declining.

Owing to old Mrs. Fawley's inability to keep punctual hours, it was nearly five o'clock before the gig was returned to its owner; but the Duke thought that he would have time to reach the Bird in Hand, and to return again before darkness fell, and he decided not to postpone his visit to Mr. Liversedge. He naturally did not inform Mrs. Appleby of his destination, being reasonably sure, from what he had learned from his market-acquaintance, that she would do what lay in her power to restrain him from venturing to such a haunt of vice. It did not seem likely, in view of Mr. Liversedge's declared requirements, that he stood in much danger of being robbed of the money in his pockets, or in any way molested, but he took the precaution of leaving the greater part of his money locked up in his chest of drawers; and he loaded one of his new duelling-pistols, and slipped it into his pocket. Thus armed, and having acquainted himself more particularly with the way to Arlesey, he mounted on to the gig, and set off at the sedate trot favoured by the stout cob between the shafts.

It was not long before he came to the lane leading from the Hitchin pike-road. He turned into this, but was soon obliged to allow the cob to slacken his pace to a walk, since the lane, once past the village of Norton, dwindled rapidly into something little better than a cart-track, and was pitted with deep holes. It was also excessively muddy; and he was forced continually to dodge unlopped branches of the nut-trees which bordered it. He met no other vehicles, which was just as well, since the track was too narrow to allow of two vehicles being abreast, and the only human being he saw was a well-grown schoolboy at the hobbledehoy stage, who came into view as he rounded the fifth bend, and splashed through a more than usually large pond of stagnant water.

He did not pay much heed to the boy at first, but as he drew towards him he noticed that he seemed to be in trouble, stumbling along in an uncertain way, as though he were ill, or the worse for drink. Then, as he came almost abreast of him, he saw that the lad, who was dressed in good but shockingly mired clothes, and seemed to have lost his hat, was extremely pale, and had a black eye. He drew up, his quick compassion stirred, and as he did so the boy's uncertain feet tripped in a rut, and he fell headlong.

The Duke jumped down from the gig, and bent over him, saying in his soft voice: "I am afraid you are not very well: can I help you?"

The boy looked up, blinking at him in a bemused fashion, and the Duke perceived that in spite of his lusty limbs he was little more than a child. "I don't know," he said thickly. "They took all my money. I fought them, but there were two, and—and I think they hit me on the head. Oh, I feel so sick!"

In proof of this statement, he suddenly retched, and was very sick. The Duke supported him while the paroxysm lasted, and then wiped his face with his handkerchief. "Poor boy!" he said. "There, you will be better now! Where do you live? I will take you to your home."

The boy, who was leaning limply against his shoulder, stiffened a little at this, and said in a gruff way: "I'm not going home. Besides, it isn't here. I shall do very well. Don't trouble—pray!"

"But where is your home?" Gilly asked.

"I won't say."

This was uttered in rather a belligerent tone, which caused Gilly to ask: "Have you run away, perhaps?"

The boy was silent, and made an effort to scramble to his feet, thrusting the Duke away.

"I beg your pardon!" Gilly said, smiling. "I should know better than to ask you such awkward questions, for people

93

have been doing the same to me all my life. We will not talk about your home, and you shan't tell me more than you care to. But would you not like to get up into my gig, and let me drive you wherever it is you are making for?"

There was another silence, while the boy made an ineffectual attempt to brush the mud from his pantaloons. His round, freckled face was still very pale, and his mouth had a sullen pout. He cast a suspicious, sidelong look at the Duke, and sniffed, and rubbed his nose. "They took all my money," he repeated. "I don't know what to do, but I won't go home!" He ended on a gulping sob that betrayed his youth, flushed hotly, and glared at the Duke.

Gilly was far too tactful to notice that unmanly sob. He said cheerfully: "Well, to be sure, it is very hard to decide on what is best to be done without having time to reflect. Have you friends in the neighbourhood to whom I could take you?"

"No," muttered the boy. He added grudgingly: "Sir."

"Then I think I had better drive you to the inn where I am putting up, and see what can be done for that black eye of yours. What is your name?"

The boy gave another sniff. "Tom," he divulged reluctantly. "I want to go to London. And I would have gone, too, only that I asked those men the way to Baldock, and they said they would put me on the road, and then—and then——" He ground his teeth audibly, and said in a kind of growl: "I suppose I was a regular green one, but how was I to tell——?"

"No, indeed, it is the kind of thing that might happen to anyone," the Duke agreed, propelling him gently towards the gig. "Up you get!"

"And I landed *one* of them a couple of wisty castors!" Tom told him, allowing himself to be helped into the gig. "Only they had cudgels, and that is how it came about. And they took my five pounds, and my watch, which Pa gave me, and when I came to myself they were gone. I don't care for having my canister milled, but it is too bad to have taken all my money, and if I could catch them Pa would have them transported!"

The Duke, having put him safely into his seat, went to the cob's head, and began to turn the gig in the narrow space available for the manoeuvre. He was not at all inclined to take his youthful protégé to an inn of such apparent ill-fame as the Bird in Hand, even though it seemed highly probable that Tom might there realize his wish of catching his assailants; and he decided that his business with Mr. Liversedge would have to be postponed until the next day. Having turned the gig, he mounted on to the box seat, gathered up the reins, and gave the cob the office to trot homewards. Tom sat slumped on the seat beside him, sunk in depression, sniffing at inervals, and wiping his nose with a grubby handkerchief. After an interval, he said with would-be civility: "I don't know why you should put yourself to this trouble, sir. I am sure you need not. I daresay I shall do very well when my head stops aching."

"Oh, you will be as right as a trivet!" Gilly said. "Had you a bag with you, and did the thieves steal that as well?"

Tom fidgeted rather uncomfortably. "No. That is—Well, the thing is I couldn't bring my portmanteau, sir, because—— Well, I couldn't bring it! But then, you know, I had my money, and I thought I could buy anything I might need."

The Duke, feeling that he had much in common with his young friend, nodded understandingly, and said that it did not signify. "I expect one of my nightshirts will not fit you so very ill. How old are you?"

"Fifteen," replied Tom, a hint of challenge in his voice.

"You are very big! I had thought you older."

"Well, I do think anyone might suppose me to be seventeen at least, don't you?" Tom said, responding to that gratifying remark, and speaking in a far less belligerent tone. "And I am very well able to take care of myself—in general. But if sneaks set upon one two to one there is no doing anything! And I shall never have such a chance again, because they will watch me so close—— Oh, it is too bad, sir! I wish I was dead! They would have been sorry then! At least, Pa would, but I daresay Mr. Snape wouldn't have cared a button, for he's the greatest beast in nature, and I hate him!"

"Your schoolmaster?" hazarded the Duke.

"Yes. At least, he is my tutor, because Pa wouldn't have me go to school, which I had leifer have done, I can tell you! And when it came to his reading to me in the chaise, not even something jolly, like *Waverley*, or the *Adventures of Johnny Newcome*, which is a famous book, only of course he took it away from me—he *would!*—but the horridest stuff about Europe in the Middle Ages! As though anyone could listen to such dry fustian! And *in the chaise*, sir! There was no bearing it any longer!"

"It was certainly very bad," agreed the Duke sympathetically. "But they will all do it! I remember my own tutor once tried to interest me in Paley's *Natural Theology* upon one of our journeys from Bath to S—— to my home!" he corrected himself swiftly.

"That sounds as though it would be just as dry!" said Tom, impressed.

"Oh, worse!"

"What did you do, sir?"

The Duke smiled. "I was very poor-spirited: I tried to listen."

"Well, I hit Mr. Snape on the head, and ran away!" said Tom, with a return to his challenging manner.

The Duke broke into his low laugh. "Oh, no, did you? But how did you contrive to do that when you were driving along in a chaise?"

"I couldn't, of course, but the thing is we changed horses at Shefford, and then when we had not gone a mile out of the town the perch broke, and we were obliged to stop. And the postilion was to ride back to Shefford to procure another chaise for us, and when he was gone old Snape said we would take a walk in the wood, and *that* would not have been so bad, but what must he do but pull his stupid book out of his pocket again, just when I had seen a squirrel's drey—at least, I am pretty sure it was one, and I would have found out if he had but let me alone! But he is such a prosing, boring beast he don't care for anything worth a fig, and he said we would read another chapter, and so I floored him. I have a very handy bunch of fives, you know," he said, exhibiting his large fist to the Duke, "and I dropped him with a flush hit just behind his ear. And if you are thinking, sir," he added bitterly, "that it wasn't a handsome thing to do, to hit him from behind, I can tell you that I owe him something, for he is a famous flogger, and is for ever laying into me. Did your tutor too?"

"No, very seldom," replied the Duke. "But he was a great bore! I fear I could never have floored him, for I was not a big fellow, like you, but I own I never thought of doing so. Did you knock him out?"

"Oh, yes!" said Tom cheerfully. "I don't think he is dead, though. I could not wait to see, of course, but I should not think he could be. And in a way it will be as well if he is not, because they would hang me for it, wouldn't they?"

"Oh, I don't suppose it is as bad as that!" Gilly consoled him. "Did you then make your way from Shefford?"

"Yes, and the best of it is he will not know which way I went, and I kept to the woods, and the fields, so all the chaises in the world won't help him. I thought I would get on the coach for London, and see all the sights there, which he would not let me do, horrid old addle-plot! Only fancy, sir! We drove up from Worthing, and we spent just one night in London, and the only thing he would let me see was St. Paul's Cathedral! As though I cared for that! Not even the wild beasts at the Exeter Exchange! Of course I knew he would never take me to a theatre, and it was no use trying to give him the bag *then*, for someone would have been bound to have seen me. But when the perch broke, and such a chance offered, I do think I should have been a regular clodpole not to have seized it! And now—now I haven't a meg, and it is all for nothing! But one thing is sure!—I won't go tamely home! If I can't get to London, but very likely I shall think of a way to do so, I shall make for the coast, and sign on a barque as ship's boy. If there had been any pirates left I should have done that rather even than have gone to London. Though I *would* like to see the sights, and kick up some larks," he added wistfully.

"Don't despair!" said Gilly, much entertained by this ingenuous history. "Perhaps we can contrive that you shall go there."

An eager face was turned towards him. "Oh, sir, do you think I might indeed? But how?"

"Well, we will think about that presently," promised the Duke, emerging from the lane on to the Hitchin road. "First, however, we must lay a piece of steak to that eye of yours."

"Sir, you are a regular Trojan!" Tom said, in a rush of gratitude. "I beg your pardon for not being civil to you at first! I thought you was bound to be like all the rest, jawing and moralizing, but I see you are a bang-up person, and I do not at all mind telling you what my name is! It's Mamble, Thomas Mamble. Pa is an ironmaster, and we live just outside Kettering. Where do you live, sir?"

"Sometimes in the country, sometimes in London."

"I wish we did so!" Tom said enviously. "I have never been south of Kettering until they sent me to Worthing. I had the measles, you know, and the doctor said I should go there. I wish it had been Brighton! That would have been something like! Only not with old Snape. You can have no notion what it is like, sir, being Pa's only son! They will not leave me alone for a minute, nor let me do the least thing I like, and everything is wretched beyond bearing!"

"But I know exactly what it is like," Gilly said. "If I did not, I suppose I should have been just like all the rest, and should have handed you back to your tutor."

"You will not!" Tom cried, in swift alarm.

Gilly smiled at him. "No, not quite immediately! But I think you must go back to your father in the end, you know. I daresay he is very much attached to you, and you will not like to cause him too much anxiety."

"N-no," agreed Tom rather grudgingly. "Of course I shall have to return, but I won't do so until I have been to London! That would be worth anything! He will be in one of his grand fusses, I suppose, and I shall catch it when I do go back, but——"

"You might not," the Duke said.

"You do not know Pa, sir!" replied Tom feelingly. "Or Snape!"

"Very true, but it is possible that if he knows you have been my guest, and if I meet your papa, and talk to him, he may not, after all, be so very angry with you."

Tom surveyed him doubtfully. "Well, I think he will be," he said. "I don't care, mind you, for I can stand a lick or two, but Pa is the biggest ironmaster in all our set, and as rich as—as Crassus, and he has the deuce of a temper! And he is for ever wanting to bring me up a gentleman, and he won't have me do anything vulgar and jolly, or know the out-and-out fellows in Kettering, and he is bound to be in a rage over this!"

"Well, that would be very terrible," said the Duke, in his tranquil way. "Perhaps you had best return to Mr. Snape after all."

"No, that I *won't* do!" declared Tom, with great resolution.

It was not long after this that they reached Baldock, and drove into the yard of the White Horse. Tom, although much revived in spirit, was physically a good deal shaken still, and was glad of the support of the Duke's arm into the inn. The waiter, whom they encountered in the lobby at the back of the house, stared at them in gloomy surprise, but the Duke paid no attention to his, merely saying: "Desire Mrs. Appleby to step up to my room, please," and leading Tom to the staircase.

When Mrs. Appleby came sailing into the Pink Parlour a few minutes later, she was not only very curious, but more than half inclined to take exception to Tom's arrival. The waiter had described his appearance in unflattering terms, and although she had been prompt to snub him, she had been equally prompt to come up and inspect Tom for herself.

She found him sitting in the armchair by the fire, while the Duke bathed his bruised head and face. He certainly looked a disreputable object, and Mrs. Appleby exclaimed in a displeased voice: "Well! And may I ask, sir, what is this?"

The Duke was quite unused to being spoken to in that tone, and he turned his head to look at her in some surprise. Without knowing why she did so, she dropped a slight curtsy, and said very much more mildly: "I understood as you wanted to speak to me, sir."

"Yes," the Duke replied. "I want a bedchamber to be prepared for my young friend, if you please. He has had the misfortune to be robbed by a couple of footpads. Sit still, Tom, and hold that wet pad to your eye: Mrs. Appleby will bring you some raw beef to put upon it directly."

"I didn't know you was going to bring any young gentleman back with you, sir, I'm sure."

"No, indeed, how should you?" said the Duke. "I did not know it myself. Have you some objection?"

"Oh, of course, sir, if he is a friend of yours——! Only it seems a queer thing, with you not mentioning it, and him with no baggage, and all!"

"It is a sad fix for him to be in," agreed the Duke. He smiled at her. "We must do what we can to make him more comfortable."

"Yes, sir," said Mrs. Applesby helplessly. "I'm sure I would not wish to be unfeeling, but I never heard of a young gentleman trapesing about the country, and no carriage, nor nothing, and seemingly quite by himself!"

"No, it was certainly unwise, but he will know better another time. I expect he would be glad of that hot-brick you brought up for me."

At this, Tom uttered a growling protest, which had the effect of drawing Mrs. Appleby's attention to him. She now perceived that he was younger than she had at first supposed, and looking extremely wan and battered. Her face softened; she said: "I will see to it, sir. Oh, dearie me, and the way his good clothes are spoilt! I do hope he has not run away from school!"

"No, I have not!" Tom said.

She shook her head, but said: "Do you take him to No. 6, sir: you will find the bed is ready made up. And if he will take off his jacket and his nether-garments I will see what can be done to furbish them up."

She bustled away, and Tom, asserting that he was quite well, and did not wish to go to bed, allowed himself to be led down the passage to a small room at the back of the house. When upon his feet he was obliged to confess that he still felt as sick as a horse. The Duke said that he would feel very much better when he had swallowed a glass of hartshorn and water, and rested for a little while, and helped him to strip off his mired clothing. Tom then lay down upon the bed in his underlinen, and the Duke covered him with the patchwork quilt.

"I did not think it would be bellows to mend with me so easily!" Tom murmured discontentedly. "But he hit me with a cudgel, after all! I am as dead as a herring! I only hope old Snape is feeling half as bad!"

He closed his eyes on this pious aspiration; and the Duke, wondering a little ruefully into what difficulties his sympathy with a fellow-sufferer might lead him, went away to ask Mrs. Appleby for some hartshorn.

CHAPTER X

THE Duke did not borrow Mrs. Appleby's gig again until the following afternoon, for the morning was fully taken up with purchasing such articles of apparel and toilet as he considered necessary for his protégé's comfort and respectability. His notions did not always jump with Tom's, since he laid what that young gentleman considered to be undue stress on the indispensability of soap and tooth-powder, and other such frivolous luxuries. Nor did Tom perceive the necessity of carrying with him on his travels more than one shirt. But the Duke was firm on these points, and after dealing patiently with a sudden and alarming fit of independence in young Mr. Mamble, in which he was informed that Pa would not like his son and heir to be beholden to anyone, he led him forth on a tour of the Baldock shops, assuring him that he would keep faithful tally of his expenditure, and present Pa with his bill in due course.

Mr. Mamble, whose resilient constitution Gilly could not but envy, had very soon recovered from his malaise, and had got up from his bed on the previous evening in time to work his way steadily through two glazed veal olives, a collop of beef, part of a leg of pork, two helpings of ratafie pudding, and a jelly. He told Gilly, after this repast, that he was now in bang-up form; and after selecting two apples from a dish on the side-table, which he set aside to be consumed when pangs of hunger should attack him later in the evening, he settled down before the fire, and poured forth a jumbled history of his life and its trials to his sympathetic host.

From this recital Gilly gathered that his mother had died when he was still in short-coats, and that his remaining parent, who seemed to have prospered exceedingly in his business, had set his heart and his considerable energy on to the task of turning his heir into an out-and-out gentleman. To this end he had engaged Mr. Snape, whose unenviable duty it was to instruct Tom in every branch of a

100

gentleman's education, to keep him out of mischief and low company, and to guard him from the chances of chills or infection. Mr. Snape appeared to be a joyless individual, whom the Duke found no difficulty at all in disliking. He very soon perceived that Tom's lot was worse than his own had been, for whereas Lord Lionel was naturally untroubled by considerations of gentility, and had been quite as determined that his nephew should learn to clean his own guns, saddle and bridle his horses (and even shoe them), carve joints, and protect himself with his fists, as that he should acquire a proper knowledge of the Humanities, Mr. Mamble was morbidly anxious that Tom should engage on no occupation which might lead supercilious persons to suppose that he was not born into the *haut ton*. Consequently, poor Tom, himself unaffected by social ambitions, had been fenced in on all sides, his natural bents frowned upon, and his overflowing spirits curbed. The Duke, listening to him, felt real pity stir his heart, and thought that if he could lighten the lot of this oddly likeable boy he would have performed the first meritorious action of his life. Whatever the outcome of his interview with Mr. Liversedge, he would, he supposed, be journeying back to London within two days. If the zealous Mr. Snape had not by that time tracked his pupil down, he would take him to London, and from Sale House write a letter to Mr. Mamble, informing him that, having picked Tom up on the road, he had carried him to town, and would render him up to his parent whenever that busy gentleman could spare the time to visit the Metropolis. The Duke knew the world well enough to be sure that the knowledge that his son had fallen into noble company would suffice to allay Mr. Mamble's wrath; and he had little doubt that if he chose to put himself to the trouble of doing it he could persuade Mr. Mamble to dismiss Mr. Snape, and send his son to school. If, on the other hand, Mr. Snape arrived in Baldock before he had left for London, the Duke, who had never made the least push to deal with his own tutor, anticipated no difficulty in dealing with Tom's. As for the desirability of setting an anxious parent's mind at rest without loss of time, he dismissed this without compunction. It would ill become him, he thought, to waste any consideration on Tom's father when he had none for his own far more estimable uncle. If Lord Lionel stood in need of a lesson, so, in greater measure, did Mr. Mamble, and he should have it. Meanwhile, he would keep Tom safely out of harm's way—and heaven alone knew what harm Tom would plunge into if allowed to wander about the countryside alone!—and gratify his longing to see all the sights of London.

Tom, whose mind knew no half-shades, had swiftly passed from suspicion of his benefactor to wholehearted admiration for him. His scruples having been relieved by the Duke's promise to render a strict account of any financial transaction incurred on his behalf to his father, he accepted a guinea to spend with alacrity, and assured the Duke of his ability to amuse himself while he was absent on his own affairs.

Accordingly, the Duke set out once more on his quest of the Bird in Hand, choosing this time to go by the pike-road as far as to the cross-road leading to Shefford. He was obliged to traverse some distance down a rough lane, but a little way beyond the village of Arlesey the Bird in Hand came into sight, a solitary alehouse standing amongst some tumbledown outhouses and barns, and displaying a weather-beaten and much obliterated sign on two rusty chains which creaked when the wind swayed them. The house was a small one, and might from its situation have been supposed to have catered merely for farm-labourers. It had a neglected appearance, but an impression that it was slightly sinister the Duke attributed to his imagination. He drew up, and alighted from the gig, tethering the cob to a post. At this hour of the day there were no signs of life about the inn, and when he reached the door, and entered the tap-room into which it led, he found no one there. The room was small, and foetid, with the fumes of stale smoke from countless clay pipes, and the droppings of gin and ale. The Duke's nostrils curled fastidiously, and he walked over to an inner door, and pushed it open, calling: "House! house!"

After a prolonged pause, a spare individual in a plush waistcoat shining with grease shuffled out from the nether regions of the hostelry, and stood staring at the Duke with his mouth open and his watery eyes popping out of their sockets. Several teeth were missing from his jaw, and a broken nose added nothing to the comeliness of his face. The sight of a well-dressed stranger within the precincts of the inn appeared to bereave him of all power of speech.

"Good-afternoon!" said the Duke pleasantly. "Have you a Mr. Liversedge staying at this inn?"

The man in the plush waist coat blinked at him, and said enigmatically: "Ah!"

The Duke drew out his pocket-book, and produced from it his cousin's card. "Be so good as to take that up to him!" he said.

The man in the plush waistcoat wiped his hand mechanically on his breeches, and took the card, and stood holding it doubtfully, and still staring at the Duke. The sight of the pocket-book had made his eyes glisten a little, and the Duke could only be glad that he had had the forethought to leave the bulk of his money at the White Horse. The presence of the pistol in his pocket was also a comfort.

He was just about to request his bemused new acquaintance to bestir himself, when a door apparently leading out to the stableyard opened, and a burly man with grizzled hair and a square, ill-shaven countenance appeared upon the scene. He cast the Duke a swift, suspicious look out of his narrowed eyes, and asked in a wary tone what his business might be. The man in the plush waistcoat mutely held out Mr. Ware's elegantly engraved visiting-card.

"I have business with Mr. Liversedge," said the Duke.

This piece of information seemed to afford the newcomer no gratification, for he shot another and still more suspicious look at Gilly, and removed the card from his henchman's hand. It took him a little time to spell out the legend it bore, but he did it at last, and it seemed to the Duke that although his suspicion did not abate, it became tinged with uneasiness. He fixed his eyes, which held no very pleasant expression, on the Duke, and palpably weighed him up. Apparently he saw nothing in the slight, boyish figure before him to occasion more than contempt, for his uneasy look vanished, and he gave a hoarse chuckle, and said: "Ho! it is, is it? Well, I dunno, but I'll see."

He then mounted a creaking stair, and the Duke was left to endure the gaze of the man in the plush waistcoat.

After a prolonged interval, the landlord reappeared. The Duke had caught the echoes of his voice raised in argument in some room above; and it seemed to him when he came downstairs that his uneasiness had returned. The Duke should have been able to sympathize with him: he was feeling a little uneasy himself.

"You'll please to come up, sir," said the landlord, with the air of one repeating a hard-learned lesson.

The Duke, who had slid one hand unobtrusively into the pocket of his drab Benjamin, and closed it round the reassuring butt of Mr. Joseph Manton's pistol, drew a breath, and trod up the stairs.

He was led down a passage to a room at the back of the house. The landlord thrust the door wide, and announced him in simple terms: "Here he is, Sa—sir!" he said.

The Duke found himself upon the threshold of a square and not uncomfortable apartment which had been fitted up as a parlour. It was very much cleaner than the rest of the house, and it was plain that efforts had been made to achieve a semblance of elegance. The curtains, though faded, had lately been washed; the table in the centre of the room was covered with a red cloth; and one or two portable objects seemed to indicate that the guest at present inhabiting the room had brought with him various articles of furniture of his own.

Standing before a small fire was a middle-aged gentleman of somewhat portly habit of body, and a bland, pallid countenance surmounted by a fine crop of iron-grey hair, swept up into a fashionable Brutus. He was dressed with great propriety in a dark cloth coat and light pantaloons; the points of his shirt-collar brushed his whiskers; his cravat was arranged with nicety; and it was only upon closer examination that the Duke perceived that his elegant coat was sadly shiny, and his shirt by no means innocent of darns. There was a strong resemblance between him and the landlord, but his countenance had an air of unshakable good-humour, which the landlord's lacked, and nothing could have exceeded the gentility with which he came forward, holding out a plump hand, and saying: "Ah, Mr. Ware! I am very happy to receive this visit from you!"

The Duke had by this time visualized the possibility of his corpse being cast into the evil-smelling pond beside the inn, but he could see no obligation on him to take Mr. Liversedge's hand, he merely bowed. Mr. Liversedge, whose eyes had been running over him shrewdly, smiled more widely than ever, and drew out a chair from the table, and said: "Let us be seated, sir! Alas, you have come upon a very painful errand! I assure you I feel for you, sir, for I have been young myself, but my duty is to my unfortunate niece. Ah, Mr. Ware, you little know the pain and grief—I may say the chagrin—you have inflicted on one whose tender heart was been so undeservedly smitten!" Overcome by the picture his own words had conjured up, he disappeared for a moment or two into a large handkerchief.

The Duke sat down, and laid his hat on the table. He said in his diffident way: "Indeed, I am sorry for that, Mr. Liversedge. I should not wish to cause any female pain or grief."

Mr. Liversedge raised his bowed head. "There," he said, much moved, "speaks a member of the Quality! I knew it, Mr. Ware! True Blue! When my niece has wept upon this bosom, declaring herself forsaken and betrayed, My love, I have said, depend upon it a scion of that noble house will not fail to do you right! I thank God, Mr. Ware, that my faith in humanity is not to be rudely shaken!"

"I hope not, indeed," said the Duke. "But, you know, I had no notion that your niece's affections were so deeply engaged."

"Sir," said Mr. Liversedge, "you are young! you do not yet know the depths of woman's heart!"

"No," agreed the Duke. "But will money allay the—the pangs of grief and chagrin?"

"Yes," said Mr. Liversedge simply.

The Duke could not help smiling at this. He said in a meek tone: "Forgive me, Mr. Liversedge, but is not a—a transaction of this nature repugnant to a man of your sensibility?"

"Mr. Ware," said Mr. Liversedge, "I shall not conceal from you that it is deeply repugnant. I am, as you have divined, a man of sensibility, and it is with profound reluctance that I have compelled myself to take up the cudgels on behalf of my orphaned niece."

"At her instigation?" murmured the Duke.

Mr. Liversedge surveyed him, a calculating look in his eye. "My niece," he said, "has been put to great expense on account of expectations raised, Mr. Ware. I need not enumerate. But bride-clothes, you know, sir, and——"

"Five thousand pounds?" said Gilly, in bewildered accents.

They looked at one another. "I am persuaded," said Mr. Liversedge reproachfully, "that you would not wish to do anything unhandsome, sir. Considering the elevated nature of my niece's expectations, five thousand pounds cannot be considered an extortionate figure."

"But I am quite unable to pay such a sum," said Gilly.

Mr. Liversedge spread out his hands. "It is very disagreeable for me to be obliged to remind you, sir, that you are nearly related to one, who, I am persuaded, would not regard such a trifling sum any more than you or I would regard a crown piece."

"Sale?" said the Duke. "Oh, he would never pay it!"

Mr. Liversedge said in a shocked voice: "I cannot be brought to believe, sir, that his Grace would grudge it!"

The Duke shook his head sadly. "I do not stand next to him in the succession, you know. I have two uncles, and a cousin before me. And my father, Mr. Liversedge, is not a rich man."

"I cannot credit that his Grace would permit his name to be dragged through the mire of the Courts!" said Mr. Liversedge, with resolution.

"And I am sure," said the Duke gently, "that you would shrink from dragging your niece's name through that mire."

"Shrink, yes," acknowledged Mr. Liversedge. "But I shall steel myself, Mr. Ware. That is, I should do so if his Grace were to prove adamant. But what a shocking thing if the head of such a noble house should have so little regard for his name!"

"I wonder what course you had the intention of pursuing if I had fled to Gretna Green with your niece?" said the Duke thoughtfully. "For I cannot suppose that an alliance for her with anyone so lacking in fortune and expectation as myself was what you had in mind!"

"Certainly not," replied Mr. Liversedge, without a blush. "But she is a minor, after all! little more than a child! The marriage might have been set aside—at a price."

The Duke laughed. "Come, we begin to understand one another better! You may as well own, sir, that your object is to squeeze money from my noble relative, no matter on what pretext."

"Between these four walls, Mr. Ware," said Liversedge cheerfully. "Between these four walls!"

"How much it must disgust a man of your sensibility to be reduced to such straits!" observed the Duke.

Liversedge sighed. "It does, sir. In fact, it is quite out of my line."

"What is your line?" enquired the Duke curiously.

Mr. Liversedge waved an airy hand. "Cards, sir, cards! I flatter myself I had established myself with every prospect of success. But Fate singled me out to be the object of vile persecution, Mr. Ware. I am—temporarily, of course—without the means to re-establish myself suitably, and you see me forced to eke out a miserable existence in surroundings which, I am persuaded, you will easily descry to be totally unfitting for any man of gentility. You, Mr. Ware, who are putting up, I make no doubt, in the comfort of the George—an excellent hostelry!—can have little notion——"

"No, no, above my touch!" murmured the Duke demurely. "The White Horse!"

"The White Horse," said Mr. Liversedge feelingly, "may not aspire to the elegance of the George, but compared with this hovel in which I am compelled to sojourn, Mr. Ware, it is a palace!"

The Duke did not deny it, and after a slight pause during which Mr. Liversedge appeared to dwell longingly on the amenities afforded by post-inns, that worthy gentleman heaved a sigh, and continued in a more optimistic tone: "However, I do not complain. Life, Mr. Ware, is full of

106

vicissitudes! Let me but once come about, and I do not despair of finding just the locality for the opening of a house where gentlemen with a taste for play may be sure of finding entertainment. In all modesty, Mr. Ware, I will say that I have a talent above the ordinary for such enterprises. If ever I should have the happiness to welcome you to any house under my direction, I fancy you will be pleased with what you will find. Nothing shoddy, I assure you, and admittance by password only. I shall pay particular attention to the quality of the wine in my cellar: nothing could be more fatal to the success of such a venture than to fob off one's patrons with inferior wine! But to achieve my object, sir, I must have Substance. Without Substance the result, if any, must be shabby, and, as such, too far beneath me to be considered."

"You are frank!" said the Duke. "My cousin Sale, in fact, is to set you up in some gaming-hell!"

"That," said Mr. Liversedge, "is to put the matter with vulgar bluntness, Mr. Ware."

"I fear I must wound your susceptibilities more deeply still! It is not your niece who makes this demand, but you, and the whole affair is a fudge!"

Mr. Liversedge smiled at him with great patience. "My dear sir, you wrong me, indeed you do!"

"I am very sure I do not! You have owned to me——"

A plump, uplifted hand checked him. "Between these four walls, Mr. Ware!" Liversedge said, with a return to his reproachful manner.

The Duke stared at him. Suddenly he said: "And what, sir, if I were to express my willingness to marry your niece? Have you thought of that?"

"Of everything!" Liversedge assured him affably. "I, of course, with my niece's happiness in mind, should be overjoyed. But it would not do for you at all, Mr. Ware, and your noble relatives, I fear, would do what lay in their power to prevent such an unequal match. Alas that it should be so, but it is the way of the world, after all, and if I were your father, sir, I confess I should strain every nerve to put a bar between you and my poor Belinda. Love-begotten, you know. Dear me, yes! Quite ineligible! You are young, and impetuous, but I feel sure your relatives must see it as I do myself."

"Mr. Liversedge," said the Duke, "I do not believe that your niece has the least notion of suing me for breach of promise! You think to out-jockey me, to take me in like a goose, in fact! This is all a hoax! I daresay your niece knows nothing of the matter!"

Mr. Liversedge shook his head sorrowfully. "It pains me, Mr. Ware, to meet with this unmerited mistrust! it pains me excessively! I did not look to have my good faith so doubted; I did not expect, in face of all that has passed between you and my unfortunate niece, to be met with what I must—reluctantly, believe me!—term callousness! If you were an older man, sir, I should be strongly tempted to request you to name your friends. As it is, I shall content myself with bringing before you irrefutable proof of the integrity of my actions."

He rose to his feet as he spoke, and the Duke followed suit rather warily. Liversedge smiled his understanding, and said: "Have no fear, Mr. Ware! A guest under my roof, you know, I must hold sacred, however moved I may be. Not, I beg you to believe, that I lay the least claim to this roof. But the principle holds! Pray be seated, for I shall not be long gone!"

He bowed with great dignity, and went out of the room, leaving the Duke to wonder what might be going to happen next. He walked over to the window restlessly, and stood fidgeting with the blind-cord. As he stood there, he had the satisfaction, at least, of seeing the landlord and the man in the plush waistcoat walking across the dirty yard with pails in their hands. From the medley of squeals in the distance he inferred that they were on their way to feed the pigs. He had not soberly supposed that either of them would be called in to overpower him, for he could not perceive any good end to be achieved through such methods, but he felt more at his ease with them out of earshot. Mr. Liversedge might be an entertaining scoundrel, but a scoundrel he certainly was, and would probably stop at very little to extort money from his victims. It was evident that he considered the supposed Mr. Ware a negligible opponent. The Duke had seen the indulgent contempt in his smile, and had done nothing to dispel it. He was by this time quite determined not to allow himself to be bled of as much as a farthing. By fair means or foul—and he would feel very little compunction at using foul means against a gentleman of Liversedge's kidney—he must wrest Matthew's letters, which Liversedge had in all probability gone away to collect, away from him. And since it seemed unlikely that this could be achieved without Mr. Manton's pistol coming into play, he was happy to see the landlord and his henchman going off to feed the pigs.

Mr. Liversedge was absent for some ten minutes, but presently the Duke heard his ponderous tread, and turned round to face the door.

It opened; Mr. Liversedge's voice said unctuously: "Come in, my love! Come and tell Mr. Ware how deeply he has wounded your tender heart!"

The Duke jumped, for this was a possibility he had not envisaged. The thought darted across his mind that if his true identity should be guessed it might occur to Mr. Liversedge's fertile brain that the Duke of Sale, held to ransom, would prove a more profitable investment than his niece's broken heart. His hand slid once more into the pocket of his coat, to grasp the butt of his pistol, and he braced himself to face the inevitable disclosure.

Into the room stepped a vision of loveliness. The Duke caught his breath, and stood staring. His cousin Matthew had certainly spoken of Belinda's beauty, but he had not prepared him for anything as superb as the creature who now stood on the threshold, regarding him out of eyes so large, so innocent, and of so deep translucent a blue as to make his senses swim for a dizzy moment. He closed his own eyes involuntarily, and opened them again to make sure that they had not deceived him. They had not. He beheld a veritable beauty. A face of rose-leaf complexion was framed in a cascade of guinea-gold curls, artlessly bound with a ribbon of scarcely a deeper blue than those glorious eyes; the brows were delicately arched; the little nose classically straight; the wistful mouth, with its short upper-lip, as kissable as it was perfect in proportion.

The Duke swallowed once, and waited. That melting gaze widened a little as it rested on him, but the lady said nothing.

"Did not Mr. Ware promise you marriage, my love?" said Mr. Liversedge, closing the door, and bending solicitously over the vision.

"Yes," said the vision, in a soft, west-country voice. "Oh, yes!"

If the Duke had been dizzy before, his senses now reeled. He could think of nothing to say. He wondered, for an unreasoning instant, if those tender blue eyes could be sightless, since he resembled his cousin hardly at all. But when he stared into them he saw a sort of speculation in their gaze, and knew that they were not.

"And did he not write you letters, my love, which you very properly gave to me, promising that he would make you his wife?" prompted Mr. Liversedge.

"Oh, yes, he did!" corroborated Belinda, smiling angelically at the Duke, and affording him an entrancing glimpse of even teeth, gleaming like pearls between her parted lips.

Mr. Liversedge spoke in a voice of studied patience.

"Were you not completely taken-in, my dear child? Was it not a crushing blow to you when he declared off, and left you forsaken?"

Under the Duke's bemused stare, the smile left Belinda's face, and two large tears welled over, and rolled down her cheeks. "Yes, it was," she said, in a voice that would have wrung pity from Herod. "He said I should have a purple silk dress when we was married."

Mr. Liversedge interposed rather hastily, patting one dimpled hand. "To be sure, yes, and other things too! And now you have none of them!"

"No," agreed Belinda dolefully. "But I shall be paid a vast sum of money for being so taken-in, and then I may have a——"

"Yes, my love, yes!" interrupted Mr. Liversedge. "You are upset, and no wonder! I would not have brought you face to face with Mr. Ware, who has so grossly deceived you, but that he doubted the depth of the wound he had dealt you. I will not compel you to remain another instant in the same room with him, for I know it to be painful to you. Go, my love, and trust your uncle to care for your interests!"

He opened the door for her, and after another of her wide, innocent looks at the Duke, she dropped a curtsy, and withdrew.

Mr. Liversedge shut the door upon her, and turned to find the Duke standing still rooted to the spot, and lost in astonishment. He said: "Ah, Mr. Ware, I perceive that you are confounded!"

"Yes," said Gilly faintly. "That is—Good God, sir, what are you about to keep such a lovely creature in this noisome alehouse?"

"No one," said Mr. Liversedge, "could regret the unhappy necessity more than I do! Alas, sir, when the pockets are to let, one has little choice of domicile! But I feel it! I assure you that I feel it profoundly. Your solicitude does you honour, Mr. Ware, and I trust it will be unnecessary for me to say more in prosecution of——"

"Mr. Liversedge," interrupted the Duke, "you ask me to believe that you hold some two or three letters I was mad enough to write to your niece, and for these you are demanding the preposterous sum of five thousand pounds! I may deplore your choice of domicile, but this cannot affect the point of issue between us!"

"Five letters, Mr. Ware," sighed Mr. Liversedge deprecatingly. "And each of them worth the very moderate price I have set upon them! I daresay your memory may not be

110

quite perfect. And so prettily expressed as your billets are! I will refresh your memory, if you will permit me! Pray be seated, sir! I should not wish you to feel that there was the least deception: five letters, and you recalled but three! Now, if I were not a man of honour, Mr. Ware, I might have allowed that to pass! You would have bought them from me, and thought yourself rid of the whole business! And I might then have driven a bargain with you for the remaining two! I know of those who would have done so. Yes, indeed, sir, I assure you there are many such shabby tricksters in the world. But Swithin Liversedge is not to be counted amongst them! Do but take your seat, and you shall see the letters with your own eyes! You may have them for a paltry sum. I will engage myself to give them up to you on receipt of bills for five thousand pounds."

The Duke sat down again at the table, opposite to his host, in a drooping posture that, while it might deceive Liversedge into believing him to be overcome by consternation, enabled him to get his hands under the table-edge undetected. "You have the letters!" he uttered.

"Yes, Mr. Ware, yes!" beamed Liversedge. "You shall count them!"

He put his hand into the breast of his coat as he spoke, and as he glanced down, the Duke gripped the ledge of the table, and drove it violently forward. It caught Mr. Liversedge all unawares, and full in the midriff. He uttered a sound between a grunt and a shout, tried to save himself, and failed. His chair tipped backwards, and he fell, snatching fruitlessly at the red table-cloth. In the same instant, the Duke, releasing the table, whipped the pistol from his pocket, and thumbed back the hammer. "Now, Mr. Liversedge!" he said, panting a little, for the table was a heavy one, and had taken all his strength to thrust forward. "Don't move! I am held to be a very fair shot!"

But the command was unnecessary. As he looked down at the portly frame at his feet, he saw that Mr. Liversedge was incapable of moving. His head had struck against the iron fender, and not only was a sluggish trickle of blood oozing from his scalp, but he was insensible. Mechanically, the Duke's left hand went to his pistol, and grasped the hammer. He pressed the trigger, as Captain Belper had taught him to do, and gently released the hammer, easing it down. Still holding the pistol in his hand, he dropped on his knee beside Liversedge, and slipped his left hand into the breast of his coat. A slim package had been already half drawn from an inner pocket. He pulled it out, and swiftly assured himself that it did indeed contain some half a dozen letters

111

directed in Matthew's hand. It was characteristic of him
that before he rose to his feet he slid a hand over Mr.
Liversedge's heart. It was beating rather faintly, but there
was no doubt that its owner still lived. The Duke hauled
his inanimate body, not without difficulty, clear of the grate,
and rose to his feet. As he did so, the door opened, and he
turned swiftly, his pistol at the ready, his thumb on the
hammer. But he did not pull it back a second time. Belinda
stood on the threshold, looking in wide-eyed surprise at her
uncle's prostrate form.

"Oh!" she said. "Is he dead?"

"No," the Duke replied. He crossed the floor to her side,
and shut the door. "He will recover: this is only a swoon!
What made you hold your peace just now? You know I am
not Matthew Ware!"

"Oh, yes!" she replied, smiling at him happily. "You are
not at all like Mr. Ware! He is much bigger than you, and
more handsome, too. I liked Mr. Ware. He said he would
give me——"

"Why did you not inform your uncle of his mistake?
What made you accept me as you did?"

"Uncle Swithin doesn't like it when I dispute with him,"
she explained. "He said I was to say just what he told me,
and I should have a purple silk gown."

"Oh!" said the Duke, a good deal taken-aback. "I am
excessively obliged to you, and if a purple silk gown is
what you desire I would I could give you one! How old
are you?"

"I think I shall soon be seventeen," she answered.

"You think! But you know when you have a birthday,
surely?"

"No," said Belinda regretfully. "Uncle Swithin's head is
cut open."

This remark seemed to be more in the nature of a statement than a reproach, but the Duke, glancing down at Mr.
Liversedge's form, saw that his pallid countenance was
ghastly in hue, and felt a certain measure of compunction.
He did not think that Mr. Liversedge was in much danger
of bleeding to death, but he did not desire his death, and
thought, moreover, that his own position might be awkward
if this should happen. He bent over him again, and bound
his own handkerchief round his head, saying: "When I am
gone, you may summon help, but pray do not do so until
then!"

"No," said Belinda obediently. "I wish you was not going!
Where did you come from?"

Her unconcern with her uncle's plight made the Duke

112

laugh in spite of himself. "I did not drop from a balloon, I assure you! I came from Baldock, and I think it is time that I returned there. Your uncle will be recovering in a moment, and since I do not care for the look of his friends belowstairs, I think I had best depart before he can summon them to his aid."

"Mr. Mimms is very disagreeable," she observed. She raised her lovely eyes to his face, and said simply: "I wish you would take me with you, sir!"

"Indeed, I wish I might!" he said. "I am very sorry to leave you in such a place. Were you fond of my—of Mr. Ware?"

"Oh, yes!" she replied, a soft glow in her eyes. "He was a very pretty-behaved gentleman, and when we were married he said I should have jewels, and a purple silk gown."

The thought that his young cousin had wounded anyone so young and so beautiful had been troubling the Duke, but this artless speech considerably allayed his qualms. He smiled, and, colouring a little, said: "Forgive me—I have very little money in my pocket, but if your heart is set upon a silk gown—I do not know about such matters, but will you take this bill and buy yourself what you like?"

He had been half afraid that she might be offended, but she smiled in a dazzling way at him, and accepted the note he was holding out. "Thank you!" she said. "I had never any money to spend of my own before! I think you are *quite* as handsome as Mr. Ware!"

He laughed. "No, no, that is flattery, I fear! But I must not stay! Goodbye! Pray do not—let your uncle use you again as he has done!"

He caught up his hat from the table, cast a final glance at Mr. Liversedge, who was beginning to recover his complexion, and went swiftly out of the room, and down the stairs. Belinda sighed regretfully, and looked in a doubtful way at her guardian. In a few more moments he groaned, and opened his eyes. They were blurred at first, but they cleared gradually. He put a hand first to his cracked skull, and then, instinctively, to his inner pocket. Then he groaned again, and enunciated thickly: "Lost!"

Belinda, a kind-hearted girl, perceiving that he was striving to pick himself up, helped him into a chair. "Your head is broke," she informed him.

"I know that!" said Mr. Liversedge, tenderly feeling his skull. "That I should have been floored by a greenhorn! For God's sake, girl, don't stand there with your mouth half-cocked! Fetch me the brandy-bottle from the cupboard!

113

Why did you not call Joe, silly wench? Five thousand pounds gone in the flash of an eye!"

Belinda brought him the brandy, and he recruited his strength by a generous pull at the bottle. His colour was by now much more healthy, but his spirits were sadly overborne.

"Done by a gudgeon!" he said gloomily. "Done by a miserable, undersized sapskull that has no more wits than to talk of marriage to the first pretty wench he meets! I was never more betwattled in my life! If I could but get my hands on your precious Mr. Matthew Ware——!"

"Oh, it wasn't Mr. Ware!" said Belinda sunnily.

Mr. Liversedge raised his aching head from between his hands and stared at her in blear-eyed surprise. "*What?*" he demanded. "Did you say it was not Mr. Ware?"

"Oh, no! Mr. Ware is a much prettier young gentleman," said Belinda. "He is tall, and handsome, and——"

"Then who the devil was he?" interrupted Mr. Liversedge incredulously.

"I don't know. He did not say what his name was, and I didn't think to ask him," replied Belinda, rather regretfully.

Mr. Liversedge hoisted himself out of his chair with an effort. "My God, what have I done to be saddled with such a fool?" he exclaimed. "If he was not Ware, why—*why*, girl, could you not have told me so?"

"I didn't know you would wish me to," said Belinda innocently. "You said I must say just what you told me, and you don't like it if I don't obey you. And I like him quite as well as Mr. Ware," she added consolingly.

Mr. Liversedge boxed her ears.

CHAPTER XI

THE Duke returned to Baldock in high fettle. For one who had never before fended for himself, he had managed the affair, he thought, pretty well. Matthew's letters were safely tucked into his pocket; he had not paid Mr. Liversedge a farthing for them; and he had not had recourse to Manton's pistol. Even Gideon could hardly have done better. In fact, Gideon would probably not have done as well, since Mr. Liversedge, confronted by his formidable size and extremely purposeful manner, would undoubtedly have conducted himself far more warily. Gilly was too modest not to realize that the success of his stratagem must be larely attributed to his lack of inches, and his quite unalarming

114

appearance. Mr. Liversedge had palpably summed him up as a scared boy within one minute of his having entered his parlour, and had not thought it necessary to be upon his guard. That had not been very wise of Mr. Liversedge, but Gilly was inclined to suspect that for all the breadth and scope of his visions, Mr. Liversedge was not a rogue of any great mental attainment. However, be that as it might, Gilly had scarcely expected to have succeeded so well, and he thought he had a very good right to feel in charity with himself. Nothing now remained to do but to burn Matthew's letters, set Matthew's anxious mind at rest, and go back to London with Tom next day. In his present mood he was rather sorry to have no excuse for absenting himself any longer from his household. Certain aspects of his stolen journey had not been altogether comfortable, but on the whole he had enjoyed himself very well, and he had derived a good deal of satisfaction from the discovery that he was not as helpless as he had feared he might be.

This mood of gentle elation suffered a set-back upon his arrival at the White Horse. The inn appeared to have become the focus of interest in the town, for a large and motley crowd was gathered before it, in the centre of which the impressive figure of the town-beadle seemed to be haranguing a heated and flustered Mrs. Appleby. Then the Duke perceived that one of the beadle's ham-like hands was grasping young Mr. Mamble by the coat-collar, and a sense of foreboding crept over him. He drew up, and prepared to step down from the gig.

Nearly everyone was too much absorbed in the strife raging between the beadle, Mrs. Appleby, a weedy man in a black suit, a farmer with a red face, and a stout lady in a mob-cap, whose voice was even shriller than Mrs. Appleby's, to have any attention to spare for the arrival of a gig; but the melancholy waiter, who had been surveying the scene with the gloomy satisfaction of one who has foreseen trouble from the outset, chanced to look up as the Duke rose from the driving-seat, and exclaimed: "Ah, here *is* the gentleman!"

The effect of these simple words was slightly overwhelming. Tom, taking advantage of an involuntary slackening of the grip on his collar, twisted himself free, and thrust his way through the crowd, crying thankfully: "Oh, sir! Oh, Mr. Rufford!"

He had scarcely reached the Duke's side, and clutched his arm, when Mrs. Appleby had seized the other arm, saying indignantly: "Thank goodness you've come, sir! Such

115

goings-on as I never saw, and me not knowing which way to turn!"

"Hif you are the cove as is responsible for this young varmint," said the beadle, reaching the Duke a bare fifteen seconds later than Mrs. Appleby, "hit is my dooty to inform you——"

The rest of this pronouncement was lost in the instant hubbub that arose. The weedy man, the farmer, and the lady in the mob-cap all broke into impassioned speech. The Duke, stunned by Mrs. Appleby's voice in one ear, and Tom's in the other, begged them to speak to him one at a time, but was not attended to. Various members of the crowd thought it incumbent upon them to take sides in the dispute, and for a few minutes the fragments of their observations reached the Duke in a confused medley. Such phrases as he caught could not be regarded as other than ominous. The words "lock-up house"—"upsetting of the Mail"—and "a-smashing of Mr. Badby's good cart" were being freely bandied about; and whereas one half of the crowd seemed disposed to take a lenient view of whatever it was that Tom had done, the other and more vociferous half was urgent with the beadle for his immediate transportation.

"I didn't! I did *not!*" Tom asserted passionately. "Oh, sir, pray tell them I did not!"

"Sir!" began the beadle portentously.

"Mr. Rufford, sir, do *you* make him attend, for listen to me he will not!" besought Mrs. Appleby.

A sudden lull fell, and the Duke realized with dismay that everyone, with the exception of the beadle, was looking at him in the evident expectation that he would instantly take command of the situation. He had never regretted the absence of his entourage more. He even wished that his Uncle Lionel could have been suddenly and miraculously wafted to the scene. The very sight of Lord Lionel's imposing figure and aristocratic visage would be enough to cause the crowd to disperse, while any well-trained footman would have cleaved a way for his Grace in a fashion haughty enough to have quelled even the beadle. But the Duke found himself bereft of all whose business in life it was to shield him from contact with the vulgar herd, and was obliged to fend once more for himself. He contrived to shake off the two frenzied grips on his arms, and to say in his usual gentle way: "Pray let us go into the house! And do not, I beg of you, all talk to me at once, for I can distinguish nothing that you say!"

His soft voice, falling upon the ears of the crowd in

striking contrast to the strident accents of the combatants, seemed to have an instant and sobering effect. Even the beadle was not unaffected by the indefinable air of dignity which wrapped the Duke round, and raised no objection to withdrawing into the coffee-room of the inn.

"Come, Tom!" the Duke said. He saw one of the ostlers standing nearby, and added: "You there! Take the gig into the yard, if you please!"

He then passed into the White Horse, and Tom, Mrs. Appleby, the beadle, the weedy man, the farmer, and the lady in the mob-cap all crowded in after him. Once within the coffee-room both Tom and Mrs. Appleby would have poured their stories into his ears, but he interrupted them, saying: "Pray wait! I will attend to you in a minute." He looked at the beadle, and said calmly: "Now will you tell me what all this bustle is about?"

The beadle was impressed in spite of himself. Unquestionably this quiet young gentleman was a member of the Quality. His experience had taught him the value of civility in dealing with such, and it was in moderated accents that he informed the Duke that four varmints, of whom young Mr. Mamble was the ringleader, had not only caused obstruction upon the King's highway, but had effected the ruin of an honest citizen's new cart, and had been guilty of the frightful crime of delaying and seriously incommoding the Mail, the penalty for which offence, as Mr. Rufford was no doubt aware, being no less than the sum of five pounds.

"Dear me!" said the Duke. "And how did all this come about, Tom?"

"I didn't do those things! At least, I never meant to, and how was I to know the Mail was approaching?" said Tom, deeply aggrieved. "You *told* me I might amuse myself!"

By this time another person had edged himself into the room, a nervous-looking man in a muffler, who awaited no invitation to describe to the Duke in detail the damage suffered by his new cart through the young cob's rearing up in alarm, and subsequently kicking in the front of the vehicle, at the unprecedented sight of two donkeys, a cow, and Mr. Datchet's old bay gelding being ridden backwards down the main street.

"It was a *race!*" explained Tom.

The beadle here took up the tale, and from his recital the Duke gathered that just as the entrants for this peculiar race reached the corner of the road, the Mail swept round it, coming from the opposite direction, and narrowly escaped an overturn. One of the leaders, in fact, got a leg over the trace, the coachman had the greatest difficulty in

117

controlling his team, and all the passengers had suffered severe shocks to their nerves.

After recounting the exact circumstances of the crime, the beadle attempted to outline to the assembled company the ultimate fate of the sporting young gentlemen, and the immediate and awful penalties they had incurred. He was at once interrupted by the lady in the mob-cap, who asserted tearfully that her Will had always been a good boy, as well Mr. Piddinghoe knew, until led astray by evil companions. She was seconded by the weedy man, who stated that nothing short of the most violent pressure could have induced his Fred so to demean himself; and by the farmer, who said loudly and belligerently that it was nobbut a boy's prank, and he would dust Nat's jacket for him, and no more said.

However, a great deal more had to be said before the Duke could settle the affair. Mrs. Appleby very unwisely demanded to be told what should get into the boys to make them take and run a race backwards, and this encouraged Tom to explain indignantly and at length the difficulties of handicapping fairly two donkeys, one cow, and an old horse. He seemed to think that he deserved congratulation for having hit upon so novel a solution to the problem, and dwelled so insistently on the excellent performance of the cow under these conditions that everyone but the Duke and the beadle allowed themselves to be diverted from the main point at issue, and either exclaimed several times that they would never have thought it, or argued that it stood to reason the cow would have as good a chance as the horse, particularly seeing as the horse was that broken-down old brute of Mr. Datchet's.

The Duke, meanwhile, detached the owner of the ruined cart from the circle, and settled his claims out of hand. Much mollified, Mr. Badby stowed away the money which the Duke paid him for the repair of his cart, and said that he had been young himself, and was never one to create a to-do over a trifle. It then transpired that the driver and the guard of the mail-coach had very handsomely forborne to lodge an official charge against Tom, so that with Mr. Badby's retirement from the lists, the beadle was left without any very powerful weapon to use against the miscreants. The Duke was then inspired to suggest that after so much alarm and excitement everyone must stand in need of such revivifying cordials as could be found in the tap-room, and invited the assembled company to refresh themselves there at his expense. The idea took well; and after the Duke had sternly dismissed Tom to the Pink Parlour, and had promised the beadle that he should be suitably dealt with, the whole party repaired to the tap-room, where liberal potations of ale, gin, or porter very soon induced even the beadle and the weedy man, who proved to be Baldock's leading tailor, to look upon the late disturbance as a very good jest. The Duke's shy smile and quite unconscious charm were not without their effect, and since he was found to have not the least height in his manner it was not long before his obvious quality was forgotten, and he was being confided in on all manner of topics, from the Spasms endured by the lady in the mob-cap, to the shocking price of serges, corduroys, shalloons, and tammies.

By the time the Duke judged that he could bid farewell to his guests without causing them to think that he fancied himself above his company, Mrs. Appleby had three times whispered to him that his dinner was spoiling in the oven. He took his leave at last, and went upstairs to the parlour, where he found Tom awaiting him in a mood of almost equally matched penitence and vainglory. Tom was ready to justify himself at length, but as his protector, instead of rating him, succumbed to a fit of pent-up laughter as soon as he had fairly shut the door, his aggressive manner left him abruptly, and he offered up a handsome apology for having been the cause of so much trouble and expense.

"Indeed, I perceive clearly that you will soon ruin me!" the Duke said, still laughing. "I don't know what you deserve should be done to you!"

"Sir, you won't send me back to Pa and Mr. Snape, will you?" Tom demanded anxiously.

"No, no, nothing short of transportation will do for you!" the Duke told him.

His mind relieved of its only dread, Tom grinned gratefully, and applied himself with his usual energy and appetite to his dinner.

When he had retired to bed, which, since he was, he said, unaccountably tired, he was induced to do at an early hour, the Duke committed his cousin's letters to the flames, and sent the waiter to obtain for him paper, ink, pens, and wafers. These commodities having been brought, the fire made up, and the blinds drawn, he sat down to write two letters. The first of these was to Matthew, at Oxford, and did not occupy him long. He sealed it with one of the wafers, wrote the direction, and was just about to scrawl his name across one corner when he recollected himself, and reopened the letter to add a postscript. "*I fear you will have to pay some sixpences for this history,*" he wrote, smiling to

119

himself, *"but it would never do, you know, for me to frank this. I hope you will not grudge it!"*

He then affixed a fresh wafer to his missive, laid it aside and wrote upon a new sheet of paper:

> White Horse,
> Baldock.

My dear Gideon,

Here the letter came to a sudden halt, it having just occurred to the Duke that he would in all probability see his dear Gideon before a letter could reach him. However, after biting the end of his quill reflectively for a few minutes, he decided that since had had nothing to read, and did not wish to retire to bed, he would write to Gideon after all. The urge to confide some part at least of his amazing new experiences to Gideon was irresistible. Besides, a description of Tom's race and its consequences would occupy several sheets, so that Gideon would be forced to disgorge large sums to the Post Office for the privilege of receiving a letter from his noble relative, and that would be a very proper revenge on him for having tried to horrify one smaller and younger than himself with a blood-curdling novel. The Duke gave a little chuckle, dipped his quill in the ink, and lost no time in explaining this to Gideon. After that he embarked on a humorous account of his stage-coach journey, and in the most high-flown terms he could summon to mind, assured his cousin that he had already slain a considerable dragon, in the shape of an out-and-out villain, whom he had tricked, outwitted, and left for dead in a haunt of thieves and desperate characters from which he himself was lucky to have escaped with his life. He could fancy how Gideon would grin when he read this, and grinned himself. *"And if you should wonder, my dear Gideon,"* he continued, *"why I shoud put myself to the trouble of writing to inform you of this when I have the intention of returning to London to-morrow, I must further inform you that I have engaged myself as bearleader to a youth of tender years, whose fertile mind suggests to him such ways of amusing himself as seem likely to keep me too fully occupied during the coming week to have leisure to spare for a visit to your chambers."*

He then favoured his cousin with the whole story of the backward-race, told him that his circle of friends had been enlarged to include a tailor, a lady who kept a pastry-cook's shop, a beadle, and three farmers, and was just about to end his letter when he remembered something else which Gideon must certainly be told about. *"By the by,"* he wrote, *"if you never hear of me again, you will know that I have fled the country, taking with me the most beautiful creature I ever beheld in my life. Alas that the notice of my engagement must by now have appeared in the Gazette! I would I could describe my inamorata to you, but no words could do even faint justice to her loveliness. The heart left my bosom in one bound! Ever your most affectionate*

Adolphus.

He closed his letter, and directed it, reflecting that it would undoubtedly bring Gideon round to Sale House at the first opportunity. It was still quite early in the evening, and the rumble of voices in the tap-room came faintly to the Duke's ears. He was just wondering whether or not to seek entertainment there when a knock fell on the door, and the waiter came in, and, bending a look upon him compound of curiosity and disapproval, informed him that there was a young person belowstairs who was desirous of seeing him. "Leastways," he added, "I dunno who else it could be, for there ain't no one else here like what she says you are, not in this house there ain't."

"A young person to see me?" echoed the Duke blankly. "You must be mistaken!" A sudden and unwelcome suspicion darted into his mind. He said: "Good God!" and changed colour.

The waiter observed his consternation with a certain satisfaction. "Ah!" he said. "And go away, which I told her to, she will not!"

"I'll come!" the Duke said hastily, and went to the head of the stairs, and looked down into the lobby. Seated on a chair, a bandbox on her knees, and another at her feet, was Belinda, her enchanting face framed in a blue bonnet, and a pelisse buttoned up to her white throat. In front of her, and in an attitude of unmistakable hostility, stood Mrs. Appleby.

Some instinct warned the Duke that he beheld Trouble. A prudent man would at this point retire to his room, denying all knowledge of the fair visitor, and leave Mrs. Appleby to get rid of her, which, he judged, she would very soon do, if left undeterred. But the Duke had either too little prudence or too much chivalry to adopt this course; he went down the stairs.

Both ladies looked up quickly, one greeting him with a blinding smile, and the other with a stare of outraged virtue. "Oh, sir, please I had to come!" said Belinda.

"This young woman, sir," said Mrs. Appleby grimly, "appears to have business with you, for all she cannot give you a name! And I will take leave to tell you, sir, that mine has always been a respectable house, and such goings-on I will not have!"

"Oh, hush, Mrs. Appleby!" begged the Duke. "I am acquainted with this lady!"

"Of that I make no doubt, sir!" retorted Mrs. Appleby.

The Duke sought wildly in his mind for an explanation likely to satisfy the landlady, and could hit upon only one. "She is Tom's sister!" he said, devoutly hoping that Belinda would not deny it. "She has come in search of him, of course!"

Belinda, who seemed to have a mind very responsive to suggestion, nodded her head at this, and smiled at Mrs. Appleby.

"In—deed!" pronounced that lady. "Then perhaps you will have the goodness to tell me what your business is, miss?"

"To find Tom," replied Belinda happily.

"I never heard such a tale, not in all my life I didn't!" exclaimed Mrs. Appleby, outraged. "Why, you're no more like him than I am! Sir, I'll have you know——"

"And I have brought all my things with me, because I dare not go back, so if you please, sir, will you take care of me?" added Belinda, turning her melting gaze upon the Duke.

"Not in my house he will not!" declared Mrs. Appleby, without hesitation.

By this time a small audience, consisting of the waiter, the boots, the tapster, and two chambermaids had gathered in the lobby, and the Duke, acutely unhappy at finding himself the centre of so much curiosity, said: "Please step up to the parlour, Miss—Miss Mamble! And do you come up too, Mrs. Appleby! I will explain it to you in private!"

Belinda got up readily from the chair. The Duke took the bandboxes from her; and Mrs. Appleby, after demanding to know if her various servants could find nothing better to do than to stand there gaping, said that no amount of explanation would reconcile her to Belinda's presence in the inn. But as Belinda and the Duke were by this time halfway up the stairs she was obliged to follow them, maintaining a threatening monologue all the way.

The Duke ushered Belinda into his parlour, set down the bandboxes, and firmly shut the door upon her. He turned to confront Mrs. Appleby.

That redoubtable lady at once broke into speech. If, she

declared, Mr. Rufford had the least hope of her keeping that Hussy under her roof for as much as one hour he was sadly mistaken! To be sure, she might have guessed, after the events of this day, that something of the sort would happen, but boys' mischief was one thing, and goings-on of this nature quite another.

"Mrs. Appleby," interrupted the Duke, "can you seriously suppose that I nourish the slightest improper design towards that child? Why, she is hardly out of the school-room!"

"I know nothing of *your* designs, sir," retorted Mrs. Appleby, "but hers are plain enough, and give her a room in my house I will not!"

"Then I must give her mine, and sleep on the sofa in the parlour," said the Duke calmly.

Mrs. Appleby fought for breath.

"You cannot," proceeded the Duke, "turn a child of that age into the street at this hour. Indeed, I am persuaded you are by far too good a woman to think of doing so."

"Let her," said Mrs. Appleby terribly, "go back to wherever it was she came from!"

"It is quite impossible that she should do so. I see I shall have to entrust the whole story to your ears," said the Duke.

He then proceeded, somewhat to his own astonishmment and considerably more to Mrs. Appleby's, to weave about the unconscious persons of Belinda and Mr. Thomas Mamble a lurid and fantastic story in which defaulting trustees, cruel stepfathers, and hideous persecution figured prominently, if somewhat obscurely. He cast himself for the rôle of secret envoy, but being quite unable to think of any reason for an envoy's presence in Baldock, took refuge in an air of mystery which so much bewildered Mrs. Appleby that she ended by weakly saying that Belinda might have a small bed-chamber at the back of the house for one night only, and that not because she believed one word of Mr. Rufford's story, but because she was not, she hoped, an unmerciful woman.

The Duke, feeling worn-out by the exercise of so much imagination, mopped his damp brow as soon as Mrs. Appleby had sailed away to prepare the small back bed-chamber, and nerved himself to enter his parlour

He found that Belinda, having shed her bonnet and pelisse, had made herself comfortable in an easy chair by the fire, and was eating one of the few apples Tom had left in the basket on the side-table. She greeted her host with her angelic smile, and said: "How disagreeable she is! Will she let me stay here, sir?"

"Yes, for to-night she will," he replied. "But I do not understand! Why have you come? What is it you wish me to do for you?"

She looked at him in surprise and faint reproach. "But you said you wished you might take me with you!" she reminded him.

The Duke, who clearly saw an abyss yawning at his feet, said with a great deal of uneasiness in his voice: "Did I? Yes, well, but—but I cannot take you with me!"

"Can't you?" said Belinda wistfully. "Then what must I do, please, sir?"

"My dear girl, how can I possibly advise you?" protested Gilly. "I do not even know why you have left your uncle!"

"Oh, he is not my uncle!" said Belinda blithely.

"Not your uncle? He is your guardian though, is he not?"

"He said he would be," agreed Belinda, "but he never gave me any of the things he promised me, and besides, I don't like it at that horrid little inn, so perhaps I won't have him for a guardian any more. I thought I might have you for one instead," she added confidingly.

"No," said the Duke firmly, "that is quite impossible!"

Belinda sighed, but appeared to resign herself to her disappointment. She took another bite out of her apple, and fixed her eyes expectantly on the Duke's face.

"Does Liversedge know you have come to me?" he demanded. She shook her head. "But how could you contrive to escape unseen? and how did you reach Baldock? You cannot have walked all the way, surely?"

"Oh, no! I only walked to the pike-road, and a kind gentleman took me up in his carriage," Belinda explained. "And he said he would be very glad to take me to his house, only that perhaps his wife would not like it. I daresay she is a disagreeable lady, like that one downstairs. Ladies are nearly always so, are they not? I like gentlemen better."

The Duke did not find this difficult to believe. He refrained from comment, however, merely repeating: "How did you contrive to escape from that place?"

"Well, Uncle Swithin's head hurt him, so he went to lie down upon his bed, and everyone else was gone into the tap-room. Besides, Mr. Mimms would not care if he saw me go, because he doesn't hold with females."

"I see. But what made you run away? Did Liversedge blame you for what happened at the inn this afternoon? Was he perhaps angry with you?"

"Oh, yes! He said he wished he had not saddled himself with me, for I am too stupid to be of the least use to him, and he says he will send me back to Mrs. Pilling!" replied Belinda, large tears gathering in her eyes.

"Pray do not cry!" begged the Duke. "Who is Mrs. Pilling?"

"She is a very cross lady, not at all kind to me, and she will very likely put me in prison," said Belinda, the tears welling over.

The Duke, who had had previous experience of the ease with which Belinda wept, watched in a fascinated way the large drops rolling down her cheeks without in the smallest degree impairing her beauty, and could not find it in his heart to blame Matthew by having succumbed to so much pathetic loveliness. After a moment, he said: "I wish you will not cry! No one will put you in prison, I assure you!"

Belinda obediently stopped crying, but said in a doleful voice: "Yes, she will, sir, for I have broken my indentures."

Light began to break in upon the Duke. "Were you apprenticed to Mrs. Pilling?" he asked.

"Oh, yes, and I was learning to trim the hats very well, but then Mr. Liversedge said that if I went away with him I should live like a lady, and have a purple dress, and a ring to put on my finger. So I went with him, but Mrs. Dovercourt was cross, and I did not like it in Oxford above half, and now I think I would like not to live with Mr. Liversedge any more. But I daren't go back to Bath, because besides putting me in prison Mrs. Pilling would very likely beat me as well."

"Does she do so?" demanded the Duke, quite shocked at the thought that anyone could so maltreat the lovely Belinda.

"Yes, because I am very stupid," explained Belinda, without rancour. "And Mr. Liversedge boxed my ears, too, though I said just what he told me I must. I am very unhappy!"

"No, no, don't be unhappy!" said the Duke, terrified lest she should dissolve once more into tears. "No one shall beat you, or box your ears, I promise! You must tell me where your home is, and I will——"

"I haven't got a home," said Belinda.

"Oh!" said the Duke, somewhat dashed. "But you have relatives, have you not, Miss—— What *is* your name?"

"Belinda," she answered, with a look of surprise.

"Yes, I know, but your other name? Your surname?"

"Oh, I haven't any other name!" she told him. "I'm a foundling."

"A foundling!" he ejaculated. "Then—you do not even know who your mother and father were?"

"Oh, no!" she said. "If you please, sir, may I have another apple?"

He handed her the basket. "Of course. But, my poor

125

child, have you no relatives to whom you can turn for help?"

"Oh, no!" she said again, shaking her head so that her golden curls were set quivering and bobbing. "Foundlings don't, you know."

"I didn't know. That is, I had never thought—— It is very dreadful!"

She agreed to this, but more with the air of one willing to please than with any particular chagrin.

"What in heaven's name am I to do with you?" said the Duke, looking harassed.

Belinda said hopefully: "You did say that you wished you might give me the purple silk dress," she suggested.

He could not help laughing. "No, no, that is not what I meant!"

She sighed, and the corners of her mouth drooped tragically. "No one ever gives me a purple silk dress," she mourned, a sob in her voice.

The Duke had never had occasion to bestow much thought on female attire, but now that he came to consider the matter dispassionately he was bound to own that there was much to be said in extenuation of all those who had refused to let Belinda have her heart's desire. The combination of those bright gold curls and a dress of purple silk would be shocking enough, he imagined, to stun all beholders. He made haste to divert her thoughts. "Belinda, have you no friend to whom you might go?"

She appeared to bend her mind seriously to this question, and after staring with wrinkled brow at the Duke for a moment or two, suddenly dazzled him with one of her brilliant smiles, and said: "Oh, yes, I have a friend that was used to work at a mantua-maker's, only she was married, and went away from Bath. I should like of all things to visit her, for I daresay she has a baby now, and I am excessively fond of babies!"

"Where does she live?" asked the Duke.

Belinda sighed. "She went to a place called Hitchin, but I don't know where it is, and I only recall it because it sounds like kitchen, and I think that is very droll, don't you, sir?"

"Hitchin!" he exclaimed, his harassed air lightening a little. "But Hitchin lies only a few miles from here! I daresay no more than six or seven, perhaps not as much! If you think you would like to visit this friend, I will take you there tomorrow! Do you know her direction?"

"Oh, no!" said Belinda unconcernedly.

Again the Duke was dashed. "Well, do you know her name?" he asked.

Belinda laughed merrily at this. "Why, of course I know her name! It is Maggie Street!"

"Then depend upon it we shall soon find her!" he said, much relieved.

At this moment, Mrs. Appleby entered the parlour, and announced that as Miss's bedchamber was now ready for her she would escort Miss to it.

"Yes, please do so!" said the Duke. "And perhaps you would be so good as to bring up a glass of milk to her, for I fear she is rather hungry."

"Very good, sir," replied Mrs. Appleby stiffly. "Come with me, miss, if you please!"

She picked up the bandboxes, and swept them and Belinda inexorably out of the room, leaving the Duke feeling extremely exhausted, but not a little thankful that he was not to be saddled with Belinda for the rest of his life, as at one moment he had feared that he might be.

CHAPTER XII

UPON the following morning, the Duke thought it wisest to visit Tom before that young gentleman had emerged from his room, to warn him that he had acquired a sister overnight. Tom was inclined to take this in bad part, giving it as his opinion that girls spoiled everything. When he learned that Belinda's presence had made it necessary for the Duke to change his plans, his face fell perceptibly, and it was only an assurance that he should eventually be taken to London that enabled him to meet his new sister without overt hostility. He evinced little curiosity, which was a relief to the Duke, and, not having reached an impressionable stage in his career, was quite unmoved by the loveliness that presently burst upon him. He ate his breakfast in unusual silence, occasionally shooting a darkling look at Belinda, and lost no time in effacing himself when he had finished. The Duke sent him off to discover where he could hire a post-chaise-and-pair to carry the whole party to Hitchin that morning, for not only was he extremely anxious to hand Belinda over to her friend as soon as possible, but Belinda herself was troubled by fears that Mr. Liversedge might pursue and recapture her. It was in vain that the Duke explained to her that since Mr. Liversedge was neither her uncle nor her guardian he had no hold over her, and would scarcely dare to coerce her: she appeared to listen to his words, but it was apparent that they conveyed little to her intelligence.

"Tell me," he said, "when you were in Oxford with Mrs. —Mrs.—I don't recall the name, but the lady who was thought to be your aunt——"

"Oh, she was not my aunt!" Belinda said. "I did not like having to live with her at all, for she was so bothersome, and very often cross with me."

"But who was she?" he asked.

"I don't know. Mr. Liversedge was very friendly with her, and he said I should stay with her and do just what she told me."

He could not help smiling. "And was that to make my— to make Mr. Ware fall in love with you?"

"Yes," she replied innocently. "I did not mind *that*, for we went pleasuring together, you know, and he was excessively kind to me, and he said he would marry me, too, and then I should have been a grand lady, and had my carriage, and silk dress besides."

"Did you wish very much to marry him?"

"Oh, no!" Belinda replied placidly. "I didn't care, if only I might have all the things Uncle Swithin said I should. He said it would be more comfortable for me if Mr. Ware gave me a great deal of money, and I think it would have been, because he was so jealous, you know, that there was no bearing it. Why, when I only went out to get a pound of black pudding from the pork-butcher, and a gentleman carried the basket for me, there was *such* an uproar! And he read poetry to me, too."

"That was certainly very bad!" the Duke said gravely. "But tell me what happened after Mr. Ware—when you were no longer expecting to marry him! Did you run away from that lady?"

"Oh, no, she would not keep me any longer, because she quarrelled dreadfully with Uncle Swithin, and she said he was a Jeremy Diddler."

"What in the world is that?" he enquired, amused.

"I don't know, but I think Uncle Swithin wouldn't pay her any money, and she said he had promised it to her for taking care of me. She was as cross as a cat! And Uncle Swithin told her how we should all of us have money from Mr. Ware, but there was an execution in the house, you know, and she would not stay there any more. It is very fidgeting to have an execution in your house, for they take away the furniture, and there is no knowing how to go on. So Uncle Swithin fetched me away in an old tub of a carriage, which was so horrid! I was stuffed to death! And we had to go in the middle of the night, and that was uncomfortable too."

"He took you to that inn? Is it possible that he meant to keep you there?"

"Well, he could not help doing so," explained Belinda. "Poor Uncle Swithin! he has so very little money left, and Mr. Mimms is his brother, so you see he does not have to pay him to stay there. And of course we was expecting Mr. Ware to send us a great sum of money, and then we might have been comfortable again. But Uncle Swithin says all is ruined, and it was my fault for not calling to Mr. Mimms to stop you when you went away. But he never *told* me I should do so!"

"Don't you think," he suggested gently, "that you will like just as well to go to your friend as to have a great sum of money?"

Belinda reflected, and shook her head. "No, for if I had the money I could *also* go to visit Maggie Street," she said simply.

This was so unanswerable that the Duke abandoned the subject, together with a half-formed resolve to point out to Belinda the reprehensible nature of Mr. Liversedge's attempts to extort money from undergraduates. Something told him that Belinda's intelligence was not of the order that readily appreciated ethical considerations.

In a short time, Tom returned to the inn, his mission accomplished. If Mr. Rufford would step down to the George, he said, to confirm the arrangement he had made on his behalf, a chaise could be hired, and would be sent round to the White Horse as soon as it was needed.

The Duke was not very anxious to visit the George, where he had several times stopped on his way to his estates in Yorkshire, to change his horses, but he did not think that he had ever alighted there, and could only hope that he would not be recognized. He desired his protégés to pack their few belongings, and sallied forth, requesting Mrs. Appleby, whom he met at the foot of the stairs, to prepare his reckoning. Mrs. Appleby allowed him to see by her manner that he had sadly disappointed her; and the waiter, hovering in the background, plainly regarded him in the light of a hardened libertine.

In the event, no one whom he interviewed at the George showed the smallest sign of recognizing him. He thought the luck was miraculously with him, until it occurred to him, on his way back to the White Horse, that, had he wished to do it, he might have found it difficult to convince the landlord and the servants at the George that an unattended gentleman, staying at the White Horse and in need of a hired chaise, could possibly be his Grace the Duke of Sale. He reflected then that it was to be hoped he would have no occasion to prove his identity, since he had taken care to leave his visiting cards at Sale House, and had handed over to Gideon his seal ring.

When he reached the White Horse again, he found that although Belinda had packed her bandboxes, Tom was by no means ready to depart, having, in fact, made no attempt to stow away the articles of apparel procured for him into the carpet-bag which was all the Duke had been able to find in Baldock for the carriage of his effects. Tom had expended some part of the guinea the Duke had given him on the acquisition of a fascinating new toy, called, not without reason, Diabolo. He had already succeeded in breaking a water-bottle, and a cherished vase of unsurpassed hideousness which Mrs. Appleby stated had belonged to her husband's grandfather and was quite irreplaceable. The Duke was greeted on his arrival with a strongly worded complaint from Mrs. Appleby, and a simple request from Belinda to buy her a Diabolo too. However, Tom, who found that he did not excel in manipulating the toy, said loftily that it was a stupid thing, and very handsomely made Belinda a present of it. But the Duke was obliged to do his packing for him, and by the time he had left Tom to strap up the carpet-bag, and had dealt with his own effects, and settled his reckoning with Mrs. Appleby, the hired chaise was at the door. He saw his charges into it, directed the post-boy to take them to the Sun Inn at Hitchin, and turned to take his leave of Mrs. Appleby.

"Mark my words, Mr. Rufford, sir," she said bodingly, "you will live to regret it, for if ever I saw a light-skirt, which I never thought to soil my lips with such a word, I see one this day!"

"Nonsense!" said Gilly, and sprang up into the chaise.

"This," declared Belinda buoyantly, "is beyond anything great, sir! To be jauntering about in a private chaise like a real lady, as fine as a star! If Mrs. Pilling were to see me now she would not credit her eyes, I daresay! Oh, if only Mr. Liversedge does not find me, and take me back again!"

"Mr. Liversedge," said Gilly, "has a great deal of effrontery, but hardly enough, I dare swear, for that! Let us put him out of our minds!" He saw that she was still looking vaguely scared, and smiled. "There is nothing more he can do, Belinda, after all! Ten to one, he is by this time, turning his mind into other channels."

But little though he knew it he had wronged Mr. Liversedge. That gentleman had found himself so very far from well on the previous evening that he had been quite unable to bend his powerful mind to any more difficult problem than how he could most expeditiously cure the shocking headache that nearly blinded him. He had gone to lie down upon his bed, and had responded to a suggestion that he would be better for a bite of supper only by a hollow groan. Mr. Mimms, regarding him with a scornful eye, offered him consolation in the form of a reminder that he had warned him that no good could come of flying at game too high for him.

"You leave them swell bleaters be, Sam!" he adjured the prostrate sufferer. "Then maybe you won't have no broken head another time!"

Mr. Liversedge opened a bloodshot eye. "Swithin!" he found strength to utter.

"Sam you was christened, and much good it done you to go a-giving yourself a silly flash name like Swithin!" said Mr. Mimms severely. "Well, if you don't want no peck and booze there'll be more for them as does, that's one thing!"

On this cheering thought, he departed, leaving his afflicted brother to spread a cold compress over his head and to take another pull at the brandy bottle.

It was some hours later before Mr. Liversedge felt able to rise from his couch, and to totter downstairs to the kitchen. He still wore the Duke's handkerchief knotted round his head, and he had by no means recovered his complexion, but the pangs of hunger had begun to attack him. He pushed open the kitchen-door, and found that his brother was entertaining a guest, a thin, wiry gentleman, who wore a riding-suit of sober-coloured cloth, and a pair of well-fitting boots that seemed to have seen much service. He had a pair of bright grey eyes, which lifted quickly and warily as the door opened. He was in the act of consuming a prodigious portion of cold beef, but he held his knife suspended for an instant, until he saw who it was that had entered, when he relaxed, and waved the laden knife at Mr. Liversedge, saying cheerfully: "Hallo, Sam, old gager!"

Mr. Mimms, who was seated on the opposite side of the table, engaged in inspecting a collection of watches, purses, fobs, and rings, cast an appraising look at Mr. Liversedge, and said: "That flash mort of yours has loped off."

Mr. Liversedge drew up a spare chair, and lowered himself into it. "Where to?" he demanded.

"I dunno, nor I don't care. How you ever come to think there was any good to be got out of such a bird-witted

131

wench downright queers me! Good riddance to her, that's what I say!"

"Bird-witted she may be," replied Mr. Liversedge fair-mindedly, "but where, I ask you to tell me, Joe, could you find a more lovely piece?"

The gentleman in riding-dress paused between mouthfuls to heave a deep sigh. "Ah, if ever I see such a rare bleached mort!" he said, shaking his head. "What a highflyer, Sam! But no sense in her cockloft, which makes her dangerous ware for a man like me. Else I would have——"

"You would have done no such thing, Nat Shifnal, as I have erstwhile made plain to you!" said Mr. Liversedge. "Nothing could be more fatal for a man in my position than to be bringing damaged goods to market!" He stretched out a hand for the dish on which a somewhat mutilated sirloin of beef reposed, and drew it towards him. "I will trouble you for the carving-knife, Joe," he said, with dignity.

His brother pushed it across the table. "She's loped off in pudding-time, that's what I say and will hold to!" he announced. "If you had of gone on the dub-lay, Sam, it's low, but not a word would you have heard out of me! Nor I wouldn't have blamed you for turning bridle-cull, like Nat here. But you took and tried to be a petticoat-pensioner, and that's what I don't hold with, and nothing will make me say different!"

Mr. Liversedge replied in a lofty tone that he would thank his brother not to use such vulgar terms to him. "There is, I will grant, a certain distinction attached to those who embrace the High Toby as their profession. But the dub-lay—or, as I prefer to call it, the very ignoble calling of a common pickpocket, is something I thank God I have never yet been obliged even to contemplate!"

"No, because every time as you're nippered it's me as stands huff!" retorted Mr. Mimms.

"Easy, now, easy!" begged Mr. Shifnal placably. "I don't say as Sam done right this time, but there's no denying, Joe, he's got gifts. For one thing, he talks as nice as a nun's hen; and for another, there ain't anyone to touch him for drinking a young 'un into a fit state for plucking."

"Then let him stick to it!" retorted Mr. Mimms. "I got nothing against that lay, but petticoat-pensioners I can't stomach!"

Mr. Shifnal regarded Mr. Liversedge curiously. "How did you come to be diddled by a greenhorn, Sam? It ain't like you, I'll cap downright! By what Joe tells me, you shouldn't have had trouble in plucking that pigeon."

Mr. Liversedge described an airy gesture with one white

hand. "The greatest amongst us must sometimes err. I own that I erred. Talking pays no toll, or I might be tempted to say much in extenuation of what I admit to have been a misjudgment."

"It wouldn't be no use talking them breakteeth words to Nat," said Mr. Mimms caustically. "He ain't had your advantages, Sam, for all he's able to pay his shot, and don't have to come down on me for the very bread he puts in his mummer."

Mr. Liversedge's bosom swelled perceptibly, but after looking hard at his brother for a moment he apparently decided to ignore his lapse from good taste. He said: "What I ask myself is, Who was he?"

"If you was to be asking yourself how you was to set about making a living, there'd be some sense in it," commented the aggressive Mr. Mimms. "It don't matter to none of us who that downy young 'un was. I'll allow he looked like a flat, but he knocked you into horse-nails, which I hope and pray as it will be a lesson to you not to meddle with swells again!" He perceived that he was not being attended to, Mr. Liversedge having fallen into a brown study, and added bitterly: "There you go! A-thinking up some more of your cork-brained lays! You won't be happy till you've got yourself into the Whit, and me along with you!"

"Be silent, Joseph!" commanded Mr. Liversedge. "I must and shall make a recover!" He passed a hand across his brow as he spoke, and rather impatiently tore off the Duke's handkerchief. "That young addle-plot was very perfectly acquainted with all the circumstances of this affair," he said. "In a word, he was deep in Ware's confidence. I hold to my original conviction that his purpose in coming here was to treat with me. Had I not, for a fatal instant, lowered my guard, I fancy I should now be in possession of a substantial sum of money—of which you, Joe, would have had your earnest, I assure you."

"That's handsomely said, Sam," approved Mr. Shifnal. "What's more, Joe don't doubt you'd have paid him his earnest, nor no one that knows you."

"No, I don't," said Mr. Mimms. "Because I'd ha' seen to it you did. But not one meg have I had out of you, Sam, and all I got is you borrowing from me to take and hire a shay to fetch that silly wench here, which I never wanted, nor don't hold with!"

Mr. Liversedge disregarded him. "He was well-breeched," he said slowly. "I perceived it at the outset. That olive coat—I caught but a glimpse of it beneath his Benjamin, but I flatter myself I am not easily deceived in such matters—was

only made by a tailor patronized by members of the *haut ton.*
Not a dandy, no! But there was an air of elegance—how
shall I put it? A——"

"He was a flash-cull," suggested Mr. Shifnal helpfully.

Mr. Liversedge frowned. "He was *not* a flash-cull!" he
said with some asperity. "He was a gentleman of high breeding. His hat bore the name of Lock upon the band: I observed it when he laid it brim upwards on the table. That
may mean little to you: it conveys to me the information
that he is one who frequents the haunts of high fashion.
During that period in my life when I acted as a gentleman's
gentleman, I became acquainted, with the nicest particular-
ity, with every detail of an out-and-out swell's attire. I recognized at a glance in this greenhorn a member of the
Upper Ten Thousand."

Mr. Shifnal being plainly out of his depth, Mr. Mimms
kindly translated this speech for him. "He was as spruce
as an onion," he said.

"If you choose so to put it," agreed Mr. Liversedge graciously. "Take only this handkerchief! Of the finest quality,
you observe, and the monogram——" Suddenly he stopped
short, as an idea occurred to him, and subjected the handkerchief to a closer scrutiny. It had been hemmed for the
Duke by the loving hands of his nurse, who was a notable
needle-woman. In one corner she had embroidered a large
S, and had had the pretty notion of enclosing the single
letter in a circle of strawberry leaves. "No," said Mr. Liversedge, staring at it. "Not a monogram. A single letter. In
fact, the letter S." He looked up, and across the table at his
brother. "Joseph," he said, in an odd voice, "what does that
single letter S suggest to you?"

"Nothing," replied Mr. Mimms tersely.

"Samuel," suggested Mr. Shifnal, after profound mental
research. He saw an impatient frown on Mr. Liversedge's
brow, and corrected himself. "Swithin, I *should* say!"

"No, no, no!" exclaimed Mr. Liversedge testily. "Where
are your wits gone begging? Joseph, what, I ask you, are
these leaves?"

Mr. Mimms peered at the embroidery. "Leaves," he
said.

"Leaves! Yes, but what leaves?"

"Sam," said Mr. Mimms severely, "it's mops and brooms
with you, that's what it is! And if it was you as prigged a
bottle of good brandy from the tap-room, and me blaming
it on to Walter——"

"Joseph, cease trifling! These are strawberry leaves!"

134

"Very likely they may be, but what you've got to get into a passion for because the swell has strawberry——"

"Ignorant wretch!" said Mr. Liversedge, quite agitated. "Who but a Duke—stay, does not a Marquis also——? But we are not concerned with Marquises, and we need not waste time on that!"

"You're right, Joe," said Mr. Shifnal. "He *is* lushy! Now, don't you go a-working of yourself into a miff, Sam! No one won't waste any time on Markisses!"

"You are a fool!" said Mr. Liversedge. "These leaves stand in allusion to the rank of that greenhorn, and this letter S stands for Sale! That greenhorn was none other than his Grace the Duke of Sale—whom Joseph, by his folly in leaving this hovel to feed a herd of grunting swine, has let slip through his bungling fingers!"

Mr. Mimms and Mr. Shifnal sat staring at him in blank amazement. Mr. Mimms found his tongue first. "If you ain't lushy, Sam, you're dicked in the nob!" he said.

Mr. Liversedge paid no attention to him. A frown wrinkled his brow. "Wait!" he said. "Let us not leap too hurriedly to conclusions! Let me consider! Let me ponder this!"

Mr. Mimms showed no desire to leap to any other conclusion than that his relative had taken leave of his senses, and said so. He filled up his glass, and recommended Mr. Shifnal to do the same. For once, Mr. Shifnal did not respond to this invitation. He was watching Mr. Liversedge, quick speculation in his sharp face. When Mr. Mimms would have broken in rudely upon his brother's meditations, he hushed him, requesting him briefly to dub his mummer. "You let Sam be!" he said. "Up to every rig and row in town, he is!"

"To whom," demanded Mr. Liversedge, suddenly, "would young Ware turn in his dilemma? To his father? No! To his cousin, Joseph! To his noble and affluent cousin, the Duke of Sale! You saw him; you even conversed with him: was not his amiability writ large on his countenance? Would he spurn an indigent relative in his distress? He would not!"

"I don't know what he done to no relative," responded Mr. Mimms, "but I know what he done to you, Sam!"

Mr. Liversedge brushed this aside. "You are a sapskull," he said. "What he did to me was done for his cousin's sake. I bear him no ill-will: not the smallest ill-will! I am not a man of violence, but in his shoes I might have been tempted to do as he did. But we run on too fast! This is not proved. And yet—Joseph, it comes into my mind that he told me he was putting up at the White Horse, and this gives me to doubt. Would he do so if he were indeed the man I believe

135

him to be? One would say no. Again we go too fast! He did not wish to be known: a very understandable desire! For what must have been the outcome had he come to me in his proper person? What, Joseph, if a chaise with a ducal crest upon the panel had driven up to this door? What if a card had been handed to you bearing upon it the name and style of the Duke of Sale? What then?".

"I'd have gone and put my head under the pump, same as you ought to this very minute!" replied Mr. Mimms, without hesitation.

"Possibly! possibly! But I, Joseph, being a man of larger vision, would have raised my price! Very likely I would have demanded not five but ten thousand pounds from him. And so he knew!"

"Are you telling us, Sam, as that young greenhorn was a Dook?" asked Mr. Shifnal incredulously.

"Look at the handkerchief! And if Joseph had but stayed within the house——"

"If I'd have known he was a Dook, which sounds to me like a bag of moonshine anyways, I'd have had more sense than to meddle with him!" declared Mr. Mimms. "That would be the way to get dished-up, that would! Why, if I'd have bored in on him we'd have very likely gone to Rumbo, the pair of us! I dunno but what it wouldn't mean the Nubbing Cheat."

Mr. Liversedge sat staring before him, his ingenious mind at work. "I may be wrong. All men are fallible. It may be that I am right, however, and am I the man to let opportunity slide? That shall never be said of Swithin Liversedge! This matter must be sifted! But he may already have departed from this neighbourhood. He had recovered the fatal letters: what should keep him longer at such a hostelry as the White Horse?"

Mr. Shifnal shook his head. "Nothing wouldn't keep him any longer, Sam," he said.

Mr. Liversedge brought his gaze to bear on his friend's face. "Nothing," he said, in a damped tone. "I am bound to confess—No!" He sat up with a jerk. "Belinda!" he ejaculated. "Where else did she go but to the man whom she allowed—for aught I know encouraged!—to fly from this place, leaving her protector for dead upon the floor?"

"She'd lope off with anyone, she would," commented Mr. Mimms dispassionately. "You had only to get talking to her when you see her at Bath, and she up and loped off with you. An unaccountable game-pullet, she is!"

"It is my belief," said Mr. Liversedge, "that she has cast herself upon his generosity! She has appealed to his chivalry!

Will he thrust her away? will he refuse to aid her? He will not!"

"Not unless he's a bigger noddy than any I ever heard on," said Mr. Shifnal. "No one wouldn't thrust a wench like that away!"

"That," said Mr. Liversedge, "I knew the moment I clapped eyes on her! Nat, it may well be that he tarries at the inn, dallying with Belinda! For he will not, I fancy, take her to London. He is hedged about by those who would wrest her from him. Who should know if I do not how close a guard they keep about that young man? There is no coming near him, never was! I must go to Baldock in the morning!"

Mr. Mimms stared at him. "It won't fadge if you do," he said. "I'll allow I didn't take much account of him, for a proper greenhorn he looked to me, but he couldn't be such a goosecap as not to burn them letters he took off of you, Sam! You ain't got nothing left to do but to bite on the bridle."

Mr. Liversedge cast him a look of ineffable contempt. "If you, Joseph, had ever had one tenth of my vision you would not to-day be keeping a low thieves' ken!" he declared.

"That's the dandy!" retorted Mr. Mimms bitterly. "Go on! Insult poor Nat as never did you a mite of harm!"

Mr. Liversedge waved his hand. "I intend nothing personal," he said. "But the fact remains that you are a hick, Joseph! Those letters no longer interest me. If all is as I think it may be, there is a fortune in it! Let me but once ascertain that that young man was indeed the Duke of Sale; let Providence ordain that he has not yet driven away to the Metropolis; let me but hit upon some stratagem to get him into my hands, and we shall not regard the five thousand pounds I was once hopeful of acquiring as more than a flea-bite!"

Mr. Mimms could only look at him with dropping jaw, but Mr. Shifnal's sharp face grew sharper still. He watched Mr. Liversedge intently, and nodded, as though he understood. "Go on, Sam!" he encouraged him.

"I must have time to consider the matter," said Mr. Liversedge largely. "Several schemes are revolving in my head, but I would do nothing without due consideration. The first step must be to ascertain whether the young man is still to be found in Baldock. Joseph, I shall be requiring the cart to-morrow!"

"Sam," said Mr. Mimms, in a tone of great uneasiness,

"if so be as he is a Dook, you don't mean to go a-meddling with him?"

"Have no fear!" said Mr. Liversedge. "You, my dear brother, shall not beforgotten."

"I wish myself backt if I have anything to do with it!" declared Mr. Mimms violently. "I've kept this boozing-ken, and my father before me, and never any more trouble than would trouble a hen, but mix myself up with Dooks I won't! I'm an honest fence, I am, and I make a decent living, as you have cause to be thankful for; and Nat here will tell you I give him a fair price for any gewgaws he may happen to bring me, like this little lot—"

"Well—" temporized Mr. Shifnal. "I don't know as how I'd say—"

"As fair a price as any fence this side of London," said Mr. Mimms firmly. "And I don't have no harmen poking and prying round this ken, so that them as earns a living at the rattling-lay, or the lift, or the High Toby, can lay up here, and not fear no one! But meddle with no Dooks I will not, for, mark my words, if we was to lay so much as a finger on such as him, we should have them Bow Street Runners here before the cat can lick her ear!"

Mr. Shifnal was still thoughtfully watching Mr. Liversedge. "It's a good fish if it were but caught," he said slowly. "He's a well-blunted young cove, I daresay?"

"Able to buy an abbey!" Mr. Liversedge assured him.

"Well," said Mr. Shifnal, "I was meaning to lope off again, but what Joe says is the truth: a cull can lay up here, and no one the wiser. Maybe I'll lay up till I see which way the wind will blow. You get off to Baldock in the morning, Sam!"

This, in spite of his brother's protests, was what Mr. Liversedge did; but owing to the late hour to which he and Mr. Shifnal sat up, and the quantity of brandy they consumed, he did not make an early enough start to reach Baldock before the Duke and his small party had left it. After carefully reconnoitring the White Horse, and ascertaining that the Duke was not within sight, Mr. Liversedge walked boldly up to that hostelry, and entered the taproom. Here he encountered the tapster, who was engaged in wiping down the bar; and after passing the time of day with him, and consuming a glass of porter, he ventured to make some guarded enquiries. The tapster said: "If it's the gentleman in No. 1 you're meaning, he ain't here, nor that doxy what came a-looking for him neither. Gone off in a chaise to Hitchin not half an hour past. Rufford, his name was."

Mr. Liversedge did not wait for more. Draining his glass, and throwing down upon the table a coin wrested from his unwilling relative, he left the inn, and made haste back to Mr. Mimms's cart. His brain seethed with conjecture all the way back to the Bird in Hand, and when he reached that hostelry, he left Walter to stable the horse, and himself hurried up to his parlour. Mr. Shifnal and Mr. Mimms, who had been on the look-out for him, lost no time in following him. They found him pawing over the leaves of a well-thumbed volume. This work, published by Thomas Goddard of No. 1 Pall Mall, was entitled *A Biographical Index to the Present House of Lords,* and it constituted Mr. Liversedge's Bible. His hands almost trembled as he sought for Sale amongst the various entries. He found it at last, ran his eye down the opening paragraph, and uttered an exclamation of triumph. "I knew it!"

Mr. Shifnal peered over his shoulder, but not being a lettered man found the spelling out of the printed words a slow business. "What is it, Sam?" he asked.

"*Sale, Duke of,*" read out Mr. Liversedge in a voice of suppressed excitement. "*Names, Titles and Creations: The Most Noble Adolphus Gillespie Vernon Ware, Duke of Sale and Marquis of Ormesby (March 12th, 1692); Earl of Sale (August 9th, 1547); Baron Ware of Thame (May 2nd, 1538); Baron Ware of Stoven and Baron Ware of Rufford (June 14th, 1675)*—Baron Ware of Rufford, mark you! I thought my memory had not erred! And our young greenhorn, my masters, has been putting up at the White Horse under the name of Mr. Rufford! I can want no further proof!"

Even Mr. Mimms was impressed by this, but he reiterated his desire to have nothing to do with Dukes. His brother paid no heed to him, but fixed Mr. Shifnal with an unwinking stare, and demanded, in a rhetorical spirit, to be told why the Duke had gone to Hitchin. Neither of his hearers was able to enlighten him, nor, after profound thought, could he discover for himself any very plausible explanation. But since Hitchin, as he unanswerably declared, could not be said to lie on the road to London, he soon decided not to allow this trifling enigma to worry him. The Duke had directed the post-boy to drive to the Sun Inn, where it would seem reasonable to suppose that he meant to spend at least one night. His taking Belinda with him precluded the possibility, Mr. Liversedge thought, of his having gone to visit friends in the neighbourhood.

Mr. Mimms, whose uneasiness was rapidly increasing, brought his fist down with a crash on the table, and demanded to be told what his brother had in mind. Mr. Liversedge glanced at him indifferently. "If Nat is willing to lend me his assistance," he replied, "I consider that it would be flying in the face of Providence not to make a push to capture this prize."

Mr. Shifnal nodded, but said: "How much money is there in it, by your reckoning?"

Mr. Liversedge shrugged. "How can I say? Thirty thousand—fifty thousand—almost any sum, I daresay!"

Mr. Shifnal's eyes glistened. "Will the cove bleed as free as that?" he asked, awed.

"He is one of the richest men in the land," responded Mr. Liversedge. "I have devoted much study to his affairs, for it has always seemed to me that for a young and inexperienced man to be the possessor of so large a fortune was a circumstance not to be overlooked or hastily set aside. But even so brilliant an exponent of the art of plucking pigeons as Fred Gunnerside—a genius in his way, I assure you, and one of whom I am not to proud to learn—has never to my knowledge succeeded in coming within hailing distance of him. In fact, poor Fred was sadly out of pocket on his account, for he expended quite a large sum of money in following him on the Continent. All to no purpose! He was closely attended, not only by his servants, but by a military gentleman to whom Fred took a strong dislike. I myself had abandoned any thought of approaching him, until my late little disagreement with the magistrates at Bath forced me to sharpen my wits. I again turned my mind towards Sale. I flatter myself that my research into his family history, and every circumstance of his own life, was at once thorough and profitable. To have laid a snare for his cousin was a subtle stroke, and one that must have succeeded but for a slight error which I freely admit to have made."

Unable to contain himself Mr. Mimms growled: "That after-clap won't be nothing compared with what will happen if you meddle any more with a Dook! I tell you, Sam, the glue won't hold!"

"It might," Mr. Shifnal said. "It might, Joe. By God, if there's thirty thousand pounds in the game, it's worth a push! Is it ransom you have in your mind, Sam?"

It was evident from the visionary look in his eye that large ideas were fast gaining possession over Mr. Liversedge's brain. He replied grandly: "I might consider the question of ransom. And yet who shall say that there may not be a still more profitable way of turning this Duke to good account? Had either of you ever looked beyond the narrow confines of the bare existence which you eke out in ways which I, frankly, consider contemptible, you would know that this Duke is an orphan, and one, moreover, who has neither brother nor sister to bear him company. His guardian, and, indeed, his present heir, is his uncle." He paused. "I have considered the question of approaching Lord Lionel Ware, and it may be that this is the course I shall decide to pursue. One cannot, however one might wish to, doubt that Lord Lionel—a very worthy gentleman, I daresay—is too stiff-necked, or possibly too bacon-brained to perceive where his best interests lie. He might, one would have supposed, have found the means in all these years to have disposed of his nephew, had he had the least common-sense. I am forced, therefore, to assume that for the particular purpose I have in mind, his lordship would be of little or no assistance to me. But his lordship has a son." He paused impressively. "A son, gentlemen, who stands next to him in the succession to a title and to vast wealth. I am not myself acquainted with this young man: it did not appear to me that there could be much profit in seeking him out. But the horizon has broadened suddenly. Immense possibilities present themselves to me. This Captain Ware is in the Lifeguards: I daresay an expensive young man: all guard-officers are so! What, I put it to you, might he be willing to pay to a man who would ensure his succession to wealth and honours which it would be idle to suppose he does not covet? Consider his position!—In fact, the more I consider it myself the more convinced do I become that in seeking merely a ransom I should be acting foolishly. He exists upon a paltry pittance; the future can hold little for him beyond an arduous military career; for he cannot doubt that his cousin will shortly marry, and beget heirs of his own body. He must think his chances of succeeding to the Dukedom so slim as not to be worth a farthing. Picture to yourselves what must be his sensations when suddenly a way is shown to him whereby he can be rid of his cousin, without the least suspicion falling upon himself! Really, I do not know why I permitted myself to waste as much as a moment on such a paltry notion as a mere ransom!"

Mr. Shifnal, who had followed this speech with some difficulty, interrupted at this point. "Sam, are you saying as you mean to put that young cove away?" he demanded.

"That," said Mr. Liversedge, "must rest with Captain Ware."

"I won't have nothing to do with it!" said Mr. Mimms forcibly. "I got nothing to say against putting away coves as won't be missed, but putting away a Dook is coming it

141

too strong, and that's my last word! Mark my words, Sam, you'll catch cold at this!"

Mr. Shifnal stroked his chin. "I'm bound to say it seems like a havey-cavey business to me," he admitted. "But there's no denying Sam's got big notions in his head, and it don't do to let a fortune go a-begging. I'll allow this Dook is a regular honey-fall, and if you don't want your earnest out of fifty thousand pounds, and very likely more, if Sam works the trick proper, as I don't doubt he will, it'll be the first time I ever knew you to hang back, Joe Mimms! But though I sees as the game's in view, it don't do to act hasty. This Dook of yours, Sam, by what you tells us, has a sight of servants and suchlike hanging about him, and it ain't to be looked for that they don't know he's in Baldock. If we goes a-putting on him away quiet, what's to say we won't have the whole pack of them—ah, and the Runners as well!— nosing around these parts a-looking for him? Joe wouldn't want for them to come poking into his ken——"

Mr. Mimms, who had been containing himself by a strong effort, here interposed to corroborate this reading of his state of mind with all the eloquence at his command. Mr. Liversedge waited patiently until he paused for breath, and then said: "Very true, Nat, very true! I had myself given some thought to this matter. It is my belief that the Duke has escaped from his household, and that no one knows where he is to be found. You ask me why? For several reasons! If he had divulged his purpose in coming here, there must have been many persons who would have thought it their duty to prevent him. If he had not left town secretly, depend upon it he could never have shaken off those of his servants who invariably accompany him on any journey that he undertakes. I well remember poor Fred Gunnerside's very moving words on this very point. The young man is surrounded by a set of elderly men who seem all of them to be devoted to his interests to a degree which one must consider to be excessive. No, I am strongly of the opinion that the Duke has taken this journey unbeknownst to anyone. Very likely he looks upon it as an adventure: young men are apt to take such fancies into their heads."

Mr. Shifnal, with the vision of untold wealth dazzling him, was not hard to convince; Mr. Mimms continued however to be inimical to the project, and it was long before he could be brought to view the matter in a reasonable light. His companions wrought with him for quite an hour before he could even be induced to lend his cart for the journey to Hitchin: indeed, only the reflection that if he refused to enter into the plot he would forfeit all right to a share of the reward caused him grudgingly to pledge a measure of support. The other two then laid their heads together, reaching certain decisions, prominent amongst them being one that Mr. Liversedge should remain as much as possible in the background, leaving Mr. Shifnal, who was unknown to the Duke, to undertake the preliminary encounter.

CHAPTER XIII

THE Duke, serenely unconscious of the design being hatched against him, occupied himself for the greater part of the drive to Hitchin in coaching his young companions in the rôles he had decided they had better assume. He had no desire to run the gauntlet of any more criticism from innkeepers and servants, and he realized that the presence of a beautiful and unattended young lady in his company would need some explanation. The best explanation that offered itself to him was that Tom and Belinda, once more brother and sister, should be travelling to visit friends, under the escort of Tom's tutor, and, of course, Belinda's maid, who must have contracted some illness on the road, and been left behind. The idea of having Mr. Rufford for a tutor struck Tom as so irresistibly humorous, that for some time he would do nothing but giggle; but when he had recovered a little he bethought him that as Hitchin was uncomfortably close to Shefford, where he had escaped from his real tutor, it would be best for him to adopt some name other than his own. He and Belinda thereafter beguiled the tedium of the journey by quarrelling over the various names that suggested themselves to them. A compromise had barely been reached by the time the chaise drove up to the Sun Inn.

The landlord of the Sun accepted the Duke's story with only faint surprise. Possibly the sotto voce altercation which was still going on between Tom and Belinda helped him to believe that they were indeed brother and sister. The Duke bespoke a private parlour, and was just congratulating himself on having cleared the first of his fences, when Tom, who had wandered off to confer with one of the ostlers, came running in with the news that a Fair had come to Hitchin, with a performing bear, a Fat Woman, a dwarf, and all manner of attractions from pony-racing to bobbing for oranges. No sooner had she heard this than Belinda clapped her hands, and, turning her sparkling eyes upon the Duke, begged him to take her there, since never in her life had she been allowed to visit a Fair. It was in vain that the Duke reminded her of their errand in Hitchin; she

143

cared nothing for Maggie Street while she could dance for ribands, or watch the sterner sex wrestling for a cheese. Tom added his voice to hers. "Oh, pray let us go, sir! It is a splendid Fair, the ostler says, with matches at singlestick, and jumping in sacks, and a grand firework display when it is dark! And we are quite safe here, because, only fancy, the ostler said there had been a stout gentleman here searching for me, and of course that was Snape! At least, the ostler didn't say it was for me, because he did not know *that*, only I could tell. And the best of it is that he did not find me here, and so now he has gone, and why should he come back? It is a famous fudge!"

The Duke was quite unable to resist the pleading looks of his protégés, and very weakly agreed to let them visit the Fair while he pursued a strict search for Maggie Street. He enjoined Tom to take care of Belinda, and not to fail to return to the Sun in time for dinner at five o'clock; and allowed them to go.

The rest of the day was spent, as far as he was concerned, in a singularly profitless fashion. He was quite unable to discover any trace of Maggie Street; and when he returned to the inn to dine, he was obliged to hire a room there for Belinda, alleging as the reason that the friends to whom he had said he was escorting her were all too full of measles to admit her into the house. After that it soon became apparent to him that if he wished to see his young friends at the dinner-table he would have to plunge into the hurly-burly of the Fair to find them. He was feeling rather too tired to be amused by the noise and the fun there, and was forced to admit to himself that amongst the advantages of rank must be reckoned an immunity from being jostled by merrymakers who all seemed to be very much too hot, and by far too friendly. He found Belinda watching a blindfold-wheelbarrow-race, in which Tom was taking part for the guerdon of a whalebone whip. She was sucking a large lollipop, and closely attended by two rustic swains, who seemed to be acting as porters, since they carried a motley collection of ribbons, oranges, sweetmeats, and toys, which they made haste to deliver up to her as soon as the Duke joined the party. Belinda thanked them sweetly, and informed the Duke that she was enjoying herself very much, her only disappointment having been the disagreeable behaviour of Tom, who had offered to draw the cork of a kind gentleman who would have taken her into one of the booths to witness a theatrical performance.

"Belinda," said Gilly patiently, "you must not—indeed,

144

you must not!—go off with strange men just because they promise you silk dresses, or some such thing!"

"He didn't," replied Belinda, opening her eyes wide. "It was to see a play."

"Yes, that is what I mean."

"Oh!" said Belinda, thoughtfully licking her lollipop.

The Duke could not feel that he had made much impression on her, but as her attention had become fixed on the closing stage of the race it was plainly of no use to persevere. She did not seem to bear Tom any ill-will, for as soon as it was apparent that he would win the blindfold race she dropped all her fairings to clap her hands in delight. He soon came over to them, brandishing the whip, and with his face smeared with the treacle which had coated a number of buns hung on strings for which competitors had been expected to bob. He said that it was the jolliest day of his life, and that he would come back to the inn as soon as he had collected his various purchases and prizes.

"And we may come back to see the fireworks, may we not?" he begged.

"Yes, yes, and the dancing!" cried Belinda, clasping her hands ecstatically.

With two pairs of imploring eyes fixed on him, the Duke found himself quite unable to say no, much as he would have liked to. He had seen many firework displays, and had not the smallest desire to see this one. He was tired from walking about the town in the search for Mrs. Street; and he disliked crowds. He realized, with a slight feeling of shame, that between himself and Mr. Dash of Nowhere in Particular there were several points of difference. He told himself that he was by far too nice in his tastes, and did his best to respond to Tom's suggestion with becoming enthusiasm. Tom then darted away to retrieve his prizes, and the Duke drew Belinda's hand through his arm, and led her out of the Fair-ground, towards the inn. Neither of them noticed the unobtrusive figure of Mr. Shifnal; and this sapient gentleman took care never to place himself in the line of Belinda's vision.

Upon reaching the Sun Inn, they found that the usual bustle attendant upon a private chaise's arrival was in full swing. An elegant chaise-and-four had pulled up to change horses, and the fresh team was just being led out of the stable. Belinda, fondly clasping the Duke's arm with both hands, gazed wistfully at this equipage, and said that she wished she might travel in a chaise-and-four, clad in a silk gown, and with a ring upon her finger. The Duke could not help laughing a little at what appeared to be the sum of her ambitions, but there was such a sad note in her voice that he was impelled to pat one of the little hands on his arm. Fortunately for his peace of mind, he was uninterested in the post-chaise, and did not so much as glance at its occupants, so that he failed to observe the strange effect the sight of himself had upon them. They were two ladies, one a stout dowager, the other a smart young woman, with crimped curls, and a high complexion, who no sooner clapped eyes on the Duke than she gave a gasp, and exclaimed: "Mama! Sale! Look!"

The dowager began to deliver a reproof to her daughter on the hoydenish nature of her behaviour in bouncing up in her seat, but the words died on her lips as she brought her hawk-like gaze to bear upon the Duke and his fair companion. "Well!" she ejaculated, her pale eyes showing an alarming tendency to start from their sockets.

The Duke and Belinda passed into the inn. "Well!" said Lady Boscastle again. "I would not have credited it! Not two days after that notice in the *Gazette!*"

Miss Boscastle giggled. "Poor dear Harriet! I wonder if she knows of this? Did ever you see such a lovely creature, Mama? *Poor* dear Harriet."

"One can only trust," said Lady Boscastle obscurely, "that it will be a lesson to Augusta Ampleforth, with her odious pretensions. I always said, and I always shall say that Sale was entrapped into it, for I am sure no man would look twice at Harriet, for she is nothing out of the ordinary; indeed, a squab little figure of a girl, and with far too much reserve in her manner. What a shocking thing it would be if Sale were to declare off now!"

Both ladies dwelled beatifically for some moments on this thought. Miss Boscastle said inconsequently: "Well, we shall be seeing Harriet in Bath, Mama, for she is gone to stay with old Lady Ampleforth, you know."

By this time the change of horses had been effected, and the chaise was on the move again, before Lady Boscastle had time to prosecute any enquiries at the Sun Inn. She resettled herself in the corner of the chaise, remarking that she hoped Harriet would not be found to be putting on airs to be interesting, and that Augusta Ampleforth would be all the better for a sharp set-down.

Meanwhile, the Duke and Belinda had mounted the stairs to his private parlour, and Belinda had cast off her bonnet, and run her fingers through her luxuriant ringlets, saying, with a grateful look at her protector: "I am so very glad you took me away from Mr. Liversedge, sir! I wish you was my guardian! I am so happy!"

He was too much touched to point out to her the slight inaccuracy contained in this speech. "My poor child, I wish indeed that you had some guardian to take care of you! Or that I could find your friend, Mrs. Street. But I have enquired at the receiving-office, and at upwards of twenty shops, and no one can give me the least intelligence of her. In fact, the only Street living in Hitchin is an old man, who is stone deaf, and knows nothing of your Maggie! Can you not——"

He was interrupted. Belinda broke into a peal of merry laughter. "Oh, but she is not Mrs. Street!" she told him. "How came you to think she was, dear sir? She was Maggie Street when she worked at Mrs. Buttermere's establishment, but then, you know, she was married!"

For one horrifying moment, the Duke recognized in himself an affinity with Mr. Liversedge, who had boxed Belinda's ears. Then the absurdity of it most forcibly struck him, and he began to laugh. Belinda regarded him in faint surprise, and Tom, entering the room at that moment, instantly demanded to be told what the jest might be.

The Duke shook his head. "Nothing! Tom, if you would please me, go and wash your face!"

"I was just about to do so," said Tom, with great dignity, and even greater mendacity. "By Jupiter, I never wanted my dinner more! I am quite gutfoundered!"

On this elegant expression, he vanished, leaving the Duke to ask Belinda, in a failing voice, if she knew what her friend's surname might now be. He was by this time sufficiently well acquainted with Belinda to feel no surprise at her reply.

"Oh, no! I daresay she may have told me, but I did not attend particularly, you know, for why should I?"

"Then what," demanded Gilly, "are we to do?"

He had no very real expectation of receiving an answer to this question, but Belinda, assuming an expression of profound thought, suddenly said: "Well, do you know, sir, I think I would as lief marry Mr. Mudgley after all?"

The introduction into his life of this entirely new character slightly staggered the Duke. He said: "Who, Belinda, is Mr. Mudgley?"

Belinda's eyes grew soft with memory. "He is a *very* kind gentleman," she sighed.

"I am sure he is," agreed the Duke. "Did he promise you a purple silk gown?"

"No," said Belinda mournfully, "but he took me to see

147

his farm, and his mother, driving me in his *own* gig! And he said he was wishful to marry me, only Uncle Swithin told me I should go away with him, and be a real lady, and so of course I went."

"Of course," said the Duke. "Did you know Mr. Mudgley when you lived in Bath?"

"Oh, yes! And he has the prettiest house, and his mother was kind to me, and now I am sorry that I went with Uncle Swithin, for Mr. Ware didn't marry me, and he didn't give me a great deal of money either. I was quite taken in!"

Here the door opened to admit both Tom and the waiter. While the latter laid the covers for dinner, Tom plunged into an animated account of his activities at the Fair, and displayed for the Duke's admiration the Belcher handkerchief he had won in the sack race. He was with difficulty deterred from knotting this about his neck at once. The waiter set the dishes on the table, and withdrew, and the Duke was again able to touch upon the question of Belinda's destination. He asked her if Mr. Mudgley lived near Bath. She replied, after her usual fashion: "Oh, yes!" but seemed unable to supply any more detailed information. Tom, surprised, demanded enlightenment, and upon being told that Belinda had forgotten Maggie Street's married name, said disgustedly: "You are the most hen-witted girl! I daresay she don't live at Hitchin at all, but at Ditchling, or—or Mitcham, or some such place!"

Belinda looked much struck, and said ingenuously: "Yes, she does!"

The Duke was in the act of conveying a portion of braised ham to his mouth, but he lowered his fork at this, and demanded, "Which?"

"The one Tom said," replied Belinda brightly.

"My dear child, he said Ditchling or Mitcham! Surely——"

"Well, I am not quite sure," Belinda confessed. "It was some place that sounded like those."

The prospect of travelling about England to every place that sounded faintly like Hitchin was not one which the Duke found himself able to contemplate for as much as a minute. He said rather fatalistically: "Mr. Mudgley it must be!"

"Yes, but I dare not go back to Bath," objected Belinda. "Because, you know, if Mrs. Pilling were to find me she would very likely put me in prison for having broken my indentures."

The Duke had no very clear idea of what the laws were governing apprentices, but it had occurred to him that in Bath he would find Lady Harriet. She might not be the bride of his choosing, but she was one of the friends of his childhood, and never in any childish exploit had she failed to lend him a helping hand whenever it had lain in her power to do so. That she might not feel much inclination to extend this hand to Belinda he did not consider. It seemed to him that since he had been forced into the position of Belinda's protector, and could not find it in his heart to abandon her, he must find for her (failing Mr. Mudgley) a suitable chaperon. He could think of none more suitable than Harriet, and he began to feel that he had been a great simpleton not to have carried Belinda to Bath at the outset.

Tom interrupted these meditations with a demand to know whether the proposed trip to Bath would preclude his being taken to London. If, he said, that were so, he thought he should be well-advised to leave the party, and to make his own way either to London, or to some likely sea-port. As it was obvious that the merest hint of returning him to his parent would drive him into precipitate flight, the Duke refrained from making this suggestion, but assured him that although he must certainly write to Mr. Mamble from Bath, he should beg to be allowed the pleasure of his son's company on a visit to the Metropolis. Tom seemed a little doubtful about this, but allowed himself to be overborne. Belinda reiterated her fear of Mrs. Pilling, and the Duke wondered whether his Harriet would also be able to deal with this awe-inspiring lady. He was just about to say that he would hire a post-chaise to take them all to Cheyney on the morrow, when it suddenly occurred to him that his arrival at any one of his houses, accompanied by Belinda, would give rise to more scandalous comment than he felt at all able to face. He decided to seek out the quietest inn in Bath, and to lose no time in calling upon Harriet, in Laura Place.

While he and his young friends were eating their dinners, Mr. Liversedge and Mr. Shifnal were taking counsel together. Mr. Shifnal's suggestion that Mr. Liversedge should also hire a room at the Sun, and should smother the Duke in his bed at dead of night, was ill-received by his partner, who demanded to know how that could serve any good purpose. He said that even supposing that Mr. Shifnal were there to give his assistance it was hardly to be supposed that they could smuggle out of a busy inn an unconscious guest. Mr. Shifnal, a little damped, was still trying to think out an alternative scheme when the Duke's party issued forth from the inn, and began walking in the direction of the Fair-ground. Protected by the tilt of the cart, the con-

149

federates watched them go, and could scarcely believe their good fortune.

"Sam," said Mr. Shifnal, "if we can't nabble that Dook while everyone's watching the fireworks we don't deserve no thirty thousand pounds!"

The Fair, when the Duke reached it again, was the scene of even denser crowds than it had been during the daylight hours. All the shopkeepers of Hitchin seemed to have thronged there, and although the open-air competitions were over, the various booths were packed with people, either staring at some monstrosity, or taking part in wrestling, boxing, or single-stick bouts. A large prize was offered to any sportsman able to knock out a professional bruiser with a broken nose and a cauliflower ear, and it was with difficulty that the Duke dissuaded Tom from instantly throwing his hat into the Ring. He took him instead to witness a stirring drama, entitled *Monk and Murderer! or The Skeleton Spectre,* which gave both him and Belinda the maximum amount of fearful enjoyment. Belinda was obliged to cling tightly to the Duke's arm from the moment of the Mysterious Monk's first appearance in Scene 2 (The Rocks of Calabria), to the Grand Combat with Shield and Battle-Axe in Scene 6, but upon being asked rather anxiously if she liked the piece, nodded her head very vigorously, and heaved a tremulous sigh.

When this stirring drama came to an end, the last daylight had faded, and the Fair-ground was lit by flares and cressets. The crowd was wending its way towards the open space where the fireworks were to be let off. The Duke, with Belinda still hanging on his arm, joined the general throng, and managed to secure good places for her and Tom on one of the forms set up in tiers round the field. He gave up his own place to a stout and panting dame, who sank thankfully down beside Belinda. With this bulwark on one side of his charge, and Tom on the other, the Duke thought that he might safely relax his vigilance, and retire from the crowd. He made his way between the forms to the back of the field, and was idly watching the struggles of determined citizens to push their way to the fore when a respectful voice said softly, yet with urgency, a little behind him: "My lord Duke!"

Instinctively he looked round. A neat man in a sober riding-dress, who had something of the look of a head-groom, touched his hat to him, and said: "I ask your Grace's pardon for intruding, but I have a message for your Grace."

Without giving himself time to consider that his cousin could not possibly have received the letter he had posted to him in Baldock that morning, the Duke leaped to the conclusion that the neat man must have come to him from Gideon. There was nothing at all alarming in Mr. Shifnal's appearance: indeed, he ascribed much of his success to his respectable air. The depth of his bow was exactly as it should have been; his manner was a nice mixture of deference and the assurance of a trusted personal servant. He glanced deprecatingly at the persons within easy earshot, and moved suggestively in the direction of one of the tents that were dotted about the edge of the field. The Duke followed him. "Well?" he said. "What do you want with me?"

"I beg your Grace's pardon," Mr. Shifnal said again, "but I was told—by your Grace perhaps knows who—to deliver my message into your Grace's private ear."

The Duke was a little amused, but still unsuspicious. Gideon must be hard-pressed, he thought, to have sent to him. Possibly Lord Lionel had arrived in London, and was threatening to cut his son off with a shilling unless he divulged his cousin's whereabouts. Mr. Shifnal was standing in the deep shadow cast by the now deserted tent; the first of the rockets went up in a glorious burst of stars; the Duke came up to Mr. Shifnal, and repeated: "Well, what do you want?"

He did not feel the blow that struck him down, for Mr. Liversedge, sliding out of the murk behind him, was leaving nothing to chance. The Duke dropped where he stood; and Mr. Liversedge, thrusting his cudgel out of sight under the tent-wall, instantly bent over him in an attitude of tender solicitude. A man, who had been staring up at the bursting rocket, glanced over his shoulder, and Mr. Liversedge at once called peremptorily to Mr. Shifnal: "You, sir! Would you have the goodness to assist me to carry my nephew to my carriage? He has fainted from this excessive heat and these crowds! My sister's son: a very delicate young man! I told him how it would be, but these young sparks! They will never listen to older and wiser heads!"

The stranger watching the fireworks at once drew near, offering his aid. Mr. Liversedge thanked him profusely, and agreed that the poor young man did indeed look pale. "Sickly from birth!" he confided. "I have known him to swoon for as much as an hour on end! But I beg you will not put yourself to the trouble of coming with me! This gentleman will perhaps help me to my carriage: ah, I thank you, sir!"

Mr. Shifnal, who had picked up the Duke's hat and malacca cane, here joined his confederate, and offered to take the poor gentleman's legs. One or two people began to be interested in what was going on, but Mr. Liversedge was spared the trouble of repeating his story by the first gentleman, who very kindly retailed it for him. While he was doing this, Mr. Liversedge and Mr. Shifnal made haste to remove the Duke to where they had left Mr. Mimms's cart, outside the field. A particularly fine display of pyrotechnics diverted the attention of those who had shown faint interest in the Duke's swoon, and as he and his bearers had disappeared from view when they again had leisure to look round they troubled themselves no further in the matter.

The Duke's inanimate body was soon hoisted into the back of the cart, and laid upon the boards. Mr. Liversedge scrambled in beside him, adjuring Mr. Shifnal to make haste and drive off before any meddling busybody could come poking and prying. He slid his hand under the Duke's coat, feeling for his heart, and was relieved to feel it beating. He was not, as he had told his friend, a man of violence, and he had suffered quite a horrid revulsion of feeling when the Duke had gone down under the blow of his cudgel. He decided, privately, that if it should become necessary to dispose of the Duke someone other than himself would have to undertake that task: probably Nat, who had little sensibility, and none of the gentlemanly qualms that troubled his friend.

CHAPTER XIV

UPON the morning of the Duke's departure from London, Captain Ware was awakened by the sound of altercation outside his door. Ex-Sergeant Wragby's voice was raised in indignant refusal to allow anyone to enter his master's room; and he was freely accusing the unknown intruder of being as drunk as an artillery-man. Captain Ware then heard Nettlebed's voice, sharpened by fright, and he grinned. He had enjoined Wragby, who had been his trusted servant for several years, not to mention the Duke's presence in Albany the previous evening to anyone, and as his batman had not been on duty he had no fear of the information's leaking out. He linked his hands behind his head, and awaited events.

"You looby, if you don't stand out of my way you'll get one in the bread-basket as'll send you to grass!" said Nettlebed fiercely.

"Ho!" retorted Wragby. "Ho, I will, will I? If it's a bit of home-brewed you're wanting, you herring-gutted, blubber-headed clunch, put up your mawleys!"

Captain Ware thought it time to intervene, and called: "Wragby! What the devil's all this kick-up?"

His door burst open unceremoniously, and Wragby and Nettlebed entered locked in one another's arms.

"See the Captain I must and will!" panted Nettlebed.

"Sir! here's his Grace's man, as drunk as a brewer's horse, and not nine o'clock in the morning!" said Wragby, in virtuous wrath.

"How monstrous!" said Gideon. "Nettlebed, how dare you?"

Nettlebed succeeded in wrenching himself free from Wragby's grip. "You know well I don't touch liquor, Master Gideon!" he said angrily. "Nor this isn't the time for any of your tricks! Sir, his Grace never came home last night!"

Gideon yawned. "Turning Methodist, Nettlebed?"

Wragby gave a snigger. This exasperated Nettlebed into saying hotly: "Think shame to yourself, Master Gideon, a-casting such aspersions upon his Grace! Don't you go saying as he takes up with bits of muslin, for he don't and never has! His Grace left his house yesterday morning, and he hasn't been seen since!"

"Ah, slipped his leash, has he?" said Gideon.

Nettlebed stared at him. "Slipped his leash? I don't know what you mean, sir!"

"Bring my shaving-water, Wragby, will you?" said Gideon. "I mean, Nettlebed, that I'm surprised he hasn't done it before. And why you should come to me——"

"Master Gideon, the only hope I had was that his Grace maybe spent the night here!"

"Well, he didn't. Nor do I know where he is. I daresay he will return in his own good time."

"Sir," said Nettlebed, staring at him in horror, "never did I think to hear you, as was always the first to have a care to his Grace, speak in such a way!"

"You fool, how should I speak? His Grace is not a child, for all you and that precious crew he has about him treat him as though he were! I hope it may be a lesson to you, for how he has borne it all these years I know not!"

"Master Gideon, have you thought that his Grace may have been murdered?" Nettlebed demanded.

"I have not. His Grace is very well able to take care of himself."

Nettlebed wrung his hands. "Never in all the years I've served him has he done such a thing! Oh, Master Gideon, I blame myself, I do indeed! I should never have allowed myself to take offence at what—— But how could I tell—— And he went out, not telling Borrowdale when he meant to come back, and we waited, and waited, and never a sign of him! Borrowdale, and Chigwell, and Turvey, and me, we

153

were sitting up all night, not knowing what to think, nor what to do! Then I thought as how he might have been with you, and I came round on the instant! Master Gideon, what am I to do?"

"You will go back to Sale House, and you will wait until his Grace returns, as he no doubt will do," replied Gideon. "And when he does return, Nettlebed, see to it that you do not drive him into flight again! You, and Borrowdale, and Chigwell, and Turvey—and a dozen others! My cousin is a man, not a schoolboy, and you have so bullied him between you——"

"Bullied him!" exclaimed Nettlebed, his voice breaking. "Master Gideon, I would lay down my life for his Grace!"

"Very likely, and much good would that do him!" said Gideon. He sat up. "Now you may listen to me!" he said sternly, and read his cousin's stricken henchman a short, telling lecture.

If Nettlebed attended to it, he gave no sign of having done so. He said distractedly: "If only he has not been set upon by footpads! I should go round to Bow Street, perhaps, only that I do not like——"

"If you do that," said Gideon strongly, "neither his Grace nor my father would ever forgive you! For God's sake, man, stop flying into a pucker for nothing!"

"It is not nothing to me, sir," Nettlebed said. "I am sure I ask your pardon for having disturbed you, but it did seem to me that his Grace would have told you—or come to you—but if he did not, then I am wasting my time, and I will go, Captain Ware, sir!"

"Good!" said Gideon heartlessly. "And strive to bear in mind that his Grace is more than twenty-four years old!"

Nettlebed cast him a look of reproach, and left him. Wragby, returning with a jug of hot water, said: "He'll set 'em all by the ears, he will, sir, you mark my words! If he don't have the Runners called out it'll be a wonder!"

"He won't do that."

Wragby shook his head. "Fair set-about he is! I couldn't help compassionating him."

"He wants a lesson," replied Gideon. "This should do them all good!"

Nettlebed, speeding back to Sale House, found that Mr. Scriven had arrived there, and, upon learning that nothing had been heard of the Duke since the previous morning, looked very grave, and said that Lord Lionel should instantly be informed. Chigwell then had the happy notion of running round to White's, to enquire of the porter if his Grace had been seen in the club. The porter said that he had not set eyes on the Duke since he had dined at the club with Lord Gaywood, and, perceiving Chigwell seemed strangely chagrined, asked what had happened to put him so much out of countenance. At any ordinary time, Chigwell would have treated this curiosity in a dignified and quelling way, but his anxiety, coupled with a sleepless night, had robbed him of his poise. He told the porter that he feared his Grace had met with an accident, or fallen a victim to footpads. The porter was suitably shocked and sympathetic, and was soon in possession of all the facts of the story. Chigwell, recollecting himself, said that he was so much worried he hardly knew what he was about, but felt sure that he could trust the porter not to mention the matter. The porter assured him that he was not one to blab; and upon Chigwell's departure, told one of the waiters that it looked like the young Duke of Sale had been murdered. He then asked every member who entered the club if he had heard the news of his Grace of Sale's disappearance, so that in a remarkably short space of time a formidable number of persons were discussing the strange story, some taking the view that there was nothing in it, some postulating theories to account for the Duke's disappearance, and others offering odds on the nature of his fate.

Chigwell, returning to Sale House, found that Captain Belper had called there in the hope of finding the Duke at home, and had of course been regaled by the porter with the story of his strange disappearance. He listened to it, at first with incredulity, and then with a look of dismay. In an agitated voice, he requested the agent-in-chief's presence. When Scriven joined him in one of the smaller saloons on the ground floor of the mansion, he found him pacing the floor in great perturbation of spirit. Upon the agent's entrance, he wheeled about, and said without preamble: "Scriven, this news has disturbed me prodigiously! I believe I may hold the answer to the enigma!"

"Then I beg, sir," said the agent calmly, "that you will tell me what it may be, for I must consider myself to be in some measure responsible for his Grace's well-being, and—I must add—safety."

"Scriven," said Captain Belper impressively, "I was with the Duke when he purchased, at Manton's, a pair of duelling pistols!"

They stared at one another, incredulity in Scriven's face, a certain dramatic satisfaction in the Captain's.

"I cannot believe that his Grace had become embroiled

155

in any quarrel," at last pronounced Scriven. "Much less in a quarrel of such a nature as you suggest, sir."

"Were those pistols delivered at this house?" demanded the Captain. "And if they were so delivered, *where are they*, Scriven?"

There was a pause, while the agent appeared to consider the matter. Then he bowed slightly, and said: "Give me leave, sir, and I will investigate this matter."

"Do so!" begged the Captain. "For my heart much misgives me! I remember that I cracked some idle jest to the Duke, when he bought the pair! God forgive me, I had no suspicion, not an inkling, that my words might be striking home!"

Mr. Scriven, who had no taste for the dramatic, refrained from comment, and left the room. He returned a few minutes later, and said gravely: "I cannot admit that the very serious suggestion you have made, sir, may be correct, but I am obliged to own to you that a package was indeed delivered at this house yesterday, and that his Grace——" he paused, and regarded his finger-nails. "And that his Grace," he resumed, in an expressionless tone, "appears to have taken its contents with him."

Captain Belper clapped a hand to his brow, ejaculating: "Good God!" He took a pace or two about the room. "He did not confide his purpose to me!" he said. "Had he done so—— Yet it struck me that he was not himself! There was something of constraint in his manner. And then his avoidance of a further meeting with me! Ah, I see it now, too late! He feared that I, knowing him as well as I flatter myself I do, must have divined his terrible purpose. Scriven, if any mischance has befallen the Duke I dare not hold myself guiltless!"

"I do not anticipate, sir, that his Grace left his house with any such purpose in mind," said Mr. Scriven precisely. "And if it were so, I would suggest that his skill with all manner of firearms would make it more likely that a mischance should have befallen his adversary."

"Very true!" the Captain said, much struck. "It was, after all, I who taught him that skill! And yet how daunting is the thought that you now present to me! Can it be that the Duke has killed his man, and fled the country to escape arrest?"

Mr. Scriven, who, in common with most of the Duke's dependants, cordially disliked Captain Belper, was extremely loth to admit the possibility of any of his theories being correct, but it was evident from his sudden look of consternation that this suggestion carried weight with him.

After a moment, he said: "I prefer not to consider such a shocking event, sir!"

"Lord Lionel should be instantly apprised!" declared the Captain, smiting his fist into the palm of his other hand.

Mr. Scriven bowed. "I have already sent one of my clerks with a letter for his lordship, sir."

"Post, I do trust!" the Captain said swiftly.

"Certainly, sir."

"Then there is little one can do until his lordship comes to town, as I make no doubt he will do. Yet some enquiries might be made with advantage. I shall at once repair to Captain Ware's chambers."

Mr. Scriven was then able to inform him, with a certain amount of satisfaction, that Nettlebed had already called in Albany, and that Captain Ware disclaimed all knowledge of the Duke's whereabouts. When Chigwell came in, to report that his visit to White's Club had been equally abortive, there seemed to be nothing left for the Captain to do. He did indeed mention the propriety of summoning the Bow Street Runners to their aid, but was speedily snubbed by Mr. Scriven, who took it upon himself to answer for his lordship's disliking such an extreme action excessively.

By the time Captain Ware strolled into White's Club that afternoon, the story of his cousin's disappearance was forming one of the main topics of conversation there. He was at once pounced upon by Lord Gaywood, who had not yet left London for Bath, whither he was eventually bound. Lord Gaywood, who was inclined to make light of the affair, called across the room: "Hey, Ware, what's this cock-and-bull story about Sale? Here's Cliveden saying he ain't been seen since yesterday morning! Is it a bubble?"

Gideon shrugged his big shoulders. "Gone out of town, I daresay. Why should he not?"

"A trifle smokey, isn't it?" said Mr. Cliveden, raising one eyebrow. "A man don't commonly leave town without his valet! By what I hear, none of Sale's servants knows what has become of him."

"I see there is a notice of his betrothal to your sister in the papers to-day, too, Gaywood," remarked a thin little man by the fire. "Very strange!"

"What's that got to say to anything?" demanded Gaywood, bristling.

The thin man, knowing that his lordship's temper was erratic, made haste to assure him that he had spoken quite idly. Lord Gaywood eyed him bodingly for a moment, and then transferred his attention to Captain Ware. "Out with it!" he recommended. "I'll lay a monkey you're in the secret, Gideon!"

"Not I!" Gideon said lightly. "I'm not Sale's bear-leader."

"Well!" exclaimed Mr. Cliveden, disappointed. "We were looking for you to settle all bets, Ware! We made sure you would be bound to know the truth. Do you tell me you haven't seen your cousin?"

"No," Gideon said, yawning. "I've not seen him, and I don't understand what all the pother is about. Perhaps Sale has gone off to Bath."

"Not without his valet, or any baggage!" expostulated Mr. Cliveden, shocked.

"Oh, lord, what does it matter?" Gideon said.

"Well, I don't know," said Gaywood. "It's a queer rig, ain't it? The porter was telling me that Sale's steward was here this morning, in the deuce of a pucker, asking if he had been in the club."

"Very likely!" said Gideon, with his most sardonic smile. "Sale's servants would run all over town seeking for him if he were half an hour late in returning to his house."

A mild-looking man in the window here ventured to suggest that the Duke might have fallen a victim to footpads, or even to kidnappers, and would have embarked on a bitter dissertation of the shocking state of the London streets and the ineptitude of the Watch, had not Gideon interrupted him with a crack of scornful laughter. "Oh, a revival of Mohocks, no doubt!" he said. "My cousin's body will in due course be recovered from the river. Or he may return from a day at the races, which would be sadly flat, but rather more probable."

"What races?" demanded Gaywood.

"Good God, I don't know!" Gideon replied impatiently.

"No, nor anyone else!" retorted his lordship. "There ain't any, as you'd know if you kept your eye on Cocker. Of course, he might have gone off to see a mill, but it ain't much in his line, is it?"

"The thing remains a mystery!" Mr. Cliveden pronounced. "I wonder that you should take it so easily, Ware, for upon my soul I don't care for the sound of it! I do trust poor Sale may not have met with foul play!"

Two more members came into the room at this moment, and were at once asked if they had heard the news. Foreseeing that the topic would not lightly be abandoned, Gideon lounged out of the room. The thin man said: "Queer, that! He seemed to set no store by it, did he? Yet one would have thought he must have been the first to have known of his cousin's intentions. And if he did not, I own

158

I should have expected him to show some degree of anxiety. For it can't be denied that this strange disappearance is of a nature to cause the Duke's relatives grave disquiet."

One of the new comers said: "Oh, depend upon it, he knows where Sale is! Sale dined with him last night."

Everyone's attention became riveted on the speaker's face. "Dined with him last night?" echoed Gaywood. "You're bamming! Ware had not seen Sale: he has just told us so!"

Sir John Aveley opened his eyes at this. "Has he, by Jupiter! Doing it rather too brown, surely! I met Sale on his way to his cousin's chambers last night."

There was a sudden silence. The thin man pursed up his mouth, and looked unutterably wise. Gaywood was frowning. After a moment, he said: "Well, if that is so, I daresay Ware had his reasons for keeping mum! Dash it, he and Sale are the best of friends! I should know! Been acquainted with 'em both since my cradle!"

The thin man coughed. "Just so, my dear Gaywood! No doubt he had excellent reasons."

The man who had come in with Sir John, and who had been wrapped in thought, looked up, exclaiming: "Good God, you don't suppose——?"

"Certainly not!" said the thin man. "Dear me, no! One only felt that Ware's reserve was a trifle marked."

"Fustian!" said Gaywood angrily. "Ten to one, Sale told him the whole, and pledged him to secrecy!"

"Which," said Cliveden dryly, "brings us back to the riddle of what *is* the whole? You will own, Gaywood, that for a man of Sale's position—indeed, for any man!—suddenly to disappear, leaving behind him no message, and no clue to his whereabouts, is something a little out of the ordinary. If rumour is to be believed, he has gone without his valet, or his baggage, or any of his horses. That may do very well for some nameless vagrant, but will hardly do for Sale! No! I must continue to hold by the opinion that there is something excessively smokey about the whole affair. And without wishing to say one word to Ware's detriment, I feel that considering the peculiar position in which he stands he would do well to be frank." He spread out his hands, and smiled deprecatingly at Lord Gaywood. "One cannot but feel it to be a singular circumstance that Aveley here should have met Sale actually on his way to dine with his cousin, do not you agree?"

"No, I do not!" snapped Lord Gaywood, and flung out of the room.

He did not find Captain Ware in the club, and learned upon enquiry that he had strolled across the street to the

159

Guard's Club not ten minutes earlier. Lord Gaywood followed him there, and sent up his name. In due course, Gideon came downstairs. Some imp of malice was grinning in his eyes, and it struck Lord Gaywood, watching him descend the staircase, that he looked rather saturnine. But he was so dark that it was, after all, easy for him to look saturnine. A smile flickered on his mouth; he said in innocent surprise: "Now what, Charlie?"

Lord Gaywood had come in search of him in the spirit of impetuosity which had more than once precipitated him into awkward situations, and he suddenly found it hard to say what was in his mind. However, it was clearly impossible to withdraw leaving it unsaid, so he drew a breath, and said abruptly: "I want a word with you, Gideon!"

Captain Ware looked more than ever amused. "By all means!" he said, and led the way to a small room, which at this hour of the day was deserted. As he closed the door, he said gently: "I murdered him, you know, and buried his body under the fifth stair."

Lord Gaywood jumped, and coloured hotly. "Damn you, Gideon, I never had such a thought in my head! Stop bamboozling! But where *is* Gilly?"

"I have not the most distant guess," replied Gideon.

"Well, if you say so, of course I believe you! But the thing is people have begun to talk, and it ain't pleasant! I thought I would warn you. Cliveden's been saying that you're mighty cool over the business, and there's no denying that it's queer, whichever way one looks at it! Naturally, if Gilly took you into his confidence there's no reason why you should be worrying. But if he did not——" He paused, but Gideon only shook his head. "Well, if he did not, don't you think he may have met with foul play?"

"No. I have a better opinion of Gilly's ability to take care of himself."

"But, Gideon, what should take him to go off like that?" objected Gaywood.

"Perhaps he found life a dead bore," suggested Gideon.

"That's a loud one!" remarked Gaywood scornfully. "Why the devil should a man with Sale's fortune find life a dead bore?"

"I think it conceivable that he might."

"I know there never was such a fellow for being hipped," agreed Gaywood, "but, dash it all, he is but this instant become engaged to my sister, and if you mean to tell me that that has cast him into despondency——"

"Oh, take a damper, Charlie!" recommended Gideon. "Gilly was never a gabster, and no doubt but that he has some very good reason for leaving town which he has not seen fit to divulge to any of us. For anything I know, he has gone to Bath, in a spirit of knight-errantry!"

"Well, I shall soon discover that," said Gaywood. "I'm going there myself." He hesitated, casting Gideon a side-long look.

"Let me know the worst!" said Gideon.

His lordship took the plunge. "Gideon, Aveley is saying that he met Gilly last night, on his way to dine with you!"

"Is he, indeed?" said Gideon.

"It seemed to me that I could do no less than tell you of it," explained Gaywood, defensively.

"I thank you, Charlie. But I have nothing to add, you know."

"Oh, very well!" said Gaywood. "But I'll tell you this! The town will be in an uproar soon!"

Gideon laughed, and his lordship, nettled, picked up his hat, and took his leave of him. Gideon went on laughing.

By nightfall, Lord Lionel had reached London, and was at Sale House, demanding an explanation of Mr. Scriven's letter to him, which he had no hesitation in calling a non-sensical piece of balderdash. "Where," barked his lordship, "is his Grace?"

Captain Belper, who, in expectation of Lord Lionel's arrival, had presented himself at Sale House some time earlier, replied earnestly: "My lord, would to God I knew!"

Lord Lionel had as little liking for the dramatic as Mr. Scriven, and he snorted. "No need to be acting any Chelten-ham tragedies, sir!" he said dampingly. "I make no doubt this is a piece of work about nothing! In fact, I was of two minds whether I should come to town, for I depended upon your having comfortable tidings by this time, and to be running about the country after my nephew is the outside of enough!"

Everyone wilted a little at this testy speech. It was left to Mr. Scriven to say: "Only we have no comfortable tidings, my lord."

"Well, well!" said his lordship, in a tone of displeasure, "I don't know why you should find it so wonderful that a young man should choose to go off on some business of his own without admitting all of you into his confidence! It vexes me that he should not have taken Nettlebed, for he should not be travelling about without his valet, and so I shall tell him. But there is nothing in that to put you all in a fidget!"

"I think your lordship does not perfectly understand," replied Scriven. "His Grace cannot have meditated a journey, for he took no baggage with him, not so much as a valise! And Nettlebed will inform you that his Grace's brushes, combs—every article appertaining to his toilet, in fact!—are still in his bedchamber here."

His lordship appeared to be quite thunderstruck by this disclosure, but as soon as he had recovered the use of his tongue, he wheeled about to direct an accusing glare at Nettlebed, and to demand what the devil he meant by it. Nettlebed could only shake his head wretchedly. "Upon my word!" said Lord Lionel terribly. "This is a pretty piece of work! A very ill-managed business I must deem it when with I know not how many of you to care for my nephew he can disappear, and not one of you able to tell me where he is gone!"

At this point it seemed good to Captain Belper to divulge his fear that the Duke had been engaged to fight a duel. Lord Lionel lost no time in demolishing this theory. There was never, he said, anyone less quarrelsome than the Duke; and how, he would thank the Captain to tell him, had he found the time to be picking a quarrel since he came to London? He brushed aside the question of the pistols: if the Duke had a hobby, it was for shooting, and if he might not purchase a pair of pistols without being suspected of having become embroiled in an affair of honour things had come to a pretty pass.

Chigwell ventured to say: "Yes, my lord, but—but his Grace took the pistols with him. The porter handed the package to him just before he left the house, and he took it into the library, and unwrapped it, for the wrappings were found upon the floor there. But not—not the pistols, my lord!"

"My dread is that my Lord Duke has had the misfortune to wound his adversary fatally," said Captain Belper, "and has perhaps fled to France to escape the dreadful consequences."

Lord Lionel seemed to have difficulty in controlling himself. An alarmingly high colour rose to his face, and after champing his jaws for a moment or two, he uttered in outraged accents: "This is beyond everything!"

"I assure you, my lord, I feel this agitating reflection as deeply as your lordship must," Captain Belper said, with great earnestness.

"Agitating reflection!" exploded Lord Lionel.

"I have been sick with apprehension from the moment it occurred to me. The thought that I might, perhaps, have prevented——"

"Never," interrupted Lord Lionel, "have I listened to such

162

fustian rubbish! I declare I am vexed to death! And if my nephew were fool enough to do any such thing, which I do not admit, mark you! pray, do you suppose that his seconds would have left us in ignorance of the event? Or do you imagine that he entered upon such an affair without friends to act for him? I do not scruple to tell you, sir, that your apprehensions are woodheaded beyond permission!"

The Captain was not unnaturally abashed by this forthright speech. Before he could come about again, Nettlebed said urgently: "No, my lord, no! Not a duel! His Grace has been foully done to death by footpads! I know it! We shall never see him more!"

"He *would* go out at night unattended!" mourned Chigwell, wringing his hands.

Lord Lionel stared at them fixedly, and for quite a minute said nothing. Captain Belper was ill-advised enough to interpolate: "It is a matter for the Runners."

A choleric eye was rolled towards him. Mr. Scriven said smoothly: "I could not feel that such a step should be taken without your lordship's knowledge, however."

"I am very much obliged to you!" said his lordship. "A fine dust you would have made, and all for nothing, I daresay! Where's my son?"

"My lord, I went to Master Gideon—to the Captain, I should say—this morning, but he has not seen his Grace, nor he knows nothing of where he may be!" Nettlebed told him.

"H'm!" Lord Lionel brooded over this. "So he didn't tell his cousin? I am of the opinion that he is up to some mischief, Scriven! When did he leave this house?"

"It was in the morning, my lord, quite early, I believe. He set out on foot, though Borrowdale here would have sent for his horse."

"I begged his Grace to allow me to send a message to the stables," corroborated the butler. "For seeing that his Grace was wearing top-boots and breeches, I assumed——"

"Wearing top-boots, was he?" said Lord Lionel. "That settles it! He had some journey in mind, though why he must needs make a mystery—— However, it doesn't signify! I daresay he meant to have returned last night, but took some fancy into his head, or was in some way detained. I do not by any means despair of seeing him walk in at any moment. Captain Belper, I am keeping you from your bed! I am obliged to you for your solicitude, but I will not have you waiting here upon my nephew's crotchets. That would never do! Good-night, sir!"

Finding that his lordship's hand was held out to him, Captain Belper had nothing to do but to take it, to reiterate his fervent desire to be of assistance, and to allow himself to be ushered out of the house by Borrowdale.

"The man's a fool!" remarked his lordship, as soon as the door was shut. "So are you, Nettlebed! You may be off too!"

"I blame myself, my lord. I should never——"

"Pooh! nonsense!" said Lord Lionel, cutting him short. "His Grace was never set upon in broad daylight, let me tell you!"

He waited until Nettlebed had withdrawn, and then said abruptly: "Was his Grace suffering from any irritation of nerves? Did he seem to you to be in his customary spirits?"

"Perfectly, my lord," responded Scriven. "Indeed, his Grace had conveyed to me a very gratifying piece of intelligence, desiring me to send an advertisement to the papers of his forthcoming——"

"Yes, yes, I saw the notice! I had looked for a word from his Grace, but I have had no letter from him." He paused, recalling his conversation with Gilly on the subject of his marriage. "H'm, yes! Well! Nothing had occurred to set up his back? some little nonsense, perhaps? He has sometimes some odd humours!"

"No, my lord, unless it be that his Grace—as I thought—did not quite relish Captain Belper's companionship," said Scriven, with his eyes cast down.

"Upon my word I do not blame him!" said his lordship. "I had not thought him to have been such a jackass! I am sorry now that I advised him of his Grace's coming. But he would not run out of town for such a reason as that!"

The steward gave a little cough. "I beg your lordship's pardon, but it has seemed to me that his Grace was not quite himself. The very evening before he—before he left us, he would go out alone. He would not have his carriage, nor permit us to summon a chair, my lord. Indeed, when I begged him to let me at least call a linkboy he ran out of the house in quite a pet—if your lordship will excuse the word!"

"Well, I daresay that might put him in a fidget, but it is nothing to the purpose, after all! I own that it is a little disturbing that he should stay so long away, but young men are thoughtless, you know! To-morrow, if there should be no word from him I will make some discreet enquiries. Captain Ware no doubt knows who are his intimates. We shall clear up this mystery speedily enough, I daresay."

On this bracing note, he dismissed Scriven. But when he was alone he sat for quite an appreciable time, an untasted glass of wine in his hand, and his eyes fixed frowningly upon the glowing coals in the grate. He remembered that Gilly had been foolishly agitated when the question of his marriage had been broached. He hoped that the boy had not made his offer against his will, and fallen into a fit of dejection. He was so quiet there was never any knowing what was in his head. Suddenly his lordship remembered that Gilly had had some odd notion of going to London alone, and of staying in an hotel. It really began to look as though he had had some plan of escaping from his household from the start. But why he should wish to do so Lord Lionel could not imagine. Had he been a wild young blade, like Gaywood, one would have supposed that he was bent on kicking up a lark, but it was surely the height of absurdity to cherish such a suspicion of poor Gilly. Lord Lionel could only hope that his son would be able to throw some light on a problem which was beginning to make him feel extremely uneasy.

CHAPTER XV

LORD LIONEL passed a disturbed night. He came down to breakfast in the expectation of finding a letter from his errant nephew awaiting him, but in despite of the fact that the sum of one pound was paid to the Post Office every year by Mr. Scriven, out of the Duke's income, to ensure the early delivery of the mail, no such letter gladdened his lordship's eyes. Matters did not, of course, appear to be quite so desperate as they had seemed during the chill small hours, but there was no denying that Lord Lionel had little appetite for his breakfast. He was curt with Borrowdale, and even brutal to Nettlebed; and when a message was brought to him that Captain Belper had called he instructed the footman to tell this unwelcome visitor that he had gone out.

In a very short time he did go out. He spent the better part of the morning at White's and at Boodle's, and, being no fool, was soon able to discern that Gilly's disappearance was the main topic of conversation amongst the *haut ton*. Interesting discussions ended abruptly with his entrance into a room; and from several hints that were dropped he discovered, to his wrath, that speculation was rife on his son's part in the mystery. He had almost gone to Albany when he bethought him of an old crony, and strode off instead to Mount Street. Whatever the *on-dits* of town might be, it was certain, he reflected grimly, that Timothy Wainfleet would know them all.

He found his friend at home, huddled over a fire in his book-room, and looking at once wizened and alarmingly alert. Sir Timothy welcomed him with exquisite courtesy, gave him a chair by the fire, and a glass of sherry, and murmured that he was enchanted to see him. But it did not seem to Lord Lionel that Sir Timothy was quite as enchanted as he averred, and, being a direct person, he said so, in express terms.

"Dear Lionel!" said Sir Timothy, faintly protesting. "Indeed, you wrong me! Always enchanted, I assure you! And how are the pheasants? You do shoot pheasants in October, do you not?"

"I have not come to talk to you of pheasants," announced Lord Lionel. "What is more, you know as well as I do when pheasant-shooting begins!"

Sir Timothy's shrewd grey eyes twinkled ruefully. "Yes, dear Lionel, but I apprehend that I would rather talk of pheasants than—er—than what you have come to talk about!"

"Then you have heard of my nephew's disappearance?" demanded Lord Lionel.

"Everyone has heard of it," smiled Sir Timothy.

"Yes! Thanks to the folly of Gilly's steward, who, I find, could think of nothing better to do than to spread the news at White's! Now, we are old friends, Wainfleet, and I look to you to tell me what is being said in town! For what I hear I don't like!"

"I wonder why I did not tell my man to deny me?" mused Sir Timothy. "I never listen to gossip, you know. Really, I do not think I can assist you!"

"You listen to nothing else!" retorted Lord Lionel.

Sir Timothy looked at him in melancholy wonder. "I suppose I must have liked you once," he said plaintively. "I like very few people nowadays; in fact, the number of persons whom I cordially dislike increases almost hourly."

"All that is nothing to the matter!" declared his lordship. "There is a deal of damned whispering going on in the clubs, and I look to you to tell me what it is I may have to fight. What are the fools saying about my nephew?"

Sir Timothy sighed. "The most received theory, as I apprehend, is that he has been murdered," he replied calmly.

"Go on!" commanded Lord Lionel. "By my son?"

Sir Timothy winced. "My dear Lionel!" he protested.

"Surely we need not waste our time in discussion of absurdities?"

"I am one who likes to see his way!" said his lordship. "If I have to remain here a week, you shall tell me the whole!"

"God forbid!" said his friend piously. "I find you very unrestful, you know: not at all the kind of guest I like to receive! Do pray understand that I do not set the least store by the whisperings of ill-informed persons! But you will agree that there is food and to spare for gossip. I am informed—of course I do not believe it!—that the last man to see your nephew was his cousin, with whom he is said to have dined. A circumstance—always remember, my dear Lionel, that I do but repeat what I hear!—which Captain Ware denies. One Aveley met Sale upon his way to your son's chambers. No one has set eyes on him since, you know! Malicious persons—the town is full of them!—pretend to perceive a link between this fact, and the notice which lately appeared in the Society journals. So nonsensical! But you know what the world is, my dear friend!"

"My son, in a word," said Lord Lionel, staring at him with narrowed eyes, "is held to have murdered his cousin upon learning that he is about to marry, and beget heirs?"

Sir Timothy raised a deprecating hand. "Not by persons of discrimination, I assure you!" he said.

"It is a damned lie!" said Lord Lionel.

"Naturally, my dear Lionel, naturally! Yet—speaking as your friend, you know!—I do feel that a little openness in dear Gideon—a little less reserve—would be wise at this delicate moment! He has not been—how shall I put it?— precisely conciliating, one feels. In fact, he preserves a silence that is felt to be foolishly obstinate. Strive to consider the facts of this painful affair dispassionately, Lionel! Your nephew—quite one of our wealthiest peers, I am sure! so gratifying, and due in great part, I am persuaded, to your excellent management of his estates!—announces the tidings that he is about to be wed; and within twenty-four hours he visits your son, who afterwards denies all knowledge of his whereabouts. He is not seen again; his servants search for him all over town; you come post from Sale; and the only undisturbed member of his entourage appears to be Gideon, who pursues his usual avocations with unimpaired calm. Now, do understand that not one word of this would you have had from my lips had you not forced me to speak, almost, one might say, at the pistol-mouth! The tale is as nonsensical as most rumours are. I advise you to ignore it. Let me give you some more sherry!"

"Thank you, no! I am going instantly to see my son!" said Lord Lionel harshly. "I collect that I have nursed my nephew's fortune so that my son may ultimately benefit? Are you sure that I have had no hand in his disappearance?"

"That," said Sir Timothy gently, "would be absurd, Lionel."

Lord Lionel left him abruptly, and strode off down Piccadilly, his brow black, and his brain seething with rage. He had naturally no suspicion of his son, but the apparently well-attested information that he must have been the last man to have seen Gilly greatly disturbed him. If it were true, he was no doubt in Gilly's confidence, but what could have possessed him to have aided and abetted Gilly in this foolish start? Gideon must surely know that his cousin could not be permitted to wander about the country like a nobody, a prey to chills, adventurers, highwaymen, and kidnappers! By the time his lordship had reached Albany, he had worked himself up into a state of anger against his son which demanded an instant outlet. This was denied him. Wragby, admitting him into Gideon's chambers, said that the Captain had gone on parade, and was not expected to return for another half-hour at least. Lord Lionel glared at him in a way which reminded Wragby of his late Colonel, and said in one of his barks: "I will await the Captain!"

Wragby ushered him into the sitting-room, endured a pungent stricture on the disorder in which his master chose to live, and only just prevented himself from saluting. Lord Lionel, however, recollected without this reminder that he had served in the 1st Foot Guards, and added a few scathing remarks on the customs apparently prevailing in Infantry regiments. Wragby, who was nothing if not loyal, nobly shouldered the blame for the untidiness of the room, said, "Yes, my lord!" and "No, my lord!" at least half a dozen times, and retired in a shattered condition to the kitchen, where he lost no time in venting his feelings on Captain Ware's hapless batman.

Lord Lionel occupied himself for several minutes in inspecting his son's library, and uttering "Pish!" in tones of revulsion. Then he paced about the floor for a time, but finding his path impeded by chairs, tables, a paper-rack, and a wine-cooler, he gave this up, and cast himself down in the chair before Gideon's desk. He had promised his wife that he would write to her as soon as he reached London, and as he had not yet done so he thought he might as well fill in his time in this way as in any other. Amongst the litter of bills and invitation-cards, he found some notepaper, and a bottle of ink. He drew the paper towards him, and then discovered that Gideon, as might, he supposed, have been expected, used a damnable pen that wanted mending. He began to hunt for a knife, and his exasperation mounted steadily. It seemed to him of a piece with all the rest, Gilly's disappearance included, that Gideon should have no pen-knife. He pulled open one of the drawers in the desk, and turned over a heap of miscellaneous objects in the hope of discovering a knife. He did not find one. He found Gilly's signet-ring instead.

Captain Ware returned from parade twenty minutes later, and learned from Wragby that his father was awaiting him. He grimaced, but said nothing. His batman made haste to unbuckle his brass cuirass, and his sword-belt; Captain Ware handed his great, crested helmet to Wragby, and lifted an enquiring eyebrow. Wragby cast up both his eyes in a very speaking way, at which the Captain nodded. He stripped off his white gauntlets, tossed them on to the table, flicked the dust from his black-jacked boots, and walked into his sitting-room.

An impartial observer might have thought him a vision to gladden any father's heart, for his big frame and his dark good looks were admirably suited to the magnificent uniform he wore. But when Lord Lionel, who was standing staring out of the window at the opposite row of chambers, turned to confront him gladness was an emotion conspicuously lacking in his countenance. He was looking appallingly grim, and his eyes held an expression Gideon had never before seen in them.

"I am extremely happy to see you, father," Gideon said, closing the door. "I hope you have not waited long for me? One of our curst parades! How do you do?"

Lord Lionel ignored both the speech and the outstretched hand. He said, as though the words were wrenched out of him: "For God's sake, Gideon, where is Gilly?"

"I have not the remotest conjecture," replied Gideon. "To own the truth, I am a trifle weary of being asked that question."

"You have not the remotest conjecture?" repeated his father. "Do you expect me to believe that?"

Gideon's face stiffened; the resemblance between them seemed to grow more marked. "I do, yes," he said in a level tone.

Lord Lionel held out a hand that shook slightly. "What, Gideon, is this?" he demanded, his hard eyes never wavering from Gideon's face.

Gideon glanced down at his hand, and saw what lay in the palm of it. "That," he said, still in that level voice, "is

Gilly's ring, sir. You found it in my desk. I am surprised you do not recognize it."

"Not recognize it!" exclaimed Lord Lionel. "Do you take me for a fool, Gideon?"

Gideon raised his eyes from the ring, and met his father's, in a look quite as hard as the one that challenged him. "I did not—no," he said deliberately. He took the ring out of Lord Lionel's hand, and restored it to his desk. He turned the key in the lock of the drawer, and removed it. "A precaution I should have taken earlier," he remarked.

"Gideon!" Lord Lionel's voice held a note almost of entreaty. "Be open with me, I implore you! *Where is Gilly?*"

"Don't you mean, sir, what have I done with Gilly?" suggested Gideon sweetly.

"No!" snapped his lordship. "Nothing would make me believe that you would harm a hair of his head! But when I came upon that ring in your desk—Gideon, do you know what is being said in the clubs?"

"Yes, I have not been so much amused this twelve-month," replied Gideon. "I own, however, that it does not amuse me very much to discover that you, sir, apparently share the town's suspicions."

"Don't take that tone with me, boy!" said his lordship, flushing angrily. "A pretty thing it would be if I were to suspect my own son!"

"Just so, sir."

"I do not!—Understand, I do not! But how came you by that ring, Gideon?"

"Oh, I drew it from the corpse's finger, of course, sir!" Gideon said sardonically.

"Stop trifling with me!" thundered his lordship. "I have told you I believe nothing against you! If I was shocked to come upon a ring in your desk which Gilly always wears you can scarcely wonder at it!"

"I beg pardon, sir. Gilly handed it to me to keep for him. I have neither the desire nor the expectation to wear it."

Lord Lionel sat down rather limply on the sofa. "I knew something of the sort must have happened. Where has that tiresome boy gone?"

"I have already told you, sir, that I do not know."

Lord Lionel regarded him frowningly. "Did he dine with you on the day he disappeared, or did he not?"

"He did."

"Then, confound you, Gideon, what the devil do you mean by telling everyone you had not seen him?" demanded Lord Lionel.

Gideon shrugged, and put up a hand to unhook his tight

170

collar-band. "Being unable to answer further questions, sir, it seemed to me wisest to deny all knowledge of Adolphus."

"I wish you will not call him that!" said Lord Lionel peevishly. "Do you mean to tell me he did not tell you what his intentions were?"

"He told me merely that he was blue-devilled, sir: a thing I had perceived for myself," replied Gideon, with a look under his black brows at his father.

"Blue-devilled!" ejaculated Lord Lionel. "I should like to know what cause he had to feel so!"

Gideon's lips curled. "Would you, sir? Then, by God, I will tell you! My poor little cousin is beset by persons who wish him nothing but good and since he has by far too sweet a disposition to send you, and Scriven, and Nettlebed, and Chigwell, and—but I forget the names of the rest of his retinue!—to the devil, he has been forced to fly from you all. I do not know where he has gone, or how long he means to stay away, or what purpose he has in mind!"

"Are you mad?" demanded his lordship, staring at him. "I have cared as much for Gilly as if he had been my own son!"

"More, sir, more!"

Lord Lionel gave a gasp. "Good God, boy, are you jealous of Gilly?"

Gideon laughed. "Devil a bit, sir! I thank God your affection for me never led you into shielding me from every wind that blew, or hedging me about with tutors, valets, stewards, and doctors, who would not let me set one foot in front of the other without begging me to take heed I did not step into a puddle!"

There was a moment's silence. Lord Lionel said, almost pleadingly: "He was left to my care, and he was the sickliest child!"

"Oh, content you, sir, no one blames you for your anxiety when he was a child! But it is time to be done with dry-nursing him, and has been so several years! You will not let him be a man: you treat him still as though he were a schoolboy."

"It is not true!" Lord Lionel said. "I have been for ever telling him it is time that he asserted himself!"

Gideon grinned. "Ay, so you have, and what have you said when he has made an attempt to do so? You desired him to learn to manage his estates, but when he tried so to do did not you and Scriven tell him that his notions were absurd, and that he must be guided by older and wiser heads?"

Lord Lionel swallowed, and said quite mildly: "Naturally Scriven and I know better than he can—— But this is nonsense, after all! You have said as much to me before, and I told you then——"

"Sir, I warned you not so long since that you would not long ride Adolphus on a curb-bit, and you would not attend to me. Well! You see what has come of it!"

Lord Lionel pulled himself together. "Be silent!" he commanded. "You will do well to remember to whom you speak, sir! Let me tell you this! You are answerable for much in having permitted Gilly to go off in this crazy way!"

Gideon lifted his hand. "Oh, no, sir! You mistake! I have no authority over Gilly! I must be the only one of us all to say so, too!"

"Gideon!" said Lord Lionel, striking his fist on the table. "This is beyond the line of what is amusing! You have let that boy go away without one soul to wait on him, or see that he does not fall into some accident, and however well that may do for another young man, it will not do for him! He has never been obliged to fend for himself; he will not know how to go on; he may become ill, through some folly or neglect! I had thought you too much attached to him to have been guilty of such behaviour!"

"Believe me, sir, I am so much attached to him that I hope he will fall into all manner of adventures and scrapes! I have a better opinion of Adolphus than you have, or indeed than he has of himself, and I think he will learn to manage very tolerably. He does not yet know his own value. He is unsure because untried. I hope he will not too speedily return to us."

"I declare I am out of all patience with such talk!" exclaimed Lord Lionel, starting up. "If you do not know where he is, I am wasting my time with you! I shall leave no stone unturned to find him! When you have come to your senses, you may find me at Sale House!"

Gideon bowed, and strode over to open the door for him. Lord Lionel fairly snatched up his hat and cane from the chair where he had laid them, and left the chambers without another word.

"God help you, Adolphus!" said Gideon, shutting the door.

Just what stones his parent found to turn over in the succeeding two days he was unable to discover. That Lord Lionel was in London still he knew, for he twice met him, and exchanged a few words with him. Lord Lionel was doing what he could to scotch the rumours that were flying about the town, but with indifferent success, his son inferred. These had reached Gideon's Colonel's ears, who stated, somewhat elliptically, that he had no desire to interfere in Captain Ware's private affairs, and supposed he knew what he was about.

"I have every reason, sir, to assure you that my cousin is alive and well," replied Gideon, very stiff.

"Well, well, no one doubts that!" said the Colonel inaccurately. "No bad thing, however, if you could prove it! Don't mind telling you I don't care for the talk that is running round the clubs!"

On the fifth day after the Duke's disappearance, a letter reached Captain Ware through the medium of the London Penny Post. It was penned by Nettlebed, and was couched in terms mysterious enough to baffle the recipient.

"Sir, and Honoured Captain," it began, in agitated characters, *"This is to inform you, Master Gideon, as is his Grace's true Friend which I do know and Nobody will convince me Otherwise, that having taken a Notion into my head I am leaving Town at this present, and having his Grace's wishes in mind not saying nothing to his Lordship, which you will Comprehend, Master Gideon, knowing the ways things are, and me not wishful to do what his Grace would not relish. Master Gideon, sir, there is One who may Know the Answer to why his Grace left us, and I do not know, Sir, why I did not Consider it before, but it come to me in the Night, Sir, but tell his Lordship I will not, being, as you know, Master Gideon, Devoted to His Grace's Interests, for which I take this Opportunity to Inform you, Sir, as I am gone away on his Grace's Affairs, and not Deserting my Post. I remain, Master Gideon, Your Respectful Servant, James Nettlebed."*

After perusing this communication, the Captain was not surprised to receive a visit from Lord Lionel, who came to inform him, explosively, that as though things were not already bad enough Gilly's mutton-headed valet had now disappeared. He was so anxious to learn what his son's opinion of this unexpected turn might be that he very magnanimously forgave him for their late tiff. But Gideon would only shake his head, and say that it was extremely odd, which made his lordship recall various grudges he had cherished against his son for years, and enumerate them in detail. But here again Gideon behaved in a very unfilial way, refusing to be drawn into a quarrel that might have relieved his parent's exacerbated feelings, and merely grinning at him in affectionate mockery.

On the sixth day of the Duke's absence, the letter he

had written from Baldock reached Albany, but since Captain Ware's correspondence was not of a nature to make early postal deliveries a matter of moment, it did not arrive until midway through the morning. The Captain came in at noon to find it awaiting him. He perused it appreciatively, and did not in the least grudge the monies it had cost him to receive it. He tucked it into his pocket-book, and, having won the battle over his worser self, sent off a brief note to his father, informing him that Gilly was alive, in health, and in mischief. He then shed his regimentals, attired himself in a costume suitable for a gentleman bent upon attending a sporting engagement, and sallied forth in his curricle to Epsom, where he witnessed a meeting between a young pugilist, whom he was inclined to fancy, with a veteran of the Ring. He did not return to his chambers until a very late hour; and as he had given Wragby leave of absence for the day Mr. Liversedge, arriving in London, and making all speed to Albany, knocked in vain on the door of his chambers. Mr. Liversedge was forced to postpone his visit until the following morning, and to put up for the night at the cheapest inn he could discover.

He was sufficiently conversant with the habits of fashionable gentlemen not to commit the solecism of calling on Captain Ware too early in the morning. Unfortunately he reckoned without Gideon's military duties, which, on this particular morning, took him out at a time when, according to all the rules, he should have been still abed. Wragby, who three times answered the door to him during the course of the day, informed him roundly that the Captain wouldn't come home until evening, and wouldn't receive such an importunate visitor when he did come home.

"He will receive me, my man," said Mr. Liversedge loftily. "It is a matter of the greatest importance!"

"It may be to you, but it won't be to him," replied Wragby, unimpressed, and shut the door in his face.

Nothing daunted, Mr. Liversedge returned to Albany at six o'clock, when the Captain was changing his dress for a convivial gathering at the Castle Tavern. He sent in his card, a circumstance which induced the reluctant Wragby to mention his existence to his master.

Captain Ware picked the card up distastefully, and studied it. "Is it a dun, Wragby?"

"That," responded his servitor, "is what I thought myself, sir, when I see this Individual first, but not at this hour it ain't, that's certain!"

"Oh, well, show him into the parlour! I'll see him!" said

Gideon, returning to the mirror, and wrestling with the exigencies of his cravat.

He joined his visitor ten minutes later. Mr. Liversedge, who had travelled post from Baldock, at his brother's expense, was a trifle startled by the formidable proportions of his host. He had been prepared to find that Captain Ware, holding a commission in the Lifeguards, was six foot tall, but his brief acquaintance with Captain Ware's noble relative had not led him to expect to be confronted by a young giant, with shoulders to match his height, and a cast of countenance which even the greatest optimist would have recognized to be uncompromising in the extreme. He rose from his chair, and executed a profound bow.

Gideon's hard gray eyes ran over him in one comprehensive glance. "What's your business with me?" he asked. "I fancy I don't know you."

Mr. Liversedge's experiences as a gentleman's gentleman led him instantly to recognize and to appreciate the True Quality. He bowed to it again. "Sir," he said, "I have sought you out on an affair of great moment."

"Have you, by God?" said Gideon. "Well, be brief, for I am engaged to dine with a party of friends in half an hour!"

Mr. Liversedge cast a conspiratorial glance towards the door. "Am I assured of your private ear, sir?" he asked.

Gideon began to be amused. He walked over to the door leading into the little hall, and opened it, and looked out. He then closed it again, and said with becoming gravity: "No prying ears attend upon us, Mr. Liversedge. You may safely unburden your soul to me!"

"Captain Ware," said Mr. Liversedge softly, "you have, I apprehend, a Noble Relative."

Quite suddenly Gideon ceased to be amused. Some instinct for danger, however, prompted him to reply lightly: "I am nearly related to the Duke of Sale."

Mr. Liversedge smiled approvingly at him. "Exactly so, sir! I fancy I do not err when I say that you stand close to him in the succession to the title, and the prodigious property which appertains to his Grace."

Not a muscle quivered in the dark face looming above him; the faint, satirical smile still hovered on the Captain's austere mouth; there was nothing in the lounging pose to warn Mr. Liversedge that the Captain's every faculty was on the alert. There was a moment's pause. "Quite close," drawled Gideon, his eyelids beginning to droop a little over his eyes, in a way which would have put his intimates on their guard. "Sit down, Mr. Liversedge!"

He indicated a chair by the table, in the full light of the

175

oil-lamp which stood on it, and Mr. Liversedge took it, with a word of thanks. He could have wished that the Captain had seen fit to lower his large frame into an opposite chair, but the Captain apparently preferred to prop his shoulders against the high mantelpiece, a little out of the direct beam of the lamp. "Go on, Mr. Liversedge!" he invited cordially.

"His Grace, I further apprehend," said Mr. Liversedge blandly, "is missing from his residence?"

"As you say," agreed Gideon.

Mr. Liversedge regarded him soulfully. "What a shocking thing it would be if his Grace were never to return to it!" he said. "His absence must, I am persuaded, be causing his relatives grave disquiet."

Gideon's lazy glance dwelled for a thoughtful moment on the strip of sticking-plaster adorning his guest's brow. Was this the dragon you left for dead, Adolphus? was the silent question in his brain. And just what mischief are you in, my little one? Aloud, he said: "I am sure you are perfectly well-informed on that head, Mr. Liversedge."

Mr. Liversedge, who had employed his time since his arrival in London in picking up the gleanings of town-scandal, admitted it, but modestly. He then heaved a sigh and said: "One must hope that no accident may have befallen him! Yet how inscrutable are the decrees of Providence, sir! You will have doubtless observed it. There is no knowing what the twists of Fortune may be! Why, I daresay you, Captain Ware,—a worthy scion, I am sure, of a distinguished house!—may never have contemplated the possibility that you might awake one morning to find yourself the heir to your noble relative's possessions!"

The Captain's drawl became even more marked. "That, Mr. Liversedge, is a reflection that is bound to intrude upon the mind of a man of ordinary common-sense. Life is, after all, uncertain."

Mr. Liversedge perceived that his visions were about to be fulfilled. It was pleasant to find that his reading of human character had not been at fault. But he had not seriously supposed that it could be. He smiled approvingly at Gideon, and said: "Yet when one considers that his Grace is a young man, and in the possession of his health and faculties, I daresay anyone would be willing to hazard a large wager against the chances of your becoming second in the line of the succession within—shall we say?—the month!"

"How large a wager?" asked Gideon.

Mr. Liversedge waved one hand in an airy gesture. "Oh,

against such odds, sir, I daresay you would venture as much as fifty thousand pounds!"

Gideon shook his head. "I never bet so far above my fortune, Mr. Liversedge. Now, had you offered me a wager that I should not be Duke of Sale within a month——!"

Mr. Liversedge considered his resources rapidly. "Well, I daresay it *could* be contrived," he said dubiously.

Gideon very nearly laughed in his face. He overcame the impulse, and said: "You know, I am not such a gamester as you believe, sir. Such wild bets hold little attraction for me. You will own that you would find it hard to raise such a sum, as you would be obliged to do if his Grace should not depart this life within the month."

"Sir," said Mr. Liversedge earnestly, "if I entered upon a bet of that magnitude it would only be in the certainty that his Grace *would* depart this life within the month!"

"How could you have that certainty?" smiled Gideon.

Mr. Liversedge drew a breath. "Captain Ware," he said. "I am not an unreasonable man. I do not waste your time with frivolous suggestions. More, sir! I do not ignore the peculiar delicacy of your position. Indeed, being myself a man of great sensibility, I have given much thought to your position. Naturally you could not contemplate, in any little arrangement between us, the smallest suggestion of—er——"

"Blood-money," supplied Gideon.

Mr. Liversedge looked pained. "That, sir, is an ugly phrase, and one which is as repugnant to me as it must be to you. All I offer you is a handsome wager. I am sure there are many seemingly more improbable bets entered in the book at White's. Not, of course, that this one would be entered there. A simple exchange of notes between us, sir, is all that would be necessary. And here let me assure you that I regard that as a mere formality, customary in affairs of such a nature. My faith in you as a man of honour, Captain Ware, makes it impossible for me to contemplate the necessity of producing your note at some future date."

"I'm obliged to you," said Gideon. "But I find my faith in you less securely rooted, Mr. Liversedge. I don't believe, for instance, that you have it in your power to make me lose such a bet."

Mr. Liversedge looked reproachful. "It pains me, sir, to encounter mistrust in one with whom I have been so frank. I might add, in one whom I am anxious to benefit. Or should I have told you at the outset that his Grace is at the moment sojourning at a little place quite in the heart of our delightful countryside? When I had the honour of seeing him last, he was wearing an olive riding-coat of excellent

177

tailoring, and a drab Benjamin over it, with four capes. He had a handsome timepiece in his pocket, too, with his crest engraved upon the back, and his initials upon the front." He sighed. "Perhaps I should have brought it to you, sir, but anything savouring of common thievery is very distasteful to me. However, I daresay you may recognize this exquisitely embroidered handkerchief." He dived a hand into his pocket as he spoke, and produced Gilly's blood-stained handkerchief.

Gideon took it from him, and for a moment stood staring down at it, his face very pale, and the lines about his mouth and jaw suddenly accentuated. The stains had grown brown, but Gideon knew bloodstains when he saw them, and his gorge rose. He laid the handkerchief down, his long fingers quivering, and raised his head, and looked at Mr. Liversedge.

Mr. Liversedge had known from the moment that he had mentioned the olive coat that he had struck home. He had not failed to remark that betraying quiver of the fingers. He smiled indulgently; he would have been excited himself, he reflected, if he realized all at once, as Captain Ware had, how close he stood to a Dukedom. Then he met the Captain's eyes, and in the very short space of time granted him for rumination he thought that they blazed with the strangest light he had ever seen in a fellow-creature's eyes. He had even a sensation of being scorched, which was perhaps not surprising, since Gideon was seeing him through a hot, red mist.

The next instant, Mr. Liversedge, no puny figure, had been plucked from his seat, and two iron hands were throttling him remorselessly, shaking him savagely as they did so. While he tore desperately at them, his starting eyes stared up in filming horror into a face dark with rage, with lips curling back from close-shut teeth, and nostrils terrifyingly distended. Before his vision failed, Mr. Liversedge read murder in this face, and knew that for once in his life his judgment had been at fault. Then, as his eyes threatened to burst from their sockets, and his tongue was forced out between his lips, he saw and knew nothing more. As he lost consciousness Gideon cast him from him, and he fell in an inert heap on to the floor.

CHAPTER XVI

THE noise of Mr. Liversedge's fall brought Wragby swiftly upon the scene. He found his master brushing his hands together, as though to rid them of some lingering dirt, and

178

his master's guest lying on the floor. He betrayed no particular surprise at this unusual scene, but casting an experienced eye over Mr. Liversedge remarked: "Well, it looks like you dished *him* up, sir. It's bellows to mend with him sure enough. But what I ask you, sir, is, how am I to get rid of him, if you've killed him? Too hasty, that's what you are!"

"I haven't," Gideon said shortly. "At least—— Here, get some water, and throw it over him! I don't want him dead!"

"Pity you didn't think of that afore, sir," said Wragby severely. "Nice sort of bobbery to be going on in a gentleman's chambers!"

He left the room, returning in a minute or two with a jug of water, which he emptied generously over Mr. Liversedge's countenance. "It seems a waste," he said, "but I don't know but what we hadn't better put a ball-of-fire down his gullet."

Gideon strode over to the sideboard, and poured out some brandy. "Not dead, is he?"

"No, sir," replied Wragby, who had been feeling for Mr. Liversedge's heart. "He's alive, but pretty well burnt to the socket." He considered Mr. Liversedge's mangled cravat, and shook his head. "Well, I thought you'd given him a leveller, sir, but I see as how you've been a-strangling of him." He loosened the cravat, straightened the sufferer's limbs, and raised his head. Gideon dropped on his knee, and put the glass he held to Mr. Liversedge's slack mouth. "Easy, now, easy, sir!" Wragby warned him. "You don't want to choke him again, and nor you don't want that good ball-of-fire to be running down his shirt! Better let me give it to him. I'll have him round in a brace of snaps."

Gideon relinquished the glass, and rose. "Wragby, his Grace is in trouble!"

Wragby paused in his ministrations to look up. "What, not on account of this fat flawn, sir? What's happened to his Grace?"

"I don't know. I think that fellow has him imprisoned somewhere. I ought to have discovered more before I choked him, but—— Here, give him some more brandy!"

"You leave him be, sir; he's coming to himself nice and gentle. He never come here to tell you a thing like that!"

"Oh, yes, he did! He came to sell him to me! For the trifling sum of fifty thousand pounds, he'll engage for it that his Grace is never seen again. He might even contrive to murder my father too. Obliging, isn't he? He brought me that to look at!"

Wragby stared at the Duke's handkerchief. "My God, sir,

what has he done to his Grace? That's blood, or I never saw blood!"

"I tell you I don't know. Trust me, I shall know soon enough! He can't be dead. No, he can't be dead!"

"Lor' no, sir, of course he ain't dead!" Wragby made haste to say. "Likely there was a bit of a mill, and his Grace had his cork drawn. Now, don't you go fuming and fretting before there's any need, sir! Not but what we might have known something like this would happen, if his Grace loped off the way he did!"

"God damn you, do you think I would have let him go if I'd thought he'd run into danger?" Gideon shot at him fiercely.

"O' course you wouldn't, sir! If you was to give me a hand, we could lay this hang-gallows moulder on the sofy. We don't want to cosset him, but on the other hand he's more apt to talk if we make him a bit comfortable. And talk he's got to! If he don't see reason, he'll have to be made more uncomfortable than what he is now, but he don't look to me like one as is hard at hand, and the less breeze we raise the better, sir."

Gideon nodded, and bent to take Mr. Liversedge's legs. This unfortunate gentleman was heaved on to the sofa, and groaned faintly. "Leave him to me!" Gideon said curtly. "I'll call you if I should need you."

Wragby looked at him doubtfully. "Yes, sir, but the way you've been handling him, and the black temper you're in, begging your pardon, it's more likely him as'll need me than you!"

"Don't be a fool! I shan't touch him. He thinks the cards are in his hands, but I am not quite at non plus! No, Mr. Liversedge! not quite!"

Mr. Liversedge opened his eyes, and lifted a feeble hand to his bruised throat. He groaned again, and Gideon poured out some more brandy, and took it to him. Wragby, in open disapproval, watched him raise Mr. Liversedge, and put the glass to his lips again. He seemed satisfied, however, that his master had no immediate intention of resorting to any more physical violence, and after remarking that there was no sense in making the fellow jug-bitten, withdrew to stand guard outside the door.

Mr. Liversedge found it rather painful to swallow, but he disposed of the brandy, and was even able to struggle into a sitting-posture. He tenderly felt his throat, uttered one or two more groans, and brought his blood-shot gaze to bear upon his host. "Very unhandsome!" he croaked. "Too hasty, sir! No need for any heat! Had but to say the word, and the matter could have been arranged to your taste. For a small sum—quite trifling sum, say thirty thousand, or even twenty-five—willing to restore his Grace safe and sound!" He tried to clear his throat, and winced. "*Happy* to do so!" he said. "Not a man of violence—taken quite a fancy to his Grace—no wish to harm him!"

Relief at learning that Gilly was not dead did much to abate Gideon's wrath. He gave Mr. Liversedge some more brandy. Mr. Liversedge took the glass, and lowered his feet to the floor. "Much better as it is," he said, his volatile spirits already beginning to turn events to good account. "I may say, Captain Ware, it is gratifying to discover very proper sentiment in you. No need to have been rough, though! In fact, foolish! Must bear in mind that without my goodwill impossible to find his Grace! A very good cognac, sir!"

"Make the most of it!" Gideon advised him. "You'll get none in Newgate."

Mr. Liversedge sipped the brandy delicately. He was beginning to feel very much better, as a gentle glow spread through him. "That, sir, is an ungentlemanly observation," he said. "Moreover, you would gain nothing if you acted hastily, you know. Let bygones be bygones, Captain Ware! Nothing will afford me more pleasure than to restore his Grace to his family."

"You canting humbug, you are trying to hold his Grace to ransom!" Gideon said.

"Well," said Mr. Liversedge reasonably, "one must live, sir, after all!"

"Be sure you have not long to do so!"

"I see what it is!" said Mr. Liversedge. "But you mistake, sir! I don't ask ransom of *you!* It will be nothing to his Grace: I daresay he will be very glad to pay it, for, you know, he might expect his price to be higher."

"Let me tell you this!" said Gideon. "His Grace is not going to be bled for as much as a farthing by any such fellow as you! Instead, Mr. Liversedge, you are going to go with me to where his Grace is! If I find him safe and un-hurt, you may escape your deserts—though I don't vouch for it!"

Mr. Liversedge leaned back, and crossed one leg over the other. "Now, indeed, Captain Ware, it is of no use to fly into your high ropes!" he said. "Do but consider for a moment! I daresay you would like to have me clapped up in Newgate, but if you were so unwise as to call in the Law, his Grace would perish. I will be open with you. If I were not to return—and that speedily—to the unworthy habitation which now shelters his Grace, I very much fear that there are those, less mild in nature than myself, who would put a period to his existence. And that, you know, would be very shocking! Yet how could you prevent it? You might indeed clap me into some disagreeable gaol, but you cannot force me to divulge his Grace's whereabouts. One dislikes to be obliged to use vulgar expressions, but I must permit myself to say that you are at a stand, sir!"

"Down to every move on the board, are you not?" said Gideon, smiling unpleasantly.

"Sir," said Mr. Liversedge impressively, "if a man would succeed in carrying out large enterprises, he must be so! I have heard it related that the Duke—I refer, Captain Ware, to his Grace of Wellington, not his Grace of Sale—once said that he made his campaigns with ropes. If anything went amiss, he said, he tied a knot, and went on. A valuable maxim, sir, and one on which I have striven to mould my own campaigns. I tie a knot, and go on!"

"Very well, if the knot holds," replied Gideon. "This one won't! If I had to search the whole of England for my cousin, I own I might find myself obliged to come to terms with you. But I have not, Mr. Liversedge. There is a card in my hand I fancy you had not thought I possessed. I received a letter from my cousin to-day. He wrote to me from the White Horse at Baldock. You and I, my engaging rascal, are going to Baldock to-morrow." He observed, with satisfaction, his guest's suddenly stricken countenance. "And when we reach Baldock, either you are going to conduct me to my cousin's prison, or *I* am going to conduct *you* to the nearest magistrate. And let me further inform you, sir, that if it took every Runner at Bow Street, and every constable in Hertfordshire, and the militia beside to do it, I would see to it that not a house nor a barn was left unsearched within twenty miles of Baldock!"

Mr. Liversedge, gazing in chagrin at his host's purposeful face, found no difficulty in believing him. Captain Ware appeared to him to be one who would not have the slightest hesitation in employing measures as extreme as they were disagreeable. He would probably, reflected Mr. Liversedge bitterly, enjoy setting Hertfordshire by the ears. And he would do it, too, for no magistrate, or constable, or Colonel of Militia would refuse to search with the utmost stringency for so important a personage as the Duke of Sale. Mr. Liversedge thought of Mr. Mimms's feelings, if a search-party were to descend upon the Bird in Hand, as it unquestionably would. Mr. Mimms's protests, when the lifeless body of the Duke had been placed in one of his cellars, had

182

been as pungent as they were unavailing. He was not a man who courted notoriety, but he had not quite escaped the notice of Hertfordshire authorities, and there was little doubt that his hostelry would be one of the first houses to be visited. Nor could Mr. Liversedge place the smallest reliance on the faulty memories of Post Office officials. Ten to one, some busybody of a clerk would recall that he had handled letters addressed to a Mr. Liversedge. One thing would lead to another, and several things, once added together, might even lead to Bath, where there were incensed persons only too anxious to lay their hands upon Mr. Liversedge. He was not a man much given to self blame, but he was inclined to own, at this moment, that he had made several mistakes. It was not, of course, his fault that Captain Ware should have proved to be blind to his best interests, but it might have been wiser to have abandoned his Grand Stratagem in favour of the simpler one of extracting ransom from the Duke himself. It was a painful reflection that had he done this he might even now bear in his pocket the Duke's draft for a handsome sum. He looked at the Captain with dislike, and could not imagine what could have induced the Duke to confide his secrets to such a repellent person. It seemed unlikely that Captain Ware had any proper feelings at all, so that it was in a voice lacking in conviction that he said at last: "I am persuaded you would not create such an ungenteel stir!"

Captain Ware laughed. It was not an infectious laugh, and it drew no answering gleam from Mr. Liversedge. It even grated upon his ear unpleasantly.

"I think you will lead me to my cousin," said Captain Ware, walking over to the door. He opened it, and found that Wragby was standing in the hall. He grinned at him. "Come here, Wragby!" he said. "We are going to take a little journey to-morrow into Hertfordshire, and we are going to take this person with us."

"You would be wiser to let me go immediately!" interpolated Mr. Liversedge desperately. "I dare not answer for the consequences to his Grace if I am any longer absent! He may be dead by the time you reach him, sir!"

"Now, what must I do to teach you that I am not such a gudgeon as you supposed?" wondered the Captain. "Those who are his gaolers will most certainly keep him alive until they know how you have fared with me. Wragby, I want this fellow kept under guard! That should not trouble you, I fancy!"

The ex-sergeant smiled indulgently. "Lor' no, sir! We'll rack up for the night, all right and tight together. And what may we be going to do in Hertfordshire, if I may make so bold as to ask?"

"We are going to extricate his Grace from a scrape," replied Gideon, his eyes alight. "I'll take the curricle, and my bays. Tell Sturry to see to it! We shall set out at the earliest possible moment."

"What, are we going to take this rasher-of-wind along with us, sir?" demanded Wragy disapprovingly.

"Sir," said Mr. Liversedge, "I would not have believed that any man of honour and breeding could have served another such a backhand turn!"

"Now, don't you waste your breath talking slum!" recommended Wragby kindly. "A regular out-and-outer is the Captain, and so you'll find afore you're much older! You come along of me! Asking your pardon, sir, if you mean to go off, you'd best see the Colonel first."

"I am going to find him now," said Gideon. "Don't let this fellow slip through your fingers!"

"What, me?" said Wragby, affronted. "It would take a better man than that silly bite to slip through my fingers, sir!"

He then haled Mr. Liversedge up a narrow, twisted stair to the kitchen, planted him in a wooden chair, and after informing him that he was a chub to have bearded such a neck-or-nothing blade as the Captain, congratulated him on his narrow escape from death by strangulation. Mr. Liversedge, never one to let opportunity slide, made several ingenious attempts to convince him that enormous benefits would be his if he chose to ally himself with his prisoner, but Wragby, after listening to him admiringly, said that he was as bold as Beauchamp, but that if he wanted a bite of supper he had best stop pitching his gammon. Mr. Liversedge, making the best of things, accepted this counsel, and pulled his chair up to the table.

Captain Ware, in spite of having chosen an unorthodox way of applying for it, had no difficulty in persuading his Colonel to grant him leave of absence. The Colonel not only considered Gideon one of his more promising officers, but he very much disliked scandal attaching to any member of his regiment. He no sooner learned that Gideon wished to go in search of his cousin than he said that he was very glad to hear it, and trusted that he would not return to town without him.

Leaving the Colonel, Gideon hesitated on the brink of paying a call on his father, and then decided that it would be wiser to write to him. He had no wish to be obliged to enter into lengthy explanations, and still less to find himself with Lord Lionel as another passenger in his carriage. It was by this time too late for his dinner-engagement at the Daffy Club, even had he not been too much disturbed by Gilly's plight to have any inclination for a convivial party. He walked into Stephen's Hotel instead, in Bond Street, where, since his was a known face, and one, moreover, that belonged to the military set, he was made discreetly welcome, and led to a vacant table in the coffee-room. The dinner which was served was well-chosen, and well-cooked, but the Captain made a poor meal. Had it been practicable, he would have preferred to have left town that evening. He had no very real fear that the Duke would be murdered by Mr. Liversedge's confederates, but he hated to think of Gilly in the hands of villains who might use him roughly, or incarcerate him in some comfortless stronghold. How he had got himself into such a situation Gideon could not imagine, although he suspected that the adventure he had hinted at had something to do with Mr. Liversedge. He had never supposed that anything other than the mildest excitement would befall Gilly, and Mr. Liversedge's disclosure had come to him as a shock that brought with it a revulsion of feeling. He now realized that he had been a fool to imagine that Gilly, all untried as he was, could fend for himself. If he had had a grain of sense he would have applied for leave a week earlier, and joined Gilly on his adventures. Then he remembered the mischievous twinkle in Gilly's eyes when he had last seen him, and his refusal to divulge his destination, or even his purpose in leaving London. Gilly had not wanted his cousin's company, and that fact alone ought to have put a sane man on his guard. Captain Ware, as the wine grew low in the bottle, began to feel little better than a murderer. His imagination played round Gilly's present lot, and it was with an effort that he refrained from jumping up, and striding out of the hotel. To remain inactive while Gilly might need him urgently was almost more than he could bear; and had there been a full moon he thought he must have set out on his journey immediately. He tried to comfort himself with the thought that if Gilly knew Liversedge's destination he would know also that his big cousin would come speedily to his rescue; but it did not seem probable that Liversedge would have told him, in which case he must have given himself up for lost.

When he reached his chambers again, he found that Wragby, by way of facilitating his task, had, as he phrased it, given his charge such liberal potations of strip-me-naked that he was now quite shot in the neck, and sleeping heavily upon the kitchen-floor.

"What a waste of good gin!" remarked Gideon.

"Ah, but it weren't the good gin, sir!" replied his henchman.

Gideon went into his sitting-room, and sat down to write a brief note to his father. He informed him merely that he had discovered a clue to Gilly's whereabouts, and was going out of town to find him. After that he went to bed, warning Wragby to be ready to make an early start next morning. Wragby said that there would be no difficulty about that, except that they might have to carry Mr. Liversedge down to the curricle, since he would undoubtedly be stale-drunk after imbibing so much bad gin.

CHAPTER XVII

THE Duke came to himself slowly and painfully. While the cart in which he was conveyed some five miles to the Bird in Hand jolted its way down the rough lane which Mr. Shifnal chose in understandable preference to the pike-road, he lay for some time unconscious, and for the last mile in a queer state between swooning and waking. He seemed to himself to be suffering some nightmare. It hurt him to move his head, and his eyelids were weighted. When he tried to open them knives stabbed behind them. At moments he was aware of movement, even of hands feeling his brow, and his wrists, and of a vaguely familiar voice speaking from a great distance away; but for long periods of time he sank back into uneasy oblivion, these merciful lapses being largely brought on by the bumping of wheels over all the inequalities of the road. Each lurch caused him exquisite torment, for Mr. Liversedge had struck hard, and with a heavy cudgel, and not only the Duke's head, but his neck and spine had suffered. He was in one of these deep swoons when he was lifted out of the cart, and carried into the Bird in Hand through the back-door, so he knew nothing of the violent altercation which raged over his body, or of the disaster prophesied by Mr. Mimms.

When he began to come more fully to his senses, it still hurt him to open his eyes, or to move his head, but he was regaining command over his faculties, and he knew that this weakness must be overcome. He forced himself to lift his eyelids, but winced as light struck against his aching eyeballs. Something cold and wet was laid across his brow; a voice said encouragingly: "That's the dandy, now! You want to bite on the bridle, lad, and you'll be as right as a trivet! Take a sup of this! Come on, now! open your mummer! There's nothing like a glass of blood-and-thunder to put a cove in high gig!"

A hand slid under his head, raising it. The Duke bit back an involuntary groan, and rather helplessly swallowed a mouthful of the fiery potion being held to his lips. Then he lifted a wavering hand to thrust the glass aside.

"Have another sup, and you'll feel as good as ever twanged!"

The Duke knew from experience that nothing aggravated his periodic headaches more than liquor. In his hazy state of mind the only thing he knew was that one of these, and an unusually severe one, had attacked him. He whispered: "No."

"Dashed if you aren't too green to know what's good for you!" remarked Mr. Shifnal, lowering him again.

"Water!" uttered the Duke.

"Well, you can have it if you *want* it," said Mr. Shifnal. "But I never knew Adam's ale do anyone a mite of good. What's more, I'll have to drink up this here blood-and-thunder, if you want to put water in your glass." He accomplished this task without difficulty, poured some water into the glass, and once more lifted the Duke's head. When he had let him sink back again on to the dirty mattress which had been laid on the floor to receive him, he lifted up the candlestick and closely studied his prisoner's face. "I'm bound to own you look like a death's head on a mopstick," he said candidly. "Howsever, I don't fancy as you'll be put to bed feet first this journey. What you want to do is to shut your ogles, and have a sleep."

The Duke was only too glad to do so, for the little flame of the candle hurt his eyes. Mr. Shifnal spread an aged horse-blanket over him, and went away, leaving him in Stygian gloom. The Duke slept, woke, and slept again.

When he woke fully, his head, although still aching, was rather better. It was propped up on a lumpy cushion, from which arose an unpleasant aroma of dirt and mildew. The Duke moved distastefully, and found that the back of his skull was badly bruised. He put up his hand, and cautiously felt the swelling, and as he did so he remembered that he had been watching fireworks at Hitchin Fair, and that he must keep an eye on Tom and Belinda. But he was not now at Hitchin Fair. In fact, he did not know where he was, though he seemed to be lying, fully dressed, on a very hard bed. He put his hand out, groping in the darkness for some familiar object, and felt cold stone. Then he must, he supposed, be lying on the floor. His hand encountered the round shape of an earthenware jar, and for a few moments the only thought in his mind was that he was parched with thirst. He dragged himself up on one elbow, feeling sick, and dizzy, and absurdly weak, and after a grim effort contrived to lift the jar. It was more than half full of water. The Duke drank deeply, and when he could drink no more pulled the bandage from his head, and dipped it into the jar. With this tied round his burning skull again, he was able, although unreadily, to fix his thoughts on what had happened to him. Fireworks, and a fat woman to whom he gave up his place: he remembered that clearly enough. He had gone to the back of the crowd, and someone had spoken to him. A neat man, in worn riding-clothes, whom he had taken for a groom, and who—— Suddenly he stiffened, recalling in a flash of comprehension that the man had said: "My lord Duke!" He had been caught off his guard; he had turned involuntarily; he had even been fool enough to follow the unknown man into the shadow of one of the tents. A blatant trap, and he had walked into it like the Johnny Raw he was. He could have wept with rage at his folly, and did indeed utter a stifled groan. How Gideon would mock at him if ever he heard of it! Then it occurred to him, rather unpleasantly, that there might be no room for mockery. Someone had recognized him, and had kidnapped him. The Duke was not so raw that he did not realize that the price of his freedom was likely to be a heavy one. And since he had taken such care not to let anyone know where he was there could be no hope of a rescue. Matthew would know that he had been at Baldock; so too would Gideon, for he remembered that he had written a letter to him from the White Horse. But neither could guess that he had gone to Hitchin; and neither would be at all alarmed at his continued absence, until it was too late. The Duke had no desire to pay a staggering ransom, and still less desire to face the reproaches of his family, but he could not remain shut up in darkness for the rest of his life. If he were obstinate, his captors might starve him, or resort to even sterner measures. He was quite at their mercy, and never in his life had he longed more passionately for Nettlebed, or Chigwell, or even for Lord Lionel. And more than for anyone did he long for Gideon, who would surely get him out of this appalling predicament. He felt ill, and helpless, and humiliatingly childish; and he was obliged to scold himself as sharply as Lord Lionel had so often done before he could shake off his crushing despondency.

After what seemed a very long time, he heard footsteps

coming down a creaking stair. A crack of light showed him where the door of his prison was. He found that he had instinctively braced himself, and flushed in the darkness. He forced himself to relax, and to lie as though at his ease, betraying none of the alarm he felt. A Johnny Raw he might be, but he was also Ware of Sale, and no common felon should have the satisfaction of seeing him afraid.

The door opened, and Mr. Shifnal came in, bearing a steaming bowl, and with a lantern slung over one wrist. The Duke recognized him at once, and remembered that it was he who had given him some potent liquor, many hours ago. He crooked his left arm under his head to raise it, and lay calmly regarding his gaoler.

Mr. Shifnal set the lamp down on the floor close to the Duke's head, and looked at him closely. "That's the barber!" he said cheerfully. "I thought you was backt at one time, guv'nor, but there's nothing like a real rum bub for a cull as has been grassed. Not but what you didn't have no more than a lick, but I doubt it done you good. I got some cat-lap here for you, seeing as how you was as sick as a cushion, and maybe used to pap. If you was to sit up, you could sup it down, couldn't you?"

"Presently," said the Duke. "Put it on the floor, if you please."

Mr. Shifnal grinned down at him. "It ain't no use for you to be cagged, guv'nor. The blow's been bit, and you'll have to stand buff if you want to get out of this cellar alive. Which, mind you, there's some as holds you didn't ought to get out alive, but I wouldn't wish you to think I was one of them, because I ain't. You drink up that cat-lap, and maybe you'll feel able to talk business, which is what I come for."

While he unburdened himself of this speech, not much of which was comprehensible to his prisoner, the Duke was taking unobtrusive stock of his surroundings. The cellar in which he lay was paved with stone flags and had no window. Its only outlet appeared to be the door through which Mr. Shifnal had entered and to which he held the ponderous key. As it opened inwards, there would be little chance of breaking out through it. The roof of the cellar was vaulted; it was quite a large room, and seemed to be used as a dumping-place for all manner of rubbish. A broken chair, several rusted cooking-pots, some sacks, an old broom, one or two cans, and a litter of broken casks and boxes and empty bottles were all it contained, except for the mattress on which the Duke lay.

Having taken this in, the Duke brought his gaze to bear

on Mr. Shifnal, who had squatted down beside him on a folded sack. He saw that he had a pistol tucked into his boot, and said: "I thought when I first saw you that you were a groom, but I fancy I was wrong: you are a highwayman."

"It don't matter to you what my lay is," responded Mr. Shifnal. "Maybe I'll be a gentleman, and live at my ease afore many days is gone by."

"Maybe," agreed the Duke. "Or maybe you'll be on your way to Botany Bay. One never knows."

"Hard words break no bones," said Mr. Shifnal. "Mind I don't blame you for feeling peevy! It ain't a pleasant thing to be bowled out, and you little more than a halfling. But don't you worry, guv'nor! You're well-equipt, you are, and there ain't nothing to stop you loping off any time you says the word. The cove as wants to carry you out feet first ain't here just at the moment. But he's a-coming back, and it would be as well for you if you were gone afore he gets here. Now, maybe it's because you're just a noddy, or maybe it's because I allus had a weakness for a game chicken, which I'll allow you are, but I've taken quite a fancy to you, dang me if I ain't! and I wouldn't like for you to be put to bed with a shovel afore your time. You grease me in the hand, guv'nor, and do it handsome, and I'll let you go afore this other cove comes back."

"How long have I been here?" asked the Duke, as though he had not attended to a word of this.

"You've been here ever since close on eleven last night, and you'll likely——"

"What's o'clock now?" interrupted the Duke, taking out his watch, which had stopped. "I must thank you, by the way, for not robbing me of my watch!"

"Ay, and it isn't many as wouldn't have had it off of you, and the ready and rhino in your pockets as well," said Mr. Shifnal frankly. "I don't see what it matters to you what time of day it is, because down in this cellar it don't make any difference, but since you're so particular anxious to know, it's close on nine in the morning. And a fine, bright day it is, with the sun a-shining, and the birds all a-singing. Just the kind of day for a cove to be out and about!"

The Duke set his watch, and wound it up. Mr. Shifnal looked at it wistfully. "It's a rare loge that," he said. "It went to my heart not to snabble it."

"Never mind!" said the Duke, sitting up with an effort. "You may have it, and the money in my pockets as well, if you leave that door unlocked."

Mr. Shifnal smiled indulgently upon him. "I had a look

190

in your pockets, guv'nor, and it's low tide with you. It ain't coachwheels I want, but flimseys."

The Duke picked up the bowl of thin gruel, and sipped it resolutely. "How much?" he enquired.

"What do you say to fifty thousand Yellow Georges?" suggested Mr. Shifnal winningly.

"Why, that I thank you for the compliment you pay me in rating me at so high a figure, but that I fear I am not worth it."

"Call it thirty!" said Mr. Shifnal. "Thirty wouldn't seem no more to a well-blunted swell like you than what a Goblin would be to me!"

"Oh, I couldn't pay you the half of thirty thousand!" said the Duke, swallowing some more of the gruel.

"Gammon!" replied Mr. Shifnal scornfully. "You could draw the bustle to twice that figure!"

"Not until I am twenty-five," said the Duke.

The tranquility in his voice took Mr. Shifnal aback slightly. It seemed very wrong to him that this frail young swell should not be made to realize the dangerous nature of his position. He pointed it out to him. The Duke smiled at him absently, and went on sipping his gruel. "It ain't no manner of use bamming me you ain't as well-breeched a cove as any in the land, because I knows as how you are!" said Mr. Shifnal, nettled.

"Yes, I am very rich," agreed the Duke. "But I do not yet control my fortune, you know."

"There's them as does as would pay it, and gladly, to have you back safe!"

The Duke appeared to consider this. "But perhaps they don't want to have me back," he suggested.

Mr. Shifnal was nonplussed. It began to seem as though his colleague's notions, which he had been inclined to think fanciful, were not so far-fetched. Yet although Mr. Liversedge might return loaded down with money-bags given him by the Duke's grateful cousin, Mr. Shifnal had a strong suspicion that his share in that wealth might not be commensurate with his deserts. It would, he thought, be a very much better plan for him to remove the Duke from his dungeon, and to pocket a ransom, before Mr. Liversedge could return from his mission. He would have the support of Mr. Mimms, he knew, because although Mr. Mimms would undoubtedly claim a share of any blood-money there might be, he did not want the Duke to be murdered on his premises; and he was mortally afraid of coming into serious contact with the Law. He shook his head at the Duke, and told him that he did not know what lay before him. But

191

the Duke could not perceive any advantage to his captors in killing him, and considered that Mr. Shifnal's references to the likelihood of his sudden taking-off were designed merely to frighten him into agreeing to the payment of an extortionate ransom. He finished the gruel, and set down the bowl.

"You better think it over, guv'nor!" Mr. Shifnal said. "You won't have nothing else to do, so take your time! I'm striking the gigg now, and you won't see no more of me, nor anyone, till I brings you your supper. I daresay you'll be thinking different by then."

He rose from the floor, picked up the bowl and the lantern, and went away, locking the door behind him. The Duke lowered himself on to his unpleasant pillow again, and bent his mind to the problem of how he was to escape. For he had made up his mind that escape he must and would.

No method immediately presented itself to him, and he wasted some time in cursing himself for not having gone armed to the Fair. His only weapon was his malacca cane, which had been propped against the broken chair, with his curly-brimmed beaver poised on top of it, and a malacca cane pitted against Mr. Shifnal's pistol would stand little chance of success. The possibility of taking Mr. Shifnal off his guard seemed remote: he plainly held the Duke to be of little account, but he did not look as though he were in the habit of being taken off his guard. Moreover, the Duke was still feeling extremely battered, and he doubted whether he would have the physical strength to stun Mr. Shifnal. He thought that the most pressing need was to recruit his forces, and with this end in view he closed his eyes, and tried so hard to go to sleep that he did so at last through sheer exhaustion.

He was awakened by the sound of footsteps again, but they did not come to his door. A heavy tread passed it; he heard a latch lift gratingly, and the sound as of a wooden case being dragged across the stone floor. Other and rather shuffling footsteps came down the stairs. The Duke heard the murmur of voices, and strained his ears in vain to catch what was being said. He failed, but as the footsteps passed his door again, a rough voice said: "Mind how you carry that, you clumsy chub! Give me them daffy-bottles!"

The Duke's brows twitched together, for the voice was familiar. For a long time he could not place it, but by dint of recalling the various persons whom he had encountered during the preceding week he at last reached the right conclusion. The voice belonged to Mr. Mimms; and if that were so it was more than likely that his cellar lay under the Bird in Hand. And if that again were so, then there could be no doubt that Mr. Liversedge had had a hand in the abduction.

It seemed a little puzzling to the Duke, and for a moment he wondered if he had been kidnapped for revenge. Then he thought that this was too foolhardy a thing for even Mr. Liversedge to undertake, and he supposed that by some means or other that astute gentleman had discovered the identity of his visitor. Why Mr. Liversedge was remaining in the background he could not imagine, unless it were that his sensibilities were too nice to permit of his openly confessing himself a kidnapper. The Duke decided that such questions as these were not of great moment, and applied his mind to the more urgent problem. If he was to attempt to break out of the cellar, and if this was indeed in the Bird in Hand, the best time for the attempt would undoubtedly be during the evening, when the tap-room might be supposed to be full, and Mr. Mimms and his satellites busy in serving drinks. In all probability there would be a good deal of cheerful noise in the tap-room, which would be helpful. The Duke considered afresh the only plan he had been able to hit upon, and thought it was worth a trial. Since money was what his captors wanted, they were unlikely to kill him, whatever he did; and if he failed he would be no worse off than he was now.

Not the most boring day spent in his tutor's company had ever seemed as long to the Duke as this one. The darkness was like a blanket, and no sound from above penetrated to the cellar. He thought that if he failed to escape it would not be long before he would agree to pay any ransom. When he heard Mr. Shifnal's quick step approaching down the stairs, he had almost given up hope of being brought any of the promised supper. He knew that he stood in need of sustaining food, however little he might relish the thought of it, for he had tried the effect of standing up, and of taking a few groping steps in the darkness, and he had felt abominably dizzy and weak-kneed. His headache, however, had considerably abated. He thought that it would be just as well that Mr. Shifnal should suppose him to be still prostrate, so he lay down, and closed his eyes, groaning artistically when the door opened.

Mr. Shifnal had brought him a plate of cold beef, a hunk of bread, and a mug of porter. He set these down, and asked him how he felt.

"My head aches," complained the Duke fretfully.

"Well, you got a rare wisty castor on it," said Mr. Shifnal.

"What you want is a nice bed, like you're used to, and a breath of fresh air. You could have it, too, if you wasn't so bacon-brained."

The Duke said: "But how could I pay thirty thousand pounds?"

Mr. Shifnal caught the note of doubt in his voice, and congratulated himself on his wisdom in having left the young swell alone all day. He explained to the Duke how the sum could be found, and the Duke listened, and raised objections, and seemed first to agree, and then to think better of it. Mr. Shifnal thought that by the following morning he would know no hesitation, and was sorry that he had fortified him with meat and drink. He had been a little afraid that so delicate a young man might become seriously ill if starved, and a dead Duke was of no use to him. He determined not to allow him any breakfast, if he should still be obdurate in the morning, and he refused to leave the lantern behind him. Continued darkness and solitude, he was certain, would bring about a marked improvement in the Duke's frame of mind. He went away again, warning the captive that it was of no use to shout, for no one would hear him if he did. The Duke was glad to know this, but he hunched a shoulder pettishly, and turned his face to the wall.

He forced himself to wait for what seemed an interminable time. When he judged that the hour must be somewhere near ten, he stood up, and felt in his pocket for the device he used to light his cigars. Under his finger the little flame sprang up obediently. He kindled one of the matches at it, and holding it carefully on high, located the position of the heap of lumber. He went over to it, and had picked up a splinter of wood before the match went out. He could feel that the wood was dry, and when he kindled a second match and held it to the splinter, it caught fire. The Duke found a longer splinter, and kindled that from the first, and stuck it into one of the bottles on the floor. The light it threw was not very good, and it several times had to be blown to renewed flame, but the Duke was able, in the glimmer, to find what he wanted, and to carry it over to the door. He built up there a careful pile of shavings of wood, scraps of old sacking, the broken chair, the broom, and anything else that looked as though it might burn easily. His tablets went to join the rest, the thin leaves being torn out, and crumpled, and poked under the wood. The Duke set fire to his heap, and thanked God that the cellar was not damp. He had to kneel down and blow the fitful flames, but his efforts were rewarded: the wood began to crackle, and the flames to leap higher. He got up, and

194

observed his work with satisfaction. If the smoke rose to the upper floor, as he supposed it must, he could only hope that it would be drowned by the fumes of clay pipes in the tap-room. He collected his hat, and his cane, buttoned up his long drab coat, and added an old boot to his bonfire. It was becoming uncomfortably hot, and he was forced to stand back from it, watching anxiously to see whether the door would burn. In a short time he knew that it would. His heart began to beat so hard that he could almost hear it. He felt breathless, and the smoke was making his eyes smart. But the door was burning, and in a few minutes more the flames would be licking the walls on either side of it. The Duke caught up the horse-blanket, and, using it as a shield, attacked the flaming woodwork. He scorched himself in the process, but he succeeded in kicking away the centre of the door. He paid no heed to where the burning fragments fell, but he did smother the flames round the aperture he had made; and then, abandoning the charred blanket, swiftly dived for his hole, and struggled through it.

One moment he spent in recovering his breath, and settling his hat somewhat gingerly on his head, and then, taking a firm grip on his cane, he stole up the stairs.

He reached the top, and knew that he had been correct in his assumption that he was imprisoned in the Bird in Hand. He remembered that there was a door leading into the yard at the back of the house, and he made for this. From the tap-room came the sound of convivial song and laughter. There was no one to be seen in the dimly lit space by the yard-door, and he thought for a moment that he was going to make his escape unperceived. And then, just as he was within a few steps of his goal, a door on his right opened, and Mr. Mimms came out, carrying a large jug.

Mr. Mimms gave one startled grunt, dropped the jug, and lunged forward. The Duke was expert in the use of the singlestick, but he employed none of the arts he had been taught. Side-stepping Mr. Mimms's bull-like rush, he made one neat thrust with his cane between his legs, and brought him crashing to the ground. The next instant he had reached the yard-door, and had torn it open, and was stumbling over the cobbles and the refuse outside the inn.

It was a dark night, and the yard seemed to be full of obstacles, but the Duke managed to get across it, to grope his way round a corner of the barn, and, as his eyes grew accustomed to the murk, to reach the field beyond. In the distance behind him, he thought he could hear voices. He thanked God that there was no moon, and ran for his life, heading in what he hoped was the direction of the village of Arlesey.

By the time he reached the straggling hedge that shut the fields off from the lane he was out of breath, and staggering on his feet. He was obliged to stand still, to recover himself a little, and he took the opportunity of looking back towards the inn. It was hidden from him by trees, but he was able to see a faint red glow, and realized that his fire must have taken good hold. He gave a panting laugh, and pushed his way through the hedge on to the lane. Mr. Mimms would have enough on his hands without adding the pursuit of his prisoner to it, he thought; and if the man in riding-dress thought the recapture of his prize of more importance than the quenching of the fire, the deep ditch beside the lane would afford excellent cover for a fugitive. The Duke walked as fast as he could down the lane, straining his ears for any sound of footsteps behind him. But he thought that he would be searched for in the fields rather than in the road.

The first cottages of Arlesey came into sight. Chinks of lamplight shone between several window-blinds. The Duke, reeling from mingled faintness and fatigue, chose a cottage at random, and knocked on the door. It was presently opened to him by a stolid-looking man in fustian breeches, and a velveret jacket, who opened his eyes at sight of his dishevelled visitor, and ejaculated: "Lord ha' mussy! Whatever be the matter with you, sir?"

"Will you allow me to rest here till daylight?" said the Duke, leaning against the lintel of the door. "I have—suffered an accident, and—I rather fancy—some murderous fellows are on my heels."

A stout woman, who had been peeping round her husband's massive form, exclaimed: "The poor young gentleman! I'll lay my life it's them murdering thieves as haunts the Bird in Hand! Come you in, sir! come you in!"

"Thank you!" said the Duke, and fainted.

CHAPTER XVIII

THE Duke left Arlesey on the following morning, unmolested, but slightly bedraggled. His hosts, upon his dramatic collapse, had carried him up to the second bedroom, and had not only stripped him of his outer garments, but had revived him with all manner of country remedies. They were very much shocked, Mrs. Shottery as much by the scorched state of his riding-coat as by his alarming pallor; and they perceived, by the fine quality of his linen, that he was of gentle birth. By the time that he had recovered his senses, the worthy couple had convinced each other that he had fallen a victim to the cut-throat thieves who infested the district, using the Bird in Hand as their headquarters. The Duke was feeling quite disinclined for conversation, and merely lay smiling wearily upon them, and murmuring his soft-toned thanks for their solicitude. Mrs. Shottery bustled about in high fettle, bringing up hot bricks to lay at his feet, strong possets to coax down his throat, and vinegar to soothe a possible headache, while her husband, having seen the glow of fire in the distance, sallied forth to reconnoitre. He came back just as the Duke was dropping asleep and told him with much headshaking, and many exclamations, that the Bird in Hand was ablaze, and such a to-do as he disremembered to have seen in Arlesey before.

In the morning, the Duke was touched to find that Mrs. Shottery had washed and ironed his shirt, and had even pressed out the creases in his olive-green coat. He said that he would not for the world have had her put herself to such trouble, but she would not listen to such foolishness, she said. Instead she showed him the scorch-marks on his drab riding-coat, mourning over the impossbiility of eradicating them. Her husband eyed the Duke with respect, and said he reckoned he knew how the gentleman had come by the marks.

"What happened to the inn?" asked the Duke. "Is it quite burned down? Really, I never thought of that!"

"Well, it ain't clean gone, but no one couldn't live in it no more," replied Mr. Shottery, with satisfaction. "And where that scoundrel Mimms has loped off to the lord alone knows! They say as he and the barman, and another cove went away in the cart, and so many bits and pieces piled up in it that it was a wonder the old nag could draw it. A good riddance to them all, is what I say!"

"If they don't come back, which they likely will!" said his wife pessimistically.

"I think they will not," said the Duke. "You may depend upon it that they are afraid that I shall lay information against them."

"Which I trust and prays, sir, as you will!" said Mrs. Shottery, in minatory accents.

The Duke returned an evasive answer. He had certainly meant to do so, but a period of reflection had shown him the disadvantages of such proper action. His identity would have to be disclosed, and he was as little desirous of having it known that the Duke of Sale had been kidnapped as of advertising his presence in the district. He discovered, too, upon consideration, that having outwitted his enemies he felt himself to be quite in charity with them. His most pressing wish was to return to Hitchin, where his two protégés must by now be fancying themselves deserted.

He drove there in a gig, beside a shy man who had business in the town, and had agreed to carry the Duke along with him. The Shotterys bade him a fond farewell, and indignantly spurned his offer to pay them for his lodging. He said, colouring like a boy, that he thought he had given them a great deal of trouble, but they assured him that they grudged nothing to anyone who could smoke out a nest of thieves, as he had done.

The day was fine, and a night's repose had restored the Duke to the enjoyment of his usual health. He was inclined to feel pleased with himself, and to think that for a greenhorn he had acquitted himself creditably. It seemed unlikely that Liversedge and his associates would dare to make any further attempt upon his life, or his liberty, and it was reasonable to suppose that he had come to an end of his adventures. Nothing now remained but to convey Tom and Belinda to Bath, and to hand Belinda over to Harriet while he himself searched for Mr. Mudgley.

He reckoned without his hosts. When the gig set him down at the Sun Inn, and he walked into this hostelry, he was met by popping eyes and gaping mouths, and informed by the landlord that no one had expected to see him again.

The Duke raised his brows at this, for he did not relish the landlord's tone, and said: "How is this? Since I have not paid my shot you must have been sure of my return."

It was plain that the landlord had had no such certainty. He said feebly: "I'm downright glad to see your honour back, but the way things have been ever since you went off, sir, I wouldn't be surprised at nothing, and that's the truth!"

The Duke was conscious of a sinking at the pit of his stomach. "Has anything gone amiss?" he asked.

"Oh, no!" said the landlord sarcastically, his wrongs rising forcibly to his mind. "Oh, no, sir! I've only had the constables here, and my good name blown upon, for to have the constables nosing round an inn is enough to ruin it, and this posting-house which has given beds to the gentry and the nobility too, and never a breath of scandal the years I've owned it!"

The Duke now perceived that he had not yet come to the end of his adventures. He sighed, and said: "Well, I suppose it is Master Tom! What mischief has he been engaged upon while I was away?"

The landlord's bosom swelled. "If it's your notion of mischief, sir, to be took up for a dangerous rogue, it ain't mine! Robbery on the King's highroad, that's what the charge is! Firing at honest citizens—old Mr. Stalybridge, too, as is highly respected in the town! He'll be transported, if he ain't hanged, and a good thing too, that's what I say!"

The Duke was a good deal taken aback by this disclosure, but after a stunned moment he said: "Nonsense! He has no gun, and cannot possibly——"

"Begging your pardon, sir, he had a fine pistol, and it was God's mercy he didn't kill Mr. Stalybridge's coachman with it, for the shot went so close to him it fair scorched his ear!"

"Good God!" ejaculated the Duke, suddenly bethinking him of his duelling-pistols.

"Ah, and well you may say so!" nodded the landlord. "And a great piece of black cloth hanging down over his face, with a couple of holes in it like a mask, enough to give anyone a turn! Locked up in prison he is now, the young varmint!"

"Did you say he missed his shot?" demanded the Duke.

The landlord reluctantly admitted that he had said this, and the Duke, wasting no more time with him, went up to his room to inspect his guns. As he had suspected, one was missing from the case. A quick inspection showed that Tom had taken the pistol which had never been loaded. The box containing powder and ball did not seem to have been tampered with, rather strangely. The Duke collected his fast dwindling capital from the locked drawer in his dressing-table, and sallied forth to see what could be done to extricate Tom from his predicament. Just as he was about to leave the inn he bethought him of his other protégée, and turned to ask the landlord where she was.

"She went away with Mr. Clitheroe," replied the landlord simply.

The Duke took a moment to assimilate this piece of information. Nothing in Belinda's artless prattle had led him to foresee the introduction of a Mr. Clitheroe into his life. A happy thought occurred to him; he said quickly: "Did Mr. Clitheroe quite lately marry a Miss Street?"

"Mr. Clitheroe ain't married at all, nor likely to be," answered the landlord. "He's an old Quaker gentleman, as lives with his sister, Ickleford way."

As it seemed to him most improbable that an old Quaker gentleman should have offered Belinda either a ring to put on her finger, or a purple silk dress, the Duke was now totally at a loss. The landlord, staring fixedly at a point above his head, added in an expressionless voice: "Mr. Clitheroe don't nowise hold with town bucks seducing of innocent young females—by what he told me."

The Duke allowed this aspersion upon his character to pass without remonstrance. It seemed reasonable to suppose that Belinda had fallen into safe hands; and a faint hope that one at least of his charges was provided for began to burgeon in his breast. He set forth to find the local Round-house.

It was one of Lord Lionel's maxims that every man, however wealthy, should be able on all occasions to fend for himself; and to this end he had had his ward taught such useful things as how to shoe a horse, and how to clean his own guns. Unfortunately he had never foreseen that Gilly might one day stand in need of instruction on the right methods to employ in dealing with constables and magistrates. Apart from a vague notion that one applied for bail, the Duke had no idea of what he ought to do to procure Tom's release; but although this would have seriously daunted him a week earlier his horizon had lately been so much broadened that he embarked on his task with a surprising amount of assurance.

This assurance stood him in good stead with the constable, whom he found in charge at the Round-house. The constable, an elderly man of comfortable proportions, treated him with an instinctive deference which was only slightly shaken by the disclosure that he was responsible for the young varmint locked up in No. 2 cell. He did indeed look reproachfully at the Duke, and say that it was a serious business which would end in Tom's being committed for trial, but since he added there was never any knowing what devilment such pesky lads would engage in, the Duke was encouraged to hope that he knew enough about boys not to regard Tom's exploit in too lurid a light.

He sat down on one of the benches, and laid his hat on the table. "Well, now," he said, smiling up at the constable, "will you tell me just what happened? I have heard what sounds to me a pack of nonsense, from the landlord of the Sun. He is plainly a foolish fellow, and I should prefer to listen to a sensible man."

"Now there," said the constable, warming to him, "you are in the right of it, sir! You might truss up Mr. Moffat's wit in an eggshell. Not but what this young varmint has gone for to commit a felony, no question. I'll have to take him up to Mr. Oare's place this morning, him being a

200

magistrate, and Mr. Stalybridge laying a charge against him, as he is entitled to do."

The Duke perceived that since Tom had not yet been haled before the magistrate his task must be to induce Mr. Stalybridge to withdraw the charge against him. He said: "Where did all this happen?"

"It were last night, just after dusk," said the constable. "A matter of a mile outside the town on the road to Stevenage. There was Mr. Stalybridge, a-riding in his carriage, with his man sitting up beside the coachman, him having been on a visit, you see, when up jumps this young varmint of yours out of nowhere, on a horse which he hires from Jem Datchet—which I am bound to say he paid Jem for honest, else Jem would never have let him take the nag, him being one of them as lives in a gravel-pit, as the saying is. And he ups and shouts out, *Stand and deliver!* quite to the manner born, and looses off this pop of his, which fair scorches the ear off Mr. Stalybridge's coachman, according to what he tells me. Well, not to wrap it up in clean linen, sir, Mr. Stalybridge was scared for his life, and he had out his purse, and his gold watch, and all manner of gewgaws for to hand over to the young varmint, when his man, which is not one as has more hair than wit, slips off of the box when no one ain't heeding him, and has your young varmint off of Jem Datchet's nag just as he's about to take Mr. Stalybridge's purse. I will say the lad is a proper fighter, for he put in a deal of cross-and-jostle work, but betwixt the lot of them they had him over-powered, and brought him in here, and give him over to me, as is proper. Ah, and he had both his daylights darkened, but Mr. Stalybridge's man he had had his cork drawn, so that it was wunnerful to see how the claret did flow! And once he found himself under lock and key, would he open his mummer? Not he! Downright sullen, that's what he be now, and won't give his name, nor where he lives, nor nothing!"

"I daresay he is frightened," said the Duke. "He is only fifteen, you know."

"You don't say!" marvelled the constable. "Well, I did use to think my own boys was well-growed lads, but if that don't beat all!"

"I thought you had boys of your own," said the Duke softly. "Full of mischief too, I daresay?"

He had struck the right note. The constable beamed upon him, and enunciated: "Four fine lads, sir, and everyone as lawless as the town-bull!"

The Duke settled down to listen sympathetically for the next twenty minutes to an exact account of the prowess of the constable's four sons, their splendid stature, their youth-ful pranks, and present excellence. The time was not wasted. When the recital ended the Duke had added an officer of the law to his circle of friends and well-wishers; and the constable had agreed to allow him to visit the prisoner.

The Duke then asked to see the pistol. The constable at once produced it, and the most cursory examination was enough to show the Duke that it had never been loaded, much less fired.

The constable looked very much taken-aback by this. He admitted that he had not cared to meddle with such a gun, since it looked to him like one of them murdering duelling-pistols which went off if a man so much as breathed on them.

"Well, it will not do so when it is unloaded," said the Duke. "Take a look at it now!"

The constable received the gun gingerly from him, and inspected it. Then he scratched his head. "I'm bound to say it ain't never been fired, not from the looks of it," he owned. "But Mr. Stalybridge and his man and the coach-man, they all say as the young varmint pretty nigh shot the ear off the coachman!"

"But what does the boy say?" asked the Duke.

"Well, that's it, sir. He don't say nothing. Proper sullen, that's what he is!"

The Duke rose. "He'll talk to me. Will you take me to him?"

When the door was opened into Tom's cell, that young gentleman was discovered seated on the bench in a de-jected attitude, his head propped in his hands. He looked up defensively, disclosing a bruised countenance, but when he perceived the Duke his sulky look vanished, and he jumped up, exclaiming with a distinct sob in his voice: "Oh, sir! Oh, Mr. Rufford! *Indeed*, I am very sorry! But I didn't do it!"

"No, I don't think you did," replied the Duke, in his serene way. "But you have been behaving very badly, you know, and you quite deserve to be locked up!"

Tom sniffed. "Well, when you went away, I didn't know what to do, for I had very little money, and there was the shot to be paid, and I quite thought you had deserted us! Why did you go, sir? Where have you been?"

"To tell you the truth, I couldn't help but go," said the Duke ruefully. "I am very sorry to have made you uncom-fortable, but I think you should have known I would not desert you. Now, tell me this, Tom! What did you do to make three persons swear that you fired at one of them?"

The cloud descended again on to Tom's face. He flushed,

glanced up under his lashes at the interested constable, and growled: "I shan't say."

"Then I am much afraid that you will be either hanged or transported," replied the Duke calmly.

The constable nodded his approval of this, and Tom looked up, his ruddy colour fading swiftly, and cried: "Oh, no! No, no, they would not! I didn't hurt anyone, nor even take the old man's purse!"

"What did you do?" asked the Duke.

Tom was silent for a moment. Then he muttered, staring at his boots: "Well, if you *will* know, it was a ginger-beer bottle!"

His worst fears were realized. The constable's jaw dropped for a moment, and then he burst into a hearty guffaw, slapping his leg with ecstasy, and saying that it beat the Dutch downright.

"*Ginger-beer bottle?*" repeated the Duke blankly.

"That's right, sir," said the constable, wiping his eyes. "Regular boy's trick! You shakes the bottle up good, and out flies the cork, just like it was a pisol-shot. Lordy, lordy, to think of three growed men scared of a popping cork! It'll be the laugh of the town, that's what it'll be!"

It was plain that Tom would almost have preferred to have owned to firing a pistol. He hunched his shoulder and glowered at the constable. The Duke said: "Well, thank God for that! What did you do with the bottle?"

"I threw it into the ditch," muttered Tom. "And you need not think I meant to steal the old man's purse, because Pa would have paid him back! And in any event it is different when one is being a highwayman."

"Now, that's where you're wrong, young man!" said the constable severely. "There ain't a mite of difference—not but that," he added, turning despairingly to the Duke, "you'll never get a young varmint like this here to believe you, tell him till Doomsday! All the same, they be, talking a pack of nonsense about Dick Turpin, and the like!"

The Duke, who could remember thinking that a career as a highwayman would be fraught with romance and adventure, refrained from comment. He merely said that the ginger-beer bottle must be searched for, to prove the veracity of Tom's story. The constable agreed that this should be done; Tom was locked once more into his cell; and the Duke set off, with a junior constable, and in a hired gig, to the point on the road where Mr. Stalybridge had deposed that he had been held up. This, fortunately, was easy to locate, and after a short search the bottle was found. It was borne back in triumph to the senior constable; and after the Duke had slid a gleaming golden coin into his hand, to compensate him (he said) for all the trouble he had been put to, no one could have been more anxious than this comfortable officer to see Tom set at liberty. He favoured the Duke with some valuable information about Mr. Stalybridge, fortified with which the Duke set out to pay a call on this injured citizen.

He found a pompous little man, who was obviously set on vengeance. He strutted about his book-room, declaiming, and the Duke soon perceived that an appeal to his charity would be useless. He let him talk himself out, and then said gently: "It is all very bad, but the boy did no more than losoe the cork of a ginger-beer bottle at your coachman, sir."

"I do not believe you, sir!" stated Mr. Stalybridge, staring at him out of a pair of protuberant eyes.

"But it will be proved," said the Duke. He smiled rather mischievously at his host. "I found the bottle, you know. With one of the constables. And it will be shown that the pistol has never been fired. I am so very sorry!"

"Sorry?" said Mr. Stalybridge explosively.

"Yes—but perhaps you will not care for it, after all! Only everyone will laugh so! To be giving up one's purse because a cork flies out of a bottle——" The Duke broke off, and raised his handkerchief to his lips. "Forgive me!" he apologized. "I am sure it was enough to frighten anyone!"

"Sir!" said Mr. Stalybridge, and stopped.

"And the boy is only fifteen years old!" added the Duke, in a stifled voice.

Mr. Stalybridge spoke without drawing breath for several moments. The Duke heard him with an air of polite interest. Mr. Stalybridge sat down plump in the nearest chair, and puffed, glaring at him. The Duke sighed, and made as if to rise. "You are adamant, then," he said. "I had best visit the magistrate—Mr. Oare, is it?"

Mr. Stalybridge swelled slightly, and delivered himself of a bitter animadversion on the jobbery that raised to posts of authority those who were demonstrably unfit to hold them. The Duke perceived with satisfaction that the constable had not misled him: Mr. Stalybridge and Mr. Oare were at loggerheads. Mr. Stalybridge eyed him in a frustrated way, and said: "If I withdraw the charge it will be out of pity for one who is of tender years!"

"Thank you," said the Duke, holding out his hand. "You are a great deal too good, sir. You must believe that I am excessively sorry that you should have been troubled by this badly-behaved boy. Indeed, he shall come up to beg your pardon and to thank you himself."

Mr. Stalybridge hesitated, but after looking very hard at the Duke for a moment or two, he took the hand, saying, however: "You go too fast, young man! I said *if!*"

The Duke smiled at him understandingly. "Of course!"

"And I don't want to see the young rascal!" said Mr. Stalybridge angrily. "I only hope it may be a lesson to him, and if you are a relative of his I beg you will take better care of him in the future!"

"I shall not let him out of my sight," promised the Duke. "And now perhaps we had best visit Mr. Oare."

It seemed for a time that Mr. Stalybridge was going to draw back, but after the Duke had artlessly suggested that nothing should be said of the ginger-beer bottle he consented to go with him, and to withdraw his charge against Tom. By the time this had been accomplished, and all the other formalities necessary for Tom's release fulfilled, the day was considerably advanced, and the Duke a good deal the poorer. But he bore Tom off in triumph, and that without having recourse to the use of his own title and consequence, a circumstance which pleased him so much that he quite forgave Tom for his outrageous behaviour. To have outwitted a band of kidnappers, wrested a potential felon from the hands of the Law, and dealt successfully with so inimical a gentleman as Mr. Stalybridge, all within twenty-four hours, gave him a much better idea of himself than ever he had had before. There had been times when he had regretted embarking on his odyssey, but although his efforts on Tom's behalf had been extremely exhausting, and although his money and his stock of clean linen were both running low, he no longer regretted it. He had made an interesting discovery: the retainers who sped to anticipate his every need, and guarded him from all contact with the common world, might be irksome at times, or at times a comfort to him, but he knew now that they were no more necessary to him than his high title: plain Mr. Dash of Nowhere in Particular could fend for himself.

So it was with the hint of a smile in his eyes that he bade Tom, over a sustaining dinner, render an account of himself.

"Well, I had not enough ready on me to pay the shot here," explained Tom.

"But you knew that I had locked my money in my dressing-table."

"Of course I did, but a pretty fellow I should be to think of robbing you!" said Tom indignantly.

"A pretty fellow you were to think of robbing Mr. Stalybridge," said the Duke quizzically.

"Yes, but that was different!" insisted Tom. "Besides I thought it would be an adventure!"

"You had your wish, then. Your scruples, I collect, didn't extend to my pistol?"

"But, sir!" Tom said very earnestly. "Indeed, I only borrowed that! And I didn't take any ball, or powder, you know, because I thought you would not like me to."

"Well, that was very thoughtful of you," said the Duke. "And it would have been still more thoughtful of you if you had remembered to keep out of scrapes, and to take care of Belinda."

"I was *trying* to take care of her, sir!" Tom pointed out. "For when you did not come home last night, the landlord said you had loped off without paying our shot, and he was deuced unpleasant, and I quite thought it would make Belinda uncomfortable, only she is such an unaccountable girl, and heeds nothing, besides being a dead bore—anyway, I thought I must see what could be done to come off all right. And I have played that trick with a bottle before, you know, and I thought very likely it would answer, and so it would have, if only that fellow had not crept up behind me! And, oh, sir, I very nearly hit the coachman! Only fancy! For I can tell you it is not at all an easy thing to aim a ginger-beer cork."

"Tom, you are a hopeless case, and I have a good mind to take you home to your father!"

"Oh, no, sir, pray do not! I swear I will not do it again! It would be too bad of you, when I took such pains not to give my name at that horrid Round-house, nor anything that could make the constable think I was *me*! For there is no knowing but that Mr. Snape might have enquired for me here. And if you had not gone off without saying anything to me I should not have done it!" He looked at the Duke with suddenly knit brows. "Where *did* you go to, sir?"

The Duke laughed. "You will never forgive me! I had a more exciting adventure than you: I was kidnapped, and held to ransom, and I only escaped by burning down my prison!"

Tom's eyes glistened enviously. He instantly demanded to be told the whole. It did not seem to him at all strange that anyone should desire to kidnap such an unimportant person as Mr. Rufford, so the questions he eagerly asked were none of them embarrassing. He expressed his heartfelt chagrin at having had no hand in the Duke's escape, and promised to guard him in future with all the might of his large fists. It occurred to him that Belinda might also have been kidnapped, and he began to make plans for her deliverance. But the Duke had made some enquiries about Belinda's new protector, and he was obliged to dash Tom's hopes. Mr. Clitheroe, according to reliable report, was an elderly gentleman of impeccable morals, who lived with his sister on the outskirts of the town, and busied himself largely with charitable works. In what circumstance he had encountered Belinda the Duke could not guess. She had gone out after she had breakfasted that morning, and had returned quite shortly under Mr. Clitheroe's escort, to collect her two bandboxes. The landlord had been unwilling to allow these hostages out of his hands, but he seemed to stand in some awe of Mr. Clitheroe. From what the Duke had been able to discover, that stern Quaker had severely rated him for admitting seducers and abductionists into his house, and had cut short all his attempts to explain that Belinda was travelling in the company of her brother and his tutor. "And what's the use of me telling him she has a brother when he's bound to ask where the brother may be, and all I can answer him is that he's clapped up in the Roundhouse?" demanded the landlord, justly aggrieved. "I'm sure I don't know how you've got him out, sir, but if it's all the same to you I'd as lief you didn't bring him here! And——"

"It is not all the same to me," had said the Duke, very gently indeed.

There was much that the landlord had meant to say, the chief item of information being that he would not harbour any of the Duke's party in his house another night, but the air of hauteur which this rather insignificant young man could upon occasion assume made him uneasy, and he decided to leave it unsaid. He told his indignant wife that he hadn't dealt with the Quality for twenty-five years without knowing when a high-up gentleman had entered his inn. "He can call himself a tutor if he so chooses," he said, nodding darkly, "but I never saw a tutor that wore a coat like that of his, nor one that looked at you as though you was two-penn'orth of nothing." He added philosophically: "Besides, he ain't staying more than one night."

So the Duke, who had now formed the intention of boarding the London stage on the following day, was allowed to remain at the Sun for one more night. Tom, delighted by this change of plan, promised very handsomely to behave with the utmost propriety, and at once began to make interest with his protector for visits to Astley's Amphitheatre, the Royal Exchange, and other such places of interest. He was just confiding to him his burning desire to witness a bout of fisticuffs at the Fives Court, and the Wax Effigies at Madame Tussaud's, when the door opened, and Belinda tripped into the parlour, carrying her bandboxes, and looking as unruffled as she was beautiful. She smiled blindlingly upon the Duke, and said: "Oh, you are come back, sir! I am so very glad to see you again! Oh, Tom, I quite thought you had gone to Newgate!"

"Much you would have cared!" growled Tom, by no means gratified by her sudden appearance.

"Oh, no, but I am so pleased Mr. Rufford is here! It is beyond anything great! How do you do, sir?"

He had risen from his chair, staring at her. "Belinda!" he exclaimed.

She untied the strings of her bonnet and cast it on to a chair. "We have been in such a pickle!" she informed him. "Only fancy! Tom was arrested for a highwayman, sir!"

"Belinda, what became of you?" demanded the Duke.

"Oh, I was never so taken-in!" she informed him mournfully. "For when you went away, sir, and Tom was put in prison, I didn't know what I should do. And I must tell you that they were all in an uproar here, so that it was excessively uncomfortable. And the landlord was *so* uncivil to me this morning that there was no bearing it! So I went out after breakfast, to look at the shops—they are the shabbiest in the world, I am sure! I saw a quiz of a hat, and was in whoops! And just as I was looking into a window where there were all manner of trinkets, but none of them in the least pretty, a very kind gentleman came up to me, and made me a bow."

"Mr. Clitheroe?" interpolated the Duke.

She laughed. "Good gracious, no, sir! I don't know what his name was, but he was quite a young gentleman, and modish, too, and handsome! And he asked me if I would like to have a ring to put on my finger."

"And what," asked the Duke, with deep misgiving, "did you reply to that?"

"I said I should like it above all things," said Belinda innocently.

"Lord, I think girls are the stupidest things!" said Tom, in disgust. "If he had asked me, I would have told him that I would rather have a pair of stilts, or something jolly like that! Oh, Mr. Rufford, there was a man at the Fair, walking on a pair so high that I daresay he could have looked into all the upper windows in the town! If I had a pair like that, I could have such larks, and frighten all the old ladies in their beds by looking in at them! Will you buy me a pair, sir?

I daresay there may be a shop which sells them, and I know I could learn to walk on them in a trice."

"No, I will not," answered the Duke, not mincing matters. "Belinda, didn't I tell you you must not speak to strange men?"

"Not even when they offer to buy me a ring?" she asked.

"Least of all when they offer to buy you a ring!"

"But how shall I ever have a ring, or a silk dress, if I must not speak to any gentlemen?" she asked reasonably.

"If only you will be good, and mind what I tell you," said the Duke," perhaps you shall have a silk dress!"

Belinda sighed. "That is what Uncle Swithin said, only he never gave it to me," she observed.

"Well, never mind that now! What happened when you told this buck that you would like a ring?"

"Oh, it was so sad!" she exclaimed, her eyes filling with tears. "He said we should go into the shop, and he offered his arm, and I am sure I had not so much as noticed Mr. Clitheroe, for why should I?"

"Wait a minute!" begged the Duke. "What has Mr. Clitheroe to do with all this? When did you meet him?"

"Why, just then, sir! He was standing on the other side of the road, though I did not notice him, for he is quite old, you know, and not at all handsome. He came smash up to us, and began to abuse the kind gentleman, and he said I should not go with him. But I would have gone with him, only that he went away, as red as fire! I thought it was so poor-spirited of him! And then Mr. Clitheroe asked me where I lived, and how old was I, and all manner of things."

"Well, I call that a great piece of impudence!" declared Tom. "You should have sent him to the deuce, only I dare swear you did not!"

"Oh, no, how could I? I told him that I did not live anywhere, but that I was staying with you, sir."

She smiled enchantingly at the Duke as she spoke, but although he found it impossible to be angry with anyone so lovely or so ingenuous, he was easily able to refrain from returning the smile. He said, in a tone of resignation: "Did you tell him that I was a very kind gentleman, Belinda?"

She nodded, and her curls danced. "Of course I did!" she assured him. "And he said that he would like to meet you."

The Duke shuddered. "I may readily believe it! I trust he may never have his wish granted!"

"Oh, no! he is a dead bore!" agreed Belinda. "Besides, I told him that you had gone away and left me, so he knew he could not meet you."

The Duke sank his head in his hands. "Belinda, Belinda,

if I do not speedily contrive to hand you into safe keeping I foresee that there will be scarce a town in England where I shall dare to show my face again! So you told him I had deserted you! And what then?"

"Then he said he should take me home with him, and give me something better than a silk dress, or a ring to put on my finger. And he said his sister would be very glad to take care of me. So I came back with him here, sir, and fetched my bandboxes, and he took me to his home. But I don't think Miss Clitheroe was glad at all, for she seemed very cross to me. However, she said I might stay, and she gave me some fruit to eat, and a handkerchief to hem, and she did say that I set neat stitches. But I do not care for hemming, so when Mr. Clitheroe came in I asked him what it was that he would give me, because I would like very much to have it. And I quite thought it would be something splendid, sir, for he said it was better than a silk dress! Only it was nothing but a take-in after all! He just gave me a Bible!"

Her face of chagrin was ludicrous enough to make her harassed protector burst out laughing. "My poor Belinda!"

"Well, I do think it was a great deal too bad of him, sir! The shabbiest trick! So I said I had a Bible already, and then I thought very likely you would have returned, so I would come back here to find you. And would you believe it, they would not let me! Oh, they did prose so!"

"But what did they want you to do instead?" demanded Tom.

"I don't know, for I didn't listen above half. I quite saw that I must run away, and I made up my mind to do so when they should have gone to bed, only by the luckiest chance they went off to a dinner-party—or was it a prayer-meeting? It was some such thing, but I wasn't attending particularly. So I didn't say anything, but only smiled, and made them think I would stay, and as soon as they were gone from the house, I slipped out when the servants were not by, and came back to the inn. And, if you please, sir, I have not had any dinner."

"Ring the bell, Tom, and bespeak dinner for her," said the Duke. "I am going to find a coach time-table!"

"Oh, are we leaving now?" asked Belinda, brightening.

"No, to-morrow, you stupid thing!" said Tom.

"Immediately!" said the Duke, walking towards the door.

"What?" cried Tom. "Oh, famous, sir! Where do we go?"

"Beyond Mr. Clitheroe's reach!" replied the Duke. "Constables and magistrates I can deal with to admiration, but not—*not*, I know well, Mr. Clitheroe!"

He returned to his charges half an hour later with the information that they were bound for Aylesbury in a hired chaise. Belinda, who was making an excellent meal, accepted this without question, but Tom thought poorly of it, and demanded to be told why they must go to such a stuffy place.

"Because I find that there is a coach which runs from Aylesbury to Reading," replied the Duke. "We may board that to-morrow, and from Reading we can take the London stage to Bath."

"It would be more genteel to go in a post-chaise," said Belinda wistfully.

"It would not only be more genteel, it would be by far more comfortable," agreed the Duke. "It would also be more expensive, and I have been drawing the bustle to such purpose this day that my pockets will soon be to let."

"Well, I would rather go on the stage!" said Tom, his eyes sparkling. "I shall ride on the roof, and make the coachman give me the reins! I have always wanted to tool a coach! I shall gallop along at such a rate! What a jest it would be if we overturned!"

This agreeable prospect made both him and Belinda laugh heartily. The Duke sent him off to pack up his belongings, devoutly trusting that there did not exist a coachman mad enough to entrust the ribbons to him.

CHAPTER XIX

While these stirring events were taking place in Hitchin, Mr. Liversedge was still knocking abortively on Captain Ware's door. He gained admittance to the chambers at about the time the Duke and his two charges set out from the Sun Inn in a hired chaise, with Aylesbury for their destination.

The gin with which Wragby had so lavishly supplied him made Mr. Liversedge feel very unwell; and a night spent upon the kitchen floor had given him, he complained, a stiff neck. An assurance from Wragby that a halter would soon cure this was received by him in high dudgeon. He spoke with great dignity for several minutes, but to deaf ears. Wragby recommended him to shut his mummer, and to make haste and shave himself, since the Captain would certainly refuse to take such an oyster-faced rogue up beside him in his curricle. Mr. Liversedge said that he had no desire to be taken up beside the Captain. "In fact," he added austerely, "the less I see of a young man whom I

211

find unsympathetic in the extreme the better pleased I shall be!"

"You stow your whids, and do what I tell you!" said Wragby.

"It is a marvel to me," said Mr. Liversedge, picking up the razor, and looking at it contemptuously, "that any gentleman should employ such a vulgar fellow as you."

"And don't give me no saucy answers!" said Wragby.

By the time the Captain was ready to set forward on the journey, Mr. Liversedge had not only shaved, but had imbibed a cup of strong coffee, which revived him sufficiently to enable him to greet his host with creditable urbanity. His optimistic temperament led him to busy himself with the forming of various schemes for turning the present distressing state of affairs to good account rather than to waste time kicking against the pricks. The day was fine, and the cool air refreshing to him. It was not long before he was complimenting Captain Ware upon his horses, and his skill in handling the ribbons.

"Devilish obliging of you to say so!" said Gideon sardonically. "You are no doubt a judge!"

"Yes," said Mr. Liversedge, tucking the rug more securely round his legs. "I fancy I may be held to be so, sir. You must know that many years ago I was employed in the stables of a notable whip—quite a nonsuch, indeed! A menial position, and one from which I swiftly rose, but it enabled me to judge a horse, and a whip."

Gideon was amused. "A groom, were you? And what then?"

"In course of time, sir, I attained what was then the sum of my ambition. I became a gentleman's gentleman."

Gideon glanced curiously at him. "Why did you abandon that profession?"

Mr. Liversedge described one of his airy gestures. "Various causes, sir, various causes! You may say that it did not afford enough scope for a man of my vision. My ideas have ever been large, and my genius is for the cards and the bones. In fact, had I not suffered certain ill-merited reverses I should not to-day be in your company, for I assure you that the business in which I have lately been engaged is wholly alien to my tastes—quite repugnant to me, indeed! But necessity, my dear sir, takes no account of sensibility!"

"You are a consummate rogue!" said Gideon forthrightly.

"Sir," responded Mr. Liversedge, "I must protest against the use of that epithet! A consummate rogue, you will allow, is a rogue from choice, and feels no compunction for his

212

roguery. With me it is far otherwise, I assure you. Particularly have my feelings been wrung by the plight of your noble relative—a most amiable young man, and one whom I was excessively loth to put to inconvenience!"

"You scoundrel, you would have murdered him at a word from me!" Gideon exclaimed.

"That," said Mr. Liversedge firmly, "would have been your responsibility, Captain Ware."

At this point, Wragby, who from his seat behind them had been listening to this conversation, interposed to beg his master to pull up so that he might have the pleasure of drawing Mr. Liversedge's cork.

"No," said Gideon. "I prefer to hand him over in due course to the Law."

"I am persuaded," said Mr. Liversedge, "that when I have restored your relative to you, as I am really anxious to do, you will think better of that unhandsome notion, sir. Ingratitude is a vice which I abhor!"

"We shall see what my relative has to say about it," replied Gideon grimly.

Mr. Liversedge, who could not feel that forty-eight hours spent in a dark cellar would engender in his victim any feelings of mercy, relapsed into a depressed silence.

But his mercurial spirits could not long remain damped, and by the time Gideon stopped to change horses, he had recovered enough to regale him with a very entertaining anecdote to his first employer's discredit. While Wragby besought the ostlers to fig out two lively ones, and made arrangements for the Captain's own horses to be led back to London, he considered the chances of escape; but even his hopeful mind was obliged to realize that these were slim. However, he was a great believer in Providence, and he could not but feel that Providence would intervene on his behalf before the end of the journey. He had not yet divulged the locality of the Duke's prison, and he had not been urged to do so. Captain Ware was taking it for granted that he would lead him to it. Upon reflection, Mr. Liversedge acknowledged gloomily that unless something quite unforeseen occurred this was precisely what he would do.

Baldock was reached all too soon for his taste, and without the slightest sign of an intervention by Providence. Captain Ware reined in his horses in the middle of the broad street, let them drop to a walk, and said: "You may now direct me, Mr. Liversedge. Unless you would prefer me to enquire the way to the nearest magistrate? It is all one to me."

Mr. Liversedge was irritated by this remark, and answered

213

with some asperity: "Now that, sir, is a manifestly false observation! It is *not* all one to you—or would not be to a gentleman of the smallest sensibility! Nothing, I am persuaded, could be further from your wishes than to create a stir over this business! In fact, the more I think on it, the more convinced I become that you and your noble relatives will be very much in my debt if I contrive the affair without anyone's being the wiser. Consider what must be the result if I compel you to call in the Law! Not only will his Grace——"

He stopped, for it was apparent to him that Captain Ware was not attending. The Captain, glancing idly at an approaching tilbury, had stiffened suddenly, and pulled his horses up dead. "Matt!" he thundered. The next instant he had perceived that Nettlebed was sitting beside his cousin in the tilbury, and he ejaculated: "Good God!"

Young Mr. Ware, on being hailed in such startling accents, jumped as though he had been shot, and dragged his horse to a standstill. "Gideon!" he gasped. "*You* here? Gideon, something has happened to Gilly! Something *must* have happened, because—oh, we can't talk here, in the road!"

"Yes, something has indeed happened to Gilly," replied his cousin. "But what the devil are you doing here, and what do you know about it?"

Mr. Ware looked extremely wretched, and said: "It is all my fault, and I wish I had never consented to let him— But how was I to guess—though I *told* him I knew something would happen to him if he persisted! And then, when Nettlebed came to Oxford, and told me——"

"I suspicioned Mr. Matthew had a hand in it," said Nettlebed, with ghoulish satisfaction. "Sitting up till all hours, and keeping his Grace from his bed, the way he was, the very day before he went off! If I hadn't been so setabout, I should have thought of Mr. Matthew sooner, no question!"

"I never asked him to do it, and I would not have!" Matthew said hotly. "He *would* go, in spite of all I could say!"

"Come to the George!" commanded Gideon. "I'd better get to the bottom of this before I do anything else. I suppose you're in a scrape again!"

"Gideon, where is Gilly?" Matthew called after him urgently.

"Kidnapped!" Gideon threw over his shoulder, and drove on towards the posting-inn.

Mr. Liversedge, who had been sitting wrapped in his own thoughts, gave a genteel little cough, and said: "Another

214

relative, I collect, Captain Ware? Possibly—er—Mr. Matthew Ware?"

"You seem to be remarkably well-acquainted with my family!" returned Gideon shortly.

"No," said Mr. Liversedge sadly. "Had I been better acquainted with them—— But it is useless to repine! So that is Mr. Ware! Dear me, yes! Strange how the dice will sometimes fall against one, do what one will! I wish I had had the good fortune to have met Mr. Ware earlier. He is just the kind of young man I had supposed him to be. I am not one of those who are unable to judge a matter dispassionately, and I will own that although I might have a personal preference for Mr. Ware, his Grace is the better man."

"You are right," said Gideon, "but what you are talking about I have not the remotest guess!"

"And I wish with all my heart," said Mr. Liversedge, with feeling, "that you might never have the remotest guess, sir!"

Both carriages had by this time reached the George. Gideon sprang down from the curricle, and strode into the house, closely followed by his agitated young cousin, but any hope that Mr. Liversedge might fleetingly have cherished of making good his escape was frustrated by Wragby, who conducted him into the inn in a manner strongly reminiscent of his days in the army.

Gideon having demanded a private parlour, the whole party was conducted to a small apartment on the first floor. Matthew was barely able to contain himself until the door was closed. He burst out into speech as soon as the waiter had withdrawn, exclaiming: "You said he had been kidnapped! But I don't understand; It was all over! He wrote to me that it was!"

"*What* was all over?" demanded Gideon.

"Oh, Gideon!" said Matthew wretchedly, "it is all my fault! I wish I had never told Gilly about it! Who has kidnapped him? And how did you come to hear of it?"

"Ah, you have not yet been presented to Mr. Liversedge!" said Gideon, with a wave of his hand. "Allow me to make him known to you! He kidnapped Gilly, and has been so very obliging as to offer to sell his life to me." He paused, perceiving that this speech had had a strange effect upon Matthew, who was staring at Mr. Liversedge in mingled wrath and bewilderment. "*Now* what is the matter?" he asked.

"So it was you!" said Matthew, his eyes still fixed on Mr. Liversedge's face. "You—you damned scoundrel! You did it for revenge! By God, I have a mind to kill you, you——"

"Nothing of the sort!" said Mr. Liversedge earnestly. "No

such paltry notion has ever crossed my brain, sir! I bore your cousin no ill-will—not the least in the world!"

"Sit down!" commanded Gideon. "Matt, what do you know of this fellow, and what's your part in this coil?"

"Ay!" nodded Nettlebed, grimly surveying Matthew. "That's what I'd like to know, sir, and tell me he will not!"

"I ought to have told you, Gideon!" Matthew said, sinking into a chair by the table.

"You are going to tell me."

"Yes, but I mean I should have told you before, and never breathed a word to Gilly! Only I thought very likely you would say something cutting, or— But I should have told you! It was a breach of promise, Gideon!"

His cousin was not unnaturally mystified by this abrupt statement. Mr. Liversedge seized the opportunity to interpolate an expostulation. Such ugly words, he said, had never soiled his pen. Wragby then commanded him to shut his bone-box, and Captain Ware, in the voice of one who has reached the limits of his patience, requested Matthew to be a little more explicit. Matthew then favoured him with a somewhat disjointed account of the affair, to which Captain Ware listened with knit brows, and an air of deepening exasperation. He said at last: "You young fool! You're not of age!"

Matthew blinked at him. "What has that to say to anything? I tell you——"

"It has this to say to it! No action for breach of promise can lie against you while you are a minor!"

There was a shocked silence. Mr. Liversedge broke it. "It is perfectly true," he said. "Sir, I shall not conceal from you that this has been a blow to me. How I came to overlook such a circumstance I know not, but that I did overlook it I shall not attempt to deny. I am chagrined—I never thought to be so chagrined!"

"Oh, Gideon, I wish I had told you!" gasped Matthew. "None of this dreadful business need have been at all!"

"No, it need not," said Gideon. "But why the devil didn't Gilly come to me?"

"It was because he was tired of being told always what he should do next," explained Matthew. "He said here was something he might do for himself, and that it would be an adventure, and that if he could not outwit a fellow like this Liversedge he must be less of a man than he believed!"

Mr. Liversedge bowed his head in approval. "Very true! And outwit me he did, sir. Yes, yes, I am not ashamed to own it! I was quite rolled-up. Your noble relative obtained possession of your letters, Mr. Ware, and without expending

216

as much as a guinea on the business. You have every reason to feel pride in his achievement, I assure you."

Both the Wares turned to stare at him. Gideon said: "How did he outwit you?"

Mr. Liversedge sighed, and shook his head. "Had he not appeared to me to be so young, and so innocent, I should not have fallen a victim to such a trick! But my suspicions were lulled. I thought no ill. Taking advantage, I regret to say, of my trust, he drove a heavy table against my legs, as I was in the act of rising, and felled me to the ground, where, striking my head against the fender of the grate, I lost consciousness. By the time I had regained my senses, his Grace had made good his escape, bearing with him, to my chagrin, the fatal letters."

A slow smile curled Gideon's uncompromising mouth. "Adolphus!" he said softly. "Well done, my little one! So here was your dragon!"

"Drove the table against your legs?" repeated Matthew. "*Gilly?* Well, by God!"

"So far, so good," said Gideon. "But how came he to fall again into your clutches?"

"That," said Mr. Liversedge evasively, "is a long story, sir. But it should be borne in mind that it is I who have been the humble instrument whereby your interesting relative has met with the adventure his soul craved."

Nettlebed, who had been listening to this interchange with scarcely concealed impatience, interrupted to say fiercely: "You gallows-cheat, you'll say where you have his Grace hid, or you'll have it choked out of you!"

"This fellow lives at the Bird in Hand, that I do know," Matthew declared. "And there Gilly found him, for he told me so!"

"Ay, that's what you say, Master Matthew, but a solid hour have we been in this town, trying to find where this place may be, and not a soul able to tell us!" said Nettlebed bitterly. "And if we can't discover it, how can his Grace have done so?"

"His Grace would appear to have his own ways of going about his business," remarked Gideon, his eyes glinting. "We need exercise no ingenuity, however, for Mr. Liversedge will now guide us to the Bird in Hand. Eh, Mr. Liversedge?"

"Sir," said Mr. Liversedge, with hauteur, "I must perforce yield to *force majeure.*"

But when, half an hour later, the curricle and the tilbury drew up outside the shell of the Bird in Hand, he was at last bereft of all power of self-expression, and could only gaze upon the blackened ruins in incredulous dismay. Both

Wragby and Nettlebed were inclined to make an end to him then and there, but his amazement was so patent that Gideon intervened to restrain them. "Well, Mr. Liversedge?" he said. "What now have you to say?"

"Sir," said Mr. Liversedge, in some agitation, "when last I saw this hostelry it was indeed a poor place, but, I assure you, intact! What can have occurred to reduce it to this pitiful skeleton, I know not! And what has become of its owner, or, I may add, its noble guest, are matters wholly beyond my powers of conjecture! I confess that they are matters which do not, at this present, exercise my mind profoundly. I have no reason to suppose, Captain Ware, that you are a man of feeling, but even your hardened heart may be touched by the reflection that the few worldly possessions remaining to me were encased in that unworthy building!"

"My hardened heart remains untouched. I want my cousin!" Gideon said brusquely, and touched up his horse. "There must be someone in the village who can tell us when this fire broke out!"

Enquiry in Arlesey led him presently to the cottage inhabited by the Shotterys. Their account of the fire was necessarily imperfect, but they knew enough to be able to convince Gideon that it had been started by his enterprising cousin. He listened to them at first in surprise, and then with his crooked smile. But Nettlebed was quite thunderstruck, and said roundly that he had never known his Grace to do the like, and didn't believe a word of it.

"Peace, fool!" said Gideon. "You know nothing about his Grace—as little as the rest of us! So he won free without our help! He is doing very well, in fact."

"Captain Ware," said Mr. Liversedge warmly, "you are in the right of it! Though I am a sufferer from his ingenuity, I bear him no malice. Indeed, it is very gratifying to see a man so young and so untried acquit himself so creditably! You will permit me to tell you that this little adventure has been the making of him. When I saw him first he was uncertain of himself: he had been too much cosseted, too carefully shielded from contact with the world. The experiences he has passed through will have done him a great deal of good: I have no scruple in asserting it, and it is a happiness to me to reflect that he owes his emancipation to me."

This was too much for Nettlebed, who advanced upon Mr. Liversedge with such deadly purpose that he had to be called sharply to order. "Master Gideon!" he said explosively, "I've known you from your cradle, and stand by while that gaol-bird gammons you with his talk I will not! And his Grace, the while in the lord knows what case!"

"If one thing is more plain than another," responded Gideon, "it is that his Grace stands in no need of our help! I own, if I had known what dangers he would run into I would not have let him set out as I did, but by God I am glad I did not know! This fellow is a rogue, but he is speaking the truth: his Grace has found himself. I wonder what took him to Hitchin?"

Matthew, who had been puzzling over it in silence, said: "Well, I don't understand any of it! Why did he not go home when he had done what he came to do? What should have kept him in Hertfordshire?"

"Ay, and it's my belief you can answer that!" said Nettlebed, addressing himself to Mr. Liversedge.

"Fellow," said Mr. Liversedge loftily, "do not try my patience too far, or you will regret it! I have so far held my peace, but if you provoke me I shall disclose certain information so damaging to the Duke's reputation that you will be sorry!"

Nettlebed wrung his hands. "Master Gideon!" he said imploringly, "it's more than flesh and blood can bear! If you won't let me make him swallow his lying words, will you give him over to the Law, and be done with it?"

"Captain Ware," said Mr. Liversedge, "if you do any such thing, I must throw my scruples to the din, and bring an action against your noble relative for abducting my ward!"

At these words, Matthew gave a start, and exclaimed: "Belinda? Good God! No, no, he would not——!"

"I never heard the like of it, not in all my days!" exploded Nettlebed. "To think I'd be standing here listening to such wicked slanders! His Grace never abducted no one, nor never would!"

"He seduced her—I say it with confidence!—with promises of rich raiment!" announced Mr. Liversedge. "And let me tell you, Captain Ware, that my ward has not yet attained the age of seventeen! An innocent flower, who has now suffered doubly at the hands of your family!"

Matthew drew his cousin a little apart, an urgent hand grasping his elbow. "Gideon, if that is so it is the most devilish coil! No, no, I don't mean he abducted her, but you don't know Belinda! Indeed, it will not do! We must instantly find them, and rescue him! She is the loveliest creature, and I'm sure I don't blame him for—— But it will not do, Gideon!"

"What nonsense, Matt!" Gideon said impatiently. "Gilly became engaged to Harriet only a week ago!"

"Yes, I know, but you haven't seen Belinda!" said Matthew simply.

Gideon suddenly remembered a passage in the Duke's letter to him. "Good God!" he muttered. "No, it's ridiculous! I never knew Gilly to be in the petticoat-line. As for abduction—fustian!"

"Well, of course, but you don't know what a fellow this Liversedge is!" Matthew said, under his breath. "He will make trouble for Gilly if he can, and he is Belinda's uncle—or so he says."

"He'll have no opportunity to make trouble," replied Gideon shortly.

"He will if you hand him over to the Law," Matthew warned him. "I don't mean he could succeed in a charge, but it would make the devil of a stir, you know! But what are we to do with him?"

"It seems to me," said Gideon, "that I had best find Adolphus, and discover just what mischief he is brewing. I'll take Liversedge along with me, and Adolphus can decide what is to be done with him. As for you, had you leave to come here?"

"Oh, yes, I told the Bag-wig I was wanted on urgent family affairs, and he gave me an exeat. But, you know, Gideon, I do think Nettlebed needs a set-down! It is the outside of enough for him to come searching for me at Oxford, and behaving as though I were a schoolboy, and threatening to go to the Bag-wig himself if I would not tell him where he could find Gilly!"

"I wish he might have done so!" said his cousin unsympathetically. "What in thunder do you mean by saddling Adolphus with your damned follies? No thanks to you he is not now being bled white! Get back to Oxford, and if you can't keep out of silly scrapes, for God's sake bring 'em to me in future, and don't encourage Gilly to risk his neck in your service!"

Matthew was so much incensed by this unfeeling speech that he embarked on a long and indignant vindication of himself. Gideon broke in on it without compunction, and told him to spare his breath. Matthew glared at him, and said: "Well, it is just as much my affair as yours, and I shall go with you to Hitchin!"

"You may do that, for it's on your way, but you'll go no farther with me!" said Gideon, turning away.

He found that he was being anxiously watched by Nettlebed and Wragby, in whom dislike of Mr. Liversedge had engendered a temporary alliance. Mr. Liversedge was seated at his ease in the curricle, his plump hands folded, and a benign, not to say saintly expression on his countenance. Mr. Liversedge saw in his sudden recollection of Belinda the hand of Providence working powerfully on his behalf, and was able to meet Captain Ware's hard eyes with an indulgent smile.

"We are now bound for Hitchin, my hopeful friend," said Gideon. "It appears to me that my noble relative might be glad to have you delivered into his hands!"

"If," retorted Mr. Liversedge superbly, "your noble relative has the least regard for justice, sir, he will see in me a benefactor!"

"Master Gideon, only let me darken his daylights!" implored Nettlebed tearfully.

This favour having been denied him, he climbed up sulkily into Matthew's hired tilbury. Gideon took his place on the box of the curricle, and gathered up the reins. Mr. Liversedge said kindly: "May I proffer a piece of advice, sir? I apprehend you are about to make some stir of Hitchin by enquiring for the Duke of Sale. Speaking as one who has his Grace's true interests at heart, I would counsel you to enquire rather for Mr. Rufford, under which sobriquet I have reason to believe him to be travelling."

Gideon, who was beginning to be amused by his effrontery, thanked him, and, upon arrival at the Sun Inn, followed his advice. The result was not happy. The landlord regarded him with patent hostility, and said that if ever he had had an inkling of the trouble which was to come upon him through giving this precious Mr. Rufford house-room he would have put up his shutters rather than have faced it.

"And if it's that pesky boy of his as you're after, it ain't no manner of use asking me," he added. "Because it's none of my business, nor never was! And if it's rooms you're wanting, the house is full!"

Captain Ware, whose autocratic temperament did not make it easy for him to swallow impertinence with a good grace, took instant exception to this form of address, and was on the point of adding to a pithy summary of the landlord's failings and probable end his own name and style when Mr. Liversedge, with his deprecating cough, laid a hand on his sleeve, and said: "Ahem! Allow me, sir! Now, my good man, attend to me, if you please! You will not deny that Mr. Rufford has lately been staying in this inn, with—I fancy—a young companion."

"If you mean as how he had Miss Belinda and that

young brother of hers with him, which he said as he was his tutor, I won't," replied the landlord. "Not but what I never saw a tutor behave like he did, nor wear a coat like his. Too smokey, by half, that's what he is, and the more fool me to let him into my house! The trouble I've had! Let alone Master Tom bringing me into disgrace through getting taken up for a common felon, the way he was, I've had Mr. Clitheroe threatening me with hell-fires for letting rakes seduce innocent females under my roof, which I never did, not wittingly, that is! And no sooner does he take himself off than there's Mr. Mamble on the doorstep, ay, and brought along the constable, what's more, which is a thing I never had happen to me, not in all my days!"

"Who the devil is Mr. Mamble?" demanded Gideon.

"Ah, you may well ask, sir! Master Tom's father, that's who he is!"

Matthew, who had been wholly bewildered by the landlord's speech, said: "But who is Master Tom? Gideon, it can't be Gilly! Liversedge! who is this Master Tom?"

"There, sir, I must own that you find me at a loss," confessed Mr. Liversedge. "I can, however, state that Belinda is without known relatives. Master Tom, in fact, is a mystery."

"Wait!" said Gideon. "Damme, why didn't I think to bring my cousin's letter with me? I fancy he spoke of bear-leading some boy or another. This would appear to be the boy."

"I don't know about bear-leading him, sir," struck in the landlord. "By what Mr. Mamble said, him and that Mr. Snape, which is Master Tom's real tutor, Mr. Rufford kidnapped Master Tom. Mr. Mamble was talking of going to London to set the Runners on to his heels, but myself I'd say it was more like Master Tom kidnapped him, for a more daring boy I hope I may never clap my eyes on! Nice goings on when the gentry take to highroad robbery, and has to be bailed out of prison! Mr. Mamble has it fixed in his head his son has got into the hands of a rogue which is using him for his wicked ends, and nothing the constable said could make him change his mind! Mind you, I never thought such of Mr. Rufford myself, and no more, didn't the constable, or Mr. Oare, which is the magistrate here."

"Highroad robbery!" gasped Matthew incredulously. "*Gilly?* Fellow, do you say that Mr. Rufford was arrested?"

"No, not him, sir. He wasn't here when that happened. Dear knows where he was, and I'm sure I never thought to see him again! It was Master Tom that set out to win a purse, and got himself locked up in the Round-house. And then what must happen but Miss went off with old Mr.

Clitheroe, which is a highly respected Quaker gentleman living in the town!"

"That," said Mr. Liversedge, shaking his head, "was a mistake. It would not answer at all."

"No, sir, and nor it did, for back she came again that very evening. But Mr. Rufford was here by that time, and it wasn't any business of mine, whatever Mr. Clitheroe may choose to say! But it was on account of Mr. Clitheroe that Mr. Rufford up and left with the pair of them last night, instead of spending it here, like he meant to. One of the waiters, which chanced to be outside the door of the private parlour, heard him say he could deal with constables and magistrates, but not with Mr. Clitheroe. And just as well he did go, for Mr. Clitheroe, he came round in such a taking as I never saw half an hour after, and for all Mr. Rufford has a high-up way with him when he chooses, I doubt Mr. Clitheroe wouldn't have taken no account of that, him being moved by the spirit the way he was."

"Gideon," said Matthew, in an awed voice, "do you think that Gilly has run mad?"

"Oh, no, sir!" said the landlord. "Not if you was meaning Mr. Rufford! A very quiet gentleman he is, and knows his way about the world. I never had nothing against *him*."

"Do you know where he went to?" Gideon asked. "Was he bound for London?"

"No, sir, he was not. He hired a chaise and pair to take the whole party to Aylesbury, that I can tell you, which is the same as I told Mr. Mamble first thing this morning."

-"To Aylesbury!" The cousins exchanged glances of startled enquiry.

"Now, what the deuce should take him to Aylesbury?" Gideon wondered.

"There's no understanding any of it!" Matthew declared. "Of course, I see why he should take Belinda with him, but what can he want with this Mamble boy? Who *is* he? I never met any Mamble! Host, who is Mamble? Do you know him?"

"No, sir, I never see him before. He ain't a native of these parts, nor he ain't what I would call true Quality." He coughed. "A great bacon-faced man, he is, as would make no more than a mouthful of Mr. Rufford—and very willing he is to do it, by what he said! He told the constable as he was an ironmaster from Kettering, and Master Tom his only son. He has it fixed in his head Mr. Rufford means to hold the lad to ransom, for he's mighty plump in the pockets, which he makes no secret of. And it seems as how Mr. Rufford, or maybe some rogue with him (not but what I never saw no rogues in his company) gave Mr. Snape, the tutor, a wisty leveller, and made off with Master Tom while he was stretched out senseless on the ground. Leastway, that's his story, and not for me to deny it."

There seemed to be no way of arriving at an explanation of Tom's entry into the Duke's life, but the landlord's frequent references to his activities led Captain Ware to demand a more exact account of them. The whole story of the attemped robbery on the Stevenage road was then poured into his ears. By the time the Duke's masterly share in the business had been described to him, his crooked smile had dawned, but Matthew appeared to be stunned. He did not recover his power of speech until they had left the inn, and then he said feebly: "He *must* be mad!"

"Not he!" said Gideon, grinning.

"But, Gideon, whoever heard of Gilly's behaving in such a fashion?" He sighed despairingly. "I do wish to God I knew what he is doing!"

"You had best accompany me to Aylesbury, then."

"Yes, by Jove, I will!" Matthew declared, brightening. "For it is on my way, after all! And there is one thing, Gideon! it is of no use your saying that it is my fault that Gilly has run mad, for *I* never had anything to do with foisting the Mamble-boy on to him, and if he had gone back to town as soon as he had recovered those curst letters of mine he would never have been kidnapped!"

Gideon only grunted, but Mr. Liversedge said kindly: "Very true, Mr. Ware, very true, but it cannot be denied that your reprehensible conduct towards my unfortunate niece lies at the bottom of all. One must hope that it may be a lesson to you, and when one considers the dangers into which his Grace has been led——"

"Well, if that don't beat all hollow!" exclaimed Matthew indignantly. "It was you who put my cousin in danger!"

"Precisely so," agreed Mr. Liversedge. "And who but yourself, sir, was it who introduced me into his Grace's life?"

"Gideon!" said Matthew, very red in the face, "if you do not have this impudent dog clapped up, I'll—I'll——"

"Tell Gilly what you'll do when you see him at Aylesbury!" recommended his cousin.

But when they reached Aylesbury they failed to discover the Duke at either of the chief hostelries in that town. The landlord of the White Hart informed them that Mr. Rufford, and his young cousins, had left for Reading on the stagecoach as soon as they had swallowed their breakfasts that morning. He added that they were not the first persons to enquire after Mr. Rufford, and expressed the hope that he had not been housing a fugitive from justice.

"But what in the devil's name is he *doing*, jauntering about the country in stage-coaches?" almost wailed Matthew, once out of the landlord's hearing.

"Fleeing from Mr. Mamble, I should think," replied Gideon flippantly.

"Well, it's no jesting matter if he *did* kidnap that boy!" Matthew pointed out. "What do you mean to do now?"

"My blood is up, and I shall follow him. Besides, he may yet need me to protect him from this infuriated parent. You will go back to Oxford."

"I suppose I must," sighed Matthew. "But what shall you do with that fellow, Liversedge?"

"Oh, take him along with me! Wragby can look after him."

"Master Gideon," said Nettlebed, with a set look on his face, "if you mean to continue searching for his Grace, I am coming with you!"

"By all means!" responded Gideon. "You will be very crowded in the boot, but you may assist Wragby to guard the prisoner. Mr. Liversedge! I fear you may not quite like it, but you are accompanying me to Reading."

"On the contrary, sir," replied Mr. Liversedge affably, "I should be sorry to leave you. Owing to the disaster which has befallen the Bird in Hand I find myself temporarily bereft of the means of subsistence. To be abandoned in this town, where I own no acquaintance, would put me to serious inconvenience. I shall be happy to go with you. Let us hope that we may be more fortunate in Reading than we have been in Hitchin or in Aylesbury!"

But when, at the end of a forty-mile drive over an indifferent road, the curricle reached Reading, Fortune (said Mr. Liversedge) seemed disinclined to smile upon its occupants. The Duke's erratic trail was lost from the moment of his alighting, with his young companions, from the stage, and an exhausting search of all the inns in the town failed to pick up the scent again. Gideon, who had been driving all day, was tired, and consequently, exasperated; and after drawing blank at the fifth inn said that he was determined to find the Duke, if only for the pleasure of wringing his neck. "What the devil has become of him, and what am I to do now?" he demanded.

Mr. Liversedge, who had been awaiting his moment, said with admirable common-sense: "If, sir, I may venture to make a suggestion, we should now repair to the Crown, which appeared to be a very tolerable house, and bespeak dinner in a private parlour, and beds for the night. I shall give myself the pleasure of mixing for you a Potation of which I alone know the secret. It was divulged to me by one of my late employers since deceased, alas!—a gentleman often in need of revivifying cordials. I fancy you will be pleased with it!"

"We must find his Grace!" declared Nettlebed obstinately.

"It will be dark in another hour," said Gideon. "Damn it, the fellow's right! We'll rack up for the night!" He yawned suddenly. "God, I am tired!"

"Leave everything to me, sir!" said Mr. Liversedge graciously. "That man of yours—a worthy enough fellow, I daresay!—is quite unfit to arrange all those little genteel details so necessary to a gentleman's comfort. In me you may have every confidence!"

"I have no confidence in you at all," replied Gideon frankly. "I foresee, however, that we shall end by becoming boon-companions! Lead on, you unmitigated scoundrel!"

CHAPTER XX

SERENELY unaware that he was being pursued by two sets of persons in varying degrees of wrath or exasperation, the Duke conveyed his charges to Bath on the stage-coach, without incident. He made no stay in Reading, arriving there with only just enough time to catch the London to Bath coach. He experienced a little difficulty in procuring places at such short notice, but by dint of bribing several interested persons, he secured one inside seat for Belinda, and two outside ones for himself and Tom. Belinda was inclined to cry when she found that she could not sit on the roof, but by a fortunate chance a delicate-looking young gentleman boarded the coach, and took his place inside. He stared at Belinda in such blatant admiration that she at once became cheerful, and spent a very happy journey encouraging his respectful advances. He did not look to be the sort of dashing blade who would endeavour to seduce her with promises of rings and silken gowns, so the Duke, thankful to be spared the embarrassment of her easy tears, handed her in with no more than a mild request that she would refrain from informing her fellow-passengers that she was travelling to Bath under the escort of a very kind gentleman. He then climbed on to the roof to take his seat beside Tom, and resigned himself to a long and uncomfortable journey. Tom, having begged in vain to be allowed to tool the coach, sulked for some few miles, but revived upon recollecting that he had in his pocket a catapult which he had found time to buy in Aylesbury. His skilful handling of this weapon led to a little unpleasantness with an old lady by the road-side, whose fat pug dog was startled into unwonted activity by a pellet in the ribs, but as no one but the Duke had seen Tom aim the catapult, and he seized and pocketed it the instant he realized what Tom was so surreptitiously engaged upon, no one was able to bring the crime home to the culprit.

"Tom, you are the most shocking boy!" said the Duke severely. "If you have any other devilish engine in your pocket, give it to me at once!"

"No, upon my honour, I have not, sir!" Tom assured him. "But wasn't it famous when the pug jumped, and ran off yelping?"

"Yes, a splendid shot. If only you will behave with propriety I will take you to Cheyney one day, and give you a day's real shooting."

A glowing face was turned towards him. "Oh, sir, will you *indeed?* I think you are the most bang-up, out-and-out person in the world! Where is Cheyney? What sort of a place is it?"

"Cheyney?" said the Duke absently. "Oh, it's one of my—— It is a house which belongs to me, near a village called Upton Cheyney, some seven miles from Bath, towards Bristol."

"Is that where we are going?" asked Tom, surprised. "You never said so, sir!"

"No," said the Duke. "No, we're not going there."

"Why not?" demanded Tom. "If there is shooting to be had, it would be much jollier than a stuffy inn in Bath! Do let us, sir!"

The Duke shook his head. He had a very lively idea of what would be the feelings of the devoted retainers in charge of Cheyney were he to arrive there in disgracefully travel-stained clothes, unheralded, unescorted, carrying a cheap valise, and leading Belinda by the hand. He supposed he would shortly be obliged to disclose his identity to Tom, but since he had no desire to be known at the quiet inn he had mentally selected in Bath, and placed little dependence on Tom's discretion, he decided to postpone the inevitable confession. He said instead that his house was too far removed from Bath for convenience.

His knowledge of Bath's hotels was naturally confined to such fashionable establishments as York House and the Christopher, in neither of which did he propose to set foot, but he remembered being led, as a boy, by the conscientious Mr. Romsey to gaze reverently upon the façade of the

Pelican in Walcot Street, which had once housed the great Dr. Johnson. This respectable inn was no longer patronized by modish people, and had the added advantage of being situated not far from Laura Place, where the Dowager Lady Ampleforth resided.

It was not to be expected that a quiet and unpretentious hotel would meet with the approval of the Duke's charges. Tom said that if they must put up at an inn he would like to choose the busy posting-house on the Market-place; and Belinda told the Duke reproachfully that she had once conveyed a bonnet to a lady staying at the Christopher, and had formed the opinion that it was a very genteel, elegant hotel, in every way superior to the Pelican. The Duke agreed to it, but gently shepherded his protégés into the Pelican. In the middle of protesting that it was a shabby place Tom was suddenly overcome by a suspicion that Mr. Rufford might not be able to afford to put up at the more fashionable houses, flushed scarlet, and loudly asserted his conviction that they would do very well at the Pelican after all. He then took the Duke aside to remind him that Pa would reimburse him for any monies expended on his behalf, and begged permission to sally forth to see the sights. As it was already time for dinner, this was refused him, but the blow was softened by the Duke's promise to let him go to the theatre that every evening. Belinda at once said that she would like to go too, and, upon being told that it would be quite ineligible, was only induced to stop crying by a timely reminder of the awful fate in store for her if, by some malign chance, her late employer should be in the audience, and perceive her. She stood in such awe of Mrs. Pilling that she trembled, and turned quite pale, and had to be reassured before she could be brought to eat her dinner.

While the covers were being set upon the table, the Duke called for paper and ink, and dashed off an urgent letter to his agent-in-chief.

"My dear Scriven," he wrote, *"Upon receipt of this, be so good as to despatch Nettlebed to me with such clothing as I may require, and two or three hundred pounds in bills. He may travel in my private chaise, and bring my footman with him. It will be convenient for me to have also my curricle, and the match bays, and these may be brought by easy stages, together with my Purdeys, also at Sale, and the grey mare. I shall send this to you express, and beg you will not delay to follow out its instructions. Yours, etc., etc., Sale."*

He was shaking the sand from his missive when it occurred to him that a little information about himself might be welcome to his well-wishers. He added a postcript: *"Pray inform Lord Lionel that I am in excellent health."*

Having, in this masterly fashion, allayed any anxiety or curiosity which his household might cherish, he sealed his letter, directed it, and arranged for its express carriage to London. After that, he joined his young friends at the dinner-table, partook of a neat, plain meal, sped Tom on his way to the theatre, persuaded Belinda to go to bed, and took rueful stock of his appearance.

No amount of wear and tear could disguise the cut and quality of Scott's olive-green coat, or the excellence of Hoby's top-boots, but a riding-coat and buckskin breeches, even when in the pink of condition, could not by any stretch of the imagination be considered eligible garments in which to pay an evening visit in Bath. A week earlier, the Duke would have shrunk from the very idea of presenting himself in Laura Place in such a guise, but the experiences through which he had passed had hardened his sensibilities so much that he was able presently to confront old Lady Ampleforth's porter, who opened her door to him, without a blush. The sound of a violin, and a glimpse of a great many hats and cloaks in the hall conveyed the unwelcome intelligence to him that Lady Ampleforth was entertaining guests. He did not blame the porter for eyeing him askance, but he said in his calm way: "Is Lady Harriet Presteigne at home?"

"Well, sir," replied the porter doubtfully, "in a manner of speaking she is, but my lady has one of her Musical Parties this evening."

"Yes, so I hear," said the Duke, stepping into the hall, and laying down his hat. "I am not dressed for a party, and I shall not disturb her ladyship. Be so good as to convey a message to Lady Harriet for me!"

The porter, having by this time taken in the full enormity of the Duke's costume, said firmly that he didn't think he could do that, Lady Harriet being very much occupied.

"Yes, I think you can," said the Duke tranquilly. "Inform Lady Harriet that the Duke of Sale has arrived in Bath, and wishes to see her—privately!"

The porter was staggered by this speech. He knew, of course, that Lady Harriet was betrothed to the Duke of Sale, but it seemed to him highly improbable that anyone so exalted would visit a lady in a crumpled coat and stained buckskins. He said cunningly: "Yes, your Grace. I will have your Grace's card carried up to my lady."

"I haven't one," said the Duke.

Upon hearing this brazen utterance, the porter saw his duty clearly marked out for him. He prepared to eject the uninvited guest, saying: "I that case, sir, you'll pardon me, but I could not take it upon myself to disturb her ladyship!"

Fortunately for the Duke's dignity, Lady Ampleforth's butler sailed into the hall at this moment. The Duke said: "Ah, here's Whimple! I hope you do not mean to disown me, Whimple. I wish to have some private speech with Lady Harriet."

The butler stared at him for an unrecognizing moment, and then gave an audible gasp. "Your Grace!"

"Thank God!" said the Duke, smiling. "I was afraid you had forgotten me, and meant to tell this stout fellow to hurl me down the steps."

"No, indeed, your Grace! I—I apprehend your Grace has but just arrived in Bath? Would your Grace wish me to announce you, or, perhaps. . . ."

"You may see for yourself that I am in no case to present myself to Lady Ampleforth. Lady Harriet, however, will forgive me for coming to her in all my dirt."

"Surely, your Grace!" beamed Whimple, much touched by this evidence of lover-like impatience. "Perhaps your Grace would condescend to wait in the breakfast-parlour, where no one will disturb you? I will instantly apprise Lady Harriet of your Grace's arrival!"

The Duke having expressed his willingness to condescend in this manner, he was ushered into a small apartment at the back of the house. While an underling lit the candles, the butler went away to find Lady Harriet. The Duke had not long to wait. In a very few moments Whimple opened the door for Lady Harriet to pass into the room. He sighed sentimentally, for he was a romantic man, and he had never before been employed as Love's messenger.

It struck the Duke that his betrothed was not in her best looks. She was even a little wan, and she seemed to be suffering from some agitation of spirit. She was tastefully attired in a robe of white crape, profusely trimmed with blond lace, and with her hair in full ringlets, but she would have been the better for a touch of rouge. As the door shut behind Whimple, she looked almost shrinkingly at the Duke, and uttered in a faint voice: "Gilly! My lord!"

He stepped up to her, taking her hand, and kissing it. It trembled in his, and he was aware of her uneven breathing. He wondered why Harriet, who had known him all his life, should be so afraid of him. He retained her hand, saying:

"Harriet, have I startled you? I am a villain to come to you in such a disreputable state!"

"Oh, no!" she murmured. "No, no!"

"Indeed, I beg your pardon!" he said, smiling at her. "But I am in the deuce of a fix, Harriet, and I have come to you to help me out of it!"

Her pallor seemed to grow more marked. She gently withdrew her hand from his. "Yes, Gilly," she said. "Of course I will help you out of it."

"You were always the best of good friends, Harriet!" he said. "But it is quite outrageous! I have no business to ask such a thing of you!"

She lifted her hand as though to silence him, and then let it drop again. Averting her face a little, she managed to say with only the smallest tremor in her voice: "You need not tell me, Gilly. You never desired it. I—I knew that at the outset. You wish to declare our—our engagement at an end, don't you?"

"Wish to declare our engagement at an end?" he repeated, quite thunderstruck. "Good God, no! Why, Harriet, what can you be thinking of?"

She began to twist into a tight rope the ends of the gauze scarf which was draped round her shoulders. "Is it not that, Gilly? Pray do not try to spare my feelings! I knew I was wrong. I should not have—— But it is not too late! You see, I *know!* And indeed I do not blame you!"

"Harriet, I have not the remotest guess at what you are talking about!" the Duke said blankly. "What is it that you know? What can possibly have done to merit this from you?"

Surprise gave her courage to look at him. She faltered: "I knew from Gaywood that you had disappeared. Of course I did not credit the wicked slanders which he said were running round town! But——"

"Good God, were there any?" he interrupted. "What did the fools say?"

"Gaywood told me that people suspected Gideon of having murdered you, but——"

He went off into a peal of laughter. "Oh, no! No, Harriet, did they indeed think that? Then I expect he *will* murder me! It is a great deal too bad!"

She looked at him wonderingly. "You see, Gilly, you left no word, and someone saw you going to Gideon's chambers the night you disappeared. And Gaywood said he would say nothing, only that he had no notion where you were. Of course, no one who knows Gideon would believe such a story!"

"He is the best of good fellows! He should have betrayed me instantly. But what has this to do with the rest, Harriet?"

Her head sank; she studied the fringe at the end of her scarf. "It was Lady Boscastle, Gilly, who—who told us the rest."

His brows knit for a puzzled moment. "Lady Boscastle? Oh, yes, I know! One of the matchmaking mamas! But what can she have told you? I have not set eyes on her since the lord knows when!"

"She has just arrived in Bath," said Harriet, beginning to plait the fringe. "She—she passed through Hitchin on her way. You did not see her, but—but she saw you, Gilly. She came to pay a morning visit here, and she—she told Grandmama and me."

She ventured to peep up at him, and was startled to see his eyes dancing. "The devil she did!" he said. "Did she tell you I had Belinda on my arm?"

"A—an excessively beautiful girl!" faltered Harriet, gazing at him in mingled hope and trepidation.

"Oh, the loveliest creature imaginable!" he said gaily. "With not two thoughts in her head to rub together! No, I wrong her! There are just two thoughts! One is of golden rings, and the other of purple silk dresses! Harriet, you goose!"

Colour flooded her cheeks; her eyes filled. "Oh, Gilly!" she uttered. "Oh, Gilly, I thought—— Indeed, I beg your pardon!"

"No, it is all my fault. I wonder you don't send me to the devil!" He saw that tears hung on her eyelashes, and put his arm around her, and kissed her. "Harry, don't cry! I swear it is all a hum!"

Her head drooped on to his shoulder. "Yes, Gilly. I have been very stupid! Only I could not help thinking that perhaps you had met a lady whom you liked better than me."

"I have not. I am sure I never could," he replied.

She blushed, and wiped the drops from her cheeks. He drew her towards the table, and set a chair for her, pulling up another for himself. "You always helped me out of scrapes, Harry!" he said. "I am in *such* a scrape now!"

She smiled tremulously at him. "Oh, no, how could you be? Tell me! What made you run away from London?"

"I was so tired with being Duke of Sale! Do you understand that, Harriet?"

She nodded. "Yes, for they worried you so. Gideon used to say that one day you would kick over the traces. Was that what it was?"

"Not quite. Matthew was in a scrape, and I thought

232

I could rescue him from it—and I was quite right: I did rescue him, and that was where Belinda came into my life. Harriet, I don't know what the devil to do with Belinda! At least, I didn't know until I thought of you, and then it seemed to me that the best plan would be to bring her to you. She is the most tiresome girl!"

There was quite a pretty colour in Harriet's cheeks; she gave a gurgle of laughter, and said: "Is she, Gilly? But who is she, pray?"

"She is a foundling," he replied. "Oh, I shall have to tell you the whole story! You will think I have run mad!"

But although Harriet was considerably astonished by the tale unfolded to her, she did not think he had run mad. She listened to him in breathless silence, her colour fluctuating as she heard of the dangers which had threatened him. But as the tale proceeded she began to perceive that his adventures had subtly altered him. She had never seen him look so well, or know him to be so gay; and there clung about him an air of assurance he had previously lacked. He chose to turn it all to a jest, and to laugh at himself for falling into such pitfalls, but it was plain to Harriet that this diffident young man to whom she was betrothed had a quite unexpected strength of character, and was very well able to take care of himself. She glowed, and although she could not help laughing at the absurdity of his position, she admired him too, and would have accepted a dozen found-lings at his hands without uttering a word of reproach.

"Oh, Gilly, *what* a scrape to be in!" she said, when he came to the end of his story. "It is the most ridiculous thing I ever heard! What *will* Lord Lionel say, if he finds out?"

"He will clap me into Bedlam, I daresay. To tell you the truth, I care very little for what he may say if only I can be rid of Belinda! I must find this Mudgley-fellow! And of course that nonsensical girl has not the least notion where he lives! But the thing is, Harriet, I can't continue at the Pelican with her, and I dare not be seen abroad with her—in this of all towns!—for fear of meeting someone I know!"

"No, indeed! Only think of *my* feelings!" she agreed, twinkling shyly at him.

"Yes, and then there is this milliner to whom she was apprenticed! Harry, I am quite ignorant about apprentices! Do you know what happens to them if they break their indentures?"

"No, but I am sure it is something dreadful. I believe they are quite bound for a number of years, almost like slaves!"

233

"Good God! what must I do to get her honourably released, I wonder?"

"Well, do you know, Gilly, I think perhaps I could do that," she confided, blushing a little.

"No, could you indeed?" he said eagerly. "I am afraid she is a very disagreeable woman. Belinda finds nearly every woman so, I own, but from what she has said to me about Mrs. Pilling I do think she is as unkind, tyrannical female. Belinda is frightened to death of her! Would she be satisfied if I offered to pay whatever is owing to her?"

"I daresay she might be, but I don't think you should appear in the matter at all," said Harriet firmly. "I have been considering, and I believe it may be something I can do for you quite easily. You know, Gilly, everyone knows that we are to be married in the spring, and all the dressmakers and the milliners want to make my gowns and trim my hats. Because it—it is a great thing to be marrying a Duke, and they think it will be the most fashionable wedding of the season. I cannot but feel that if I were to go to Mrs. Pilling's establishment, and tell her that I wish her to make me several hats to go with my bride-clothes she would be very willing to forgive Belinda."

He was much moved. "Harriet, you are the best-natured girl in the world! But from her direction I cannot think that she is at all a modish milliner! You will not like to buy hats from her."

"I shall not mind, dear Gilly," replied Harriet simply.

He kissed her hand. "But your mama! What would she have to say?"

"I—I shall not mind that either, if it is for you," said Harriet. "And I think I shall drive there in Grandmama's barouche, and take my footman as well as my maid. I expect Mrs. Pilling would like that. And then, you know, she will let it be widely known that she is to make several hats for me, and it will bring her a great deal of much more fashionable custom than perhaps she has ever had."

He was not very conversant with feminine foibles, but he was dimly aware that his betrothed was making a considerable sacrifice for him. He thanked her warmly, adding after a moment's thought: "And if you do not like them you may throw them away after all!"

She laughed at that. "Oh, no, how extravagant! I think Mama would certainly have something to say at such shocking waste of money!"

"Would she?" he said, dashed. A happy thought occurred to him. "It doesn't signify! You may throw them away as soon as we are married, and buy some new ones. Should

234

you like to go to Paris? They have very good bonnets there. If only we can contrive to go without my uncle's foisting Belper on to us!"

She said earnestly: "Gilly, no one can foist *anyone* on to you any more!"

He smiled a little ruefully. "Do you think so?"

"I know it. Only if you let them, and you will not."

"Now I come to consider it," he remarked, "even my uncle would not expect me to take my tutor with me on my honeymoon! Harriet, I think we should go to Paris! We could have the most diverting time! Should you care for it?"

"Yes, of all things," she said, looking tenderly at him. "But first we must provide for Belinda!"

"So we must! I was forgetting about her. How vexatious it is! Are you sure you do not mind having her to stay with you until I have found Mudgley?"

"No, indeed!" she assured him.

He looked a little doubtful. "Yes, but I have just bethought me of your grandmother. What shall you tell her?"

"I shall tell her the truth," Harriet replied. "For, recollect, she already knows that that horrid Lady Boscastle saw you in Hitchin with Belinda! And, if you do not very much object to it, Gilly, I shall tell her about your adventures, because I think she will be very much amused, and pleased." She smiled a little. "Grandmama is not at all like Mama, you know, and she has been saying to me that although she likes you very well she would like you better still if you were not so *very* conformable and well-behaved! Of course I shall not tell her about Matthew! And I daresay she would like you to bring Tom to visit her, for she dearly loves anything that makes her laugh. She will be in whoops when she hears of the backward-race! I wonder, will he get into mischief here?"

"My God, I hope not!" exclaimed the Duke. "Perhaps I had best go back to the Pelican, for if he comes home from the theatre and does not find me heaven alone knows what he may take it into his head to do!"

"Perhaps you had," Harriet said regretfully. "And I must go back to the drawing-room, or people will begin to wonder. Grandmama will let me bring her carriage to fetch Belinda in the morning. What shall you do then? Do you mean to remove to Cheyney?"

"Oh, no, I don't wish to bury myself there! When Nettlebed has brought me my clothes, and I am fit to be seen again, I think I shall go to the Christopher. Do you attend the dress-balls? Will you stand up with me for all the country-dances?"

She laughed. "Oh, yes, but what will Tom do?"

"Good God, Tom! I must send off an express to his father. I fear he is shockingly vulgar, and will forgive me for my atrocious conduct merely because I am a Duke!"

She rose, and gave him her hand, saying playfully: "It will be well for you if he does, Gilly!"

He kissed her hand, and then her cheek. "Yes, very true! He sounds a terrifying person, and would no doubt make short work of a plain Mr. Dash of Nowhere in Particular. Thank God I am a Duke!"

CHAPTER XXI

WHEN the news was broken to Belinda that she was to go to stay with a kind lady in Laura Place, she looked very doleful, and said that she would prefer to stay with Mr. Rufford, because ladies were always cross, and she did not like them.

"You will like this lady," said the Duke firmly. "She is quite a young lady, and she is never cross."

Belinda looked beseechingly at him. "Please, I would like to find Mr. Mudgley!" she said.

"And so you shall. At least, you shall if I can discover where he lives."

Belinda sighed. "Mr. Mudgley would not let Mrs. Pilling put me in prison," she said. "He would marry me instead, and then I should be safe."

"I shall do my best to find him for you," promised the Duke.

"Yes, but if you don't find him I shall not know what to do," said Belinda sadly.

"Nonsense! We will think of something for you."

"Oh!" said Belinda. "Will *you* marry me, sir?"

"No, that he will not!" declared Tom, revolted.

"Why not?" asked Belinda, opening her eyes at him.

"He is not such a gudgeon as to be thinking of marrying, like a stupid girl!" Tom said contemptuously.

The Duke intervened rather hastily. "Now, Belinda, you know you don't want to marry me!" he said. "You want to marry Mr. Mudgley!"

"Yes, I *do*," agreed Belinda, her eyes filling. "But Uncle Swithin took me away from him, and Mr. Ware did not marry me either, so what is to become of me?"

"You will go with Lady Harriet, and be a good girl, while I try to find Mr. Mudgley."

Belinda's tears ceased to flow. She looked very much awed, and asked "Is she a *lady*, sir?"

"Of course she is a—— Oh, I see! Yes, she is Lady Harriet Presteigne, and she will be very kind to you, and if you do as she bids you she will not let Mrs. Pilling send you to prison. And what is more," he added, perceiving that she still seemed unconvinced, "she is going to fetch you in a *very* genteel carriage! In fact, a lozenge-carriage!"

"What is that?" asked Belinda.

"The crest on the panel—a widow's crest."

"I shall drive in a carriage with a crest on the panel?" Belinda said, gazing at him incredulously.

"Yes, indeed you will," he assured her.

Tom gave a guffaw. "Stupid thing! He's bamming you!" Her face fell. The Duke said: "No, I am not. Tom, if you cannot be quiet, go away!"

"Well, I shall. I shall go out to see the sights. Oh, Mr. Rufford, there are some famous shops here! The waiter told me! Would you be so very obliging as to lend me some money—only a *very* little!—and I swear I will not get into a scrape, or do the least thing you would not like!"

The Duke opened his sadly depleted purse. "It will be no more than a guinea, Tom, for buy some cravats I must, and I am pretty well run off my legs."

"What a lark!" exclaimed Tom. "Won't you be able to pay our shot, sir? But Pa will do so, you know!"

The Duke handed him a gold coin. "I trust it will not come to that. There! Be off, and pray do not purchase anything dreadful!"

Tom promised readily not to do so, thanked him, and lost no time in sallying forth. The Duke then persuaded Belinda to pack her bandboxes, and went out to send his express to Mr. Mamble. By the time he had accomplished this, and returned to the Pelican, Belinda had finished her task, and was indulging in a bout of tears. He strove to reassure her, but it transpired that she was not weeping over their approaching separation, but because she had been gazing out of the window, and Walcot Street, which she knew well, put her so forcibly in mind of Mr. Mudgley that she now wished very much that she had never left Bath.

"Well, never mind!" said the Duke encouragingly. "You have come back, after all!"

"Yes, but I am afraid that perhaps Mr. Mudgley will be cross with me for having gone away with Uncle Swithin," said Belinda, her lip trembling.

The Duke had for some time thought this more than possible, and could only hope that the injured swain would be melted by the sight of Belinda's beauty. He did not say so to Belinda, naturally, but applied himself to the task of giving her thoughts a more cheerful direction. In this he was so successful that by the time Lady Ampleforth's barouche set Harriet down at the inn, the tears were dried, and she was once more wreathed in smiles.

Having seen the carriage from the window, the Duke left Belinda to put on her bonnet, and ran down to meet his betrothed. She was looking much prettier, he thought, than on the previous evening. There was quite a colour in her cheeks, and she was wearing a very becoming hat of chip-straw, trimmed with lace and rosebuds. She gave him her hand, encased in a glove of lavender kid, and said with a mischievous smile: "Grandmama was excessively diverted. She would have come with me, I do believe, if she could have done so. But she does not go out very much now, and never before noon. And I must tell you, Gilly, that I thought it best not to tell Charlie that you had come to Bath, for I am sure he would roast you dreadfully if he knew the whole! Then, too, although he is the dearest of brothers, he could never keep a secret, you know."

"You are very right!" he said. "I had not thought of it, but I foresee that I must spend my time dodging any acquaintance whom I may see until Nettlebed makes me respectable again. Will you come upstairs? Belinda is waiting for you in the parlour. I must warn you that she is a little afraid of you, and fears you may be cross!"

"Afraid of me?" Harriet said, surprised. "Oh, I am sure no one ever was!"

"I am sure she will not be when she has seen you," he returned, handing her up the stairs.

He ushered her into the parlour, saying: "Here is Lady Harriet come to fetch you, Belinda!"

The two ladies stood for a moment, staring at one another, Belinda in childlike curiosity, Harriet blinking as though she had been dazzled. She had expected to be confronted by a beauty, but she had formed no very definite picture of Belinda from the descriptions afforded her, and was unprepared for such a radiant vision. She knew a pang, for it seemed to her incredible that the Duke should not have fallen a victim to Belinda's charms. She could not forbear stealing a wondering glance at him. She found that he was looking at her, and not at Belinda, an enquiring lift to his brows. She blushed, and stepped forward, saying in her soft voice: "How do you do? I am so glad I am to have the pleasure of your company for a while! I hope you will be comfortable with me."

"Oh, yes, thank you!" said Belinda dutifully, curtsying. "But I do not like hemming handkerchiefs, if you please."

"No, indeed! It is the most tedious thing," agreed Harriet, her eyes twinkling.

Belinda began to look more cheerful, but it was plain that she was not entirely reconciled to the prospect of staying in Laura Place, for she asked: "Shall you keep me for a very long time, ma'am?"

"Oh, no, only until the Duke has found Mr. Mudgley!" said Harriet, guessing that this was the assurance most likely to be welcome.

Belinda looked bewildered. "But I don't know any Dukes!" she objected. "I thought Mr. Rufford would find Mr. Mudgley for me. You *said* you would, sir!"

"Oh, dear, I beg your pardon, Gilly!" Harriet said, in a good deal of confusion. "I thought—I meant to say Mr. Rufford, Belinda!"

"But he is not a Duke!" exclaimed Belinda, quick shocked.

Looking quite as guilty as Harriet, Gilly said: "Well, yes, Belinda, as it chances I am a Duke! I had meant to have told you, but it went out of my head. It doesn't signify, you know."

Belinda gazed at him, an expression in her face of mingled incredulity and disappointment. "Oh, no, I am sure it is a hum!" she exclaimed. "You are teasing me, sir! As though I did not know a Duke would be a much grander person!"

Harriet said in a stifled voice: "He—is very grand when he wears his robes, I assure you!"

"Well!" Belinda said, quite disillusioned. "I thought a Duke would be very tall, and handsome, and stately! I was never so taken-in!"

The Duke bowed his head in his hands. "Oh, Belinda, Belinda!" he said. "Indeed, I am very sorry: I only wish I may not have destroyed your faith in Dukes!"

"But do you wear a coronet, and purple robe?" asked Belinda.

"No, no, only one of scarlet cloth!"

"Cloth! The shabbiest thing!" she cried. "I thought you would have worn a velvet one!"

"Ah, but it was lined with white taffeta, and doubled with four guards of ermine!" he said gravely.

"Gilly, don't be so provoking to the poor child!" said Harriet, controlling a quivering lip. "You know that was only your parliamentary dress! I am sure you have a crimson

239

velvet mantle for state occasions, for I know Papa does. Don't look so sad, Belinda! Indeed, it is a very grand dress, and I will show you a picture of it presently, in a book belonging to my grandmama."

"I should like to see it," said Belinda wistfully. "And of course, if you are truly a Duke, sir, no wonder you do not wish to marry me, if you cannot find Mr. Mudgley! It would not do at all, for whoever heard of a Duke marrying a foundling? It would be the most shocking thing!"

He said gently "I am sure it would be a very lucky Duke who did so, Belinda, but, you see, I am already betrothed to Lady Harriet."

She was quite diverted by this, and after exclaiming at it, and looking speculatively from him to Harriet, politely wished them both very happy. The information seemed in some way to reconcile her to her immediate fate, and she went away presently with Harriet perfectly complacently.

She much enjoyed the experience of driving in a barouche, and a tactful suggestion from her hostess that they might go shoppnig together in the afternoon made her clasp her hands tightly together, and utter in palpitating accents: "Oh, ma'am, do you mean it? In the modish shops on Milsom Street? I should like it above anything great!"

"Then of course we will go," Harriet said, her kind heart touched.

This promise had the effect of casting Belinda into a beatific dream. Visions of silken raiment floated before her eyes, and brought into her flower-like countenance so angelic an expression that several passers-by stared at her in patent admiration, and Lord Gaywood, sauntering down the steps of Lady Ampleforth's house just as the barouche drew up there, stood rooted to the spot, his jaw dropping, and his eyes fairly starting from his head.

In her desire to be of assistance to the Duke, Harriet had not paused to consider what would be the effect upon her susceptible brother of Belinda's charms, but when she saw him apprently stunned by them she felt a little dismay stir in her breast. She said, as she alighted from the carriage: "Charlie, this is a friend of mine, who is coming to stay with me for a few days. My dear, it is my brother, Lord Gaywood."

Lord Gaywood recovered himself sufficiently to make his bow. Belinda said, with a happy smile: "Only fancy! Now I have met a Duke *and* a lord! I daresay they would never believe it at the Foundling Hospital, for I am sure such a thing never happened to any of the others!"

His lordship was considerably taken-aback by this artless speech, but he was not one to worry over trifles, and he responded gallantly: "I am excessively glad to make your acquaintance, Miss—er—Miss——?" He rolled a fiercely enquiring eye at his sister, and was astonished to perceive that her face had become suffused with blushes.

"Oh, I am not Miss anything!" said Belinda, not in the least discomposed. "I am Belinda. I haven't any parents, you know, so I have no name."

Lord Gaywood swallowed once or twice, but soon pulled himself together. "Belinda is the prettiest name I ever heard!" he declared. "Allow me to offer you my arm up the steps!" He added out of one corner of his mouth: "Does the old lady know of this?"

"Yes, of course! Pray hush!" whispered Harriet, red to the roots of her hair.

"Well, if it don't beat all!" he ejaculated.

"What does?" enquired Belinda, looking up at him innocently.

"Why, you, of course!" he responded, without hesitation. "Dash it, you beat 'em all to flinders! Why haven't I seen you before? You can't have been in Bath for long, I'll swear!"

"Oh, no! Mr. Rufford brought me here yesterday!" she told him.

"Mr. Rufford? Who's he?" demanded lordship.

"Charlie, pray do not!" Harriet begged, in a good deal of distress. "You should not ask such impertinent questions! You know you should not!"

"I was forgetting," explained Belinda. "He said he was Mr. Rufford, but all the time he was a Duke. And now I don't know what his name is, for I was so surprised I never asked him! Oh, ma'am, do please tell me!"

"*What?*" gasped Lord Gaywood, stopping dead upon the top step. "Harriet, what in thunder——?"

"Gaywood, I beg you will be quiet!" Harriet said. "I will explain it presently! Belinda, I will take you up to the bed-chamber that has been made ready for you, and you will like to take your bonnet off, I daresay, and your pelisse. And then you must make your curtsy to my grandmama."

"Harriet!" said his lordship, in martial accents, "I order you to come downstairs again, and talk to *me!*"

"Yes, yes, I will do so directly!" promised his harassed sister, propelling Belinda towards the stairs.

When she came down again some few minutes later, she found Lord Gaywood awaiting her in the doorway of the book-room. He promptly seized her by the hand, and led her in, saying: "Harriet, tell me this! Is that out-and-out beauty the game-pullet Sale had with him at Hitchin, or is she not?"

Harriet replied with a good deal of dignity: "Pray do not pull me about so, Gaywood! I don't know what a game-pullet is, and I am sure I don't want to, for it sounds to me a horribly vulgar expression!"

"It's precisely what you think it is, so don't be missish!" retorted his lordship.

"Well, you should not say such things to me. And she is *not!*"

"Then who is this Duke who calls himself Rufford?" demanded Gaywood. "Now I come to think of it, Rufford's that place of Gilly's in Yorkshire! Well, by God, this is a new come-out for him! And all the time bamboozling everyone——"

"He did not!" she said hotly. "You are quite, quite mistaken! He has behaved in the noblest way!"

"Harry!" he exploded. "How can you be such a fool as to let him pitch his gammon to you! Didn't that old cat tell us how she saw him with a girl hanging on his arm, in the most——"

"Yes! And it was you who said, Charlie, that you did not believe a word of it, because she was for ever cutting up characters!"

"Well, I didn't believe it," he admitted. "But if that's the little ladybird, I do now!"

"It is untrue!" Harriet said. "He rescued her from a very awkward situation, and because she is an orphan, and has nowhere to go, he brought her to me!"

"Well, of all the brass-faced things to do!" exclaimed Gaywood. "When *I* see Sale—— Where is he?"

"He is in Bath, but—but he is very much occupied at the present. You will see him presently, I daresay, but if you mean to insult him, Charlie, I shall never, never forgive you!"

These terrible words from his gentle sister quite astonished the Viscount. He looked at her in some concern, and said that he did not know what had come over her. "Of course, you're such a silly little creature, Harry, that you will believe any bubble," he said kindly. "Mind you, there's no harm in Sale's having a mistress in keeping, but to be flaunting her about Bath, and having the dashed impudence to cajole you into giving her countenance is coming it rather too strong, and so I shall tell him!"

"Very well, Gaywood!" said Harriet, with determined calm. "If you are set on making a great goose of yourself, you must do so! Perhaps you will tell him as well that you do not like his *flaunting* a schoolboy about Bath either!"

"What schoolboy?" demanded Gaywood.

She was obliged to divulge some part of the Duke's adventures. Fortunately, Gaywood was so much entertained by a description of Tom's behaviour that she was able to gloss over Belinda's part in the story. She was grieved to think that she had exposed the Duke to her brother's ridicule, but she knew the erratic Viscount well enough to feel tolerably sure that amusement would effectually banish righteous indignation from his mind.

The Duke, meanwhile, had sallied forth to buy himself some neckcloths and handkerchiefs. He was careful to avoid the fashionable quarter of the town, and had therefore the greatest difficulty in finding any neckcloths which Nettlebed would not instantly have given away to an underfootman. On his return to the Pelican he ran into Tom, who said that he had spent all his money, and was hungry. The Duke took him off to a pastry-cook's shop, where, as it was a good three hours since he had partaken of a breakfast consisting of ham, eggs, about half a sirloin of cold beef, and a loaf of bread, he was able to do justice to a meat-pie, several jam-puffs, and a syllabub. Tom was inclined to think poorly of Bath, which city offered few attractions to a young gentleman of his tastes. He said, with a wistful gleam in his eye, that it would enliven the town to put aniseed on the hooves of some of the fat carriage-horses he had seen in Milsom Street, but added virtuously that he had refrained from purchasing any of this useful commodity, his intuition having warned him that putting aniseed on horses' hooves was a pastime of which his protector would not approve. The Duke assured him that his instinct had not misled him, and rewarded him for his saintly conduct by giving him sixpence, and sending him off to the Sydney Gardens, with a promise that he would find there bowling-greens, grottoes, labyrinths, and Merlin swings. He set him on his way, accompanying him as far as to Argyle Buildings, and watching him traverse Laura Place towards Great Pulteney Street; and then turned with the intention of walking down Bridge Street. But just as he had crossed the river again, he caught sight of a lady who looked alarmingly like one of his aunt's friends, and he promptly dived down a side-street. A very large gentleman who, with two companions, had been observing him narrowly, ejaculated: "That's the scoundrel, you mark my words! A little dab of a man in an olive-green coat! After him, now!"

The Duke, having removed himself from the vicinity of

his aunt's acquaintance, saw no need for haste, and was walking sedately along the narrow street. The sound of heavy-footed and somewhat hard-breathing pursuit made him turn his head, but as he did not recognize any of the three persons thudding behind him he did not connect their chase with himself, but merely looked rather surprised, and stepped aside to allow them to pass him. The foremost of them, whom he perceived to be a constable, reached him first, and shot out a hand, ejaculating: "Halt! Name of Rufford?"

"Yes," said the Duke blankly. "What——"

The large man, who was puffing alarmingly, exclaimed: "Ha! He owns it! Impudent rogue! Officer, arrest him! You villain, where is my son?"

"Good God!" said the Duke. "Are you Mr. Mamble?"

"Ay, my lad, I am Mr. Mamble, as you'll find to your cost!" said the large gentleman grimly. "Snape, is this the fellow who gave you a ding on the head?"

The third gentleman, who was nearly as brawny as his employer, said hastily: "I never saw the man, sir! You know I told you I was taken unawares!"

"Well, it don't make any odds!" said Mr. Mamble. "He admits he's this Rufford. Ay, and I'll soon Rufford you, my lad! Why don't you arrest him, you fool?"

"On what charge?" asked the Duke calmly.

"Charge of kidnapping!" the constable informed him. "You come along quiet, now, and no argy-bargy!"

"Nonsense!" said the Duke. "I haven't kidnapped your son, Mr. Mamble. In fact, I have just sent you an express concerning him."

Mr. Mamble's countenance slowly assumed a purple hue.

"You heard that, Snape?" he said. "He's sent me an express! By God, if ever I met such a brazen rogue! So you want a ransom, do you, my cully? Well, you ain't going to get one! The man hasn't been foaled as can diddle Sam Mamble, and when he is he won't be a snirp the like of you, that I can tell you!"

"I don't want a ransom, I did not knock Mr. Snape on the head, or kidnap your son, and my name is not Rufford!" said the Duke.

"Now, that won't do!" the constable said severely. "I axed you, and you admitted it! You'll come along to the Round-house, that's what you'll do!"

"I wish you will not be so hasty!" the Duke said, addressing himself to Mr. Mamble. "If you will accompany me to the Pelican Inn, I will engage to satisfy you on all counts, but I really cannot do so in the open street!"

"You perceive, sir, what an artful rogue he is!" Mr. Snape said, plucking at Mr. Mamble's sleeve. "Do not trust him!"

"Sam Mamble never trusted no one!" announced Mr. Mamble comprehensively. "Where's my son, villain?"

The Duke opened his mouth, and shut it again. He had taken an instant dislike to the unctuous Mr. Snape, and felt that to betray Tom's whereabouts at this stage would be a dastardly act.

"Ha! So you think you won't say, do you? We'll see to that!" said Mr. Mamble.

"On the contrary, I am perfectly willing to restore your son to you," replied the Duke. "But I have a few things to say to you first!"

"If I have to listen to any more of this fellow's impudence, I'll bust!" said Mr. Mamble. "What the devil makes you stand there like a fool, Snape? Go and call up a hack!"

Mr. Snape said obsequiously that he had only been awaiting a command to do so, and hurried off. The Duke tried to remove the constable's hand from his shoulder, failed, and said wearily: "You are making a mistake, you know. If you must have it, I'm the Duke of Sale!"

This disclosure produced anything rather than the desired effect. Both his auditors were for the moment struck dumb by such effrontery, and then combined to revile him. Upon reflection, he was obliged to own that their disbelief was not surprising. Several passers-by had by this time gathered round, and rather than run the risk of creating a scene in the street the Duke abandoned the attempt to argue with his captors. When Mr. Snape presently reappeared in a hackney, he got into it without protest, and allowed himself to be driven to the Round-house. Mr. Mamble was urgent with the constable to seek out a magistrate directly, but the constable seemed to think that the matter first called for closer investigation. So the whole party trooped into the Round-house, where the Duke speedily learned that he was being accused of having (with or without accomplices) laid a cunning plot to kidnap Tom, felled Mr. Snape to the earth, and made off with his charge with intent to hold him to ransom. He glanced contemptuously at the tutor, and said: "Yes, I had thought from what Tom told me that you were a shabby, mean sort of a fellow, and I suppose it might be expected that you would concoct some such tale to protect yourself! It was Tom who hit you on the head, and I think you know that, and are hoping that he will be too much frightened to tell the truth."

"Sir, I am persuaded I have no need to deny such a

wicked charge!" said Mr. Snape, looking appealingly at his employer.

"The truth," said the Duke, ignoring him, "is that I came upon your son, sir, near Baldock. He informed me that he had escaped from his tutor, and was desirous of going either to London, or to the sea-coast, where he had some notion of shipping on a barque as cabin-boy. He had had the misfortune to fall in with a couple of foot-scamperers, who had man-handled, and robbed him. He was in a sad case, and I took him back to the inn where I was putting-up." He smiled. "Perhaps I should have insisted on his returning to you then and there, but I had a great deal of sympathy with him, for I was much beset by tutors myself." He added reflectively: "And I don't know that I could have made him do it, for he would undoubtedly have run away had I suggested any such thing. Altogether it seemed to me that he would be safer in my company than wandering alone about the country. I had intended to have taken him to London, but various unforeseen circumstances arose which made it imperative for me to come instead to Bath. That is the whole matter in a nutshell."

Mr. Mamble, who had listened in fulminating wrath, expressed the opinion that he was a practised rogue, and besought the constable to do his duty. The constable, who had been slightly impressed by the Duke's manner, said in an aloof way that he knew his duty without being told it, and asked the Duke for his full name.

"Adolphus Gillespie Vernon Ware," responded the Duke coolly. "Would you wish me also to recite my titles to you?"

Mr. Mamble roared out: "Stow that foolery, will you? Your name's Rufford!"

"No, that is merely one of my minor titles," said the Duke.

The constable laid down his pen. "Now, look'ee here!" he said mildly. "If so be you're his Grace of Sale, you'll have to prove it, because it don't seem a likely tale, and you don't look like no Duke, nor you wouldn't be staying at the Pelican!"

Mr. Snape smiled with malign satisfaction. "No doubt you have your visiting-card upon you, sir?" he said.

"Ay, that's the dandy!" agreed the constable, brightening, and looking hopefully at the Duke.

The Duke, now quite confirmed in his dislike of Mr. Snape, said, flushing slightly: "No. I have not. I—I am travelling strictly incognito."

Mr. Mamble gave a crack of sardonic mirth. "Ay, I'll be bound you are! How much more time am I to waste kicking my heels here?"

"But I have got my watch!" suddenly remembered the Duke, drawing it from his pocket, and laying it upon the table. "You will perceive that it is engraved with my arms on one side, and with the letter S on the other."

All three men closely inspected the timepiece, and the constable began to look uneasy. However, Mr. Snape pointed out that such a daring rogue would make nothing of picking pockets, and was felt to have scored a point. The constable then had a happy thought, and said with some relief: "It's easy settled, and it won't do for me to go making no mistakes. I'll have a man go out to Cheyney, which is his Grace of Sale's place, and if this gentleman is the Duke he can easy be identified by them as knows him!"

Mr. Mamble, who had been watching the Duke, said shrewdly: "Don't like the sound of that, eh, my fine fellow?"

The Duke did not like the sound of it at all. It seemed to him more than probable that those in charge of Cheyney would spurn with contumely the suggestion that he might be in the Round-house at Bath; while if it was disclosed to them that he had come to Bath with one coat and no attendants they would quite certainly refuse to believe it. He was not really at all anxious that they should believe it, either, for they would be very much shocked, and he would find himself obliged to enter into long and fatiguing explanations.

"No, I do not like it," he said. "I've no desire to sit here for the rest of the day, while someone goes to Cheyney and back. I have a better notion than that." He turned to the constable. "Are you familiar with Lord Gaywood?" he asked.

The constable said bitterly that he was very familiar with Lord Gaywood, and added some pungent criticms on high-spirited young gentlemen's notions of amusement.

"Does he box the watch?" asked the Duke sympathetically. "I don't do it myself, but I feel sure Gaywood does, when he is in his cups. Let me have a pen and some paper, if you please."

Mr. Mamble at once protested against this further waste of time, but the constable, on whom (for all his dislike of that young gentleman) Lord Gaywood's name was working powerfully, fetched some writing materials, and told Mr. Mamble it would be as well not to act hasty.

The Duke drew up his chair to the table, and began to write a note to his betrothed.

"My dear Harriet," he scrawled rapidly, *"I fear you will utterly cast me off, for I am now under arrest for being a*

247

dangerous rogue. Unless I can convince Mr. Mamble that I am indeed myself, nothing short of my instant incarceration in a dungeon will satisfy him. I beg your pardon for putting you to so much trouble, but pray tell Gaywood the whole, and desire him, with my compliments, to come to the Round-house and identify me. Ever yours, Sale."

He folded this missive, wrote Harriet's name and direction upon it, and handed it to the constable with instructions to have it conveyed immediately to Laura Place. The constable said he would do this, and added apologetically that duty was duty, and he hoped, if he should have made a mistake, that it would not be held against him.

The Duke reassured him on this head, but Mr. Mamble exploded with wrath, and said that all this tomfoolery was not helping him to find his boy.

"Well, I will help you to find you, provided you go to look for him yourself, and do not send this objectionable fellow to bully him into saying what he wants him to," said the Duke. "You may then ask him if I kidnapped him, and I hope you will be satisfied that I did not."

"Where is he?" demanded Mr. Mamble.

"Are you going to go yourself?"

"Damn your impudence, yes, I am!"

"His is Sydney Gardens, probably lost in one of the labyrinths. And don't storm and roar at him, for it doesn't answer at all!"

"I don't need you to tell me how to treat my own son!" said Mr. Mamble angrily.

"That is precisely what you do need," replied the Duke, his serene tones in striking contrast to Mr. Mamble's explosive method of speech. "Presently I shall have a good deal to say to you on that score, but you had best find Tom first. I don't know where you are putting up in Bath, but you may send this fellow to await you there. I've no wish for his company."

Mr. Mamble glared at him, but he was a fair-minded man, and, having endured Mr. Snape's unadulterated society for several days, he could not but admit the reasonableness of the Duke's request. He told Mr. Snape to go back to the White Horse, since he was of no use to anyone, being a muttonheaded fool, no more fit to be in charge of a guinea-pig than of a growing lad. He then said that if the Duke was trying to fob him off while his accomplices spirited Tom away he would rend him limb from limb, and departed, calling loudly for a hack.

The Duke resigned himself to await Lord Gaywood's arrival. As the minutes crawled by, it began to be borne in upon him that the messenger had not found Lady Harriet at home. He hoped very much that her return to Laura Place would not be long delayed, for not only did he find the chair on which he was sitting excessively uncomfortable, but he fancied that the constable was regarding him with increasing suspicion.

After about three quarters of an hour a diversion took place. Tom, looking heated and pugnacious, bounced into the room, and launched himself upon the Duke, grasping him by the arm with painful violence, and crying: "They shan't arrest you! They shan't! I'll fight them all! Oh, sir, don't let Pa take me away, for I won't go with him, I *won't!*"

Mr. Mamble, who had followed his son into the room, said: "You young rascal, that's a pretty way to talk! And me your Pa! Ay, and as for you, Mr. Whatever-your-name-is, if you didn't kidnap my boy—which, mind you, I'm not by any means sure you didn't;—you've properly cozened him out of his senses with your smooth talk! And what's more, he says you're no more the Duke of Sale than what I am!"

"No, he doesn't know I am," said the Duke.

"Sir, you're *not!*" said Tom, apparently feeling that it must be to his discredit.

"Well, yes, Tom, I'm afraid I am," said the Duke apologetically.

"You're Mr. Rufford! Oh, do say you are, sir! I know you are only bamming! Dukes are grand, stuffy people, and you aren't!"

"No, of course I am not," said the Duke soothingly. "I cannot help being a Duke, you know. You need not let it distress you! I am still your Mr. Rufford, after all!"

The sullen look, which indicated that he was very much upset, descended upon Tom's face. He said gruffly: "Well, I don't care! I won't go home with Pa, at all events! I hate Pa! He has spoiled everything!"

"That is not a proper way to speak of your Papa, Tom, and it is moreover quite untrue," replied the Duke, removing the clutch from his arm.

"What you need," Mr. Mamble informed his son bodingly, "is to have your jacket well dusted, my lad! Ay, and it's what you'll get before you're much older!"

"And that," said the Duke, "is hardly a felicitous way of recommending yourself to your son, sir."

What Mr. Mamble might have replied to this was never known, for at that moment the constable who had been sent to Laura Place ushered Lady Harriet into the room.

The Duke leaped to his feet, exclaiming: "Harriet!"

She put back her veil, blushing, and saying in her soft shy voice: "I thought I should come myself. Gaywood is gone out, and you know how he would roast you! I am so very sorry you have been kept in this horrid place for so long! I had gone out with Belinda, and this poor man was obliged to stay till I returned.

The Duke took her hand, and kissed it. "I would not have had you come for the world!" he said. "Indeed, I don't know what I deserve for dragging you into such a coil! You did not come alone!"

"No, indeed, the constable brought me," she assured him. "I beg your pardon if you do not like it, Gilly, but I did not wish to bring my maid, or James, for they would have been bound to gave gossiped about it, you know. What is it I must do to have you set at liberty?"

She looked enquiringly towards the senior constable as she spoke, who bowed very low, and said that if it was not troubling her ladyship too much he would be obliged to her for stating whether or not the gentleman was the Duke of Sale.

"Oh, yes, certainly he is!" she said. She blushed more than ever, and added: "I am engaged to be married to him, so, you see, I must know."

Mr. Mamble drew a large handkerchief from his pocket, and mopped his face with it. "I don't know what to say!" he announced. "To think of my Tom going about with a Duke, and me being so taken-in—— Well, your Grace will have to pardon me if I might perhaps have said anything not quite becoming!"

"Yes, of course I pardon you, but do pray withdraw the charge against me, so that I may escort Lady Harriet home!" said the Duke.

Mr. Mamble hastened to do this, and would have embarked on an elaborate apology had not the Duke cut him short. "My dear sir, pray say no more! I wish you will go with Tom to the Pelican, and await me there. I hope you will give me your company at dinner, for there are several things I wish to talk to you about."

"Your Grace," said Mr. Mamble, bowing deeply, "I shall be highly honoured!"

"But it isn't dinner-time yet!" objected Tom. "I don't want to go back to the Pelican! Pa took me away from those jolly gardens before I had even seen the grotto! And I had paid my sixpence, too!"

"Well, ask your Papa for another sixpence, and go back to the gardens—that is, if he will permit you to."

"You do just what his Grace tells you, and keep a civil tongue in your head!" Mr. Mamble admonished his son. "Here's a crown for you: you can take a hack, and see you ain't late for dinner!"

Tom, his spirits quite restored by this generosity, thanked him hurriedly, and dashed off. The rest of the party then dispersed, the Duke handing Harriet up into a hackney, and Mr. Mamble setting out in a chastened and bemused frame of mind to walk to the Pelican.

Having given the direction to the coachman, the Duke got into the hackney beside Harriet, and took her in his arms, and kissed her. "Harry, I don't know how you found the courage to do it, for you must have hated it excessively, my poor love, but I am very sure I am the most fortunate, undeserving dog alive!" he declared.

She gave a gasp, and trembled. "Oh, Gilly!" she said faintly, timidly clasping the lapel of his coat. "Are you indeed sure?"

"I am indeed sure," he said steadily.

Her eyes searched his face. "When you offered for me, I did not think——" Her voice failed. She recovered it. "I know, of course, that persons of our rank do not look for—for the tenderer passions in marriage, but——"

"Did your mother tell you so, my love?" he interrupted.

"Oh, yes, and indeed I do not mean to embarrass you with—with——"

"Infamous! It is precisely what my uncle said to me! Was that what made you so shy, that dreadful day? I know I was ready to sink! My uncle told me I must not look for love in my wife, but only complaisance!"

"Oh, Gilly, how could he say so? Mama said it would give you a disgust of me if I seemed—if I seemed to care for you very much!"

"What very odd creatures they are! They should deal extremely together. As extremely as we shall!"

She sighed, and leaned her cheek against his shoulder. "How comfortable this is!" she said. "And so delightfully vulgar! Does plain Mr. Dash put his arm round ladies in hackney coaches?"

"When not in gaol he does," the Duke responded.

CHAPTER XXII

WHEN Tom returned from his second visit to Sydney Gardens, he was relieved to find his parent in a subdued frame of mind. He had been half afraid that he might discover

Mr. Snape at the Pelican, but when he peeped cautiously into the private parlour he saw only the Duke and his father, seated on either side of a small coal fire, and drinking sherry. Mr. Mamble had not imbibed enough to put him at his ease, and he was sitting rather on the edge of his chair, and treating his host with a deference which the Duke disliked even more than he had disliked his earlier manner. He had not neglected, however, to turn Mr. Mamble's reverence for a title to good account, but had lectured him with great authority on his mishandling of his son.

"He's my only one, your Grace," Mr. Mamble explained. "I never had any advantages, not being one who came into the world hosed and shod, like you did, and by the time I was as you see me now—and I fancy I'm as well-equipped as anyone!—I doubt it was too late for me to be thinking of learning to be a fine gentleman. They say black will take no other hue, and black I'll remain to the end of my days. But if it busts me I'll see my boy a regular out-and outer! I won't deny I've been disappointed in Snape—though, mind you, he came to me out of a lord's house, and he was mighty well spoken of, else I wouldn't have hired him, for I'm one as likes good value for my money, ay, and gets it, what's more! But a tutor he must have, like the nobs, for if he don't, how will he learn to behave gentlemanly, and to speak the way you do?"

"Send him to school," said the Duke.

Mr. Mamble eyed him suspiciously. "Begging your Grace's pardon, was that what your father did with you?"

"My father died before I was born. I hope he would have, had he lived. As it was, my guardian had so great a care for me that he saddled me with a tutor. But I was very sickly, which Tom is not. Even so, I can assure you that it is wretched for a boy to be educated in such a way. I used to envy my cousins very much, for they were all at school."

"Ah, I daresay, your Grace!" said Mr. Mamble gloomily. "But the sort of school I want for Tom maybe wouldn't have him, on account of me not being a gentleman-born."

"I expect," said the Duke diffidently, "I might be able to help you. I fancy I have an interest at one good school at least."

Mr. Mamble drew a breath. "By God!" he said, with deep feeling, "if your Grace will speak for Tom there's no saying where he won't end!"

Thus it was that by the time Tom came in for his dinner, his parent greeted him with the tidings that if he would be a good boy, and mind his book, and abjure low company, he should go to a school of his Grace's choosing.

Tom was at once amazed and overjoyed by this unexpected piece of good fortune, and as soon as he could master his tongue expressed his readiness to conform in every way to his sire's wishes.

Mr. Mamble grunted, regarding him with a fond but sceptical eye. "Ay, I daresay! Prate is prate, but it's the duck lays the eggs," he observed. "You be off, and make yourself tidy! You ought to know better than to come into his Grace's room looking like a clodpole!"

"Oh, bother, he don't give a fig for that!" said Tom cheerfully. "Oh, sir, shan't I go to London with you, after all?"

"Yes, indeed you shall, if your Papa will let you," the Duke said, smiling at him reassuringly. "Perhaps you might come to me after Christmas, and see the pantomime, and all the famous sights. I will invite two of my young cousins as well—only you must not lead them into mischief!"

"Oh, no!" Tom said earnestly. "I promise faithfully I will not!" Another thought occurred to him; he said anxiously: "And shall I go shooting at your house here? You *said* I should!"

"Yes, certainly, unless your Papa wishes to take you home directly."

Mr. Mamble, who was ecstatically rubbing his knees at the thought of his son's approaching visit to a ducal mansion, said that he didn't know but what he might not remain in Bath for a few days after all. The Duke mentally chid himself for the feeling of dismay which invaded his breast.

Mr. Mamble became more loquacious over dinner, and by far more natural. He even ventured to ask the Duke why he had elected to wander round the country under a false name.

"Because I was tired of being a Duke," replied his host. "I wanted to see how it would be to be a nobody."

Mr. Mamble laughed heartily at this, and said he warranted some people didn't know when they were well-off.

"Oh, Pa!" exclaimed Tom, looking up from his plate. "He isn't! But I told him you would pay him back for all the money he spent on me, and you will, won't you?"

Mr. Mamble said that he would certainly do so, and showed an embarrassing tendency to produce his purse then and there. The Duke hastily assured him that his difficulties were only of a temporary nature.

Mr. Mamble begged him not to be shy of mentioning it if he would like the loan of a few bills. He said that he knew that the nobs were often at low tide through gaming and racing and such, which, though he did not hold with them himself, were very genteel pastimes. He then said in

253

a very lavish way that he hoped that the Duke would not trouble himself about his shot at the inn, but hang it up, since he would count himself honoured to be allowed to stand huff, and would question no expense.

"No, no, indeed I am only awaiting a draft from London!" the Duke said, in acute discomfort. "And pray do not try to reimburse me on Tom's account! I should dislike it excessively!"

Mr. Mamble, fortified by several glasses of burgundy, then set himself to discover the extent of the Duke's fortune. The Duke, who had not previously encountered his kind, gazed at him quite blankly, and wondered of what interest his fortune could be to anyone but himself. Mr. Mamble said that he supposed it was derived mostly from rents, and asked him a great many questions about the management of large estates, which, while they certainly showed considerable shrewdness, reduced the Duke to weary boredom. The covers were removed, the port had sunk low in the bottle, and still Mr. Mamble seemed to have no intention of taking his leave. A horrible suspicion that he had brought his baggage from the White Horse to the Pelican, and meant to take up his quarters there, had just entered the Duke's head when the door was opened, and he looked up to see his cousin Gideon standing upon the threshold. The expression of gentle resignation was wiped from his face. He sprang up, exclaiming: "Gideon!"

Captain Ware grinned at him, but stepping across the room grasped him urgently by the shoulders, and shook him, saying: "Adolphus, I think I will murder you!"

The Duke laughed, wrenching the big hands from his shoulders, and holding them hard. "I'm told you're already thought to have done so! Oh, but I am glad to see you, Gideon! How the devil did you know where I was?"

"I have tracked you all the way from Arlesey, my abominable cousin—and a rare dance you have led me!"

"From Arlesey!" The Duke stared up at him, the liveliest astonishment in his face. "Good God, how comes this about? You cannot have known that I was *there!*"

"But I did know it. Your amiable friend Liversedge very handsomely offered to sell you to me. He thought I might like to succeed to your dignities. I don't know what mischief you have been brewing, Adolphus, but if ever you cause me to lose so much sleep on your account again I will make you sorry you were ever born!"

"No, that you won't!" suddenly interjected Tom, who had been gazing upon this scene with strong disapprobation. He doubled his fists, and eyed Captain Ware belligerently. "I won't let anybody touch him, and so I warn you!"

Gideon was amused. "Famous! Now, had I known you had such a stout bodyguard, Adolphus, I need not have worried about you!"

"Well, you let him alone, for I mean it!" said Tom.

The Duke laughed. "No, no, Tom, you must not pick a quarrel with my big cousin, for he takes very good care of me, I promise you! Gideon, I must make you known to Mr. Mamble, who is Tom's father. Mr. Mamble, Captain Ware!"

Mr. Mamble got up ponderously from his chair, and executed a bow. Tom, a fanatical light in his eye, demanded: "Is he a soldier?"

"Yes, he is," said the Duke.

"Cavalry?" said Tom anxiously.

"Lifeguards!" said the Duke, in thrilling accents.

Tom drew a deep, worshipful breath, and uttered: "And you never told me! Sir, were you ever in a battle?"

"I was in a skirmish at Genappe, and in a battle at Waterloo," replied Gideon.

"Wounded?" Tom asked hopefully.

"Just a scratch," said Gideon.

"Tell me all about it, sir, *please!*"

"Yes, some other time he will," said the Duke, recklessly committing his cousin. "But not, I think, to-night, for it is growing late, and——" He broke off suddenly, catching sight of his valet, standing in the doorway, and dumbly regarding him. "Nettlebed! But, good God, how in the world——?"

"I brought him along with me," explained Gideon. "Found him with Matt, in Baldock, hunting for you."

"My lord!" said Nettlebed, in a queer voice. "My lord! I thank God I've found your Grace! I shall never forgive myself, never!"

"Oh, no, no, no!" said the Duke, laying a hand on his arm, and shaking it playfully. "Now, Nettlebed, pray don't be upset for nothing! You see I am very well! Yes, and extremely glad to have you with me again, for I have missed you very much, I assure you. But I do wish you had not left London! I sent an express to Scriven last night, desiring him to tell you to come to me, with all my gear!"

"My lord, I had to do it!" Nettlebed said. "But I will never do anything your Grace does not wish again, if only your Grace will forgive me!"

"But I have nothing in the world to forgive," the Duke said gently. "Oh, are you thinking how cross you were with me on the morning I ran away from you all? Well, I meant

255

you to be cross, so perhaps it is I who should be begging your pardon. Now, do pray go and set all to rights in my room, Nettlebed! I am not the least hand at keeping my traps in order, and I shall be very glad to have them tidied for me again."

This request had the desired effect of making Nettlebed pull himself together. His eye brightened, and he assured the Duke that he had no longer any need to trouble his head over such matters. Before he left the room, he swept the cloth from the table, which the waiter had neglected to do, made up the fire, and straightened the cushions on the sofa, as though in the performance of these acts of service his wounded soul found balm. After that, he withdrew, but saw to it that his presence should still be felt by sending up the waiter with another bottle of port, and one of brandy.

The Duke, who wanted to be alone with his cousin, was then guilty of a piece of strategy. He told Tom that it was time he went off to bed. This aroused Mr. Mamble from some dream of grandeur, and he not only endorsed the command, but said that it was time he went back to the White Horse. He seemed undecided whether to remove from this house to the Pelican on the morrow, or to wrest the unwilling Tom from the Duke. The possibility of having Mr. Mamble as a fellow-guest wrought so powerfully on the Duke's mind that the first thing he said to his cousin, when he returned from seeing one Mamble off, and the other to his bedchamber, was: "There's only one thing to be done! I'll send them both to Cheyney! I promised Tom he should go there to shoot, and I expect his father would like of all things to stay in a Duke's house."

Gideon grinned. "No doubt he would! What very queer company you are keeping, Adolphus! I wonder how Mamble and Liversedge will deal together?"

The Duke stared at him. "Liversedge?"

"Not knowing what else to do with him," explained Gideon. "I have left him at Cheyney, in Wragby's care—"

"Gideon, you have not brought that fat rogue here with you?" the Duke said incredulously.

"But I have," replied Gideon. "He awaits your judgment, my little one."

"But I don't want him!" objected the Duke, looking harassed. "Really, Gideon, it is quite absurd of you! I have enough on my hands without your adding Liversedge to the rest!"

Gideon was amused. "Are you aware that he not only

kidnapped you, but would have been prepared to murder you, for a suitable recompense?"

"Yes, you told me so. I am glad I did not know it while I lay in that cellar! I should have been frightened out of my wits! I supposed that ransom was what was wanted of me, but now I come to think of it the other fellow did utter a number of dark threats, which I set no store by. Did Liversedge really think you would pay him to murder me? He is the most amusing villain!"

Gideon regarded him with a flickering smile. "Am I to understand that you are going to condone his villainy?"

"Well, what else can I do?" asked the Duke reasonably. "If I hand him over to justice, what a stir there would be! Now, Gideon, if you had been captured by a veritable child's trick, and stowed away in a cellar, would you wish the whole world to know of it?"

"I would not, I own. At the same time, I should desire to discourage any more such attempts."

"Oh, I am not so green as to fall a victim twice! And I burned down his house, or, at any rate, the only lodging he seemed to have—and took Belinda away from him, so I think he has been pretty well punished, don't you?"

"I must have a more vengeful disposition than you, Adolphus. No."

The Duke smiled. "Well, he did you no service, after all. But I cannot but feel that he did me a great deal of service. Only wait until I have told you the sum of my adventures! You will be bound to agree that but for Liversedge nothing in the least out of the way would ever have happened to me. No, no, it would be the shabbiest thing to hand him over to the Law! Besides, he made me laugh!" He looked speculatively at his cousin. "And if you forced him to lead you to my prison, Gideon, I will hazard a guess that you used him very roughly first."

"Yes, was it not odd of me?" retorted Gideon. "But this will not do, my child! He is not less villainous for making us laugh. If you had not written to me from Baldock, I should not have known where to look for you, and all might have gone very ill indeed with you."

"Nothing of the sort!" said the Duke, with one of his impish smiles. "*You* did not rescue me from my cellar, Gideon! I rescued myself! You can have no notion of how much I am set up in my own esteem! Liversedge shall go free. I have more important things to think about."

Gideon poured himself out a glass of port, and sat down, stretching his long legs before him. "Very well, let it be as you please! But what is to be done with him? He appears to be penniless, and has informed me, with his engaging candour, that of all towns in the world Bath is the one where he least desires to show his face. It would not surprise me if you found it hard to be rid of him. He has effrontery enough for anything!"

"Oh, let him make himself useful at Cheyney, until I have time to consider what must be done with him!" said the Duke carelessly. "If I can induce Mamble to take Tom there, they will be glad of an extra servant in the house. I daresay he may make an excellent butler."

This made Gideon choke over his port, but when he had recovered he admitted that there was much in what his cousin said, as well he knew, since the moment of his reaching Reading on the previous evening Liversedge had taken it upon himself to act as a major-domo. "I have no doubt he was intent only on softening my hard heart, but I will own that no one could have been more zealous to discover some trace of you, Adolphus. In fact, I owe it to him that we did at last pick up the scent, for when no one could be brought to remember a little fellow in an olive-green coat, he enquired for your inamorata, describing her in terms which has given me an over-mastering desire to meet her. There was no difficulty then: no one, it seems, could fail to remember the lady!"

"No, very true! She is the most dazzling girl! You shall certainly see her, but mind, Gideon! you are not to seduce her with promises of a purple silk gown!"

"Good God, could I?"

"Yes, she will go off with anyone who does so. Oh, Gideon, I am glad you have come! I have so much to tell you!" He refilled the glasses, and sat down opposite his cousin. "No sooner am I clear of one scrape than I fall into another! Harriet had to rescue me from the Round-house here only this afternoon, and you would not believe what an odious reputation I have in Hertfordshire!"

"Would I not? You forget that I sought for you in Hitchin! But begin at the beginning, Gilly! By the by, I sent that young fool, Matt, back to Oxford with a flea in his ear. He ought to be flogged for embroiling you in his silly starts!"

"Poor Matt, he did not embroil me: I embroiled myself. But how came he into the business?"

"Nettlebed recalled that he had been closeted with you the night before you disappeared, and went after him. I met the pair of them in Baldock. Never mind that now! Proceed with your story!"

Thus adjured, the Duke settled down to regale his cousin with the entire history of his adventures. Gideon interpolated

258

so many questions, and laughed so much that the candles were burning low in their sockets before the Duke had ended the tale. Then he demanded to know Gideon's share in it, and this amused him quite as much as his own part had amused Gideon. When he heard of Lord Lionel's discovery of his ring in Gideon's desk, he gave such a crack of mirth that a fellow-guest in the adjoining room thumped indignantly on the wall.

"Yes, excessively droll, no doubt!" said Gideon, thrusting a hand into his pocket, and bringing out the ring. He tossed it into the Duke's hand. "Take your ill-omened bauble! And now, little cousin, I will break to you a trifle of knowledge you do not appear to have been informed of before! No action for breach of promise can lie against a minor."

For a moment the Duke stared at him. Then he said blankly: "Do you mean that I did it all for nothing?"

"That is what I mean, Adolphus," replied Gideon, grinning at him.

This struck the Duke as being so exquisitely humorous that the gentleman in bed in the next room was obliged to thump on the wall again.

"Oh, but I am glad I didn't know it!" gasped the Duke, wiping his eyes. "Yes, I know you think it ought to be a lesson to me in future to ask my big cousin's advice, but I would not have missed my adventures for a fortune!"

"No," said Gideon, regarding him under his drooping eyelids. "I have a notion you are not going to ask anyone's advice in the future, Adolphus. Shall you be sorry to return to all your dignities?"

"Yes—no! I had a most diverting time, but some of it was most uncomfortable, and I own that I do not care to be without a valet, or a change of raiment! I do trust that Scriven will not delay to send someone here with my baggage!"

"I fancy you need not be anxious on that head," said Gideon dryly. "What is more, I have my own guess as to who will appear in Bath before we are much older!"

"Good God! Not my uncle? What the devil shall I do with him, if you are right? I must find this fellow, Mudgley, and I am sure my uncle will be the greatest hindrance to me!"

Gideon's eyes gleamed appreciatively at the unconscious change in his cousin which made it possible for him to contemplate the possibility of his being able to do anything at all with Lord Lionel, but he replied gravely: "You had best send him to join your new friend at Cheyney."

"Yes, I think I had," said the Duke, quite seriously. "He

dislikes hotels, so perhaps he will choose to go there. I wonder, will he think Mamble preferable to the damp sheets he is convinced all landlords put upon their beds? And then there is Liversedge! Gideon, I charge you most straitly not to say one word to your father about Liversedge! He would raise such a breeze! And for heaven's sake, try to think of some plausible tale for me to fob him off with! It would never do for him to know the truth."

"Turning him up sweet? You won't do it!"

"I must do it. There is Matt to be thought of, remember! But first I do think I should get rid of Mamble. If he stays in Bath I shall never be able to shake him off. Gideon, you shall drive him and Tom out to Cheyney for me tomorrow!"

Gideon groaned. "And tell Tom how I got my wound? I thank you!"

"Nonsense! It will not hurt you to tell him about a battle, and you are just the sort of fellow to give him other ambitions than highroad robbery."

"Rid your mind of the hope that you are going to fob your hell-born babe off on me!" recommended Gideon.

But the Duke only smiled at him with deep, if rather sleepy, affection, and murmured: "*Kind* Gideon! Not really a hell-born babe, you know: just a trifle wild! I daresay he will mind you tolerably well. I *am* glad you are come to Bath!"

He said the same thing when he took himself off to bed, and found Nettlebed waiting to attend on him. Nettlebed had contrived, in some inexplicable way, to make his bed-chamber much more comfortable, and there would be no denying that it was extremely pleasant to find candles already burning there, the fire made up, his nightshirt laid out in readiness, and a devoted servitor to pull off his boots, pour out hot water for him, and tenderly divest him of his raiment. He said: "It has done me a great deal of good to be without you, Nettlebed, for it has made me appreciate you as I never did before! Can anything be done, do you think, to make me respectable enough to be seen abroad?"

"Now, don't you worry your head over that, your Grace!" Nettlebed admonished him. "I will soon have your coat fit to wear, never fear!"

"Thank you. I brought some new neckcloths to-day, so——"

"Your Grace won't have to wear *them*," said Nettlebed repressively.

"I was afraid you would not quite like them," said the Duke, in a meek voice.

Nettlebed was not deceived; he was still to much chastened to treat this demure mischief as it deserved, but he shook his head at the Duke, and said severely, as he drew the curtains round the bed: "Ay, right well your Grace knew I wouldn't like them, and a good thing his lordship isn't here to see the case you're in! Now, you go to sleep, your Grace, and no more of your tricks!"

CHAPTER XXIII

IN the morning it was discovered that not only had Nettlebed removed the stains and the creases from the Duke's coat, but he had also furbished up Tom's apparel. Nettlebed by no means approved of Master Mamble, but if his master chose to take under his wing a youth of vulgar parentage there was nothing for it but to do what lay in his power to make him respectable. From having attended the Duke and his various cousins in their boyhood, he was perfectly well able to deal with even so recalcitrant a subject as Tom, even succeeding in sending him in to breakfast with his neck clean, and his hair brushed.

Tom, no sufferer from matutinal moroseness, enlivened the board with a ceaseless flow of conversation. As much of this took the form of pertinacious questions addressed to Captain Ware, his victim revised his overnight decision, and grimly informed the Duke that he would obey his behests with the utmost willingness. "And how you have borne it for close on a week, I know not, Adolphus!" he said.

The Duke laughed, but bade Tom postpone his questions. "For my cousin is always very cross at breakfast," he explained, "and you will have, besides, plenty of opportunity to ask him what you like presently. I have been thinking that you might like to go out to Cheyney, and stay there for a day or two. Captain Ware will tell my headkeeper to look after you, and you may take a gun out, and very likely see Shillingford's ferrets, and go ratting as well."

The magnificence of his proposal served not only to render Tom speechless for quite ten minutes, but to make him assail his parent, upon his arrival at the Pelican, with such eager entreaties to him to permit him to accept the most splendid invitation of his life that Mr. Mamble was almost dazed by them. When he understood more clearly what the invitation was, he protested that he did not wish to be any longer separated from his heir. This made it easy for the Duke to extend the invitation to him, and so adroitly did he do it that Mr. Mamble had no suspicion that he was being got rid of, and Gideon had to hide an appreciative

261

grin. Fortunately for the success of the Duke's scheme, Mr. Mamble had fallen foul of the landlord, the boots, and one of the waiters at the White Horse, and had already declared his intention of shaking the dust of this hostelry from his feet. If he thought an invitation to stay at Cheyney while its owner remained in Bath irregular, this consideration was outweighed in his mind by the prospect of being able to floor his oldest crony and chief rival in Kettering with the careless announcement that he had been visiting the Duke of Sale at his house near Bath. He accepted with a low bow, and in a speech in which the words Condescension, Your Grace, Distinguishing Attention, and All Obligation occurred so frequently that the Duke could only be grateful to Tom, who interrupted it without ceremony, demanding to know when they might set forward on the journey.

"You may come with me there at once," said Gideon. "We will go ahead of your father in my curricle, and see all in readiness."

"Oh, *sir!* and may I drive it? May I? Do, pray, say I may!"

His parent bade him mind his manners, and recommended Captain Ware to give him a clout if he should be troublesome. Gideon, however, nodded, and bade him make haste and pack up his valise. Tom dashed off at once, and in a very short time the Duke was alone, and able to set forth on his quest of Mr. Mudgley.

He found it disagreeably reminiscent of his earlier quest for the Bird in Hand. None of the more obvious places of enquiry seemed ever to have heard of Mr. Mudgley, and visits to two gentlemen who bore names slightly resembling Mudgley proved abortive. The Duke drove back to the Pelican in the gig he had hired for these visits in a mood of considerable misgiving. He found that his cousin had returned from Cheyney, and that Nettlebed had had the forethought to bespeak suitable accommodation for them both at the Christopher. He nodded absently, and said: "Yes, very well, when my baggage has arrived. I must go round to Laura Place."

"What's amiss, Adolphus?" enquired his cousin.

"The devil's in it that no one has heard of Mudgley. If I can't discover him, I shall be in a worse scrape than any! That unfortunate child has nowhere to go, and no relatives who will own her, and what in thunder am I to do with her?"

Gideon raised his brows. "From what you have told me,

I should suppose that she will pretty speedily find a nest to settle in," he said caustically.

"That is the very thing I am seeking to prevent!" said the Duke, irritated.

"Is it worth the pains?"

"Good God, can you not understand that I made myself responsible for her? She is only a child! A pretty fellow I should be if I were to abandon her at this stage! I must try if I cannot induce her to recall more particularly where Mudgley lives. Did you leave all well at Cheyney?"

"I left your servants a trifle stunned by your guests, but it seems probable that Liversedge will assume control of the household. He informed me that I might have the most complete confidence in him. By and by, that bailiff of yours —Moffat, is it?—is overjoyed to learn that you are in Bath, and trusts that you will go to Cheyney. He has all manner of matters to lay before you."

"If Moffat wants to see me, he must come to Bath. I have no time to go out to Cheyney now."

"I told him so, and he said that he would come to you," said Gideon. "There is no escape for you!"

"You might have fobbed him off!" complained the Duke.

"Your retainers are not so easily fobbed off. If you are going to Laura Place, I shall come with you. I can no longer exist without a sight of the fair Belinda. Besides, I dote on the Dowager! I wonder if she has bought a new wig? When last I saw her she had a red one—devilish dashing!"

But when they arrived in Laura Place, and were taken up to the drawing-room on the first floor, they found that wiser counsels had prevailed with the Dowager Lady Ample-forth, and she had exchanged the red wig for one of iron-grey. But as she chose to set a turban of rich violet silk, shot with orange, on top of these new ringlets the effect was still extremely colourful. She was a handsome old lady, with a beak of a nose, and a wicked eye. In her day she had been, as she had not the slightest hesitation in inform-ing her acquaintance, a great rake, but gout, and increasing years, now largely chained her to her chair. She tolerated her son, despised her three daughters, and cherished to-wards her daughter-in-law a violent animosity. Since she belonged to a more robust and by far less prim a generation than theirs she had no difficulty at all in shocking her descendants, a pastime to which she was greatly addicted.

She received the Duke indulgently, and his cousin with acclaim. Gideon corresponded exactly with her notions of what a young man should be like, and she received his outrageous advances in high delight, encouraging him in

every extravagant flattery, and adjuring him to murmur into her ear all the more scandalous stories current in military
circles. She was able to regale him with quite a number of
warm anecdotes herself, and it was not long before she had
signed to him with one twisted hand to draw his chair
closer to hers. This left the Duke free to confide his errand
to Harriet. She was concerned to learn that he had been
unable to discover Mr. Mudgley. "It is not that I do not
wish to keep her with me, Gilly," she explained, "but I
know Mama will never permit me to, and there is another
circumstance which makes me feel a little uneasy. I am
afraid Charlie admires her excessively!"

"Good God!" said the Duke. "I had not thought of that!
What is to be done?"

"Well, Gilly, I do think we should find a suitable establishment for her, but pray do not be worried! Charlie is
not staying here, you know: he has a lodging in Green
Street, and I have explained to him that he must be good.
But nothing would do but he must squire us to the theatre
last night, and I fear he did flirt rather dreadfully with
Belinda! I was a goose to go with him, but Belinda wanted
so very much to see the play that I did not know how to
refuse. But I won't let him be alone with her, I promise. I
must go with Grandmama to Lady Ombersley's party to-
night, but Charlie told us himself that he has promised to
some friends of his own, which is why he cannot go with
us. I hope you will not think I did wrong to go to the play!"

"No, no, how could you do wrong? I am only distressed
that you should be put to so much anxiety, my poor Harry!
Is Belinda in? Would it be of the least use for me to ask
her if she cannot cudgel her brains a little?"

"Oh, yes, she is trimming a hat for herself! I will fetch
her down directly. But, Gilly, I don't know how it will
answer! She is the strangest creature! It does seem as though
this Mr. Mudgley and his mother are the only people who
have ever been kind to her, and I own that she speaks of
the young man with a wistful look that quite touches one's
heart, but she has not the least notion of constancy! It is
quite dreadful! And, oh, Gilly, by the unluckiest chance we
saw a purple gown in one of the shops on Milsom Street,
and I do believe it has put everything else out of her head!"

He laughed. "Harriet, do pray buy it for her, and set it
to my account! Perhaps if she had her purple gown——"

"Gilly, I *could* not!" said Harriet earnestly. "You have no
idea how unsuitable it would be! It is of the brightest
purple satin, with Spanish sleeves slashed with rows of gold
beads, and a demi-train, and the bosom cut by far too low!

Dear Gilly, I would do anything for you, but only conceive of a young girl's wearing such a gown! Even Grandmama would be shocked!"

He was awed by this description of the gown's magnificence, and could not but acknowledge the justice of Harriet's objection to it. To insist on her lending her countenance to a young female clad in such startling raiment would, he realized, be unreasonable. He acquiesced therefore in her decision, and held the door open for her to pass from the room.

The Dowager watched him critically, and said, as he came back into the room: "Well, Sale, I'm sure I don't know what you uncle will have to say to your raking, but it has done you a great deal of good, and my granddaughter too! I've no doubt you've been deceiving her monstrously, but the dullest dog alive is ever your virtuous young man! Which I thought you were, I own. However, I see there's more of your grandfather in you than I knew. Lord, what a dashing blade he was, to be sure! He can't have been a day older than you when he ran off with Lyndhurst's wife. They hushed it up, of course, but I remember what a scandal it was at the time! They say it cost his father—your great-grandfather, you know—a pretty penny to get him out of such an entanglement, and I daresay it did. Then he married one of the Ingatestone gals: a sickly creature, she was, always in the megrims! Lord Guiseley was her *bel ami* for years. They used to say that the second daughter—your aunt Sarah, I mean—was none of Sale's, but I never set any store by it myself: she hadn't the spirit of a hen! But your grandfather used to be the biggest rake in town. All the Mamas used to forbid us to dance with him at the assemblies, for he never kept the line, and there was no sense in encouraging his advances once he was tied up in marriage, you know."

The Duke received these engaging reminiscences of his progenitors without protest, merely smiling at the old lady, and murmuring that he hoped no careful parent would feel compelled to warn her daughter against him; but Gideon instantly demanded to be told more about Aunt Sarah, whom he cordially disliked. The Dowager was nothing loth, and was in the middle of a highly libellous story when Harriet came back into the room with Belinda.

Belinda, becomingly attired in one of Harriet's cambric gowns, bestowed a ravishing smile upon Gideon, favouring him with one of her wide, speculative stares. She seemed genuinely pleased to see the Duke, but she was looking a little wistful, and her lovely mouth drooped at the corners.

265

Whether she was pining for Mr. Mudgley, or for the purple gown, he was unable to discover, since her thoughts seemed to be equally divided between them. She was plainly in awe of Lady Ampleforth, and was minding her manners so painstakingly that she spoke only in a subuded voice, and sat on the extreme edge of a chair, with her feet together, and her hands folded in her lap. He guessed that, in spite of Harriet's kindness, her surroundings were oppressive to her. She was terrified of doing something wrong. He felt more sorry for her than ever, and redoubled his determination to find her swain for her.

But she was of very little assistance to him. She had only once visited Mr. Mudgley's farm, on a day when Mrs. Pilling had gone to Wells to see her sister; and although she was able to describe in great detail the big kitchen there, the dear little chicks in the yard, and a calf which had licked her fingers, she had no idea how far the farm lay from Bath, or in which direction. But there had been a stream, with primroses growing beside it, and Mr. Mudgley had very obligingly stopped to let her get down from the gig to pick a great bunch of them.

The Duke felt defeated, and for a moment said nothing. Belinda sighed. "Perhaps he went away, like Maggie, and I shall never see him any more," she said.

He did not think this was likely, and shook his head. Belinda sighed again. "I daresay he is married now, because he was *very* handsome, and it was such a nice house, with a garden, and beautiful red curtains in the parlour. I am very unhappy."

Both he and Harriet said what they could to console her, but she seemed to have sunk into a mood of gentle resignation. She said simply: "I wish I was not a foundling! It is very hard, you know, because no one cares what becomes of one, and one has nowhere to go, and when I thought that Uncle Swithin would make me comfortable I was quite taken-in. And so it is always!"

This sad little speech brought the tears to Harriet's eyes, and she took one of Belinda's hands in hers, and clasped it, saying: "No, no, do not say so! The Duke and I will always stand your friends, I promise!"

"Yes, but it is not the same," said Belinda unanswerably.

The Duke could only reiterate his determination to find Mr. Mudgley. Belinda smiled gratefully at him, but without conviction, and, catching Gideon's eye, he rose to take his leave.

"Well," said Gideon, as they walked towards Bridge Street together, "she is certainly a nonpareil, Adolphus, and

I think you are wasting your time. She is destined to become a Covent Garden nun."

The Duke compressed his lips, returning no answer. Captain Ware glanced quizzically down at him. "I have offended you, Adolphus?"

"No. I expected you to say something of the sort. You have never the least sympathy for those born in less easy circumstances than yourself—witness your contempt of Matt!"

Captain Ware blinked. "Phew! What can I do to atone?"

"Find Mudgley for me!" said the Duke tartly.

"Yes, your Grace!" said Captain Ware, in servile accents. This made the Duke laugh. He slid a hand in his cousin's arm, pressing it slightly, and saying: "I have learnt some few things in this week that I never knew before, you see, Gideon. Did you ever think how it would be to be without a single relative in the world?"

"I did not, I own. I thought you had done so, however, and envied those in that happy state."

"I have discovered my mistake," replied the Duke.

Gideon could not help smiling at this. He said: "I hope you will still think so when my father arrives in Bath!"

This event took place that evening, just as Nettlebed had brought sherry and Madeira into the private parlour, drawn the blinds, and made up the fire. The door was suddenly opened, and Lord Lionel stalked into the room, before the trembling waiter had had time to announce him.

His lordship, having passed through every stage of anxiety, was suffering from the inevitable reaction, and looked to be in anything but a conciliatory mood. His eagle-glance swept past his son and became fixed upon the Duke. "Ha!" he ejaculated explosively. "So you have seen fit to inform us of your whereabouts, Sale! Extremely obliging of you! And now perhaps you will have the goodness to explain the meaning of this caper?"

The Duke, rising quickly from his seat by the fire, fancied that he could detect fresh lines on his uncle's face. He went forward, holding out his hands, and saying: "Dear sir, I am so very glad to see you! Forgive me!"

Lord Lionel champed upon an invisible bit. With all the air of a man constrained against his will, he took the outstretched hands, and gripped them. "I want none of your cajolery, Sale!" he announced, his penetrating gaze searching the Duke's face. "I do not know what the devil you mean by behaving in this way. I am very angry with you, very angry, indeed! How dared you, sir?"

The Duke smiled up at him. "Indeed, I don't know how

I dared! But I did not mean the fools to worry you with my capers!"

"Let me tell you that I have better things to do than to worry over your conduct!" said his lordship inaccurately. "Are you quite well, Gilly? Yes, I see that you are. It would have served you right if I had found you laid down on your bed with one of your sickly turns, let me tell you! Where have you been, and what the devil are you doing in this place? Let me have a plain answer, if you please!"

"Oh, I have been in all manner of places, sir, trying to discover if I am a man, or only a duke!" responded the Duke.

"Balderdash!" pronounced his lordship comprehensively. He released the Duke's hands, and discovered Nettlebed's presence in the room. His exacerbated feelings found a certain measure of relief in the utterance of a severe rebuke to him for having left Sale House without notice or permission. He then turned his attention to his son, and having condemned his manners and morals in a few blistering sentences, felt a good deal better. He eyed the real culprit measuringly. "I know very well when you have been in mischief, sir!" he said grimly. "Don't think to fob me off, or to hide behind Gideon, for I mean to have the truth! If you were but five years younger——"

"No, no!" protested the Duke, his face alive with laughter. "You never flogged me after I was sixteen, sir!"

"I collect," said Lord Lionel, with a fulminating glance cast at his son, "that you mean to tell me that it was *I* who drove you into this nonsensical affair?"

"To tell you the truth, sir," said the Duke, coaxing him into a chair by the fire, "I do not mean to tell you anything at all! Oh, no, don't frown at me, and pray do not be so angry with me! You see I have taken no hurt, and I promise I will not cause you such anxiety again. Nettlebed, be so good as to tell them to lay covers for three, and fetch another wine-glass for his lordship!"

"I do not dine here," stated his lordship, his brows still alarmingly knit, "and nor do you, Gilly! I do not know why, when you have a house very conveniently placed, you must needs install yourself at a common inn: I daresay it is of a piece with all the rest! You will accompany me to Cheyney at once!"

Gideon leaned his shoulders against the wall, and waited with interest to hear what his cousin would reply to this command.

"Oh, no, do stay to dine with me!" said the Duke. "I must explain to you that I have guests staying at Cheyney—rather odd guests perhaps you may think!"

"Yes, I do think it!" said Lord Lionel. "I have already been to Cheyney, Sale! I am well aware that it no longer any concern of mine if you choose to fill your house with a parcel of vulgar tradesmen, and to give an overgrown schoolboy carte blanche to shoot every bird you have on the place, but I should be glad to know where you acquired your taste for low company!"

"The thing is," replied the Duke confidentially, "that I haven't a taste for low company, sir. I owed Mamble some degree of extraordinary civility, for I fear I did aid and abet his son to escape from him."

"I do not know what you are talking about!" complained his lordship. "And if it is your notion of extraordinary civility to invite a man to stay in your house when you are not there to entertain him, I can only suppose that I have failed, in all these years, to teach you common courtesy! I am ashamed of you, Gilly!"

"But I couldn't endure him, sir! It is very bad, but what was I to do, when he would toadeat me so, and there was no getting away from him? He means only to stay there for a day or two because I promised Tom he should have some shooting. Should you object very much to entertaining him for me?"

"I should!" barked Lord Lionel. "You will stop talking flummery to me, and come to Cheyney!"

The Duke poured out some sherry into the glass Nettlebed had just brought into the room, and handed it to his uncle. "No, I cannot spare the time to go to Cheyney now," he said. "I am removing to the Christopher, however. Did you bring my baggage with you from London, dear sir?"

"Yes, I did, and it is awaiting you at Cheyney. Now, Gilly——"

"Then it must be sent to the Christopher to-morrow," said the Duke calmly. "It is very tiresome! I am *so* sadly in need of a change of raiment!"

"Gilly!" said his lordship awfully.

"Yes, sir!"

Lord Lionel glared at him. "Gilly, what is the matter with you?" he demanded. "What made you do it, boy? Be a little plain with me, I beg of you!"

The Duke sat down beside him, and laid a hand on his knee. "It is very ridiculous," he said, in his soft voice. "I found it a dead bore to be Duke of Sale, and I thought I would try how it would be to be nobody in particular."

"Upon my word! I should have thought you would have had more sense."

"But I hadn't, sir."

Lord Lionel gripped the hand on his knee. "Now, my boy, don't be afraid to own the truth to me! You know I have nothing but your welfare at heart! If you went off on this start because of anything I may have said to you—in short, if you did not like the arrangement I had made for you, there was not the least need for you to have offered for Lady Harriet! I never had any desire to force you into what you had a distaste for. Indeed, if your mind misgives you—though it will be a damned awkward business!—I will see to it——"

"No, sir, I am very happy in my engagement," the Duke interrupted. "Much happier than I ever thought to be! She is an angel!"

Lord Lionel was slightly taken aback. He stared at the Duke under his bushy brows, and remarked dryly: "This is a different tune from the one you sang at Sale, when I first broached the matter to you!"

"I was not then aware what a treasure you had chosen for me, sir. But I told you I had been learning some few things of late."

Lord Lionel grunted. "Well, if you have learnt to have a little more common-sense, I am glad of it, but why you must needs run off without a word to anyone is past my understanding! If you had wanted to go out of town, I am sure it was quite your own affair, and you might have done so without question."

Gideon spoke. "But not, sir, without Nettlebed, Chigwell, Borrowdale, Turvey, and the rest of his retinue."

"You," said Lord Lionel crushingly, "have behaved throughout in an insolent, heedless, and callous fashion, and may now have the grace to remain silent!"

"There is much in what you say, sir," admitted Gideon, with a wry twist to his mouth.

"Well, well, that will do!" said his lordship, mollified. "There is no harm done, after all, and I shall not enquire too particularly into what Gilly has been doing. I am not one of those who expect a young man to lead the life of a saint! You are looking very well, Gilly, very well indeed, and that, I must own, makes up for everything!"

The Duke's hand turned under his, and clasped it. "You are very much too good to me, sir, and I don't know what I deserve for causing you so much anxiety."

"Pooh! nonsense!" said his lordship testily. "I know your coaxing ways, boy! Don't think to cozen me with them! But it is the outside of enough, when you give every idle gossiper in town cause to say that Gideon has murdered you!

Not but what it was quite his own fault, and I have no sympathy to waste on him, none at all!"

"But I cannot have you so cross with Gideon," said the Duke gently. "He is quite my best friend, you know, and, besides, what could he do when I had sworn him to secrecy? And when he heard that I was in a scrape he came to rescue me from it, so it is very hard that he should be scolded now!"

"What scrape have you been in?" demanded Lord Lionel.

"Well, I didn't mean to tell you, sir, but I think you are bound to hear of it, for rather too many people know it. I was so foolish as to allow myself to be kidnapped, by some rascals who thought to hold me to ransom."

"That is just what I had feared might happen!" Lord Lionel exclaimed. "All this rubbishing talk of finding out whether you are a man or only a duke, and you are no more fit to fend for yourself than a child in short coats! Well, I hope it may be a lesson to you!"

"Yes, sir," said the Duke demurely, "but, as it chances, I did fend for myself."

"Gilly, don't tell me you let the villains bleed you!" exclaimed his lordship.

"No, sir, I burned down my prison, and came off scatheless."

Lord Lionel stared at him in great surprise. "Are you trying to humbug me, Gilly?" he asked suspiciously.

The Duke laughed. "No, sir. I thought I had to bestir myself, for I didn't know that Gideon was coming hotfoot to the rescue. They were not very clever villains, perhaps, which was fortunate. But they did me a great deal of good!"

"Did you a great deal of good?" exclaimed Lord Lionel. "What nonsense you talk, boy! How came it about? Tell me the whole!"

If the Duke did not comply exactly with this request, he told Lord Lionel enough to astonish and shock him very much. But it was evident that he was also pleased to think that his nephew had behaved with such spirit, and he forgot, in his interest in the affair, to enquire how Gideon had come by the knowledge that Gilly had been kidnapped. But he was not at all pleased to learn that nothing had been done to lay the villains by the heels, and roundly denounced such foolish clemency. "They must be brought to book!" he declared. "You will inform the magistrates, Gilly: you should have done so before you left the district, of course!"

"No, sir, I think not," the Duke replied tranquilly.

"What you think is of no consequence!" said his lordship. "A pretty state of affairs it would be if all such rascals were to go unpunished! You owe a duty to society, as I have been for ever telling you! Now, do not argue with me, I beg of you!"

"Certainly not, sir: you know I can never bear to do so! I am very sorry for society, but my mind is quite made up. I beg your pardon, but I could not endure to have such a stupid story made known to the world!"

Lord Lionel had been about to scarify him soundly, but this utterance gave him pause. He frowned over it for a moment or two, and at last said grudgingly: "Well, there is something in what you say, but I cannot like it! And there is another thing, Gilly! I do not understand why you have engaged a new steward, without a word to anyone. You will naturally be enlarging your staff, but it will be better to leave such matters in Scriven's hands. He is far more able to judge of what will suit you than you can possibly be. Not but what," he added fairly, "this man of yours seem to know his work very well, and to be just the sort of fellow you should have about you. I have nothing to say against him but in future I advise you to let Scriven attend to the hiring of your servants." He perceived that his son was struggling not to laugh, and directed one of his quelling glances at him. "Now, what do you find to amuse you in that, pray?"

"Nothing, sir!" gasped Captain Ware, wiping his eyes.

Lord Lionel found that his nephew was similarly affected. "Well, well, you are a couple of silly boys!" he said indulgently. "So you wish to remain in Bath, do you, Gilly? You will be squiring Harriet to the balls at the Assembly Rooms, I daresay, and certainly it would not do for you to be driving out to Cheyney late at night. But you would be more comfortable in a set of lodgings, my dear boy, than in an hotel! There are some very tolerable ones to be had, and you may have your own servants to wait on you, and be sure of the beds!"

"Thank you, sir, I shall do very well at the Christopher. It would not be worth the trouble of finding lodgings, for I only stay until Harriet goes to Ampleforth, you know. Shall you join me there, perhaps?"

"No, no, you know very well that I detest hotels! I may as well stay at Cheyney for a few days. It is some time since I was there, and it will do no harm for me to see how things have been going on. Besides, it is quite improper for that fellow, Mamble, to be there without either of us in residence!"

The Duke felt a twinge of remorse. He said contritely: "It is too bad of me! I'm afraid you will dislike it excessively, sir!"

"I daresay," said Lord Lionel dryly, "that I shall not dislike it as much as you would. I have not lived in the world for fifty-five years without learning how to deal with fellows of that stamp, I assure you. But how came you to fall in with him, and what is all this nonsense about aiding his son to escape from him?"

By this time, the waiter had come in, and began, under Nettlebed's severe surveillance, to lay the cover for dinner. It was tacitly assumed that Lord Lionel would partake of this meal, which he did, even going so far as to say that the mutton was not so ill-cooked, and the burgundy—of its kind—quite potable. Nettlebed, who despised all the servants at the Pelican, would not permit the waiter to attend upon his master, but received the various dishes from him in the doorway, so that the Duke was able to regale his uncle uninterrupted with the story of his dealings with Tom. It was not to be expected that his lordship would approve of such unconventional conduct, and he had no hesitation at all in prescribing the proper treatment for boys who played such pranks, but he listened appreciatively to the Duke's part in them, putting several shrewd questions, and nodding at the answers as though he were well satisfied. Indeed it was felt by both cousins that he had expressed a high measure of approbation when he said: "Well, Gilly, you are not such a fool as I had thought."

Encouraged by this encomium, the Duke said in his meekest voice: "There is one other little matter which perhaps I should tell you, sir. I daresay you will be paying your respects to Lady Ampleforth?"

"Certainly," said his lordship.

"Then I think I had better tell you about Belinda," said the Duke guiltily.

His uncle lifted his brows at him. "Oho! So now we come to it, do we? I thought there was a petticoat in it!"

"No," said Gideon lazily. "Adolphus has merely been playing the knight-errant. He has been ready to eat me for telling him he is wasting his time. I hope you may have better success with him."

But Lord Lionel, when he had listened to as much of Belinda's story as his nephew saw fit to impart, was rather amused. Schoolboys of plebeian parentage were to be deplored, but the intrusion into the Duke's life of beautiful damsels he regarded as inevitable, and not in the least blameworthy. Whether he believed in the propriety of the Duke's dealings with Belinda seemed doubtful, but all he said, and that in a tolerant voice, was: "Well, well, it has all been highly romantic, no doubt, and I consider that Har-

273

riet has behaved with great good sense. She is a well-trained girl, and will make you an excellent wife! But this Belinda of yours should now be got rid of, my boy."

"Yes, sir. I—we—hope to establish her creditably," said the Duke.

Lord Lionel nodded, ready to dismiss the matter. "That's right. You can afford to be generous, but do not run to extremes! If you do not like to set about the business yourself, I will do it for you."

"I think, sir, that it will be better if I settle it," said the Duke firmly.

"As you please," said his lordship. "It will not hurt you to get out of this scrape by yourself, though I daresay you will be humbugged into paying her far too much. Never be deceived by a pretty face, my boy! All the same, these ladybirds!"

He then favoured his awed young relatives with several surprising reminiscences of his own youth, pointed the moral to them and said that it was high time he drove back to Cheyney. Gideon saw him to the Duke's chaise. He paused for a minute or two in the doorway of the inn, and said, in a burst of confidence: "You know, Gideon, the boy has not managed so ill! I own, I had not thought he had so much resolution! I begin to have hopes of him. I should not be at all surprised if he turns out to be as good a man as his father. It is a thousand pities he is so undersized, but you may have noticed that he has his own dignity."

"I have frequently noticed it, sir."

"It would not have been wonderful if he had been daunted by all these constables, and kidnappers, and beadles, but no! Mind, he should not have done such a foolish thing, but as it chances no harm has come of it, and I shall say nothing more on that head. You are both of you past the age of being scolded."

"Yes, sir," said his son, grinning affectionately at him.

CHAPTER XXIV

THE Duke's chaise, with his footman and all his baggage, having been despatched by Lord Lionel from Cheyney at an early hour on the following morning, Gilly lost no time in removing to the Christopher, where he instantly discarded his travel-stained raiment, and gratified Nettlebed by telling him that he might give the olive coat away, since he never wished to see it again. Not to be outdone in generosity, Nettlebed said that another such coat could be ordered from Scott

274

—if his Grace preferred his cut to Weston's. He then eased the Duke into a coat of blue superfine, carefully smoothed his nakeen pantaloons, flicked some quite imaginary dust from his Hessians, and added that if his opinion were asked, he would feel himself obliged to say that no one could cut a coat with quite that refinement of taste shown by Weston. The Duke, glancing at the reflection of his trim figure in the mirror, admitted that there was a good deal of truth in what he said, and went off, knowing that he had amply recompensed his servitor for any anxiety he had previously caused him to feel.

He found his footman hovering in the passage, waiting, apparently for no better purpose than to open the door for him into his private parlour. This well-trained individual wore a more than ordinarily inhuman expression, not even permitting himself one furtive glance at his master. But the Duke paused outside the parlour-door, and said smilingly: "I have not thanked you for contriving so very cleverly for me, that day in London, Francis. I am very much obliged to you."

The footman, bringing his gaze down, found that the Duke was plainly waiting to slide a coin into his hand. He accepted this with becoming gratitude, and the Duke said: "I hope they did not ask you a great many awkward questions!"

"No, your Grace, they never asked me any," replied Francis, encouraged by the twinkle in the Duke's eye to relax his quelling rigidity. "And if they had, I wouldn't have said a word, not if they offered me fifty pounds, I wouldn't!"

The Duke was a trifle startled by this evidence of devotion. "You are a very good fellow: thank you!" he said.

This unlooked-for courtesy threw Francis quite off his balance. He turned a dull red, and uttered in far less refined accents: "It weren't nothing! I would be main glad to serve your Grace anyways you might wish!"

The Duke murmured a suitable acknowledgment, and passed into the parlour. Francis, discovering that the coin in his hand was a golden one, instead of the shilling that was his due for any extraordinary service, drew a profound breath, and fell into a blissful reverie.

The Duke found his cousin in the parlour, glancing through the *Morning Post*, which had just arrived from London by the mail-coach. He said, in an awed voice: "Gideon, the most dreadful thing! I have been quite deceived in that footman of mine!"

Captain Ware lowered the newspaper. "Good God, what has he done?"

"Why, nothing! But I thought he did not care a button what became of me, and I find he is as bad as all the rest! They must have drummed their nonsense into his head, for I never did the least thing to attach him to my interests! It is the most disheartening thing! He will grow old in my service, and become a dead bore to my sons!"

Captain Ware roared with laughter. "Dismiss him instantly, Adolphus, dismiss him instantly!"

"Oh, I couldn't do so! It would be the unkindest thing!" said the Duke involuntarily.

"Then I fear that until you can bring yourself to do unkind things you must submit to being the idol of your servants. Tell me, would you be content to accept a Rudgeley for your Mudgley?"

"Are you trying to roast me? What do you mean?"

"Only that in obedience to your commands I have been pursuing some few enquiries. I am credibly informed that the receiving-office here has frequently handled letters addressed to a Mr. Rudgeley residing at Little End, Priston. Could Belinda have been mistaken in the name, do you suppose?"

"Oh, very easily! You are the best of good fellows, Gideon! Where is Priston?"

"Somewhere to the south-west, I'm told. Not very far, but off the pike-road."

"I'll go there at once. What a curst nuisance it is that my curricle is not yet arrived in Bath! Oh, well! I'll take my chaise! Francis! Francis! Oh, there you are! Tell them to bring my chaise to the door, if you please! I shan't need more than a pair, but the postilion must acquaint himself with the road to Priston. Gideon, do you come with me?"

"No, I thank you! I am going to promenade in the Pump Room. I think I shall drive out to dine at Cheyney later, to take dutiful leave of my parent."

"Oh, no, must you? Do you go back to town so soon?"

"To-morrow, if I am not to face a court-martial."

"Well my uncle always dines early in the country, so you may join us at the Dress Ball later," said the Duke.

"Yes, if I had provided myself with evening-dress I might!" retorted his cousin.

"It is too bad: I shall miss you!" said the Duke absently.

"I hesitate to say it Adolphus, but you are a liar!"

The Duke laughed. "Oh, no!" he protested, and went off to collect his hat and overcoat.

Nettlebed was assisting him to put on this garment when Francis came to his room with the news that his bailiff had arrived from Cheyney and respectfully begged to see his Grace.

The Duke groaned. "No, no, I cannot! He will keep me kicking my heels for an hour or more! Why could he not carry his troubles to my uncle? Tell him to go to the devil!" He perceived that Francis was about to carry out this command, and added hastily: "No, do not! Tell him that I am very much occupied, and cannot see him until noon, or perhaps even later!"

Francis bowed, and withdrew. Nettlebed said severely: "You shouldn't have sent him off, your Grace. A very good man is Mr. Moffat, and one as has your interests at heart."

"Well, I have more important business to attend to," replied the Duke impenitently.

But he was once more doomed to disappointment. When, after being misdirected twice, he reached Little End, which was a small but respectable house beyond Priston, and was admitted to the presence of its master, he was dismayed to find himself confronting a gentleman greatly stricken in years. A stammering enquiry elicited the information that Mr. Rudgeley was a bachelor, and had no young relatives corresponding even remotely with Belinda's description of her swain. There was nothing to be done but to extricate himself as gracefully as he could from a situation that had become unexpectedly awkward. Mr. Rudgeley seemed inclined to take his visit in bad part, and the Duke, sinking back in his chaise again, was obliged to wipe a heated brow. He drove back to Bath in a mood of considerable despondency, which was not alleviated by the news that his bailiff was patiently awaiting his pleasure.

"Oh, damn the fellow! I don't want to see him!" he said pettishly.

Nettlebed was shocked. "Is that what your Grace wants me to tell him?" he asked, taking his hat and Benjamin from the Duke.

"No, I suppose not," sighed the Duke. "Is he in the parlour? I'll go to him. Tell them to send up some wine, and biscuits, will you?"

He was looking rather cross when he entered the parlour but when his bailiff—yet another of those who had known him in his infancy—rose to meet him with a smile of simple affection, he was ashamed of his ill-humour, and shook hands with Moffat, saying: "Well, and how do you do, Moffat? I am sorry to have kept you waiting this age. Sit down, and tell me how you have been going on! And Mrs. Moffat? It is a long time since I saw you last!"

This friendly greeting naturally led to all manner of questions, and reminiscences which stretched back over an alarming number of years. Not until the bailiff had drunk his wine did the Duke feel it to be possible to lead him tactfully to a discussion of the business which had brought him to the Christopher. Moffat apologized for troubling his Grace, explaining that he had not been up to the house since the previous morning, and so had not known of Lord Lionel's arrival there. "Not but what," he said, confidentially, "I was wishful to see your Grace in person. It won't be so very long now before your Grace will be of full age. And right glad everyone will be! Not meaning anything disrespectful to his lordship!" he added hastily. "I'm sure no one could be held in greater esteem! But to see your Grace properly in the saddle, as one might say, is what we are all looking forward to. There will be some changes I dare swear, your Grace—if I may say so—not being set in the old ways, like his lordship and Mr. Scriven. So I made so bold as to bring a few paper I would like fine to have your Grace look over before they go to Mr. Scriven."

"Do you expect me to override my uncle, Moffat?" asked the Duke, smiling, and drawing up his chair to the table. "I am not in the saddle until the spring, you know! What is it? Roofs again?"

"No, your Grace. Just one or two little matters!" replied Moffat, preparing to expound at length.

The Duke resigned himself, and bent his mind to the problems laid before him. They seemed none of them to be very pressing, and he was obliged to stifle several yawns before Moffat jerked him out of his bordom by saying, with a little hesitation: "The only other thing, your Grace, is young Mudgley's affair, and I own I should be very glad if you would condescend to—"

"What?" exclaimed the Duke, starting up in his chair.

The bailiff was slightly alarmed. "I'm sure I beg your Grace's pardon, if I've done wrong to bring the matter up!" he faltered.

"Did you say *Mudgley?*" demanded the Duke sharply.

"Why, yes, your Grace, but indeed I would never——"

"Don't tell me the man is one of my tenants!"

"Well, your Grace, he is, and then again he isn't!" said Moffat, looking at him in considerable perturbation.

The Duke dropped his head in his hands. "And I have been hunting high and low for the confounded fellow! Of course, if he lives near Cheyney, his letters must all go to Bristol, not here! No wonder I could discover no trace of him! Good God, and I very nearly said I would not see you!"

278

"Hunting high and low for young Mudgley, your Grace?" said Moffat, in a stupefied voice. "But—but does your Grace wish to see him?"

"Yes, I tell you! I have come all the way from Hertfordshire for no other purpose!"

Moffat stared at him in great misgiving. "I beg pardon, but—but is your Grace feeling quite well?" he asked, concerned.

The Duke began to laugh. "No, no, I haven't run mad, I assure you! I can't explain it all now, but I have most urgent need of the man! Where does he live? You said he was one of my tenants."

"Not exactly, I didn't, your Grace. He's a freeholder, but he rents the Five-acre field from your Grace. It was on account of that I was wishful to speak to your Grace."

"Where's the Five-acre field?"

"If you will allow me," said Moffat, spreading open a map upon the table, "I will show your Grace. Now, it's right here that Mudgley's farm lies, hard by Willsbridge."

"But I don't own any land west of the river, do I?" objected the Duke, looking at the map.

"Well, that's just it, your Grace. It isn't part of the estate and never has been. It came into the family when your Grace's grandfather acquired it. They do say that he won it at play, but I don't know how that may be. There was a tidy bit of it when I was a boy, but your Grace's father, he never set much store by it, and it was cut up, Sir John Marple buying the house, and the demesne, and the rest going piecemeal, all but a few fields and such, of which the Five-acre is one." He paused, and glanced deprecatingly at the Duke. "If it had been part of Cheyney, I ask your Grace to believe I wouldn't have thought of such a thing, let alone have mentioned it!"

"But what is it that you want?" asked the Duke.

"It's young Jasper Mudgley as wants it, your Grace!" said Moffat desperately. "Maybe I shouldn't be speaking to you of it, seeing that Mr. Scriven won't hear of letting it go, nor his lordship either, by what Mr. Scriven writes to me, the both of them setting their faces against selling any of your Grace's land, as is right and proper. But young Mudgley's father and me was boys together, and I've always kept an eye over Jasper, as you might say, since his father was taken. He's a good lad, your Grace, and the way he's worked his farm up is wonderful, and things not always easy for him. But he's by way of being a warm man now, and he'd be right glad to buy the Five-acre off of your Grace, if you'd be willing to sell it. I told him my lord wouldn't hear of it, but it seemed to me as I might venture just to mention the matter to you."

"Of course! You did just as you should!" said the Duke enthusiastically. "Only tell me one thing, Moffat! Is he married, or single?"

"Single, your Grace. He lives with his mother, him being her only one."

"The Five-acre shall be his bride's dowry!" said the Duke, rolling up the map, and handing it to the astonished bailiff.

"But, your Grace, he's got no thought of marriage!" protested Moffat.

"Then I must put one into his head," said the Duke.

"Your Grace won't do that, by what Jane Mudgley was telling me," said Moffat. "Seemingly, there was a wench in Bath he fell head over ears in love with back in the spring, but she went off somewhere unbeknownst, and he doesn't seem to be able to put her out of his mind. Not but what she didn't sound to me the kind of wench I'd have chosen for a steady young fellow like Jasper."

"She is the bride *I* have chosen for him!" said the Duke, his eyes dancing. "Does his mother dislike it excessively? I imagine she might! Do you think I can persuade her to accept the girl? Perhaps I had best see her before I take Belinda to her."

"But—but——" stammered Moffat.

"That was why I wanted to find Mudgley!" explained the Duke. "The girl is under my care, and I have promised that I will find him for her. You may take me out to the farm. How did you come into Bath?"

"I rode in, your Grace. But——"

"Very well: only give me time to change my dress, and I will ride back with you! Francis must find me a horse! Sit down, Moffat: I shall not keep you waiting many minutes!"

"Your Grace!" Moffat, looking extremely worried, made a detaining esture.

"Yes, what is it?" the Duke said impatiently.

"Your Grace, I don't know how to say it—and I beg your Grace's pardon for what may offend you! But I know young Mudgley, and—and he wouldn't—not for a moment!—he wouldn't be agreeable to—to——"

The Duke's puzzled frown vanished. "He wouldn't take my leavings, eh? Excellent fellow! No, no, Moffat, it's nothing of the sort, I promise you! She is staying in Bath under Lady Harriet Presteigne's protection. I do hope Mudgley will believe me! Is he a fine, lusty fellow? Well, I shall depend upon you to guard me from his vengeance, if he doesn't believe me!"

He vanished leaving his bailiff to start after him in great perplexity.

Nettlebed, upon being summoned to lay out his master's riding-breeches and coat, demurred at once. He said that his Grace would be quite knocked-up with all this dashing about the country, and a ball on the top of it.

"Help me out of this coat!" ordered the Duke.

"Now, your Grace, do but listen to reason!" begged Nettlebed.

"Nettlebed, do you wish me to run away from you again?" demanded the Duke.

"No, no, you wouldn't do that, your Grace!" said Nettlebed, quailing.

"That, or engage a new valet," said the Duke inexorably.

This terrible threat utterly subjugated Nettlebed, and in almost trembling haste he helped to array his master in his riding-dress.

"I am *not* in the least fatigued," said the Duke, straightening his cravat.

"No, your Grace!"

"I shall *not* be knocked up," said the Duke, walking over to the door.

"No, your Grace!"

"I shall dance into the small hours."

"Yes, your Grace!"

"And," pursued the Duke, opening the door, and casting a mischievous look at his cringing servitor, "I shall *not* engage a new valet!"

"Now, your Grace!" said Nettlebed, in quite a different voice.

But the Duke had gone.

He rode out towards Willsbridge beside his bailiff in a mood of gay good-humour, which much rejoiced that worthy man's heart. By his request, they gave Cheyney a wide berth, the Duke having no desire to encounter his uncle while going upon an errand of which Lord Lionel would violently disapprove, and Moffat understanding this without the Duke's having the least need to explain it to him. They reached Furze Farm without meeting anyone with whom the Duke was acquainted, and, tethering the horses to the gate-posts, walked across the yard to the open kitchen-door. A girl in a cotton apron and a mob-cap, who had stepped out to empty a pail of water, dropped a curtsy to Moffat, and informed him that Missus was in the kitchen, rolling out the pastry. Her voice brought a spare, middle-aged woman to the door. She had a worn, kindly face, and after casting the Duke a doubtful look, smiled at Moffat, and said: "Come you in, Mr. Moffat! Now, if I'd but known you would be passing this way to-day——!"

"Mrs. Mudgley, ma'am, I've brought his Grace to see your Jasper," said Moffat, indicating his companion.

She gave a gasp, and made haste to curtsy and to wipe the flour from her hands at the same time. "Your Grace! Oh, Mr. Moffat! And me all unprepared, and Jasper out in the fields, and you bringing his Grace to the kitchen, instead of round the front, as it fitting! I do not know what to say, your Grace, but I'm sure I beg your pardon! If you would please to step into the parlour, I will send directly to fetch my son!"

"Will you let me rather come into your kitchen, and talk to you, Mrs. Mudgley?" he said, with his shy smile.

She looked rather wildly at Moffat, faltering that it was not fit. The bailiff said in a heartening tone: "Take his Grace in, ma'am: I'll warrant he will like it very well!"

She dropped another curtsy, and the Duke stepped over the threshold, and laid his hat and gloves down on a chair, saying, as he looked round the room: "Yes, indeed I do. How comfortable it is! Am I disturbing you?"

"Oh, no, indeed, your Grace!" she assured him. She saw how young he was, and suddenly felt less nervous. She set a chair for him, whisked her pastry up into a damp cloth, and said diffidently: "If your Grace would partake of a little refreshment after the ride? Just a cup of my cowslip wine, belike?"

"Thank you: you are very good!" he said, hoping that it would not disagree with him as much as he feared it would. "Moffat, while I am talking to Mrs. Mudgley, will you be so good as to find her son for me?"

Mrs. Mudgley looked a little scared at being left without support, but by the time she had poured out a glass of her wine for the guest, and he had tasted it, and said how good it was, and had asked her how it was made, she began to forget his exalted status, and even allowed herself to be persuaded to sit down in a chair opposite him.

He said: "Moffat has been telling me about the Five-acre field. I am sorry my agent would not let your son buy it, but, you see, he has had to be so very careful while I was a minor."

She murmured something about her son's being able to give a fair price for it.

"Well, I think I shall not sell it to him," said the Duke. "I should like to give it to his bride for her dowry."

She looked at him in a puzzled way. "Your Grace is very good, but——"

"Mrs. Mudgley, I didn't come for that reason, but to ask you if you recall a girl named Belinda?"

She jumped. "Belinda!" she exclaimed. "Yes, and indeed I do, your Grace! Jasper was that taken with her he'll not look at another wench! Poor thing, it wasn't what I wished for him, sir, but seeing him so set on her, and him no more changeable than his father was before him, I would have let him wed her, and said naught, for she was so pretty you couldn't but compassion her, and good-natured besides, even if she hadn't much sense in her head, which dear knows she hadn't! But she ran off from the woman she was apprenticed to, and try as he would my boy could never discover what had become of her. Why, sir, it couldn't be that you know where she is?"

"Yes, I do know," he replied. "She fell into the hands of a plausible rogue, who wished to use her for his own ends, and I think she has been very unhappy since she ran away from Bath. But although she has been drifting about the country, and is a very silly girl, I am quite sure she is still quite an innocent girl." He paused. "I think I ought to tell you all I know of her," he said, meeting her startled blue eyes candidly. "You won't judge her harshly, I believe, and—and it would not be right not to tell you!"

She looked anxiously at him, but said nothing. But as he gently unfolded Belinda's story to her the anxiety faded. She shook her head over it often, and clicked her tongue in censure, but at the end sighed, and said: "It all comes of her being a foundling, your Grace, and no one to bring her up right. Not that they don't do their best at the Foundling Hospital, I'm sure, but it's not the same, and never could be. It's like as if the poor children don't have the feelings they would with homes of their own, and folks to care for them. It always seemed to me that Belinda was just like that leaf that's just blown in through the door, sir, cast about she didn't know where, and nothing to hold to, if your Grace takes my meaning." He nodded. "I never thought she was a bad girl, for all the silly notions she had in her head."

"No, that I know she is not," he replied. "But she has the most dreadful way of going off with anyone who offers to give her silk dresses, or trinkets, I can't deny!"

"Ah, but they did say at the Foundling Hospital, where my father went to ask if they had no news of her, that her father was Quality, which would account for it, sir, the Quality being very easy in their ways," explained Mrs. Mudgley simply. "A love-child, she was. I wouldn't be telling the

283

truth if I was to tell your Grace I'm wishful my son should wed with her, but see him in the dumps like he's been ever since he lost her, I can't. She won't go trapesing off once she's got a home of her own, and babies, and I daresay I shall be able to show her the way she should go on, for she was mightily taken with the farm, and they did teach her to bake and make at the Foundling Hospital, that I will say!"

"Yes" he said, looking round. "She would be happy here. She is not happy in Laura Place, I think. It's strange to her, and she is a little afraid of Lady Ampleforth. And she thinks a great deal of your son, and of you." He smiled. "You were very kind to her: she told me, finding it strange that any woman should show her kindness."

Her heart was touched; she said: "Poor little dear! Do you bring her to me, sir, and don't let her fear to be scolded, for it's no manner of use scolding a pretty silly creature like her!"

A shadow darkened the doorway; the Duke looked up, and saw a sturdy young man confronting him, in breeches, and leggings, and with his shirt-sleeves rolled half-way up his tanned arms. He had a stolid, open countenance, in which a pair of widely set grey eyes squarely met the Duke's. His mother jumped up, and went to him, chiding him for not having put on his coat and washed his hands before coming into the house, but he put her gently aside, saying, with his eyes still fixed on the Duke: "Mr. Moffat told me his Grace of Sale had news of Belinda, Mother."

"Yes, yes, but make your bow, Jasper, do!" she adjured him. "His Grace has been so kind, you would not believe!"

"Has he?" said Mr. Mudgley heavily.

"Jasper, will you mind your manners? I don't know what his Grace must be thinking of you, standing there like a gowk! And him giving the Five-acre to Belinda, as he will!"

The lines about Mr. Mudgley's jaw seemed to harden. "I don't care for that," he said. "Nor I don't rightly know why he should do any such thing, Mother."

The Duke rose. "Not for any such reason as you have in your head," he said. "Walk out with me: we shall do better to talk this over alone."

"I'm agreeable," said Mr. Mudgley, in a level tone, and stood aside for him to pass out of the kitchen.

"Oh, deary me!" said Mrs. Mudgley, to Moffat, who had slipped quietly into the house behind his young friend. "I do hope my Jasper won't offend his Grace! You know what he is, Mr. Moffat! As stiff-necked as his father, and move him you can't, once he's taken a notion into his head! Whatever will become of us if he should say something which his Grace might take amiss?"

"His Grace won't take offence," Moffat said. "He's not like his uncle, high in the instep, as the saying is. I've known him since he was a sickly boy, hardly out of short-coats, ay, helped him out of trees when he got stuck, and taught him to handle a gun, and there never was a lad with a sweeter nature, that I'll swear to! What's more, ma'am, he's got a way with him, for all he's not to much to look at, and if he don't have your Jasper out of his high ropes I shall be fair astonished!"

He was not destined to suffer astonishment. After walking up and down the lane for long enough to make Mrs. Mudgley feel very uneasy, the two men came in, apparently on the best of terms. Mrs. Mudgley saw that the set look he had worn for so long had vanished from her son's face, and shed tears, which she dried hastily, however, explaining that she didn't know whether she stood on her head or her heels. None of the three men found this very comprehensible, but they were relieved to see that she had stopped crying, and encouraged her in their several ways, her son patting her on the shoulder, Moffat saying There, there! in a helpless way, and the Duke announcing that it had been decided that he and Lady Harriet would bring Belinda out to Furze Farm as soon as was possible.

Mrs. Mudgley then poured out cowslip wine all round, and after he had heroically swallowed his portion, the Duke took his leave of his hosts and rode back to Bath, feeling that a weight had dropped from his shoulders.

He had been invited to dine in Laura Place, before attending the Dowager and Lady Harriet to the Assembly Rooms, and when he reached the Christopher he found that his cousin had driven out to Cheyney some time earlier. He walked upstairs, to be met by Nettlebed, who took his hat and gloves from him, expressing the hope that he would rest before he changed his dress.

"Yes, perhaps I will," he said yawning. "What's this?" He picked up a letter from the table as he spoke, and saw that it was addressed to him in Lord Gaywood's dashing handwriting.

"My Lord Gaywood's man left it here for your Grace, not half an hour ago," responded Nettlebed disparagingly. "He said there was no answer expected. And a fly-by-night fellow he is! I wonder his lordship would have such about him."

The Duke broke the wafer, and spread open the letter. It was quite brief.

"Dear Sale," it ran. *"Don't put yourself to any more trouble over your fair Cyprian, for I'm taking her off your hands. It would be a curst sin to tie such an out-and-outer up to some Somerset bumpkin. You may fob Harriet off with what tale you please, and believe me, Your devilish obliged servant, Gaywood."*

CHAPTER XXV

FOR a full minute after he had read this missive the Duke knew an impulse to wash his hands of the whole affair. Then a cold, unaccustomed rage took possession of him, and, as he raised his eyes from the letter in his hand, his valet was startled to see in them an expression so reminiscent of the late Duke in one of his rare fits of anger that he could almost have supposed that the Duke's father and not himself stood before him.

The Duke crushed the letter into a ball, his mouth tightening. He glanced at Nettlebed, and spoke. "My chaise, and four good horses," he said curtly.

Nettlebed knew that voice, though he had never heard it issuing from this Duke's lips. He was frightened, but he felt himself bound by his love and duty to protest. "Now, your Grace!" he began, in a scolding tone.

A sudden flash of anger in the Duke's frowning eyes silenced him. "You heard what I said!"

"Yes, your Grace," said Nettlebed miserably.

"Do as I bid you, then! It is to be ready for me within twenty minutes. I am going round to Laura Place now. Call me a hackney!"

Devoutly trusting that Lady Harriet would be better able than himself to dissuade his master from undertaking whatever grim project he had in mind, Nettlebed said: "Yes, your Grace!" again, and hurried out of the room.

The Duke bade the hackney-coachman wait for him outside Lady Ampleforth's house, and ran up the steps to the door. It was opened to him by the porter, who at once ushered him upstairs to the drawing-room, where he found the Dowager seated beside the fire, with her gloved hands clasped on the head of her ebony cane, a bonnet overpoweringly bedecked with curled ostrich plumes, tied over her improbable ringlets. At the writing-table in the window, Lady Harriet, also in walking-dress, sat agitatedly scribbling on a sheet of hot-pressed note-paper. When the Duke was announced, she turned quickly, half-rising from her chair, and exclaiming in a faint voice: "Oh, Gilly!"

"For heaven's ·sake, girl!" snapped the Dowager. "Let us have no die-away airs, I beg of you! One would suppose the end of the world to be upon us! Well, Sale, you are come in a good hour! That fancy-piece of yours had found another fool to run mad over her blue eyes."

"Gilly, I have been quite unworthy of your trust in me!" Harriet said, in a conscience-stricken tone. "I am so mortified, and I fear you will think I have been dreadfully to blame!"

He trod over to her swiftly, and raised her hands to his lips, and kissed them both. "No, no, I could never think that!" he said. "I should not have saddled you with such a tiresome burden!"

"Very true!" said the Dowager.

"Do you *know*, then, Gilly?" Harriet asked, her eyes searching his face.

"Yes, I know. Belinda has run away again."

"I was just writing a note to tell you of it. I have been driving out with Grandmama and when we returned, I discovered—Gilly, is it—is it Charlie?"

"Yes."

She saw the same tightening of the mouth which had alarmed Nettlebed, and timidly laid a hand on his sleeve. "You are very angry! Pray do not be! I think—I think Charlie did not exactly understand the nature of the affair!"

The irrepressible old lady by the fire gave a croak of sardonic mirth. "Small blame to him! I have no patience with these missish tricks, girl! One would say a young man had never before mounted a mistress!"

"Oh, Grandmama, hush! Of course I know—— But I promised Gilly I would let no harm befall Belinda!"

"Harm, indeed! The minx does very well for herself, I vow! I see no occasion for these tragedy airs!"

Harriet clasped her hands together. "I had not thought that he had been alone with her, Gilly, but I have been questioning the servants, and it seems that when he would not go to Lady Ombersley's party with us, saying that he was engaged with some friends of his own, he spent the evening here, with Belinda. But I do not believe the mischief was concerted between them then! Belinda was very unhappy, you know, when you told us how you had been unable to find Mr. Mudgley——"

"I have found him," he interrupted.

"Oh, Gilly, no! When she may have gone off with Charlie! It makes it worse! What shall we do?"

"I am going after them. I came only to discover if you knew more than I do, and to inform you that I have received a communication from your brother, apprising me of the event. Obliging of him!"

She winced at this, but the Dowager thumped her cane on the floor, and ejaculated: "Are you crazy, Sale? Let me tell you that you are well-rid of the girl! My grandson will know better how to deal with her! I wonder you will concern yourself in this ridiculous fashion over such Haymarket-ware! *I* knew her for what she was the instant I clapped eyes on her!"

"Grandmama, it is only since she had the misfortune to break your Sèvres bowl that you have thought so!" said Harriet pleadingly.

"You are wrong, ma'am," said the Duke. "She is not yet Haymarket-ware, and I do not mean her to become so."

This put the old lady out of all patience, and she delivered herself of a scathing denunciation of the namby-pamby behaviour of the present generation. Since her tongue was always salted, and never more so than when she lost her temper, she brought hot blushes to her granddaughter's cheeks. The Duke, however, heard her out with chill civility, bowing slightly when she stopped for want of breath, and turning to address his betrothed. "You do not know when Belinda, left this house, my love?"

"No, for no one saw her, but I think it cannot have been very long since. It was the unluckiest thing that I was obliged to go with Grandmama to Monkton Combe, for we have been away from the house since noon. Whimple has told us that Gaywood was here shortly after we drove away, and I fear that it must have been then that he—that the mischief was planned. You know how it is when Belinda is not quite happy, Gilly! She cries, and she looks so very lovely—not in the least like other people!—and poor Charlie must have been led astray, and have offered to take care of her, without, perhaps thinking——"

"Nonsense, Harriet!" the Duke said. "It was not Gaywood that was led astray!"

She hung her head. "It is very bad of him, I know," she faltered. "Indeed, I am very sorry!"

He dropped a hand on her shoulder. "*You* have nothing to be sorry for!"

"She might be sorry to be such a fool, and you too, Sale!" interpolated the Dowager.

He paid no heed to this, but said: "I am going after them, of course. I imagine Gaywood will have taken her to London, for he will scarcely have the effrontery to be seen with her in Bath, under our noses! I beg your pardon,

288

Harriet, and yours, ma'am: I shall be unable to escort you to the Assembly Rooms to-night. I hope you will forgive me."

"Oh, Gilly, as though I cared for that! Indeed, I have no wish to go! If—if you should not dislike it very much, I will go with you to fetch Belinda back!"

"Hoity-toity, what next?" demanded the Dowager. "*That* would be the outside of enough, girl! Junketing about the country like any hoyden! You will do no such thing!"

Harriet flushed, but looked beseechingly up at the Duke. "Would it be improper, Gilly? You must be the judge, but I wish very much to go with you."

He pressed her hand. "No, not improper, but I could not permit it, love. There is not the least need, moreover."

"No. Oh, no! Only that—when he is vexed, poor Charlie has such a dreadful temper, and—and you are angry too, Gilly!"

"Oh, you need have no fear on that score!" he said reassuringly. "We shall not brawl in public, I hope!"

"I do not wish you to quarrel!" she said piteously.

"My dear, you are being absurd!" he said. "I might give Charlie a trimming, but I do not intend to come to pistols with him!"

"*You* would not, I know, but he——!"

"No, no!" he said. "He is not such a fool!"

She was obliged to be satisfied, and he took his leave of her, promising to visit her immediately upon his return to Bath.

When he reached the Christopher again, he found his chaise waiting for him. He determined to drive first to Lord Gaywood's lodging in Green Street, to learn what he might there, but as he had no expectation of finding Belinda there, and believed it to be possible that he might have a long drive before him, he went first into the hotel to provide himself with an overcoat. He ran up the stairs, and was brought up short on the landing by the sight of Tom, coming out of his parlour. "Good God! What are you doing in Bath, Tom?" he demanded, misgiving in his heart.

"Oh, sir, I thought you was never coming!" Tom cried, grasping his hand with painful enthusiasm. "I have been waiting for you this age, and that fusty old Nettlebed would not tell me where you was gone to! It is such a lark, and I *know* you will be pleased with me this time!"

"But what are you doing here? No, never mind! I can't stay now, Tom. You shall tell me about it another day."

"No, no, you don't understand, sir! Oh, do come into the parlour! I *must* tell you!"

He exerted all his lusty strength to tug the Duke to the

parlour. He was plainly in a state of considerable excitement, and big with portentous tidings.

"Well, be quick, then, for I have an important engagement out of town!" said the Duke. "Does your papa know you are here?"

"No, but that don't signify! It is too bad! He says we must go home to-morrow, and I might bid you farewell on our way through Bath! The shabbiest thing, for I know how it would be, with the chaise waiting, and Pa in one of his fusses to be off! And I have so much to tell you, sir!"

"Yes, Tom, but indeed I cannot stay to hear it now!"

"Oh, no! But you asked me why I was in Bath, you know. I have rid in, and your groom *said* I might take the roan cob, and you would not mind!"

"No, but——"

"And I thought I had better come to Bath to-day, perhaps, because, as it chances, I shot a sheep," explained Tom airily. "I did not do it on purpose, sir, and I daresay it is not much hurt, and I expect it is your sheep and I know *you* will not be angry for a thing like that, but Lord Lionel might not be quite pleased, perhaps, if he hears of it. So I thought I would come to see you, sir."

"Yes, Tom, but——"

"I thought you would tell Lord Lionel that you do not care for the sheep," suggested Tom tentatively.

"Do you wish me to give you a note informing Lord Lionel that you have my permission to shoot sheep?" asked the Duke, unable to help laughing. "Much good would it do you! Now, Tom, be a good boy, and go back to Cheyney!"

"But I haven't told you what has happened!" Tom protested. "I know you will like to hear it, sir, and I only did it at least; for the most part—because I thought you would be pleased! Because you were vexed when Belinda went away with that old gentleman in Hitchin, and you were for ever saying she must not talk to strange men!"

"Belinda?" the Duke said sharply. "What's this, Tom? Have you seen Belinda to-day? Tell me at once, if you please!"

"I *am* telling you, sir!" Tom argued, aggrieved. "You were not here, when I rode in, and the waiter said you was gone off somewhere with your bailiff. He is a famous fellow, sir! He took me——"

"Never mind that! What is this about Belinda?"

"Oh, *that!* Well, when I heard you was gone out, I thought I would go to those gardens again, and so I rode off down Bridge Street. And just as I came to Laura Place, I saw Belinda coming down the steps of one of the houses.

She did not see me, for I was not near, only I could not mistake, you know, because of her yellow hair, and besides that she had both those stupid bandboxes. So I didn't go up to her, because she is such a bore, sir! And I was just going on my way when a fine beau jumped out of a hack that was standing close by, and he went smash up to' Belinda, and took the boxes, and said something to her, and handed her into the hack, and got in after. And even then, sir, I didn't think of what a lark I could kick up! Only, of course, I knew you would not like her to go off in a hack with the beau, so I thought I would follow it, and very likely rescue her, if she would like it, or at any rate see how it would be to be a Runner, or a spy, or some such thing. And only fancy, sir! the hack drove past the Pelican! And it went on for ever, almost out of the town! It stopped at last at a big inn, and Belinda got down, and the beau, too, and I could see they were arguing about something, though of course I was not near enough to hear what they said, but you know how Belinda looks when she does not like a thing! I really did think then that she would like to be rescued, and I dismounted, and tethered the cob, and went past the inn, pretending just to be sauntering along, you know. And I saw them through one of the front windows, and they *were* arguing—at least, the beau was, and Belinda was just sitting. So I thought I would make a plan to steal her away, and I was just on the point of hitting on something famous, I daresay, when the beau came out of the inn, and jumped into the hack, and shouted to the jarvey to drive to Milsom Street. I could see he was in a furious rage, and I quite thought Belinda had sent him to the right-about, only that she never does, and he was a regular dash, I can tell you: complete to a shade! And of course she had not, but only to buy her a purple gown! Such stuff! I think girls are the stupidest things! For you must know, sir, that when the beau drove off I went in to rescue Belinda." He paused and gave a disgusted sniff. "It would have been a splendid adventure, but she doesn't care for anything jolly, and she wouldn't go with me, not even when I told her you would not like her to talk to the strange beau. She said she was going to live in London, and have a grand lodging, and a carriage, and all sorts of trash, and she would not go back to the cross old lady, and you could not find Mr. Mudgley, so what else was she to do, and much more beside, but all fustian! I told her she would not go to London in a hack, for it was a great way off, and she said she was going in a chaise-and-four, like a lady, and *that* was what she was arguing about with the

291

beau, for he wanted to drive her in his curricle, but she would not have it! Only fancy, sir! You would not have supposed that even Belinda could be so stupid! I wish *I* could drive to London in a curricle! I would gallop at *such* a rate! I would take the shine out of them all! I would——"

"Yes, yes, but what happened then?" interrupted the Duke.

"Oh there was no doing anything with her, sir! She said the beau was a lord, but I daresay that was a hum, and he had gone off to hire a chaise, and to buy this stupid dress for her. So I went away, and the more I thought of it the more I *knew* you would not like it. And then I thought of the most famous plot!" Tom's eyes sparkled with reminiscent delight as he spoke; he looked appealingly at the Duke, and said: "You wouldn't have liked it, would you, sir?"

"No, not at all. What was your plot?"

"Well, *first*," said Tom, relishing every moment of his recital, "I went back into the inn, and asked for the landlord, only when he came it wasn't—I mean, it was a landlady, but it didn't signify. I told her the smokiest story, sir! She was completely taken-in! I said I knew Belinda very well, and how I had seen her get into that hack with the strange beau, and that was quite true, at any rate. And then I said the beau was a lover Belinda's pa didn't like, and that they were off to Gretna Green, because Belinda was a great heiress, and the beau a wicked adventurer. I read a story like that once, only it was a stupid tale, with hardly any fights, and I never thought I should be glad I'd read it. It just *shows* one, doesn't it, sir? The landlady was excessively shocked! I said there would be the deuce of a bobbery when it was discovered, and I thought I should go to warn Belinda's pa. The landlady was frightened for her life, and she said it would be a bad thing for the house, but she could see Belinda was only a child, and it was a shame, and ought to be stopped. So then I said I would fob the beau off, if she would engage to keep Belinda out of the way, and make the ostlers swear they would tell the beau the same story that I did, if he should question them. But he was in such a taking that he never did! Only to ask the head ostler in the fiercest voice you ever heard if a chaise with yellow wheels and four gray horses had stopped at the inn, and of course the ostler said yes, grinning like mad, because it had, you know!"

"Tom, Tom, you are going too fast for me! What has the chaise to do with it?"

"Oh, yes! Well, the landlady cajoled Belinda to go with her into a parlour at the back of the house, because she said she would be more comfortable there, and then I wrote a letter in the sort of way I thought very likely Belinda would. I wrote that *you* had come for her sir, and would give her a better gown than the one in Milsom Street, and so she was going to London with you instead. And I put in that she was very much obliged to him, because I thought she would say that, to be civil. And then I went out into the road to wait, and after an age the beau drove up in a post-chaise-and-four, and jumped down, and I went up to him, and asked him in the sort of voice a stable-boy would if he was Lord Gaywood, which Belinda said he was. And he said yes, so I gave him the note, and said a young lady with yellow curls had given me a shilling to do so. And, oh, sir, I do think it was the most first-rate lark I've ever kicked up, for he flew into the deuce of a passion, and he looked as though he would like to murder someone! And he asked what horses were you driving, and I could see it was you he wanted to murder, so I said gray ones, like I told you, because there *was* a chaise with four splendid grays, and yellow wheels, and they were famous steppers, so that I should think he will not easily catch them, and so you will have time to fetch Belinda, and be off before he can come back. For he set off after the other chaise in a twinkling, sir, and told the post-boys they should have double fees if they caught up with it. Sir, *are* you pleased with me?"

"Tom, I am delighted with you!" the Duke assured him. "My only regret is that I cannot see Gaywood's face when he does overtake that yellow-wheeled chaise! When you come to stay with me in London, you shall go to all the theatres, and the wild beast shows, and to Vauxhall to see the fireworks, and anything else you may happen to have set your heart on! I am eternally obliged to you—and if my uncle should hear about the sheep, you may tell him that I told you to shoot it! Will you do one thing more for me?"

"I should think I would!" asseverated Tom, dazed by the thought of the treats in store for him.

"Then ride back to Cheyney now, and tell them that I am coming out to dine there, and may be a little late, so that they will please to set dinner back. Don't tell anyone of this adventure!" He saw a slightly chagrined look on Tom's face, and smiled. "Well, only tell Captain Ware!" he amended. "You will find him there, you know."

It was plain that the prospect of again meeting this heroic personage was a lure Tom found hard to withstand. But he set his jaw, and said staunchly: "No! I shall come with you, sir, in case the beau should have returned!"

The Duke laughed. "Thank you, Tom, but even if he has returned I don't think I stand in need of protection!"

"Yes, but you don't know, sir," said Tom earnestly. "He is much bigger than you are, and in such a temper beside!"

"My dear Tom, I know him very well indeed, and I assure you I am not afraid of him! Indeed, you must go back to Cheyney, or your papa will be in what you call one of his fusses, and that might end painfully for you, you know! Be off with you, and don't forget to tell them that I am coming to dine there!"

He succeeded in getting rid of his young friend, and having seen him mount, and ride off, turned to his waiting chaise, and directed the astonished postilions to drive him to the George inn, on the London road. They exchanged speaking glances, but it was not for them to question the eccentricities of the Quality, and if the Duke chose to be driven a distance of little more than a mile in a chaise-and-four no doubt he would grease their palms handsomely.

The Duke found Belinda waiting patiently in a small parlour at the George, her bandboxes at her feet. She was surprised to see him, but not in the least chagrined. She said: "Oh, sir, Lord Gaywood is such a very kind gentleman, and he is going to set me up in style in London, and give me that gown I saw in Milsom Street, and drive me in a chaise-and-four!"

"Lord Gaywood is deceiving you, Belinda," he said. "He will do none of these things. You know, it is very bad of you to have run away with him. Didn't I warn you that you must not go with strange gentlemen, however kind they may seem to be?"

"Oh, yes, sir, but indeed I thought of you, and how you told me it was a take-in!" Belinda explained. "And *this* time I did just what you would like, for I said I wouldn't go to London if he did not give me that lovely purple dress *first!* And he has gone to Milsom Street to buy it, so you see that he *is* a kind gentleman, after all!"

"Belinda," he said gravely, taking her hands, and holding them, "do you like Lord Gaywood better than Mr. Mudgley?"

"Oh, *no!*" she cried, the ready tears springing to her eyes. "But you cannot find Mr. Mudgley, and Lady Ampleforth boxed my ears, and I was very unhappy in that house. And Lord Gaywood said he would take care of me, and no one should be angry with me!"

"But I have found Mr. Mudgley" he said gently.

Her tears ceased to flow abruptly; she stared at him with her eyes very wide open.

"I promised that I would bring you to him. He wants you very much, and his mother does too. Which is it to be, Belinda?—a purple gown, or Mr. Mudgley?"

"Will you take me *now!*" Belinda asked urgently, her cheeks softly flushed. "Oh, *please,* will you take me now?"

"Yes, I'll take you now," the Duke replied, absurdly relieved at this instant decision. He added, feeling that her sacrifice deserved reward: "In a chaise-and-four!"

She clapped her hands in delight, saying that Mr. Mudgley would not be able to believe his eyes when he saw her drive up in such an equipage. The Duke, trying not to feel disappointed at this naïve remark, led her out to the chaise, and handed her up into it. He found a nervous, and considerably bewildered landlady hovering beside him, and turned to her. "If the gentleman who escorted this lady to your house should return presently," he said, "will you be so good as to give him a message for me?"

"Yes, sir," she said doubtfully. "That is——"

"Tell him, if you please," continued the Duke, "that the Duke of Sale thanks him for his letter, but does not need any assistance from him in the management of his affairs!"

CHAPTER XXVI

THE Duke drove Belinda to the Christopher, and installed her in his parlour there while he dashed off one of his scrawls to his betrothed. It had occurred to him that he had told Mr. Mudgley that Lady Harriet would bring Belinda to him. To drive her to Furze Farm a day earlier than could have been expected, and without Lady Harriet, might, he felt, reawaken the mistrust he had been at such pains to allay in Mr. Mudgley's breast. So he begged his Harriet to prevail upon the Dowager to allow her to go with him, and to dine afterwards at Cheyney, offering as sops to that erratic old lady's possible scruples the presence of Lord Lionel at Cheyney, a promise to escort Harriet back to Laura Place at a seemly hour and a reminder that there would be moonlight. He sent this missive off by the hand of his footman, and having assured himself that his elusive charge had no immediate thought of wandering away again, went into his bedchamber to change his dress.

Nettlebed, upon learning of the projected dinner-party, did his best to persuade him into knee-breeches, but he was not really surprised when the Duke said that he should wear pantaloons and Hessians, and, for the first time in his long association with the Duke, bowed to this decree without either grumbling, or reminding his master that Lord Lionel always wore knee-breeches in the evening.

Much heartened by this evidence of the beneficial effects to be obtained by treating his servants with brutal severity, the Duke hurried into his clothes, and had packed Belinda and her bandboxes into the chaise again before Francis had had time to return with the answer to his letter. So emboldened by his victory over Nettlebed was he feeling that he drove round to Laura Place with the intention of being extremely high-handed with the Dowager, if she should dare to thwart him. Happily (since the Dowager was more than capable of holding her own against far more formidable males than he would ever be), this trial of strength proved to be unnecessary. When he was admitted into Lady Ampleforth's house, he found his Harriet already descending the stairs, with her hat on, and a cloak hiding her muslin gown.

He started forward to meet her saying: "Do you go with me? Will Lady Ampleforth trust you to me? How pretty you look!"

If she had not been in her best looks before, this impulsive exclamation naturally made her glow into something approaching beauty. She smiled tremulously, blushing, and murmuring: "Oh, Gilly, do I? I do not know how you can say so, when you have been with Belinda!"

He acknowledged the force of this, but said seriously: "I do not know how it is, Harriet, but I would rather look at you than at Belinda. You have more *countenance!*"

She now knew that whatever happiness might be in store for her this must rank as the most memorable day in her life. To conceal her swelling pride, she said in a rallying tone: "You are trying to flatter me, Gilly!"

"No," he said. "I know you too well to suppose that flattery would be acceptable to you."

Without making the slightest attempt to disabuse his mind of its curious misapprehension, Harriet said simply: "I am glad you think I have countenance, dear Gilly. I want only to be worthy of you."

"To be worthy of me!" he said, quite thunderstruck. "But I am the most commonplace creature! Indeed, I do not know how you can look twice in my direction when you have known my handsome cousin!"

"Gideon?" she said in surprised accents. "Of course I have a great regard for him, for I am sure he has always been very kind, and *you* love him, which must recommend him to me, you know. But surely no one in their senses could think of him when you were by, Gilly!"

Preys to their blissful delusions, they walked slowly out of the house to the waiting chaise.

"I was half afraid your grandmama would not let you come with me!" the Duke said foolishly.

"Oh, Gilly, was it very wrong of me? I was obliged to use a little stratagem, for she was so cross, and I could see she meant to say it would be improper for me to go! I—I said I knew Mama would not permit it! Not quite like that, you know, but letting it be seen that that was what I thought. It is very dreadful! She doesn't like Mama, and I knew very well that I had only to put *that* into her head, and she would say I might go with you!"

She sounded conscience-stricken, but the Duke laughed delightedly, so that any filial qualms that were troubling her gentle soul were instantly laid to rest. He handed her into the chaise where Belinda greeted her without the smallest sign of guilt.

"Oh, my lady!" said Belinda. "Mr. Rufford—I mean, the Duke!—has found Mr. Mudgley!"

"Dear Belinda, you must be very happy!" Harriet said, laying a gloved hand on her knee.

"Oh, yes, ma'am!" agreed Belinda blithely. She paused, and added on a more wistful note: "But I wish I might have had that beautiful dress!"

"I am sure you would not wish for it rather than to be established so comfortably," Harriet suggested gently.

"No, indeed! Only that I might perhaps have stayed until Lord Gaywood came back, you know. For he went to buy it for me, and it *does* seem very hard that I must not have it after all!"

Harriet, quite dismayed, strove to the best of her ability to give Belinda's thoughts a more proper direction. The Duke, a good deal amused, intervened, saying: "Useless, my love! If you would but do what you may to convince her that this last adventure must be kept a secret between the three of us, it would be very desirable!"

"It seems very dreadful to be teaching the poor child to deceive the young man!" Harriet replied, in an under-voice. "I own, it might be wiser—— But to have a secret from the man to whom one is betrothed is very wong, and surely quite against female nature!"

"Dear Harriet!" he said, finding her hand, and raising it to his lips. "*You* would not do so, I know! But if she blurts out the whole to these people——? For they are simple, honest folk, and could not understand, perhaps."

"I will do what you think right," she said submissively, and thereafter tried her utmost to impress upon Belinda the wisdom of banishing Lord Gaywood alike from her thoughts and her conversation. Belinda was so much occupied in ecstatically recognizing and pointing out to her companions remembered landmarks that it seemed doubtful whether she attended with more than half an ear to the kindly advice bestowed upon her, but she was a very persuadable girl, and by dint of Harriet's dwelling strongly on her unfortunate contretemps with the Dowager she was soon brought to the conviction that her sudden descent upon Furze Farm was due not to any traffic with Lord Gaywood, but to her having broken a cherished Sèvres bowl.

But when the chaise drew up by the farm, Harriet could almost have believed that these precautions had been needless. For Mr. Mudgley was just shutting the big white yard-gate, and he turned, and stood still to watch the chaise, with the setting sun behind him, striking on his uncovered head, and catching the auburn lights in his thick thatch of curly hair. He was still wearing his working-clothes, with his sleeves rolled up, and his shirt open to reveal the tanned, sturdy column of his throat, and he presented such a fine figure of a man that not even Harriet, with twenty years of strict training behind her, could wonder that Belinda no sooner saw him than she gave a little scream of joy, and, without waiting for the steps of the chaise to be let down tumbled headlong into his arms. It did not seem probable, after that, that any explanations would be asked for or proffered.

The Duke and his betrothed did not linger for many minutes at the farm. Mrs. Mudgley was sufficiently mistress of herself to do the honours of the house, but her son could scarcely be brought to take his eyes from his long-lost love, and Belinda, her eyes like stars and happy laughter bubbling on her lips, darted about, recognizing and exclaiming at first this object, and then that, and paid very little more heed to her late protectors than if they had been a part of the furnishings of the big kitchen.

"And I was conceited enough to fear that she liked me a little too well!" confided the Duke, once more bowling along in the chaise. "I am quite set-down!"

"Do you know, Gilly," said Harriet thoughtfully, "I am much inclined to think that Belinda is perhaps one of those people who are very pretty, and amiable, but do not care profoundly for anyone. It is very sad! Will Mudgley discover it, and be unhappy, do you think?"

"Why, no! She is good-natured, and affectionate, and

although he may be an excellent fellow I do not imagine his sensibilities to be over-nice. They will deal very well together, I daresay. *She* will always be silly, but he appears to have considerable constancy, and we must hope that *he* will always be fond!"

Harriet, accepting what he said, was content to forget Belinda. She sat cosily beside the Duke, her hand in his, while the chaise covered the little distance between Furze Farm and Cheyney. He was tired, and she was happy; they exchanged few remarks, and those, for his part, in lazy murmurs. Once the Duke said: "Let us be married very soon, Harriet."

"If you wish it, Gilly!" she said shyly.

He turned his head against the squabs that lined the chaise, and looked at her mischievously. "Of course I do. I see that you mean to be a *very* good wife, you are so conformable! Do you wish it?"

She nodded, blushing, and he laughed, beginning to tease her about the hats she must buy in Paris when it was discovered that those she had already ordered from Mrs. Pilling made her look like a dowd. She was still protesting when the chaise drew up before the doors of his house.

"I have no extraordinary liking for this house of mine," the Duke said gaily, handing her down from the chaise, "but still I shall say Welcome to your home, dear Harriet! How strange it seems to be rid of all my embarrassments! I shall not know how to go on, I daresay!"

He led her up the few shallow steps to the doors. These were flung open to them by an embarrassment he had forgotten. The Duke paused, a rueful look in his eye, and exclaimed: "The devil! I must do something about you, I suppose!"

Mr. Liversedge had, naturally, no livery with which his office might be dignified, but the lack of it was scarcely noticeable. His carriage was majestic, and his manner to perfection that of a trusted steward of long standing. He bowed very low, and ushered the young couple into the house, saying: "I trust your Grace will permit me to say how very happy we are to receive you, *and* her ladyship! I venture to think that you will find everything in readiness, though, to be sure, as your Grace well knows, the staff at present residing here is of a scanty, not to say inadequate nature. I should add that Master Mamble—a good lad, but addlepated!—forgot to inform us that her ladyship would be accompanying your Grace. But I will instantly apprise the housekeeper of this circumstance. If your Grace should care to take her ladyship into the library while I perform this office, you will, I fancy, find the Captain there, and such refreshments as I ventured to think might be acceptable to you after the drive. Lord Lionel, I regret to say, stepped out a little while since with Mr. Mamble, not being in the expectation of receiving her ladyship. He will be excessively sorry, I assure your ladyship."

He led the way, as he spoke, across the wide hall to the library door, and set this open, smiling benignly upon the Duke and informing him in a confidential undervoice that he need entertain no fear that the diner being prepared would disgrace him in the eyes of his future Duchess. "For," he said, "I deemed it proper at the outset to give the matter my personal supervision."

The Duke found himself saying thank-you in what he knew to be a weak way.

His cousin was lounging in a chair beside the fire. He looked up lazily, and, when he saw Harriet, got to his feet, his brows lifting. "Your very obedient servant, ma'am!" he said, laughing, and shaking hands with her. "How very like Adolphus not to tell us that he meant to bring you with him! You may blame him for it that you find me very unsuitably dressed to receive you. How do you go on, Harry? You look very becomingly!" He drew forward a chair for her. "I have been laughing this hour past, Adolphus, at your protégé's crowning devilry! Oh, yes, I was dragged out into the shrubbery to be regaled with it! I will own that he is a youth of parts. What have you done with the fair Belinda?"

"We dropped her—quite literally, you know!—into the arms of her precious Mr. Mudgley, and there left her. Gideon, when I said that that fellow might make himself useful, I never meant that he should take upon himself the entire conduct of my house! What is to be done with him? Borrowdale himself never bade me welcome in a more fatherly spirit!"

"You had better turn him off then. *I* have no objection, since I am not residing here, but I think it only right to warn you that he has won my father's approval—as much by his firm handling of Mamble as by his undoubted excellence as a steward and butler."

The Duke could not help laughing. "He is incorrigible! Only conceive of my uncle's feelings if he knew the truth! I bear him no malice—indeed, I am grateful to him for so much enlarging my experience—but I will *not* permit him to rule my household!" He saw that Harriet was looking from him to Gideon in a little perplexity, and added: "My love, it is the most ridiculous situation! That is the fellow

300

who cast me into a cellar, and offered to sell me to my wicked cousin!"

She was very much shocked, and exclaimed in a faint voice. It was incomprehensible to her that anyone should be amused by such a circumstance, but both Gilly and Gideon plainly thought it excessively funny, so she smiled dutifully, realizing the truth of her mama's dictum, that there was never any knowing what stupidities men would find diverting. But she could not forbear to implore the Duke not to keep such a dreadful person near him. "Indeed, he ought to be put in prison!" she said earnestly.

"Undoubtedly he ought, my dear, but you must hold me excused from denouncing him, if you please! He is by far too amusing! Besides, he did me no harm, but, on the contary, a great deal of good."

It was not to be supposed that Harriet could regard with anything but horror one who had cast her Gilly into a cellar, but she perceived that the Duke's mind was made up, and said no more. Liversedge himself came back into the room a minute or two later, with an offer to escort her to the housekeeper, and so bland and respectful was his manner that she could almost have supposed the whole affair to have been a mistake. She rose from her chair, and said meekly that she would like to take off her hat.

"I warn you, Harriet, you will not escape from Mrs. Kempsey for an hour at least!" Gideon told her, mocking his cousin. "She will tell you how weak a chest Adolphus always had, and what remedies were tried, and how she nursed him once when he had the measles. She nursed me too, but she won't waste a moment on my sufferings, though I swear I was much more full of measles than Adolphus!"

The Duke smiled. "But you brought them home from Eton and I took them from you!" he reminded his cousin. "How could you expect to be forgiven such shocking conduct? Don't let her bore on for ever, Harry!"

"Indeed, I shall not think it a bore!" she said. "I hope she will tell me what she likes, for I mean to get upon terms with all your people, Gilly."

He walked beside her to the door, handing her cloak to Liversedge, and saying, as he did so: "When you have taken her ladyship upstairs, come back to me: I must settle with you."

"I will certainly do so, your Grace," Liversedge responded with a bow. "But possibly you will excuse me for a few minutes while I cast my eye over the kitchen. I fancy you will be pleased with my way of serving woodcocks à la Tartar, but the menial at present presiding in the kitchen is not to be trusted with rare dishes. There is, moreover, the question of a sweet, which the presence of a lady at the board makes indispensable. I doubt whether the individual aforementioned has a mind fit to rise above damson tart and jelly, but I hope to contrive a Chantilly Basket which will not disgust her ladyship."

He bowed again at the conclusion of this speech and sailed away without giving the Duke time to answer him.

"If I must consort with rogues," remarked Gideon, pouring out some sherry, "I own I like them to be in the grand manner. It's my belief you'll never be rid of this one, Adolphus."

He was mistaken. When Liversedge presently returned to the library, it soon became evident that he had no desire to remain at Cheyney. He found the life there too circumscribed.

"Had it been your Grace's principal residence, I might have been tempted to consider the propriety of establishing myself in some useful capacity," he explained, with one of his airy gestures. "Although, I must add, servitude, however genteel in its nature, has little charm for me. It does not, if I may say so, offer sufficient scope for a man of my vision. Not that I would have your Grace think that it was with reluctance that I assumed the control of this establishment. On the contrary! I have the greatest regard for your Grace—indeed, I may say that I was much taken with you at the first moment of setting eyes on you!—and I have been happy to feel that I was being of service to you."

"Before you succumb to this eloquence, Adolphus," drawled Gideon, "I would remind you that this admirer of yours would have murdered you for a paltry sum."

"There, sir," instantly replied Liversedge, "I must join issue with you! For fifty thousand pounds I might have been able to overcome my natural repugnance to putting a period to his Grace's life, but for a lesser sum I could not have brought myself to contemplate it. Those nobler instincts which even the basest of us have must have revolted."

The Duke regarded him curiously, his chin in his hand. "Would you really have murdered me?" he asked.

"If," said Mr. Liversedge, "I were to seek refuge in a lie, you, your Grace, would not believe me, and I should have debased myself to no purpose. I shall not seek to deceive you: for fifty thousand pounds I must have steeled myself, if not to perform the deed, at least to order its execution. I do not deny that it would have been a struggle, for I am not a man of violence, but I am inclined to think that the temptation would have been overmastering. A man of your

302

wealth, sir, has no business to offer himself to be the prey of those less fortunately circumstanced, and that, you will allow, is precisely what you did. It was neither politic nor right, but I shall say no more on that head. Your Grace is young, and, when you came, incognito, into my orbit, you were—if I may say so without offence—shockingly green! I flatter myself that through my exertions you have gained in experience, and will not err again after that fashion."

"You had better reward the fellow!" interpolated Gideon.

Mr. Liversedge was quite unabashed. "Captain Ware, though scarcely in sympathy with me, touches the very nub of the matter," he said. "Consider, your Grace! If we are to balance our accounts, which of us is the gainer?"

"I perceive that you are of the opinion that I stand in your debt," replied the Duke, faintly smiling.

"Certainly," said Liversedge, inclining his head. "Can it be in doubt? You were, I fancy, in search of adventure: I gave it to you. You were green: I compelled you to put off the boy and to assume the man. Let us glance for a moment at the other side of the ledger! You snatched from me the letters which I had acquired from your young cousin; you stole from me the means whereby I might have hoped to have acquired other such letters—I refer to my adopted niece; you burned down the wretched hovel which was my sole shelter; you drove into miserable seclusion the individual who owned it, and is nearly related to me; and by these several acts—unthinkingly, I daresay, but none the less painful in their consequences—reduced me to a state of penury which makes it impossible for me to depart from this house."

"If I made it possible for you to leave this house, what would you do?" asked the Duke.

"God grant me patience!" groaned Gideon.

The Duke ignored him. "Well, Liversedge?"

"It would depend," replied Liversedge, "on the extent of your Grace's generosity. My ambition has ever been to preside over a genteel establishment where those with a taste for gaming may be sure of select company, elegant surroundings, and fair play—for my experience has taught me that nothing could be more fatal to the ultimate success of such a venture than to make use of such shifts as the concave-suit, fuzzing, cogging, or in a word any of the Greeking transactions by which novices in this form of livelihood too often think to make their fortunes. That kind of thing may answer for a space, but can never lay the foundations of a permanent establishment of the refinement I have in mind. I attempted something of the sort in this country, but the difficulties are great, and the sordid precautions one is obliged to take against unwarrantable interference set too heavy a drain upon one's resources. If the means lay within my grasp, I should repair to Strasbourg, a town where my talents could flourish, and one, moreover, where I own acquaintances who would count themselves fortunate to acquire my assistance in the management of their houses. A small beginning, you may think, but I do not doubt of rising swiftly from it."

"Strasbourg," said the Duke meditatively. "I remember I disliked the place excessively. I was never more bored! I will revenge myself on Strasbourg, Liversedge, by sending you there to batten upon its citizens. But if any other peer should chance to come into your orbit again, do not kidnap him, for that might come to my ears, you know, and I should feel that it was time to make an end of you."

He rose to his feet as he spoke, and walked towards the desk that stood in the window.

"Sir," said Liversedge, "I am not of those who do not profit by their mistakes. In departing from an occupation at which I excel I erred. Kidnapping is too crude a trade for any man of taste and sensibility."

"You are wise," said the Duke. "If such a greenhorn as I could——"

"Careful, Gilly!" Gideon said under his breath, his eyes on the doorway. "The fat, I fear, is now in the fire!"

The Duke turned his head. Mr. Liversedge had neglected to shut the door securely upon his entrance into the library, and it now stood wide. Lord Lionel stood on the threshold, as though transfixed, an expression of such wrathful amazement in his face that any hope his nephew might have cherished that he had not overheard enough to make plain to him the whole died on the spot.

"So!" uttered his lordship terribly. "I am now in possession of the truth, am I? I might have doubted the fidelity of my ears had I not already had reason to suppose that you have taken leave of your senses, Sale! I came to find you, to request that you will give me an explanation—— But that can wait! Give me a plain answer, yes or no! Is this the rascal who tried to hold you to ransom?"

"You know it is, sir," said the Duke.

His lordship drew an audible breath. "If you have not actually lied to me, sir, you have practised the grossest form of deceit! I would not have believed you capable of it, for with all your faults——"

"Shall we leave my faults for discussion at some more convenient time, sir?" interrupted the Duke.

Lord Lionel was a just man. Even as he opened his mouth to blister his nephew he realized that the rebuke had been deserved, and shut it again. He said with strong restraint: "You are very right! You will not, however, expect me tamely to acquiesce in your extraordinary schemes! Don't try to put me off, Sale! I came in time to hear more than enough! As well that I did so, since you have apparently succeeded in cajoling Gideon into permitting you to indulge your whimsicality in a manner——"

"What, in the name of all that is wonderful, have my affairs to do with Gideon?" demanded the Duke. "Indeed, what have they to do with anyone save myself? I am not a child, sir!"

"You are——" His lordship recollected himself, and stopped. He shut the door ungently, and strode into the middle of the room. "There has been enough of this nonsense!" he said. "If you cannot see what is the proper course to pursue, I can! This villain is to be handed over to those who will know how to deal with him! Either you will give orders for a constable to be fetched from Bath to take him in charge, or I will!"

The Duke moved to the desk, and sat down at it, and drew a sheet of paper towards him. "I have no power, sir, to prevent you from sending for whom you wish," he said, his soft voice even, and rather chilly. "I think it only right to warn you, however, that I am making no charge against Liversedge, and shall deny whatever allegation you might feel yourself compelled to utter.

Gideon's black brows went up, and one corner of his mouth too. He glanced at his thunderstruck parent, and said warningly: " 'Ware riot, sir, 'ware riot, I do beseech you!"

"Be silent!" Lord Lionel rapped out. "Gilly, *why!*"

"I have already told you, sir," the Duke replied, dipping a pen in the inkstand, and beginning to write. "I do not choose to advertise my own folly."

Mr. Liversedge, who had been listening with an expression of great interest to this animated dialogue, coughed in a deprecating way, and said: "If I may say so, sir, such a decision is a wise one, and does you credit. It would indeed be undesirable to apprise the vulgar world of this affair. Setting aside all consideration of your dignity—not that I would for an instant advocate anyone's doing so!—one cannot but reflect that the knowledge of *my* failure might inspire some more fortunate conspirator to lay a plot against your Grace that would achieve success. And that," he added earnestly, "is a thing I should deprecate as much as the most devoted of your relatives."

Lord Lionel brought his staring gaze to bear upon him. "Upon my soul!" he ejaculated. "This passes all bounds!"

It was at this inopportune moment that Mr. Mamble came into the library, rubbing his hands together, and saying with a satisfaction unshared by his hosts: "I thought I should find you here! Well, your Grace! Eh, but you look different than when I saw you in that shabby old coat you was wearing when I had you arrested for a dangerous rogue!" He chuckled at the memory, and advanced into the room. "Well, his lordship and I have become a pair of downright cronies, as I daresay he has been telling you. He has his notions, and I have mine, and maybe we've both learned summat we didn't know before. But I'm fairly put out by that young rascal of mine! It's mercy it was no more than a sheep, and your Grace kind enough to pardon it, else I would have dusted his jacket rarely for him!"

"How do you do?" murmured the Duke, half-rising, and extending one hand. "I beg you will forget the sheep! I stand so much in Tom's debt that one sheep's life seems a small price to be called upon to pay."

"Well, I don't know how that may be," responded Mr. Mamble, shaking the hand, "but it wasn't as bad as that! What's o'clock? I'm beginning to feel sharp-set, I can tell you, and ready for my dinner. Ay, there's the Captain pouring out the sherry, I see, and right he is! A glass of sherry is the very thing I was needing, for I've been riding out with your good uncle, your Grace, looking over your estate. It's not so large as mine, by Kettering, but he tells me it ain't more than a tithe of what you're possessed of."

Mr. Liversedge rose nobly to this as to every other occasion. He bowed politely to Mr. Mamble, sweeping him in some irresistible fashion known only to himself towards the door, and saying in a voice in which authority and civility were nicely blended: "I shall have a bottle of sherry sent up to your room, sir, on the instant. You will be desirous of changing your raiment before sitting down to dine with his Grace. The hour is already far advanced, but have no fear! Dinner will be held until you are ready to partake of it."

Mr. Mamble might fancy himself to have achieved habits of easy intercourse with Lord Lionel, but he was not of the stature to compete with Mr. Liversedge, and he knew it. He allowed himself to be bowed out of the room, saying that he had not known it was so late, and must certainly change his dress.

Lord Lionel's exacerbated feelings found relief as soon as the door was fairly shut behind him. "Intolerable upstart!"

Mr. Liversedge said soothingly: "I beg your lordship will not trouble your head over him! A good man in his way, but vulgar! One cannot but feel that his Grace was misguided in extending the hospitality of Cheyney towards him, but old heads, as your lordship well knows, are not found upon young shoulders."

Lord Lionel found himself so much in sympathy with this observation that he was almost betrayed into applauding it. He stopped himself in time, and was just about to scarify Liversedge for daring to open his mouth, when the Duke spoke.

"Liversedge!" he said, shaking the sand from the few lines he had written.

"Your Grace?" responded Liversedge turning deferentially towards him.

"You will accompany me to Bath this evening. I will furnish you with the means to buy yourself a seat upon the mail-coach to London. When you reach London, go to Sale House, and give this note to Scriven, my agent, whom you will find there. He will comply exactly with its instructions. I have requested him to advance you the sum stated in whatever coinage may be most convenient to you. Don't delay to quit this country! I assure you it might yet become unfriendly to you."

"Sir," said Mr. Liversedge, taking the letter from the Duke's outstretched hand, "no poor words of mine could convey to your Grace the sense of the deep obligation I feel towards you! I venture to prophesy that you will live to become an Ornament to the Peerage, and if—with my hand on my heart I say it!—I should not again have the felicity of setting eyes upon your face, I shall cherish the memory of my all too brief association with you to the day of my demise! And now," he continued, tucking the Duke's letter into his pocket, "I will, with your Grace's permission, repair to the kitchens, where I dare not hope that my surveillance is not long overdue."

With these words, the magnificence of which apparently made Lord Lionel feel that any attempt at expostulation must come as an anticlimax, he bowed again, and left the room with an unhurried and a stately gait.

"I am far from approving of your conduct, Adolphus, but I will own that I should be sorry to see your enterprising acquaintance in Newgate," said Gideon. "He comes off with the honours!"

His father rounded on him. "How many more times am

I to tell you not to call him by that name?" he demanded, venting an irritation of spirit that had no relation at all to anything Gideon had said.

"I must leave that to yourself to decide, sir," replied Gideon, willing to draw his parent's fire.

But the Duke intervened. "Oh, no, sir, don't forbid him to call me Adolphus! He is the only person who does so, and how much I should miss it if he ceased!"

He rose from the desk, and came to the fire. Lord Lionel said angrily: "How could you be such a fool as to reward that fellow? If you wished to let him to free—well, I have nothing to say to that! Certainly we can none of us desire this lamentable episode to be made public! An episode, I would remind you, that sprang solely from your own thoughtless and ill-judged behaviour! But to reward the villain, as though he had rendered you some signal service, makes me fear for your reason!"

"He has," said the Duke, stirring the smouldering log in the hearth with one foot. He looked up with his mischievous smile. "No, do not ask me how, sir, for I could not explain it to you. Only do not be so vexed with me! I must sometimes be allowed to make my own decisions, you know."

"No one has ever been more urgent with you to do so than myself!" replied his lordship, in perfect sincerity. "I have been foolish enough to have indulged the hope that you had come to years of discretion! I don't scruple to tell you that I find myself sadly mistaken! When this abominable affair came to my knowledge, I was in search of you, to demand from your own lips an explanation of the extraordinary intelligence conveyed to me not an hour since by Moffat!"

The Duke regarded his fingernails meditatively. "Ah, yes! The Five-acre field," he said. "So Moffat has already told you, sir? Well, he would have done better to have left it to me, perhaps, but it makes little odds. I have the intention of bestowing it upon Jasper Mudgley, for a bride-gift."

"You need not put yourself to the trouble of telling me that, Sale! I have had the whole story from Moffat. I wonder I should have found the patience to have heard him out! Understand me, boy! while I hold the reins you will not sell or give away one foot of your lands!"

The Duke raised his head, and met his uncle's fierce look with one so icily aloof that Lord Lionel was startled. "I have borne enough!" he said, his voice still level, and low-pitched, yet with anger throbbing in it. "I will not endure any longer this ceaseless thwarting of my every wish! I am fully sensible, sir of the great debt I owe you for your un-remitting care of me, of my interests, but my gratitude would be increased tenfold if you would bring yourself to believe that I am neither a child nor a fool!" He paused, his chest rising and falling rather quickly, but Lord Lionel did not speak. He was still staring at his nephew, his expression hard to read. After a moment, the Duke continued: "You are aware of my reason for thus disposing of a part of my land. I would have explained this to you, had not Moffat forestalled me. I am persuaded that I have no need to re-mind you that this paltry patch of ground is not part of the Cheyney estate, and I trust that I have even less need to assure you that I have not the most distant intention of cutting up my inheritance It is not I who stand in danger of forgetting that I am Ware of Sale! You have said that while you hold the reins—my reins!—I shall not give away one foot of my land. I shall not attempt to persuade you to alter that decision, sir: you will do as you please. But in a short space of time now I shall have reached my twenty-fifth birthday, and on that day, believe me (for I was never more in earnest!), Mudgley will receive from me the deed of gift that will put him in possession of the Five-acre field!"

He stopped, and for a moment or two there was complete silence in the room. The Duke continued to meet his uncle's stare, his eyes as stern as those older ones. Gideon, stand-ing still by the fire, glanced from one to the other of the combatants with a wry twist to his mouth.

"By God!" Lord Lionel said at last, slowly. "I never saw you look so like your father before, boy! So you mean to unseat me? Well, well, you are an impudent dog, but I am glad to see you have so much spirit in you! If you are so set on this business, I suppose you must have your way, but don't imagine that it has my approval, for it has not! Ware of Sale, indeed!" He laughed suddenly. "There, stop glaring at me, Gilly! I have a very good mind to box your ears!"

The rigid look vanished from the Duke's face. He put out a hand that was not quite steady, and said quickly: "No, no, how could I say such things to you? Forgive me! You are the best, the kindest of uncles!"

Lord Lionel was amused. "Very pretty talking, upon my word! Don't think to cajole me with your caressing ways, you young rascal, when I know well you are determined to have your own way in spite of me!"

The Duke gave a shaken laugh. "Yes. Yes, I am. But I need not have spoken to you so!"

"Oh, I never liked a man the less for being ready to sport his canvas!" Lord Lionel said coolly. "But this fellow

309

Liversedge, Gilly! Do you expect me to submit to being waited on at table by a villain?"

The Duke smiled sweetly at him. "Well, he may as well make himself useful while he is still under my roof, sir. I am sure he will wait on us excellently. Besides, Harriet is here, and I really cannot have an indifferent dinner set before her!"

"Harriet here!" exclaimed his lordship. "Good God, Gilly, why could you not have told me that before? Here am I in all my dirt, for I had not meant to change my dress since we are alone, and one must keep that fellow Mamble in countenance! Where is Harriet?"

"I dare swear in Mrs. Kempsey's room, sir. She will not regard your riding-dress, I assure you."

"I would not be guilty of such discourtesy as to sit down to the table with her in it!" declared Lord Lionel, hurrying towards the door. "Really, you are a great deal too thoughtless! You will make my excuses to Harriet, and say that I shall be down directly!" He opened the door, but checked on the threshold, perceiving that Liversedge was in the act of opening the double entrance-doors. "Now, who the devil can be visiting us at this hour?" he said testily. "I hope that fellow has the sense to deny us!"

Liversedge was given no opportunity of doing so. As soon as the doors were fairly open, Lord Gaywood thrust unceremoniously past him into the hall, saying through his teeth: "Inform the Duke that Lord Gaywood desires speech with him! And don't tell me he is not at home, for I know very well he is!"

"Well, Gaywood, what's all this?" demanded Lord Lionel. "If you want Sale, he is here, and will no doubt be glad to see you. I see no occasion for these stable-manners you young men delight in assuming. Put down your hat and coat, and do not give me any of your black looks!"

Lord Gaywood was in a towering rage, but this reception from one of whom he stood in the liveliest awe acted as a check upon him. He stammered: "I didn't know you were here, sir!"

"I daresay you might not, though what that has to say to anything I know not! Come in, Sale is in here. Gilly, here is Gaywood in some nonsensical pucker!"

The Duke took the door-handle in his own hand. "Yes, sir, so I see."

The Viscount rolled a fiery eye at him, and said with painstaking civility: "I must beg the favour of a word in private with you, my lord Duke!"

"Certainly," replied the Duke. "Come in!"

Lord Lionel's brows shot up. "Now, what's the matter be-tween you two?" he asked. "I'll have no quarrelling here, understand! Don't put on airs to be interesting, Gaywood, for they don't impress me!"

Lord Gaywood ignored him contemptuously. "I said, in private, my lord Duke!"

Lord Lionel began to look rather grim. He turned, as though to come back into the room, but found that the Duke's hand had been laid detainingly on his arm.

"If you please, sir!" the Duke said.

"Now, Gilly, I don't know what may be amiss, but I am not going to permit you——" He stopped, meeting the Duke's eyes. "Oh, very well!" he shrugged. "Settle it be-tween you! You will not do anything foolish, my boy!"

He went off, and the Duke, still holding the door, looked across the room at his cousin. "Gideon!"

Captain Ware grinned at him. "Content yourself with your signal victory over my parent, Adolphus! Nothing short of physical violence will remove me, and you would be very unwise to attempt anything of that nature, you know!"

The Viscount achieved a sneer. "Hide behind Gideon if you choose!" he said. "You will not thus escape me!"

"You know, Charlie, when you have gamed away all your fortune, you may take to the boards and be sure of suc-cess!" said Gideon admiringly.

"Oh, be quiet, Gideon!" said the Duke wearily. "I wish you will go away! What is it, Gaywood? Have you come to offer me an apology? I promise you, you owe me one! If I were not about to be married to your sister I should be sorely tempted to call you to book! You are a curst nuisance!"

"*You* call *me* to book!" gasped Gaywood. "By God, if that don't beat all! You foist your bit of muslin on to my sister—and I can tell you I was within an ace of calling you out for that alone! and you——"

"Belinda is not, and never was, my bit of muslin, and if you were not a rattle-pated fool you would know it!"

"Doing it a trifle too brown, my lord Duke! Do you take me for a gudgeon?"

"Good God, yes!" replied the Duke. "I have taken you for a gudgeon any time these past ten years!"

"Now, by Jupiter, that's too much!" exploded the Viscount, starting forward.

He found his passage barred by Gideon's broad shoulder. "Oh, no, my boy!" said Gideon. "Nothing of that sort. You'd best take a damper!"

"Gideon, will you have the goodness to allow me to manage my own affairs?" said his cousin.

Gideon looked at him for a moment, and then stepped back. "As you wish, Adolphus!"

"I am obliged to you. Now, Gaywood, we'll make an end to this nonsense, if you please, for I have quite come to the end of my patience!"

"You served me the shabbiest trick, Sale, and by God, you shall answer for it! You're a damned dog in the manager, sir! You did not want the girl yourself, but you could not bear that anyone else should have her! So you——"

"On the contrary, I have given her into the care of the one man alive who does truly want her!" retorted the Duke.

"Don't try to bamboozle me with that tale! I make no doubt you have her hidden away somewhere!" said the Viscount furiously. "Where is she?"

"Oh, in the arms of that Somerset bumpkin, of course!"

The Viscount stared at him suspiciously. "She is, is she? I should like to know who the devil gave you the right to meddle in my affairs!"

"I do not care a button for your affairs," replied the Duke. "It was Belinda's affairs that were my concern. You knew the truth, for Harriet told you it! How dared you, Gaywood, try to seduce a girl under my protection?"

"Seduce her! That's a loud one!" ejaculated his lordship with a short bark of laughter. "Much you know of it! Why, she fell into my hand as readily as any ripe plum!"

A gleam of amusement shone in the Duke's eyes. "Did she so?" he said dryly. "But not so readily, I fancy, that she could be persuaded to go with you until she had sent you running up Milsom Street in search of a purple gown!"

The wanton provocation of this remark made Gideon open his eyes a little, and caused the smouldering flames of the Viscount's wrath to leap up again. He flushed hotly, and almost audibly ground his teeth. "You'll answer to me for what you have done this day, my lord Duke!" he said. "Name your friends! They shall hear from mine!"

Gideon moved suddenly, as though again he would have stepped between them. The Duke flung out a hand. "Be quiet! Do you imagine I stand in need of a bodyguard? So you would like to call me out, Gaywood! Famous!"

"You dare not refuse to give me satisfaction!" Gaywood declared.

"Satisfaction! You fool, if I went out with you, much satisfaction you would get from the encounter! I own, there was a moment to-day when I would willingly have met you, yes, and have put a bullet through you! Had you not been

Harriet's brother—— But you are her brother, and though you may forget it I shall not!"

"I'm not afraid of your damned marksmanship," said Gaywood, white with anger. "You'll accept my challenge, Sale!"

"He will not meet you," Gideon interposed. "No one but a madman like yourself would expect it of him!"

"Who made you my spokesman?" demanded the Duke. "I'll meet you, Gaywood, and I will tell you just what will happen at that meeting! We shall fire at twenty-five paces, I in the air, you where you please!"

The Viscount appeared to fight for breath. "Delope? You would not! Why, I might kill you!"

"You are welcome to try!" retorted the Duke.

"I hardly dare to open my mouth," drawled Gideon, "but there is much in what he says, Gaywood. I don't reckon myself a mean shot, but I would think twice before I engaged in pistol-play with Sale. And you won't hit him, you know. He is such a little fellow, and you are such a damnably bad shot!"

What the infuriated Viscount might have been goaded into replying to this was never known, for at that moment Tom bounced into the room, in an extremely muddied condition, and announced that he had been helping to dig out a badger. He then caught sight of Gaywood, and exclaimed: "Oh, Mr. Rufford, that's the beau that ran off with Belinda! Did you know?"

"I *thought* as much!" said the Viscount, grasping Tom by the collar, and shaking him viciously. "Not content with the rest, you must needs set this whelp of yours to bubble me, Sale! By God, you might at least——"

"He did not!" interrupted Tom, struggling to free himself. "I thought of it myself, and I'm glad I hoaxed you, and I'll do it again if ever I have the chance!"

"Gaywood, let that boy go!" the Duke said, grasping the Viscount's wrist. "Your quarrel is with me, not with a schoolboy!"

"No, it ain't!" declared Tom, twisting himself out of the Viscount's slackened grip, and squaring up to him purposefully. "You'll have to settle with me before you touch my Mr. Rufford!"

"That's the spirit, bantam!" approved Gideon, much entertained. "No flourishing, now! Let's see some of the homebrewed!"

"For God's sake, Gideon, will you be quiet?" said the Duke, half laughing, half exasperated. "Tom, go and make yourself tidy! You cannot start a mill in my library!"

"I'm not afraid, if he is!" said Tom, observing with disgust the Viscount's strategic retreat behind a chair.

"Hey, what's all this?" suddenly demanded Mr. Mamble's voice from the doorway. "What's he been doing, your Grace? I'll teach him!"

"Nothing!" replied the Duke, struggling not to break into the mirth that was consuming him. "A—a slight misunderstanding with Lord Gaywood!"

Mr. Mamble executed one of his low bows in the Viscount's direction, and begged him to state what devilry the pesky boy had been engaged on. He then cuffed Tom, and told him he should think shame to come into his Grace's presence looking like a pauper brat.

"Well, I couldn't help getting my clothes muddied, Pa!" said Tom sulkily. "It was a badger!"

"You say Papa, like you hear his Grace! How dare you go plaguing this gentleman with badgers? Now, you tell me this instant where you've put it, and no more tricks! I know you!"

The Viscount's face of astonishment proved too much for the Duke. He sank into a chair, covering his eyes with one hand, and making a helpless gesture with the other.

"What the devil——?" exploded the Viscount, quite bewildered. "Who said anything about badgers! If that damned boy is your son——" He stopped, suddenly perceiving into what disclosures a complaint against his youthful tormentor would lead him. "Oh, never mind, never mind!" he said irritably.

"You tell his lordship you're sorry for what you've done!" Mr. Mamble adjured his offspring.

"I ain't sorry!" said Tom recalcitrantly. "I did it because I knew Mr. Rufford would be pleased, and he *was!* And I won't let him bully Mr. Rufford, not if you tell me for ever! He shan't touch him!"

Mr. Mamble looked suspiciously at the Viscount. "Oh, so that's the way it is, is it?" he said. "Seems to me it's his lordship as is wanted here! I don't hold with duelling, and I'll be bound he don't either, for he's a sensible man! I'll wager he'll know how to handle it!"

"Here, I say, no!" exclaimed the startled Viscount, seeing him about to go in search of Lord Lionel. "You can't do that! *Gilly——!*"

"Lord or no lord," said Mr. Mamble firmly, "I know where my duty lies!"

The Duke pulled himself together, raising his head from his hand, and saying faintly: "You are quite mistaken, Mr. Mamble! Lord Gaywood and I have no intention of fighting a duel. In fact, Lord Gaywood and I are shortly to become brothers!"

Mr. Mamble still looked unconvinced, so Gideon said kindly: "Have no fear, sir! I will not let the children harm each other! They will have their little differences, you know. Pray forgive me, but should you not take Tom upstairs to brush the mud from his clothes?"

"Ay, that I *will* do!" said Mr. Mamble, seizing Tom by the lobe of one ear, and leading him forth.

"For God's sake, Gilly!" said the Viscount, momentarily forgetful of the point at issue, "where *did* you pick up that fellow?" He recollected himself, and tried to whip up his dying wrath. "Not that I care for that!" he said hastily. "When we were interrupted, my lord Duke——"

"Oh, Charlie, don't start calling me my lord Duke again!" begged the Duke. "You will set me off laughing once more, and my ribs are aching! Do stop making such a cake of yourself! You know very well that by to-morrow you will be thanking God you are so well out of a scrape! You have no notion what a tiresome girl Belinda is!"

"Oh, haven't I?" retorted the Viscount. "Let me tell you that she made me go all the way to Milsom Street for a gown all over gold beads, and of the most shocking colour you ever laid eyes on! But I don't mind that! Damme, I never saw a lovelier creature in my life! But that was a dog's trick you served me, Gilly! To send me off after a damned chaise with an old harridan in it, and her pug-dog——"

The Duke gave a little crow of joy. "Oh, no, Charlie, was it indeed an old harridan? If only I might have seen you! But it was none of my doing, I swear! My peerless Thomas planned and executed the whole!"

"I wish I'd choked the brat!" said his lordship. "Oh, yes, it's very well for you to laugh, but it is a great deal too bad, and here am I with this damned purple gown on my hands, besides all else!" He glanced round as the door opened to admit his sister, and blinked. "Good God, how came you here, Harry?"

"Gilly brought me," she replied. "Charlie, I do not like to be cross and scolding, but I am quite *vexed* with you! How could you behave so? It was too bad of you!"

The Duke led her towards the fire. "No, no, don't be vexed with him, Harry! The poor fellow is left with a purple gown upon his hands, and has no one upon whom to bestow it!"

"I have been thinking about that," she replied seriously. "It quite serves Charlie right, but, you know, Gilly, I think I will buy it from him, and give it to poor Belinda for a bride-gift. It would make her so very happy, and perhaps if only she had it she would be content!"

"You are an angel, Harriet," said the Duke, pressing her hand. "She will look quite shockingly in it, you know, but I daresay Mudgley will not think so. Should I give her a ring to put on her finger, do you think?"

"No, for Mr. Mudgley will do that," she pointed out. "I expect, however, that it would be proper for you to offer to stand sponsor to their first child," she added thoughtfully.

"I make you my compliments, Harriet!" said Gideon. "I perceive that you will be an excellent Duchess, and become universally looked up to!"

"Oh, no!" she said, blushing. "How can you say so? Only I mean to try to do my best, and I shall have Gilly to tell me how I should go on, you know."

"What, will you do as he bids?" exclaimed Gideon.

"Of course!" she said simply.

"Adolphus," said Captain Ware, picking up his sherry-glass, "from my heart I felicitate you! The days of your bondage are clearly at an end! I drink to your future career, wherein you will doubtless assert yourself, tyrannizing over your family, bullying your servants, and filling your house with foundlings, Newgate-scoundrels, hobbledehoy school-boys, and whatever scaff and raff of society your fancy prompts you to befriend! Adolphus, my little one, I salute you!"

THE ROMANTIC NOVELS OF

Georgette Heyer

02601	**April Lady**	75c
02891	**Arabella**	75c
11000	**A Civil Contract**	75c
11771	**Cotillion**	75c
24825	**The Foundling**	75c
25300	**Friday's Child**	75c
30241	**The Grand Sophy**	75c
69891	**The Quiet Gentleman**	75c
71301	**The Reluctant Widow**	75c
77832	**Sprig Muslin**	75c
79351	**Sylvester Or, the Wicked Uncle**	75c
81640	**The Toll Gate**	75c
84665	**The Unknown Ajax**	75c
86111	**Venetia**	75c

Available wherever paperbacks are sold or use this coupon.

GOTHIC MYSTERIES BY

DOROTHY EDEN

All now 75c

07972	Bridge of Fear
08182	The Brooding Lake
12352	Crow Hollow
13881	The Daughters of Ardmore Hall
14191	Death is a Red Rose
47402	The Laughing Ghost
57802	The Night of the Letter
67852	The Pretty Ones
77122	The Sleeping Bride
86600	The Voice of the Dolls
94390	Yellow is for Fear

Available wherever paperbacks are sold or use this coupon.

Spine-Tingling Mysteries

02273 **And Hope To Die**
Charbonneau   60c

02276 **Angel of Death** Loraine   75c

03125 **Assassin Who Gave Up His
Gun** Cunningham   75c

07921 **The Bride Wore Black**
Woolrich   60c

12200 **Crimson Madness of Little
Doom** McShane   60c

14155 **The Old English Peep Show**
Dickinson   75c

14258 **The Depraved** Rome   75c

28920 **The Girl Nobody Knows**
McShane   75c

54710 **The Murder League**
Fish   75c

65225 **Passenger on the U**
Aveline   95c

67110 **The Pleasant Grove Murders**
Vance   60c

77855 **The Spy Who Hated Fudge**
Hershatter   60c

Available wherever paperbacks are sold or use this coupon.

ace books, (Dept. MM) Box 576, Times Square Station
New York, N.Y. 10036
Please send me titles checked above.

I enclose $..................Add 10c handling fee per copy.

Name ....

Address ....

City..................... State.............. Zip........

Please allow 4 weeks for delivery.   . 6